The Group

The Group

LARA FEIGEL

JM ORIGINALS

First published in Great Britain in 2020 by JM Originals
An imprint of John Murray (Publishers)
An Hachette UK company

2

Copyright © Lara Feigel 2020

A CIP catalogue record for this title is available from the British Library

Hardback ISBN 9781529305005
eBook ISBN 9781529305029

Typeset in Bembo by Palimpsest Book Production Ltd, Falkirk, Stirlingshire

Printed and bound in Great Britain by Clays Ltd, Elcograf S.p.A.

John Murray policy is to use papers that are natural, renewable and recyclable
products and made from wood grown in sustainable forests. The logging
and manufacturing processes are expected to conform to the environmental
regulations of the country of origin.

John Murray (Publishers)
Carmelite House
50 Victoria Embankment
London EC4Y 0DZ

www.johnmurraypress.co.uk

For Georgia

Stella

March

We worry about not knowing our friends well enough, but sometimes we see their lives with a clarity that feels like a form of betrayal. This afternoon at Priss's, where the five of us congregated: there were the newly upholstered antique armchair, the home-made elderflower muffins, the absent husbands, the unfamiliar children we pretend to delight in while noting their close-set eyes and dissatisfied requests for more cake, more attention, more room in an already over-crowded world.

I felt vulnerable arriving at Priss's, because half an hour earlier I'd slipped in the rain and banged my head on the car. I'd been walking round to the driver's side after strapping Maggie in, and then I slid forwards, knocking my head on the back door. It felt over-charged because I bought the car from Chris yesterday. We agreed, when we split up, that we'd share it, but that meant me having it all the time except for when he needed it, and he'd suddenly started asking for it more often and at short notice. He kept taunting me, telling me to buy him out, and then yesterday I took the bait. So as I carried Maggie to Priss's front door, I was worried that I'd got concussion from the fall and worried that I'd fallen over because I couldn't do it, being a single car-owner as well as a single mother. I didn't have the strength. The sight of Priss's house made it worse – that symmetrical front garden with its hand-made tiles and neat flowerbeds and hedge (where do they keep the bins?). It reminded me that I'd once lived in a similar house and I felt angry with Priss for taking the sturdiness of her surroundings for granted.

All this meant that I entered the house resenting Chris, resenting the friends gathered in Priss's sitting room, whose lives seemed suddenly so much better ordered than mine, and resenting the monochrome sogginess of this March in which spring still fails to arrive. As I put down our things, Priss took Maggie from me and then Priss and I brushed cheeks across the baby. I wondered if I ought to be pressing my lips into the shape of an actual kiss of the kind I press noisily on my children's faces but hardly ever on my friends', and wondered whether Priss and Helena do this more naturally. Priss looked stylish, as always, her blonde hair escaping artfully from a bun. But the hollows underneath her eyes were deeper and darker than I remembered them, and I caught a glimpse of myself in the hallway mirror, my hair greying and flattened by rain. These peculiarly unfamiliar middle-aged faces made me miss the illusions, the excitement that was so close to falling in love, of that undergraduate summer when we became a group.

It began with a picnic on a meadow, lit up with a fairytale sheen that I distrust as I recall it, though I think I'm right in remembering that it really was coated in yellow. I have never seen as many buttercups as we used to see there. Helena and Polly and I had agreed to share the James Street house in our second year, then Helena had invited Priss to join us, and I'd invited Kay, so this was a chance for the five of us to meet. Kay and Polly and I were already there, picnicking among the buttercups, the river visible behind us. I can picture Polly's eyes, so blue against the water and sky that they could have been transparent windows on to the world behind. We were meant to be revising but we'd escaped and allocated ourselves two hours of fun. Polly was telling us, I remember, about the latest of her dismissive, controlling boyfriends, but her voice was bright with cruelty as she catalogued his faults, and there was a sense that it didn't matter because her real, sustained life was with us, her friends.

The others arrived on bicycles, both wearing white, with Priss's long blonde hair and dress blowing up around her in the breeze. She was as stylish then as she is now, which excited me. There was a sense that your friends' appearances could be yours by proxy, as there is now with our husbands'. It's hard to recall how impressed I was by her in those days, because since then I've realised that there's a kind of disconnect between the extraordinary way that she looks and the more ordinary things that she says, which tend to be a version of what the people around her are saying. Over the last few years, this has made me reluctant to talk in her presence, because I don't want my thoughts to be stolen. But that day I was delighted by her, and by my life in general. I hadn't been very popular at school so it felt like an unexpected triumph to find myself sitting on the grass with four girls I admired so much, planning to live together, forming a posse of the kind I'd felt excluded from in the past. I thought back to the low point of my school career, when I'd fallen out with my best friend just before the camping expedition and ended up having to share a tent with the other two rejects of the moment, shy and unappealing girls who snored at night more loudly than they were prepared to speak by day.

Kay and I lay on the grass, as we often did together in those days, describing the clouds above us, and the others joined us, feet and arms overlapping carelessly, making me crave more of it, as touch always does even when it's as innocuous as it was then, fearing the moment when it will be withdrawn. It felt so wonderfully timeless, so much the kind of thing that we might have been doing fifty years earlier, on that same patch of grass, on an identical May day, that we escaped time. We overran our two hours as we drank the miraculously chilled Pimm's that Helena produced from her bag. I don't think I'd drunk Pimm's before university, and its sugary brightness still evokes for me the relieved sociability that I felt then, easing into the new sense of myself as someone with friends. Thus the group was formed, and since then there's been a restful quality in group life that enables the otherwise insistent noise of my thoughts to quieten. That's why I miss it now. There was a warmth between the five of us that day that had nothing to do with the intellectual connection I usually seek in friendship and was much more about just living alongside each other.

The memories of that afternoon stayed with me as I dried off and joined the others on the floor of Priss's colour-coordinated sitting room, while our children weaved among us. There can't have been many times we've sat together on the ground like that since university. These days we hardly ever meet as a group, all five of us together, without new acquaintances, without husbands or lovers.

Do you remember, I said, that picnic? The day when we first met?

I felt suddenly shy, in case they didn't remember, in case I proved more invested in our past than they were, though that's not usually my role, it's Priss's. I tend to assume it's her lack of career that makes her live so much in the past. In crueller moments, I think of it as a kind of over-investment in her teenage self, because she's never inhabited herself fully as a woman. But writing this, I'm reminded that Helena also cares about the past more than I do, though she's the only one of us who's famous. Anyway, luckily, they did remember. Kay said that she'd thought about it recently too, and missed it, missed living with us, missed the freedom of those days when we didn't know ourselves to be free.

We talked about the afternoons and late nights we spent watching films, about the collective expeditions to Sainsbury's, about the times when Helena's uncle Vince used to arrive from London with a huge basket of expensive food. He'd cook us all dinner, making us cocktails with the shaker he produced from his basket, and the feeling that we were all his nieces made us surrogate sisters, all able to make believe that we were from a family as sophisticated and large-hearted as Helena's. It wasn't just make-believe: Vince did take us all on as his family. He got me my job – he's the publishing director at the publishing house where I work.

What did we do all day? Polly asked, though as a medical student she was the only one with a full schedule. I feel so envious of myself then, she said, sleeping for eight hours every night if I wanted to, all that sitting around, talking about whether truth was a good in itself, as though if we just came up with the right philosophy we could change everything.

When I think of myself then, I feel protective, rather than envious, Kay said. I want to look after the young woman better, because then maybe I'll stop her turning into me now.

I picked up Maggie, who was propped up on a pile of

cushions and playing with her furry caterpillar, her arms puppet-like in their movements because she has not yet learnt how to bend her elbows at will. She smiled bashfully, grateful for the attention, and I laughed, loving the way that she treats each smile she receives as a new in-joke. I looked around, expecting the others to find her as delightful as I do, but Kay's baby Alisa started showing off her skills at waving and saying 'bye bye', and everyone became absorbed by playing with her. I told myself that it's because Alisa's older that she's more fun to engage with – even Priss's daughter was leaning in, trying to make Alisa wave at her. But I worried suddenly that Maggie would never be accepted by the others, and then, as though to emphasise her difference, Priss turned to me, and said, How often does Chris see Maggie now? Does he like her?

I remembered the conversation with Priss and Kay, before I got pregnant, when they both told me they thought it was a mistake. Chris and I had agreed to split up, he'd produced his younger woman on cue as he approached fifty; she was more normal, more pliable than me. I was going along with it. I was pretty sure by then that we'd split up one day, so why not now, when it was him who was instigating it. But there was that one blastocyst left in the fertility-clinic freezer, the third of three, our child in the making. It mattered, that cluster of five-day-old cells, more to me than the marriage, mattered already almost as much as my living daughter. And Priss and Kay, at a lunch they'd arranged ostensibly to see if I was all right, leant across the restaurant table to ask if I'd really thought about it, as though I might have just forgotten to do so. You're free now, Kay said, beleaguered by her own second pregnancy. You've only got one child, Chris will have her half the time, you'll have your life back, that's not really

6

worth giving up. Priss said that she didn't think it was fair on the child, to have a baby in circumstances where I couldn't be sure if its father wanted it. Chris was too decent to forbid me to do this, but surely he didn't want it, when he was about to try to have a child with someone else. He must want this baby, I insisted, he was the one who'd longed for a second child so urgently, two years before I had, and who'd then blamed me for the delay when it took another three years to get to the point we were at now, with a blastocyst waiting patiently in the freezer for us to give her the chance to live.

The conversation ran through my head now, making me feel frightened, making Maggie seem more precarious to me, as though the question of whether she was going to exist or not was still unresolved. I clutched her to me and said Of course he likes her, she's his daughter.

Is he seeing anyone else? Priss asked. Are you seeing anyone else?

I wasn't prepared for the question. It felt too early to tell them about Tom. So I said no. I resented her for exposing the distance between us, because twenty years ago I'd have told them all about every man I met, it would never have been too early. Now there are other friends I tend to confide in first, people I know less well but can trust more easily than these old friends I can't quite forgive for their knowledge of me. I was resentful partly because I knew that Priss is still centred by our university group – she and Helena still think of each other as best friends – in a way that I suspect makes for a happier life.

Then Seb started asking Kay for more cake. She began by arguing logically with him, they'd agreed two slices, he couldn't have more, but then she got bored and gave in.

There was a kind of blankness in her voice that felt unfamiliar. He started the slice but didn't finish it, and went off to the bay window where Priss's daughter Lena was pulling out costumes from the chest and putting them on. I wanted, so desperately, to feel connected to these women. I felt the need for us to be a group again, and to have a best friend from among them – it would be Kay I suppose, it's her I see most often, though I'd probably prefer it to be Helena.

I said: Actually, there is someone I like, a friend of a colleague. I've been making friends with him. I don't know if it's flirtatious or not, but I like talking to him. We talk on the phone most nights at the moment.

I felt shy, saying it. Then, feeling the urge to confess, to show them who I am in the present so they could add it to their knowledge of my past, I told them about banging my head and how it had made me worry that I couldn't cope as a single car-owner or a single mother. I thought they might think that I was thinking too much. But Chris used to say that. I have to trust my women friends not to say it.

Polly and Helena leant over to examine my head, to check there were no bumps. I felt looked after by them, and reassured by Polly's medical training. In my gratitude, I wanted to cry, wondering if it would be awkward if I allowed myself to do so. Helena saw the tears in my eyes and hugged me. I always feel that she's more invested in our friendship when I'm fragile, which brings out an urge in me to make myself more vulnerable with her.

We sat down again, cross-legged, upright on the floor.

Helena said that Chris is cruel, expecting so much of me, when he must know how hard it is being on your own with a four-month-old baby. Cruel was the wrong word to use and the editor in me wanted to correct her, requiring her to be more precise. Instead I defended him. I said that we couldn't begin to understand how confusing he must find this. It's hard being on your own with a baby, but it's even harder rarely seeing your baby, and not feeling that she's fully yours.

It's so difficult, Helena said, to know if you're getting it right.

I had an image of us as five stalks of wheat who had emerged into maturity. Most of us are thirty-nine now, Polly is already forty, we have come of age together and stand firm in the wind. But we are exposed to the elements, there is nothing to protect us, and I felt them feeling this as well.

Then it was three o'clock. The children had started arguing about the dressing-up costumes. I needed to go and collect Cleo from school and take Maggie home for her nap. When I went back to the car, I became convinced that there was a new bump on the back door, where I'd banged my head earlier, and wondered if the car had done equivalent damage to me. But I told myself that it's impossible to tell if a mark is new. The car is full of lumps and dips – each new dent used to occasion a marital argument because Chris saw my inept driving as wilful carelessness that contained aggression towards him. But then at some point, about a year ago, the car became so dented that the new bumps either went unnoticed or were simply accepted, making this the only area in our marriage where imperfection was becoming more tolerated rather than less.

This evening, I've been thinking about us as a group. I've been thinking that, when I was pregnant, I knew that Polly and Helena supported me, but I could never be sure of Priss and Kay. They are the other mothers among our group, which added to the pain of feeling judged by them. I felt excluded from their circle of motherhood, even as Priss gave me Babygros (carefully named though she is unlikely to have another child) and made food (I have never been so grateful to be cooked for) for my freezer. Part of the problem is that now I'm becoming more inclined to share their doubts. I distrust my own wilfulness: my wanting of a child and my determination to fulfil my want. Should we have children, should we not? I hate the way these become choices. I distrust, too, the way that I thought life could be plotted out in advance like the books that I edit. But I have to remain loyal to who I was then. Because at the time there was no choice about it. In my mind, as in the mind of the most virulent anti-abortion lobbyist, a person had been created. We could not just turn off the freezer – it makes me cry now to imagine it. Was that really what Kay and Priss wanted me to do?

The circumstances of Maggie's birth still seem no worse to me than anyone else's, however hard things become. If it's likely that a marriage is going to end, and if divorce becomes harder for children the older they are, then why not end the marriage while they're in the womb? Why not make the moment of rupture one they're not there to witness? So that all the baby sees of the marriage are its rippling after-effects, as she becomes the unwitting spectator of the unsharing of the badly shared car.

Of course I've found it frightening, knowing for the last four months that she's my responsibility to keep alive. On the days when I've been feverish with mastitis or exhausted by the night wakings, I've wondered if I'm up to it. Perhaps that was all Priss was suggesting today, perhaps there was no disapproval in her voice, just sympathy. It may be that I impute callousness to her because I feel guilty about my own behaviour towards her.

I have to remember that the others are vulnerable too. They feel this terrifying and exhilarating thin-skinnedness as well. It's something about this phase of life, when we confront the knowledge that there can be no more practising, that this is the only run we have at it. We are all bumpable and dented beneath our sturdiness, uncertain in our independence, liable to hurt each other when we should be looking after each other, because we feel insecure beneath each other's scrutiny and wonder how our choices will hold up. Marriage, divorce, procreation, careers: we compare the ways we have done these, or not done them; the choices we have made, or failed to make, or not known we were making.

Write about that then, Tom said on the phone this evening, when I was complaining about my difficulties in writing the novel that calls out to be written while thwarting me with the falseness of its made-upness, as though there hasn't been a century of writers grappling with these questions. He said that the form would come to me in six months, or in three years, which maddened me, because I'm too impatient to wait, and because people said exactly that to me when I was trying to get pregnant with Maggie. When it ended up taking three years to have a baby it came at the cost of the marriage whose ending I'm still prepared to describe as a cost, however much I insist on it being exactly the right thing to have happened. There must now be no more costs.

So here we are then. Five exact contemporaries who once shared a cluttered, thin-walled student house off the Cowley Road, all privileged, white, middle-class, all vestigial hangers-on, left over from an era when we received free educations at our elite university and then emerged into a world where we could still just about find jobs and buy flats, provided with opportunities for selfishness and leisure by our cleaners and our childminders. Nothing very eventful happens to us, but that gives more room for the ethnographer in me to get to work. I hope that we can spend more time together again. I want to sit in that circle, to feel Maggie and Cleo included there among their children. And I hope that when I write about them, there might be a form of clear-sightedness that feels less like betrayal than love.

Kay

March

Kay as I've said is thirty-nine, thin, quite tall, with dark brown hair greying slightly less than mine is and dark almond-shaped eyes. She's pretty, in a way that depends on her not acknowledging it: plain clothes, no make-up, not much recognition that she has a body at all. Kay studied English too and she was awarded the second first in our year. That's crucial, still, to who she is, because she'd be happier with her life, as a secondary-school English teacher married to a famous novelist, if it wasn't for that tangible reminder of her early promise, and the knowledge that she could be teaching in a university, or publishing better books than I do, or writing better novels than Harald does. Her high first was a tribute to the precision of her mind, which I envied then and value now, though sometimes I feel there is no room in it for the contradictions of daily life.

She and I met doing drama, which seems unlikely, because we are both self-contained. But I directed her in a play in our first year, an obscure comedy by Jean Anouilh, which must have been recommended to me by someone. I can remember her auditioning, she was so restrained and untheatrical she seemed not to be acting at all, just emanating a confidence in herself as this other person, a woman twenty years older than she was. At first I admired her without thinking that we'd become friends, but then there was a post-rehearsal drink where I warmed to her, surprised by how much she could drink and by the sense that she, in a different way from me, was without conversational taboos, or at least shared my frank curiosity about the details of sex, as we delineated the inadequacies of recent encounters. I was attracted to her, I think. There had been an unusually large lesbian contingent at my school and in those days, more than now, I was often sexually attracted to girls. Certainly there were months when our developing friendship was a source of excitement in my life. When she decided to move out of college and asked if she could join the shared house I was planning to rent, it felt like a kind of conquest.

She met Harald on the drama scene as well: theirs is the only marriage among our group that began then. Harald was an American graduate student who acted well. He was noisy, good-looking in that large-featured American manner; at one point he even had side-burns. I met him first and was attracted to him as well – I think Kay and I often have similar taste in men. We flirted at parties and there were a couple of times when I managed to leave alongside him and we walked fast through the night together, our shoes clicking in time, but he wasn't interested in me. And then he and Kay met on stage in our third year as, of all combustible combinations, Macbeth and Lady Macbeth. It's a sign of how absurdly seriously we took ourselves that *Macbeth* was being done as a student play at all. Harald at that point was going to be an actor. Kay was going to be a novelist. It made sense of her combination of withdrawn observation and stagey wit. She wrote methodically every day and Harald, who was appealingly ambitious for them as a couple, even found an agent who was interested in her, an American woman who'd walked straight out of 1950s New York. It's a sign of good taste in him that when he was ready to send out his first novel he didn't go to the same person, he found his own agent, though it might have been a sign of better taste, by which I may just mean decency, not to turn to novel writing at all.

But he did, and it was soon after his first novel was published that Kay, without telling any of us, enrolled to train as a teacher. I've hardly ever heard her mention his books but I know that she found that first book as bad as I did – a story of coming of age in the early days of internet porn. It made him well known and that was the end of her writing. It was all or nothing for her and she wasn't going to be the less successful writer in the house. She had no real ambitions in other spheres, so instead there has been the teaching and more recently the children: Seb, aged three, and Alisa, a baby a little older than Maggie. She has found mother-hood harder than I have, on the whole, but then it's been a surprising discovery that I find the early stages of mother-hood easier than most of my friends do, whether they enjoy it more or less than me. Kay enjoys it less.

So this is an ordinary domestic afternoon at home in March. Home is a large, featureless house near the river in Chiswick, bought with Harald's large advances and astute investments (he's the only writer I know who understands the stock market), chosen to be near her parents, filled with tasteful, forgettable furniture, the walls a tasteful, forgettable shade of grey. She is sitting straight-backed at her desk with her pile of marking beside her. Next door the baby, who she's just collected from nursery, is asleep in her cot. Downstairs there is the reassuring noise of the hoover. There is no danger that Ana is going to want to chat. Ana has no interest in anything that interrupts her cleaning and Kay gains strength from her when she is there – from the knowledge of shared industriousness in their separate spheres.

The essays, piled up on her desk, are on *Hamlet*. This is the tenth consecutive year that she has marked essays on *Hamlet*. Somehow, even with two maternity leaves, she hasn't managed to miss out on them. It's possible, as with driving along the motorway, to mark the essays without paying any attention to what she is doing. Driving, she opens the window, blasting her brain into attentiveness with cold air. She does the same now, in her study, relishing the discomfort of the chilly air on her face and neck. If there's a pleasure to be had in this setting, then it's in the austerity of self-denial.

When asked, Kay admits that she dislikes her students. She says that this is because they've become more privileged over the years, as the fees have risen, and less grateful for receiving a better education than their peers are getting at neighbouring schools. Used to servants, they treat their teachers as staff, paid to provide them with A-stars and enable their journey to university, where they will study the same canon of texts that we studied with less investment in them and therefore less riding on the precision of their opinions, which makes it less likely they will develop genuine opinions at all.

Also, having children herself has depleted Kay's maternal resources. She only has enough affection for her own progeny and so finds it harder to see the rows of girls lined up for instruction as full, embodied people in need of her attention and care. At school yesterday, while she listened to them laboriously reading the play-within-the-play scene in *Hamlet*, she looked at the ten seventeen-year-olds seated around her and wondered what it would be like if she desired her students, craving to touch the smooth skin and developing hips, and if that would make her a better teacher. Perhaps sensual yearning could awaken her to the life inside these quickening minds, perhaps then she'd have been able to say something about *Hamlet* that would make them see the urgency of the scene they were bringing into being, and make their own feelings of grief and love and confusion come into focus through the text. But as it is, she has no interest in whether one month's essay is better than the last.

When asked, Kay also admits that she dislikes *Hamlet*. I assume that this dates from the time that Harald played Horatio at the RSC, when we were in our mid twenties. They'd recently married, partly in order to get Harald citizenship. He was still pursuing a career as an actor and it was his big break. I remember going to their tiny Hampstead flat and hearing him pacing around, reciting not just his own lines but everyone else's. I was co-opted – we all were – into running through the scenes with him. Once after I went home from a late dinner, leaving the kitchen crowded with fetid fishbones, I remember thinking of Kay, trying to write, unable to escape the sound of iambic pentameter bouncing off the walls at her.

She loved him then, though. I think she attached more fully to him than any of the rest of us could have attached to anyone at the time. And she loved that small flat, with its views down over the roofs of London. Perhaps she was happy, lying in bed while he paced round the bedroom naked, reciting his lines, and then climbed in to fuck her, somewhere between the doubting Horatio and the angst-ridden prince. Perhaps it gave her life a vigour and embodiment it would otherwise have lacked, just her and the blank page. But at some point during that long run, during the weeks of going to bed alone and welcoming home a man who smelt of Ophelia's perfume, she came to hate *Hamlet*. That was his first affair and it was a horrible cliché. She could have protested but she was more committed to good taste than to her own happiness, so she didn't want to provoke embarrassing scenes. And she still doesn't, even when she finds receipts from London hotels in the wastepaper bin in their bedroom, even when her friends let on (though this hasn't happened for a few years) that he has tried to kiss them.

She's marked ten essays now. Each is scattered with methodical ticks and suggestions for improvement. She has to stop herself giving higher and higher marks as she comes to the end of the sequence. A small smile comes and goes from her face as she catches herself doing this and then holds off. She's hoping to get the final six done before the baby wakes up or Harald returns after picking up Seb from nursery. Downstairs, Ana is still moving from room to room and it's because of the noise of the hoover that Kay doesn't notice Harald and Seb arriving earlier than usual. When she does hear the footsteps, rushing to her door, she's alarmed, and then Seb comes into the room, asking for biscuits.

No, you can't have biscuits before dinner, she says, wishing that he'd just come in and hug her, that he'd give her the chance to feel the rush of affection for the child she hasn't seen all day, before she has to start getting irritated with his demands.

Daddy says I can, he says, and she feels it beginning again, the battles that characterise the four-way interaction in the household. With just the baby, it's possible to avoid conflict altogether; there are days when there isn't even any crying. Kay has started to associate this with Alisa being a girl.

Harald comes in now, carrying Alisa. He kisses Kay on the lips and then lifts Alisa high in the air and sticks his tongue out. The baby smiles and sticks hers out in return. Kay feels an irritable superiority in knowing that she can provoke more sustained smiles just by kissing Alisa's cheeks.

Let's go to the kitchen, she says to Seb, giving up on her essays and her solitude, and we'll find you a snack.

They file downstairs. This – all four of them in one room – is the family life that has always mattered so much to Harald, as it did to Chris. Kay, an only child as I am, finds this hard to grasp, though she's more prepared to perform family life than I was, deterred by the example of my marriage ending.

Kay gives Seb an oatcake and sits Alisa on her mat while Harald, apparently having had enough contact with his children, mixes gin and tonics without first asking her if she wants one. She sips hers and finds that she enjoys the rush of combined clarity and relaxation it brings. She opens the fridge. Meatballs, tomatoes, red pepper.

She announces that they will have meatballs on pasta, preparing herself to cook yet another meal too ordinary to be appetising. Remember that I'm going out, Harald says. She hadn't, but she now sees that this is why he collected Seb early. She asks where he's going and is told that it's a reading for a literary prize, which they want him to judge next year. She asks if that's the prize for experimental fiction, not bothering to hide her scepticism. He says that, yes, he's seen as experimental now, it shows that he was ahead of his time. But you're not experimental, Kay says.

There's a chant of Mummy, Mummy from Seb. Alisa has started whimpering too, bored by being the only one on the floor. Kay looks at Harald, wondering if he might think it's his duty to attend to either child, but he seems unaware of the noise, focused on his drink and his thoughts. He says that he is experimental, that you can be experimental without abandoning the sentence. He experiments with genre. Kay wonders if perhaps it will never arrive: the review that she's always expected to be written, exposing Harald as a fake.

She picks up Alisa and breastfeeds her, too tired now, more because of the prospect of the hours ahead than because she's done anything tiring, to find a creative way to placate her. Fed, she will sit on her mat again for another half hour. As the milk lets down from her breast she feels a moment of ease, her restlessness briefly quelled, but then her mind is on the move again, thinking of the next task. She says to Seb that she'll save the meatballs and just make pasta and broccoli, planning to boil them together in the pan. He retorts at once that he wants meatballs and then repeats his request more loudly.

She gives in, wondering if Harald is genuinely oblivious that he is responsible for this evening in which she will end up cooking a meal she doesn't want to cook, a meal marginally better and more effortful than the meal she'd have had to cook if she'd known from the start that she was to be the only adult present. Questioned, he'd say that she knew he was going out, that she was careless about putting things in her diary. She might respond that she doesn't need a diary because she has nothing to put in it. She has no life. It has all been taken away from her by him, in his insistent need for these children that she never actively wanted.

Alisa has finished sucking. Kay burps her and the baby sits still in her arms, smiling up at her. When Kay smiles back at her and kisses her nose, Alisa beams. Harald goes upstairs and Seb asks her for the toy car on the counter, which has a loose front door. She gives it to him, reminding him that it's fragile. Within seconds, the car door breaks and he becomes instantly distraught, asking her to fix it. Kay explains that there's nothing she can do now, but she could try sellotaping it later. She stirs the meatballs on the hob, holding Alisa in her other arm, the fat spitting into their faces. Seb orders her to sellotape it now, he needs it. When she doesn't respond he throws it at her and it brushes against Alisa's head. Kay puts the crying baby back carefully on the mat and bends down to confront her son. His face is curiously inexpressive, dark eyes framed by neat blond hair. This compact little person, so sure of his own rights, seems to have arrived in her house as a fully formed stranger and to have nothing to do with the creature she grew in her body.

She shouts that he must never throw anything at her or Alisa again. He doesn't answer, so she shakes his shoulders. He continues to stare at her. Say sorry, she commands. Sellotape it now, he shouts back. Immediately, she slaps him, hard enough to leave a red mark on his cheek.

That's it, she says, I'm throwing it in the bin.

She picks up the little red car where it has landed on the floor and wrenches the other front door off, with some difficulty. Alisa's cries have become screams now and Seb starts shouting too, words giving way to noises.

Go upstairs, she shouts, pushing him to the door. Go and wait for your dinner, I will never buy you a car again.

With Seb gone, she picks up Alisa and the baby is immediately quiet in her arms. She squeezes the small body to her and cries into the tangled brown hair, hating herself, loving the baby, still unable to access love in herself for the boy who she now hears running around the sitting room above her head with Harald, screaming in excitement, apparently unaffected by their scene. She wonders if Seb will tell Harald what she's done and how she will defend herself if he confronts her. Then Ana appears in the doorway.

I can't, I can't work like this, she says. I've just finished that room. Now they run around it. Mr, he wear shoes. The toys go everywhere.

Kay apologises, feeling more in control. She tells Ana not to worry, that they know she's done it and it's all right if it gets messy again. But Ana insists that she will have to redo it straight away.

And so it is that when Harald has gone out and Kay has persuaded Seb to eat the dinner he insisted she cook for him, after sending him once in tears to his room, the noise of the hoover continues, as Ana prolongs her battle against attrition. Kay does not say goodbye to her. With Alisa in bed, she gives in to Seb's demands that she should follow Harald's example and lie with him until he's asleep. She's relieved to find tenderness within her now that he's small and docile in his bed, and she lies her head close to his, their breaths synchronised. It's nine o'clock when she emerges from his room, her head thick with mistimed sleep, and walks around the spotless house. She always expected that they would have to change the cream carpets on the stairs soon after having children, that this act of faith from the previous owners would quickly be undermined by their occupancy. But somehow Ana has kept them spotless and fluffy, turning their house into a show home, which in its perfection seems to chastise Kay for never having liked it.

Seeing you doesn't make me less crazy. It just makes me more aware of the craziness. Which may exacerbate it. Not that I can see you. I don't know if I like lying here any more.

Kay is with Moser, our psychoanalyst. We don't seem to want to think of him as Harry. We started seeing him in the same week. I recommended him before I'd started my sessions – if I'd begun already I don't think I'd have suggested him, I'd have seen that too much time would be spent wondering about each other. But then if the psychoanalytic encounter models other encounters, if it's desirable therefore to spend half the session talking about your relationship with the analyst, perhaps we might as well make it as multi-dimensional as possible.

Unlike me, she started on the couch, determined to have the full psychoanalytic experience. I want it too but want first – and we have talked about this at some length, of course – to learn his facial expressions, by way of decoding him.

Would you like to move to the chair? His voice today feels aggressive in its quietness. She's becoming more hysterical and he succeeds in retaining his calm.

Harald was saying yesterday that he thinks the whole analytic thing has become a hoax. Your silences, your delays in replying to my emails, are all because you think that's what analysts do. All analysts are TV analysts, in a period drama set in turn-of-the-century Vienna.

Do you think that too? he asks.

He sounds weary at last, which comes as a relief, though she knows that she might be imagining it. There are things to talk about. She spent much of the previous day learning Bulgarian grammar from the internet in order to improve her text message communication with Ana, who's written announcing her intention to resign. In Ana's first long message, which Google translate mashed up but Kay has now disentangled, she complained that there is no respect for her in the house. The children are allowed to mess it up at will. Harald walks around in muddy shoes.

When Kay called Harald in the flat he rents to write in, he said that they were better off without her. According to him, she was like a librarian who hated readers. She wanted the house to herself with no children in it. This is true, but what Kay is now telling Moser is that she too wants the house to herself, with no children in it. Increasingly, corresponding with Ana yesterday, she came to share her vision of empty carpeted rooms as the ideal environment in which to live; to imagine what it would be like to walk softly with clean bare feet over clean pale carpets, making almost no imprint on her surroundings. 'I didn't sign up for this either,' she wrote back to Ana in what she was fairly sure was perfect Bulgarian.

How would you describe your feelings for her? Moser asks.

I don't know, she says. I like her. Perhaps I love her. We use love to mean so many different things. There's a form of intensity, even passion — without liking — that I'd call love. That's what I feel for her.

She is proud of herself, here, perhaps more than anywhere else. She is exact. She is appropriately crazy, given the setting. She has an unpredictable unconscious.

I think I'm good at this, she says. I think I'm probably better at it than Stella.

It matters to you to be good at it? he asks, and she says that yes, there's not much that she prides herself on being good at any more. Harald gets the sparkling career, neither of them think she's a particularly good mother, she doesn't think she's a particularly good teacher. It's what she admires in Ana. That there's something she's good at and she does it rigorously.

You don't think you're a good mother?

No, she says, maybe because Harald doesn't, which is unfair, because she invests more time in it than he does into fathering. He wouldn't say it, but when she argues with Seb it comes across that Harald is disappointed in her. He may be right. There are times when she feels nothing for either her husband or her son, and last night, when they were playing together noisily in the kitchen, she imagined herself banging their heads together, hard. Good mothers probably don't have those kinds of imaginings.

Did you want to hurt them? Moser asks.

I'm often unnerved by how violent, how quickly violent, my feelings about both of them are, she says. But without the violence there'd be nothing. At least the violence is a sign of love. It's possible I still love Harald, even if I despise him too. I don't want to have sex with anyone else, though it might be easier if I did, because then things would even out. Maybe he'd be able to love me more if he felt less guilty. But maybe I'd want to have sex with other men if Harald hadn't had so many affairs and disgusted me with it. He's taken away my interest in sex by turning it into something so childishly gluttonous, like eating too many sweets.

Have you lost interest in sex?

Yes. But haven't most women, in long marriages, if they admit it? I think it's too much that we're expected to like sex. I like the sharpness of the changes it brings. The way the tension rises and deflates. But all the fuss seems too much, if all we want is orgasms. I can't understand why Harald puts so much effort into it. But I can't see why he puts so much effort into his writing either. Maybe my standards are too high. Is that what I'm learning here? To have lower standards?

Let's leave that as an open thought, Moser says. But it's a

productive one, I think, though there won't be an easy answer. You have five minutes left.

The five-minute warning was my idea. It solved the problem of how to relinquish control by not clock watching, while not feeling too panicky about the lack of control. I told Kay about it and so now he does it with her as well. Does he talk about this with the wife who we occasionally hear in the background? Does he have a good marriage? That careful attention to language might help.

Kay looks around at the room she will leave in five minutes. The tasteful grey walls, rather like her own house, the abstract painting, the books of poetry that are just surprising enough in their extensiveness to suggest that he has risked not being quite neutral in this corner of the room. In the silence, she can feel her heart beating and is not sure where it's coming from – it doesn't seem to be her chest. She moves her hand around and finds that the pulse she can feel is just below her ear. It's faster than she'd expect, but she remembers thinking this before and checking it. She feels suddenly that there's a lot to say. She wants to talk more about Ana. She says that she has started to fantasise about buying a new home, just for herself and Ana. It will be furnished with a single table and chair. She will sit there, writing the great novel that everyone has given up on her writing. And around her, Ana will hoover, finally in control of the battle against entropy. What does Moser think? He probably thinks it's a fantasy about living with him.

Is it? he asks.

Kay runs a sponge along the kitchen worktop, wondering why she's doing this when it will soon be messy again, thinking that this is Ana's life, making brief interventions of order only to be subsumed by the stronger forces of chaos.

This will be the best beef they've ever had, Harald says. Once he'd have said 'you've ever had' but now Kay – is this inevitable in marriage? – is too much a part of him for him to want to impress her. At most they can collude in impressing others, in this case a group of his literary friends.

She goes upstairs to change her clothes. She's waited to change till the last minute, because Harald's cooking will coat everything she's wearing in grease. She sniffs the purple top she's taken off, which smells unpleasantly of Sunday pubs. She puts on a silk black shirt and a pair of trousers and looks in the mirror at the end of their walk-in wardrobe, taking no satisfaction in her appearance. She tries a closed-lipped smile but feels that she is confronting a ghost.

Downstairs, Nina Simone is playing and Harald is dancing as he cooks, his stomach wobbling as he lurches from side to side in a parody of exuberance. She stands in the doorway watching him, jolted out of disapproval by her envious admiration of the pleasure he's able to take in the world on his own. This was what attracted her once, what still attracts her, and reveals that she would not be better off elsewhere, however much she fantasises about lone austerity. It matters that at least one adult in the house should be capable of joy.

He sees her standing in the doorway and dances over, laughing as he wiggles his shoulders and hips. She is the static, awkward girl at a school dance, rescued into animation. In his arms, she dances well, better than you'd expect, given that her back and hips are so rigidly straight in daily life, and it surprises her that this is still possible and that her body is still connected to her mind at all. This is the wordless communication they are capable of but rarely have in bed now. She is twisting, somewhere between woman and cat in his arms, willing him to keep going, to send her into a state of dizziness where the inner observer is finally silenced.

There's a ring on the doorbell. Whoever it is will probably have walked past the windows at street level, looking into the basement, and will have seen them dancing. She isn't sure if she likes the thought of offering this scene as a window on to their marriage.

It's me, her friend Stella. I sit down alone, and she finds it strange seeing me without Maggie, and strange to encounter me in reality when I have been present for her as an imaginary figure during her sessions with Moser. She pours three glasses of the wine that Harald has decanted but just as we are about to sip them he produces the cocktail shaker, forbidding us our glasses. This is stylishly done and Kay decides to succumb to the attraction of the drink itself.

Are you drinking much? she asks me, and I explain that I've cut down on breastfeeding a bit so everything is becoming possible again. Harald looks at us distastefully, as though to forbid us being mothers at his dinner party, reminding me that I'm here in my professional capacity as a publisher. To reinforce this, he asks how work is and then, laughing, asks what news there is of Vince, Helena's uncle and our publishing director. I remind him that I'm still on maternity leave, evading the question about Vince, because I only heard yesterday what's happened.

Cliff, our CEO, called to tell me that Vince has been accused of exposing himself to an author in a hotel room at a literary festival. Apparently Vince denies it, though he admits inviting her to his room. At the moment, I find it all hard to believe. He's slept with enough women consensually that he surely wouldn't need to force himself upon them. And as allegations go, it feels so unoriginal at the moment.

But Vince is close enough to retirement, and Cliff is worried enough about the reputation of the company, that he may be gently forced out. Harald has heard this already, and hopes, misguidedly, that I might at that point choose to publish his own books; he sees in us the prestige he still seeks. That may be one reason why he's decided, lavishly, to feed me tonight. I'm tempted to tell him not to bother. I've only read one of his novels and didn't get much out of it. I look for a kind of urgency in books that I almost never feel in Harald, even in conversation, though I feel it all the time in Kay.

By way of acknowledging our shared world, I ask him who's coming. He lists the guests: three novelists and a journalist. He doesn't know if they're bringing partners. His dinners are informally enough catered that the numbers don't need to be fine-tuned in advance.

The doorbell rings. The three novelists, all male, have arrived at once, already in animated conversation, which they continue on their way downstairs. They take their cocktails. They all have beards and are the same sort of height, with hair different combinations of salt and pepper, paunches varying from slight to large. Kay failed to listen to their names upstairs but remembers one being called Bill and one Stephen. It's possible that two are called Stephen. Why have we allowed ourselves to live in a world where everyone is so close to being the same?

They are talking about adultery in literature. No one has done it as well as Henry James, one of them says. Kay looks over at me, wishing to exchange a glance of recognition that we are still talking about Henry James after all these years, but I am looking into my glass, preparing myself to summon a likeable and articulate social persona for the next three hours, when really I'd most like to talk to Kay about our babies.

He's so judgy, though, says the other one in a tone Kay categorises distractedly as camp.

In the best novels he's judging them as people, not for their actions, she says, hearing in herself the clipped tones of the schoolmistress but caring enough about what she's saying to continue. She explains that in *The Golden Bowl* the adulterers are wrong to take advantage of their spouses' innocence, but they're not wrong to transgress the marital bond. Everyone looks at her. The camp man smiles and stares, as though beginning to take her in. She notices that his beard is slightly less manicured than the other men's.

Whose side is James on, he asks, Maggie or Charlotte? She says that it's both. James isn't too clever for goodness, but he also values the honesty of the intelligently bad. Her guest smiles more eagerly. He has focused on her now and appreciates her. She wishes that she could remember his name. The conversation continues and she finds that she's able to talk about this book she hasn't read for twenty years. She thinks that she might actually be enjoying herself, and realises that she is eating one of the fishy canapés with relish, as though it has been made by someone else in someone else's kitchen and she is not going to be responsible for the washing up.

Do you write? the man asks abruptly. She can feel me looking at her, curious as to what she'll say.

No, she says, clasping her hands neatly in front of her as she explains that one writer is enough. He advises her to do so. With her definite opinions, she might write something original.

Watching them, I feel irritated that he doesn't know how

obvious this is. It's as though he's just discovered a fresh talent, rather than observing a talent that has been slowly wasting for twenty years.

I feel sick when I go into bookshops, she says, because there are so many books published. Usually when Harald wants to go into one I wait outside, or hide in the children's section. When Stella sends me the books she publishes, I look at them, with their tasteful covers and tasteful prose, and wonder why it feels like a valid use of a life to publish them. I look at Harald's manuscripts before he submits them, printed and stacked up, and wonder how he's so confident that the world needs another banal story about made-up people.

The room is silent as she says this, because Harald has appeared in the doorway with a young blonde woman who Kay didn't notice him going to let in. She looks at the woman who's now being introduced as Nella, wondering with neutral curiosity if she has already had sex with her husband. The man continues the conversation with an intensity that she now finds inappropriate, given that all these people are listening. He's telling her that the world may need her books more. She laughs, provoked into more speech by his presumption.

I probably do think that, she says. People think it's because I'm modest that I say these things. And that I don't write. But it's not that. It's because I'm so arrogant. If I was a novelist, I'd be the kind who'd say that all my contemporaries are dead, that I write for future generations rather than my own.

That's what Stephen thinks too, he says, which may mean that this one is not called Stephen. She wonders how much more of this she can bear.

Nella, speaking for the first time, asks Kay which is her favourite of Harald's novels, and there's so much wrong with the question and its timing that it seems easiest just to answer it.

White Rain, Kay says.

She wonders if this is true. It's certainly true that she liked his writing then, when he published his first book, more than she does now, if only because he was still an actor who was also writing. Though it's too long ago to remember clearly, she believed in his genius as an actor in a way she has never believed in his genius as a writer. As an actor, he was a chameleon. He didn't need psychological insight. Now, as a writer, he's still a chameleon, acting the part of an insightful writer with a mixture of snap judgements and comedy, and no one but her seems to have noticed the difference between being a writer and pretending to be one, perhaps because there isn't a difference after all.

Nella says that she hasn't read that one and asks Harald if he has a copy. Harald explains to the room that Nella's doing a profile of him next weekend, and then produces the colourful aubergine-based starters, while we make appropriate noises of appreciation.

Kay is seated between me and one of the novelists. She asks me how it's going with Moser, which surprises me in its intimacy. I say non-committally that I think being an editor has made me too self-conscious about language to enjoy psychoanalysis and that it's strange to think of us both there.

I'm so competitive that this has made me competitive with you, Kay says. I want to know I'm better at it.

The admission makes us warm to each other.

I'm sure you are better, I say.

Kay says that she feels more rivalrous about Moser than she does about Harald now, and we both turn to look down the table at Harald, talking to Nella. I agree that it's hard to maintain jealousy in a marriage. And we both reflect on the peculiar way that my marriage ended, with Chris presenting his younger woman to me, like a cat bringing in a bird. In the new intimacy of his confession I felt more love for him than I'd felt for years. But I condoned the relationship, because it turned out that my desire for freedom was stronger than my possessiveness.

It is not true, though, for Kay. The dancing, that shared knowledge and contact, was more real than anything else. However much her respect for her husband has waned, she still has the physical need that makes jealousy possible. Certainly she feels more desire for him than for anyone else at the table. She envies me for what she identifies, rightly I think, as my capacity for desire. She sees me as looking in any room for a man to desire, and gaining energy from the process. Now I am testing out the man next to her, aware of him listening as we talk.

The good thing about us both seeing him – Moser – is that you're always there in the room as a point of comparison, she says. It makes me see what I'm lacking. My failure to turn my life into what I want it to be, bending other people to my will like you have with Chris and at work, to get everything you want out of them. And my failure as a sexual being. I thought of you earlier, getting dressed. Thought that you'd have enjoyed it more than I was. That you desire yourself. It's been years since I did that.

Trying not to be hurt by her taunts about my selfishness, I say that I probably do still desire myself, though I haven't thought about it. I enjoyed getting dressed this evening,

33

partly because I've been out so much less, since Maggie was born. Kay's neighbour leans in, and I feel myself becoming more attractive under his stare, and wonder why I am more susceptible to this than Kay is, and what I would gain, how I would use the extra mental space, if it stopped. He asks if we're old friends and I say that yes we are, from university. There's a whole group of us left, I explain, who shared a house in our second year and who still see each other now. Kay was the cleverest.

Kay doesn't contradict me. There is no need for self-deprecation, when she has profited by her cleverness so little. It feels like a childish accomplishment, the way I describe it now, that cleverness that grown-up men and women devoted so much effort to cultivating in all of us. It feels as though I have said that she was good at doing handstands, or curling her tongue, as our children are now learning to do.

The beef appears. Harald tells everyone that it's the best beef, with the confidence in his own ability to give pleasure that is just about likeable enough to make self-deprecation unnecessary for him as well. Kay reflects that this may be what attracted her and Harald to each other initially: their childish delight in their own skills. Neither has managed to turn them into something more dignified.

Do you enjoy having this standard of cooking in your own home? Nella asks, and Kay feels like she's being assessed by a journalist as a subject after all.

Yes of course, but it's driven the cleaner away, she says, repenting now for her churlishness over his books.

Enjoying the anecdote, Harald tells everyone that Kay has learnt Bulgarian to try to get her back. She puts more effort into communicating with her than she does with me, he says.

Kay is furious with him for turning this into a story. It

robs her of seriousness in her relationship with Ana, which is one of the few areas of life that she still takes seriously. But she has to smile in shared amusement at her eccentricity. There's a cry on the baby alarm from Seb. She looks at Harald, who doesn't seem to have heard. No one pays any attention and it's tempting just to leave it, to let Seb continue as a clamouring extra guest in the room. The shouts alternate Mummy and Daddy by way of instituting the gender equality they do not have.

She says that she'd better go up, turning it off and smiling with false brightness. The guests' smiles all seem empty of sympathy and she takes refuge in the parent's rage at the obliviousness of the childless.

I want milk, Seb says, because Harald gives it to him in the night, believing, unlike Kay, that he's really hungry (before we became mothers, were we able to vouch for the hunger of others?) when he asks for it. She refuses, offering only the beaker of water she has taken up with her, and he doesn't protest, instead sipping slowly and leaning sleepily towards her. She lies back against his pillow, taking his weight on her in his furry pyjamas, and she strokes his hair as she moves the beaker from his mouth. She pictures the faces of the men downstairs, wondering if she seems as much a type to them as they do to her.

I love you Mummy, he says, and it's a new expression that he seems to be trying out.

I love you, Seb, she says.

More than Alisa?

More than the whole world, she responds, pleased with the formulation. She pulls away gently, letting him flop into the bed. This has turned out to be the thing that she has done most competently all day.

She walks past their bedroom with its neatly made bed on the way down, and is tempted to lie down, feeling that her presence makes no difference downstairs, though half an hour earlier she felt involved. The fun of the dinner party strikes her now as dutiful and bleak. She thinks that she'd like to leave the house and walk out, fast, in a straight line, quelling her restless energy as she leaves the streets of self-satisfied Victorian houses behind. She wonders if the moon is out above London and pictures it in its bony brightness, though she can't remember when she last saw it, during these weeks of housebound evenings. As she comes in, I exchange a look of sympathy with her, and she shrugs her shoulders.

It was relatively easy, she says, sitting back down to the cold remains of her beef. Do you have children, Stephen? she asks in the direction of the novelists, who are all now sitting in a row.

No, two of the novelists say at the same time. I laugh, catching her eye, expecting her to laugh too, at Harald's comedy dinner party, but she is still half inhabiting the scene upstairs so her sense of the comic is slightly outside the grasp of her conscious mind.

It must be very fulfilling, says Nella, and we all smile at her, willing her to continue. She adds that her boyfriend thinks they need to wait till they're thirty, but she'd like to start now. Kay notes the lack of relief in herself at the public mention of the boyfriend, wondering if this means that she wouldn't mind her having an affair with Harald.

We should all have as many children as we can as young as possible, Harald says, and it doesn't seem to strike him as absurd that he is saying this having just failed to acknowledge the child upstairs as his responsibility.

Kay, by way of reorientating herself within the room,

brings up the subject of Vince again, disregarding my awkwardness. She is loyal to him, too, on account of Helena, but she doesn't have enough gossip in her life at the moment so she asks if there's any news. Everyone leans in appreciatively; it seems this is the conversation they have all been waiting for since Harald announced where I work.

No, I say, but we have to presume he's innocent until proven guilty.

Kay asks if it's a formal allegation and Harald says that he's heard it is. Excited, Nella reports that she's heard that Vince has had sex with at least ten women, authors and employees, and they're all coming forward. I am shocked that the rumours have already reached this level. Kay points out that those must have been consensual, and I'm pleased that, if she is going to bring it all up, she is making this point.

It's still an abuse of power, Nella says.

It's how we all used to live, Harald says, getting the toothpicks out of the drawer, while you were still at school. But now everything's changed. Men are going to have to find something other than women.

Kay smiles at him, though she's irritated by his habit of picking his teeth in public, which he's doing now. They are on the same side here because, however she feels about his adultery, she is committed to the principle of interpreting the law as accurately as possible. There is no law against sleaze. She worries, though, surprised to find herself in league with Harald against the younger woman, that Nella will put his comments in her newspaper profile. She explains to Nella that it's not that they don't disapprove of sleaze, but that in those cases he hasn't contravened a law, and hasn't even contravened his employment contract. So it all depends what's proved in this particular case.

37

It's ten o'clock when the beef is cleared away. Ice cream is produced in a range of original flavours and Kay and I both eat it greedily, pulling back from the conversation. It may be because we're both still enclosed in new motherhood that our social energy is limited to a two-hour stretch. We're ready now for a silent sofa, and yet the conversation continues, filled with literary gossip I'm expected to join in with. But I can't remember who has won what prize recently, who might be sleeping with whom. Increasingly, I feel that there is a desperation in these conversations given that we all suspect that literature will have ceased to have much status within a decade or two.

Harald suggests that we should go up to the sitting room with brandy. I announce that I'm going home. Kay walks upstairs with me as I summon my Uber.

I'm tired, she says.

I say that it would be fine for her to go to bed.

It makes no difference whether I go to bed or not. I'll still be tired tomorrow and the day after. I think I'll be exhausted for the rest of my life.

You should write, I say, and it doesn't strike her as irrelevant.

All those writers, she says, gesturing towards the kitchen downstairs, and listening to her I have the feeling of them as dirt, clogging up the clean surfaces of her house.

I insist that she'd be different. She'd have things to say about the world. I feel that I strike her as absurdly naive and am relieved that my phone beeps to tell me that the car is there, promising that I will be in bed by midnight as planned. We kiss goodbye, her smile self-mockingly apologetic, and we agree that we will meet soon, on our own. As I am on my way down the corridor to the front door I hear them all coming upstairs and I speed up so that I don't have to say goodbye again, mentally already back in my flat with Maggie.

In the sitting room, Kay has given up on her longing for sleep, putting aside this need like so many others. She takes refuge instead in the brandy and the shock of its warmth. She is drunk, now, and there's a satisfaction in this that allows her to feel brief solidarity with the people around her, with the three men she has given up on trying to distinguish from each other, and with the woman who may or may not have slept with or be planning to sleep with her husband. Unexpectedly, Harald sits down next to her on the sofa and takes her hand. Kay observes them as a couple, as though from outside, and likes herself.

Stella

April

That dinner was a week ago. I sent my thank-you text but haven't heard from Kay. As so often at the moment, my main thought as I got into bed was that it wasn't worth the babysitting money or the time away from Maggie or the tiredness that would follow. I have so little energy now for social interaction. At least I knew what I was doing in the days when I was out to impress successful figures in the literary world or to half seduce whichever man I found myself next to.

But the next morning, lying with Maggie cradled on my chest as she sucked her milk, thinking of Kay doing the same with Alisa, a few miles west, also tired and a little hungover, also half relishing this and half wishing that she didn't have a baby still young enough to wake so early, I realised that it was for Kay that I'd gone and must continue to go, and that the old friendships, however arbitrary, are the ones that matter now, because they originate from a time of energy and commitment and because otherwise I am so alone.

When the marriage ended, I lost the shared memories of my twenties and thirties, the years I lived alongside Chris. It's not only that we can't reminisce together, it's that it's impossible for memories to retain their happiness when you are picturing someone you now dislike. Those are years that my friends witnessed. They shared my excitement when I met him and joined us for collective holidays and expeditions. So I rely on these women now, and it matters for all of us I think that we can see the twenty-year-old in the forty-year-old, can remember each other's bodies before our hips and stomachs began to sink earthwards. We know each other's families, have watched each other's parents carrying our boxes of books and make-up in from the car, exposing ourselves to each other as petulant daughters. Five years ago, I was trying to untether myself from these friends, more excited by the new people I was meeting in my professional life. But now, living alone with my children, sometimes uncertain if my mental state matters to anyone except the psychoanalyst I pay, I need these people for whom my presence is a given.

I was thinking this, sleepily, when Maggie suddenly vomited her milk in a thick white stream, all over the respectable nightie that I wear now I sleep alone, fearing that I might have to rush outside if there's a fire in the night, and all over my duvet and her hair. She wailed as I ran her a bath, unable to tend to her at the same time as stripping her clothes and my bed. Worrying about what was wrong with her, I started to feel sick myself, and washed her hair three times, though she hated it, because I was convinced I could still smell the milk in it. Then Cleo came in, asking if she could have a different breakfast because she didn't like the cereal I'd left out for her, though it's the one she has most days, and I shouted at her unfairly, saying that it should be obvious I was busy, telling her she was old enough to get her own breakfast, that I couldn't do everything on my own.

I saw Cleo burrowing inside herself as she retreated into

the kitchen, pulling her long brown hair tightly down behind her ears. I knew that she'd be sitting in silence, not eating, and I wanted to go after her to reassure her that I still see her needs and want to meet them, but I couldn't leave Maggie who was howling. I felt then as though all the imagined companionship with Kay had been an illusion, because in those circumstances she would have summoned Harald to help with the baby and to discuss what was wrong. I resented her for her easier life, while also wishing that we were still close enough in a daily way that I could call to tell her what was happening. It's hard to believe we all lived in the same house once, hearing each other's boyfriends snoring through the thin walls, eating each other's leftovers. Perhaps we even shared menstrual cycles. Perhaps that was the closest I've been to participating enthusiastically in family life.

It's a week later now and I've just got back from a drink with Vince. I went into the office to say hello to everyone and show off pictures of Maggie. Before we left, Vince gave me his fountain pen. He said that he'd edited over five hundred books with it and doesn't know how many more he has in him, so I can have it as a return-to-work present, in lieu of baby clothes.

It's black, plumper than any pen I've ever owned, the enamel tarnished and the nib darkened. I put it in my desk drawer. I'll use it. Vince and I have had our differences over the years but they feel irrelevant now that we are so palpably on the same side. He knows this without my saying. The twenty-five years between us feel so small compared to the ten years separating me from Harald's journalist Nella and her generation, when it comes to these arguments about sex. Thinking about Vince and his alleged act of exposure, I think of Norman Mailer in that scene with Germaine Greer. I'll take out my modest little Jewish dick and put it on the table and we can all spit and laugh. Surely Vince, too, and his presumably circumcised dick, could be laughed off. But I just can't believe in the allegation. His sense of humour is too strong for him not to find it a funny thing to do. He's too charming, too lacking in aggression to be so crass.

We went to our usual basement wine bar on Endell Street, which Vince finds difficult to enjoy now because he's always worried it will be our last time there before they strip it out and turn it into a gastropub or a cocktail bar. It was a warm evening and usually I'd have demanded to be outside somewhere but it felt right, with his middle-European moustache and his insistently warm jacket, that we should be there. He flirted with the new blonde waitress, asking her where she was from.

Am I wrong to do that? he asked, after she'd gone, and I was surprised to see him so lost, without the professional carapace he's always assumed around me. He asked if we could still talk to strangers and I said that we could. The world is changing so fast, he said. I'm glad I'm my age and not yours.

There is no suggestion between us that it will be good for me if he goes, even though I'll probably be given his job. It feels like a sign of shared humanity that we can assume with such mutual confidence that this isn't something I want to happen, in these circumstances. It was only at the end that we talked about the situation. He told me that he wasn't allowed to discuss it, but that I should know that he was all right. He had half an olive trapped in his moustache as he said it and I didn't know whether to point it out. Luckily it fell on to the table when he wiped his mouth with his hand.

The funny thing is that I was on their side, he said. The women. Me too, I've been saying, me too, thinking I could join them at the barricades. I didn't think I was disqualified just because I'd slept with a lot of them.

I know, I said, laughing, though I didn't know, and this wasn't what I was expecting him to say. He'd never admitted his promiscuity to me before – on some level, I suppose, I'm still his niece's friend, and I don't think anyway that he's the kind of man who'd confide in women he hasn't slept with. He said that he was relieved no one had mentioned rape, which is the most barbaric act of all. He said that he's been proud, over the years, that whatever his wife has had to put up with from him, he's adding more to the world, more pleasure and more love, than he's taking away. And then he said that he was sad that the young men won't have a chance to find out about women, and how much more wonderful they are than men.

I had tears in my eyes then, because I was moved that he'd chosen to say this to me, and that he had both missed the point and made the only point, and because I could see that he is going to have to leave, that there can be no place now for someone who thinks these things so unregretfully. And it will be my role to wield the disinfectant, cleaning out what remains of him in the office, committing to a world that has no room for him, aligning myself with the Nellas.

This seems, writing in bed, in that brief hour of lucidity between putting Maggie to bed and becoming too tired to write, the moment to say more about Tom, though part of the problem is that I don't know what to call him. Your boyfriend, Moser said a couple of weeks ago. I was strident in refusing the term. *Boyfriend*, I said, was too infantilising, it was a problem of the English language, a reason to get married, though husband with that claiming 'band' was not much better. It's true, but it was the *your* I was objecting to as well. In the exhausted aftermath of the marriage, I have found it hard to imagine ever being able to claim or be claimed as *my* anything again.

But I liked it when, staying at his house in the absurdly rolling Cotswold countryside on Sunday for the first time, we went swimming in his friends' pool after lunch and it felt like a scene in a French film, as pool scenes always do, and he stood on the side watching me swim up and down in my Speedo costume, more serious in my pursuit of exercise than was appropriate given the children surrounding me, and when I asked if he was coming in, he said I like watching my girlfriend swimming. I liked him using the word, and liked him watching, and with the sun shining it felt like perhaps I could be claimed, perhaps this was all more straightforward than I'd made it feel. We kissed when I got out, my body wet against his clothed one. We are the same height and almost the same age, our brown hair greying together, matching. It feels like a sign that I have grown up that I no longer need a larger, older man.

Then after lunch there was a call from Andreas. I could hear Andreas shouting, the electronic German accent breaking into the English idyll. Tom walked round the corner from the pool and paced up and down on the grass, framed by two rows of trees. I followed, not sure if it was appropriate or not to eavesdrop on this young man I have never met channelled through the older man whose shoulders, bent forwards over the phone in worry, already feel almost as familiar as my own body, and certainly more familiar than those of the man whose bed I shared for fifteen years but who now seems to me a stranger when we accidentally touch.

Andreas had lost his keys, he was locked out of home, and somehow Tom, in Oxfordshire, was meant to tell his son where his mother was and why she wasn't there to welcome him in. Tom offered to ring Carla too but there was nothing he could do while on the phone to Andreas and the conversation went on and on, repetitively, until eventually Tom persuaded him to ring the neighbours' bells and see if he could get into the building. Afterwards, as we waited for news, I saw, in a way I hadn't before, that Tom's unease about Andreas is there all the time. This makes me feel my unease about Cleo as a life sentence – the way that she constantly creates new needs and ailments as tests of a love that I can never sufficiently prove because the thing that she really wants is to return to the marital home as an only child.

Perhaps this is what Kay means when she says that we don't put enough thought into having children; we don't know what we're taking on. Our friend Susanne, the mother of our friend Mark from university, says that we plan it too much now, where her generation just had accidentally unprotected sex and coped with the consequences. But Kay may be right that the burden of responsibility for another life is unbearable, if you really feel responsible, as I think Tom does all the time, feeling that Andreas's depression and uncertainty is something that Tom's forced him to live out, day after day, by giving him life.

Priss

April

Priss is thirty-eight, shorter than me and Kay, with blonde hair, smooth, pale skin, green eyes, and an easy affinity between her body and the world around it. I suppose that's why she's so stylish; clothes become part of her body more easily than they do for the rest of us. She studied history and was very good at it, though I think she was as unoriginal academically as she is conversationally. But for reasons that may become apparent, I find it hard to see her clearly.

At university I thought, more admiringly than jealously, that Priss was the prettiest in our group and I found her the most restful to spend time with, able to stop listening to my inner voice in her company. When we lived together, it was with Priss that I most often sat drinking tea in the late morning, missing lectures we'd half planned to go to, or watched films on TV in the afternoons. When I was going out with men I feared might be embarrassing, I'd invite her to come along, knowing that she wouldn't blame me if she didn't like them or if we had a tedious evening, just as now I can inflict my children at their grumpiest on her and know that she'll cope. She's able to see the best in people without having a whole philosophy about it.

Now Priss is married to Ben, a literary agent who repre-
sents about half a dozen of my authors. She met him in her
mid twenties and I met him through her; it was useful to
get to know a successful agent as I started my career as an
editor. He's ten years older than her, like Chris with me,
and they met, predictably, at the marriage of his friend to
her sister. Like me and Chris with our matching dark curly
hair, they look right together. He is the male equivalent of
an English rose, pale and blond as she is. He was charmed,
I suppose, by her spontaneity, impressed by that self-assured,
joined-up quality that her appearance usually imparts. They
may have danced together at that wedding. Like Harald and
Kay, they dance well as a couple, though it's less surprising
in this case. Priss has that lightness of bearing which leads
you to expect movement.

After university, she had a succession of jobs in arts admin,
publicising one arts organisation after another. They were
badly enough paid that it was quite easy to justify giving
them up when she had Robert, who is now six, and then
three years later she had Lena and became accepted as the
non-working mother among us. I think Ben assumes that
she won't work again. I used to disapprove of this but since
having Maggie I've seen how straightforward it would be
for a mother of two children to fill the time between nine
and three-thirty. It's not surprising that, in the absence of
worldliness or vocation, she should decide not to work,
though it's also perhaps not surprising that I, who define
people too much by what they do, should have gradually
ceased to think of her in any substantial way as my friend.

They live in that large, tall house in Islington – she and
Kay have the two grandest houses of all of us, this one bought
largely with Priss's inherited money. It's seven o'clock but

the evenings are bright enough that it could be any time in the afternoon. She's sitting on Robert's bed while he falls asleep and she's thinking about meeting our old friend Mark when she did the school run earlier.

Usually it's Mark's mother Susanne who picks up her grandson on Tuesdays, but today one of Mark's psychoanalytic patients had cancelled so he was doing it and Priss felt that he'd been looking out for her in the playground. She hasn't been close to Mark since our undergraduate days, but today, as he chatted about his father, who is dying, while Lena climbed on the playground pirate ship, she remembered that Helena used to tell her that he was in love with her. She was trying to work out whether he was upset about his father beneath his usual blitheness, and whether he needed her sympathy, when the children came out and he realised he'd forgotten his son's after-school snack.

I come here trying to impress all the mummies, he said when Priss offered to share hers. I rush around, wanting to show how male and athletic I am and caring as well. But then I don't know where to stand, because I haven't done it for so long and they've changed it all again, haven't they, the place where Year 2 comes out, and I don't have a snack, because it turns out that I'm not capable of nurturing my son after all. But it's ok because one of the mummies will give me hers, and maybe in fact this is the best way to impress her, maybe I do have a chance.

Priss laughed with genuine appreciation while he said it, enjoying as she always has his ability to turn life into a sitcom. She blinked self-consciously each time their eyes met, surprised as she is every time she sees him, by how dark a blue his are. As they left the school with their respective children, he invited her to a lunch party next weekend, saying that Kay and I would be there, and Priss wondered, disappointed, if he has come to think of her primarily as our friend. On the way home, she asked herself what her life would be like if it was Mark who she'd married rather than Ben. She decided that it may not have altered very much.

She thinks now, as her son pulls the duvet up over his head, that Mark does still care about her – he doesn't just think of her as an adjunct to her more intellectual friends. She trusts her own response to his energy in the playground and to the way he waited while she checked her diary, really wanting to know if she could come. The evening has felt different, not just more manageable but shimmering gently with potential at the edge of her vision, because of the knowledge that there was an attractive man attracted to her at half past three. She wonders if those of us who work have this every day in some form or another, and if this is a shallow way to thrive in the world or if she is missing out on something that matters.

She goes back downstairs again, considering what to do with the two hours before she goes to bed, wondering if Ben will be home before she goes to sleep. The sofa, she notices when she returns to it, still has a dent from where Ben sat last night when they watched TV. There's a kind of companionship in it, now, and it's this that makes her decide to read Kirsty Kennedy's book, which Ben agents. The launch of her new novel is coming up next week and Priss would like to read the first one beforehand, partly to be sure that she has something to say amid the small talk, though she knows that Ben won't mind, won't be shaken in his pride in her, if she doesn't.

Priss is convinced, now, that Ben loves her, which she wasn't sure of a couple of years ago. There's a pride when he introduces her, an ease in their time alone together. He seems more jealous than he used to be, though it's a long time since anyone has pursued her. She isn't sure what has made him more attentive to her again but it's probably to do with the children. He loves the world he finds each day on reaching home and has come to accept her: her lack of ambition, and her lack of enthusiasm for sex, as the children get older, is less important than her role in making this life possible. She in turn has developed a kind of charged maternal energy that he responds to, enjoying her confidence about her own primacy in the domestic sphere.

She's asleep on the sofa when Ben gets home. It's half past eleven. Waking, she knows that she's been dreaming and that she was in the Peak District. She can feel it in her whole body, the feel of the landscape of her childhood, warm rock and hills of tufty grass.

You're here, he says, and she stands up to hug him. He goes upstairs to inspect the sleeping children.

She puts the kettle on. He never feels ready to go straight to bed when he comes in, so if she wants to go to bed with him, she'll need to stay up for another hour. This seems to be one of the reasons they don't have more sex, why many couples don't have more sex – because it's rare for them to get into bed at the same time. He's stopped initiating it at other moments, presumably because of her frequent lack of responsiveness, and she has become too shy to initiate it outside of bed. There's a kind of forcedness in doing so and, if she thinks explicitly about sex, which she doesn't often, then she thinks that she'd rather have the kind of sex you have when you're already in bed together than the kind you might have starting fully clothed in the sitting room. She doesn't want all the talking and looking. But she does want him to desire her, and is bothered now by the speed with which he's gone off to see the children, without wanting to talk to her first.

He comes down and they sit on the sofa drinking peppermint tea, though she would have preferred a glass of wine.

I started Kirsty's book, she says.

It's sent you to sleep, he observes.

Oh Ben, she says, I'm sorry! I was tired. I'd been arguing with Robert before he went to bed. I liked it, though. I like the characters, I like how young they are.

Yes, exactly, he says, suddenly animated. That's why she's done so well I think. Because she's young, but she's not pretending to be more grown up than she is. She's writing about being young. But in a voice that's mature in spite of all that.

She can hear Ben saying this at the party he's just been at, can picture people nodding at him. She resists the image of all those people; she wants to keep the grass and water she was dreaming about as the resting image in her mind. She takes his hand and he lifts it to stroke hers, tracing the bones from the knuckles to the wrist, each in turn. She leans into him and he puts down his mug and touches her hair and back. It seems possible that sex can just be more of this. Can be her whole body being stroked. She lies face down across his lap and as he caresses up and down from her shoulders to her buttocks, she pictures them as hills and valleys. He's very good at this. You wouldn't expect it, observing his slightly awkward manner in social situations, that he's so natural, physically, in a more intimate setting. It seems a waste that he doesn't get to display these gifts more often. She turns around and leans up and kisses him. They kiss gently, their lips opening more wetly than she expected into each other's mouths.

She lies back and smiles at him, happy in the knowledge that this is a moment – there are not enough of these in marriage – where sex is possible but not necessary. She decides to leave it to him to choose. By way of signalling his decision, he picks up his tea again, sips it and then rests it on her stomach. She feels pleased at the togetherness in the gesture while a little offended by his easy use of her body as a surrogate table. She wonders what domestic object she'd like to be more than a table: definitely not a fridge, perhaps a rug.

How was your day? he asks. They talk about Robert. She likes it that Ben is interested enough in their children to know how they would respond to any particular situation. Her updates on her days are, if anything, more interesting for him than his updates on his days are for her. Yet now, having made the question of whether to have sex his decision, she minds that he hasn't pressed for it, minds that he seems just as contented to talk about Robert as to continue kissing her. She sees in this an intimation of what life would be like if Ben's desire for her could no longer be taken as a given. With real need, now, and with the memory of being looked at by Mark still hovering within view, she leans up again to kiss him and prises open his lips with her tongue, feeling her way around his mouth.

Kirsty's party is in a large, rather grand room in a hotel near Russell Square. We are all mingling. That two-hour constellation that we have all learnt, over the years, to perform together. I have given a speech, insisting that Kirsty's youth is no longer important, that she's now a major writer: one of our major writers, I have said, enjoying the old-fashioned phrase. There are a lot of her relatives around. They want to meet me, they want to meet Ben. Priss joins in alongside Ben, wearing an asymmetrical blue dress that she bought, riskily, online. She charms Kirsty's relatives more easily than I do. But then she tires – of what? – of being a wife? Of mingling? She likes mingling, on the whole, but both the children woke up in the night so she is tired, and hates the feeling that each conversation is a kind of test in which she must manufacture opinions that she doesn't really have.

There are three aunts gathered around her. One of them has asked her what exactly Ben does for Kirsty. She is explaining what agents do, wondering if it seems unnecessary to them. They like her, and they want to respect Ben, but they are finding it a challenge.

So he posts the manuscript to Stella?

Well he won't post it, will he? He must email it.

He emails the manuscript to Stella?

Well it's obviously helpful, Kirsty said so in her speech.

Priss wanders towards the drinks table, where she enjoys the calm of not having to sustain a conversation. She's good at standing back like this and she knows it. She never looks awkward because she is so gracefully centred within her own body, as though she's in a ballet of her own devising. Now she thinks that it might be preferable to slip away at this point, but she knows that Ben likes to have her there, even if he doesn't talk to her. She looks around for him. He is gesturing, in mid flow, talking to two men. She is pleased that they've been having more sex this week. It gives her more claim over him. She looks back at the drinks table, and sees a man loitering, like her. He is attractive enough – tall and sloping – to interest her, so she smiles.

He says that he doesn't know anyone there, that he and Kirsty are connected through their families. His voice seems to slope downwards like his body does. They try talking about the book but he tries too hard and she wants to tell him that she isn't someone he needs to do this for, she'd rather talk about something else. She smiles at him, enjoying the fact that their eyes can have a conversation that seems almost wholly independent of the things they're saying, thinking that this is an experience she needs to have more often. He asks how she knows Kirsty and she explains who Ben is and who I am. He seems disappointed that she's less out of place here than he is, so she carries on talking, saying that she's not really a book person and that she doesn't know what to say to most of the people here.

What do you do? he asks.

At the moment I'm at home with the children, she says, but soon I'm going to open a café.

That sounds useful. More useful than books.

Yes, she says. I'd like to make something, but I'm not very good at making anything, so I'd like to make a place where people are happy to be.

I'll be happy to be in your café. Save me a table by the window where I don't have to talk to anyone.

She wonders if this is a sign that he wants to end the conversation. They seem anyway to have come to the end of what they have to say and they stand in silence for a few seconds, their eyes still asking questions while they give each other a chance to leave. Then they introduce themselves.

I'm Priss, she offers.

I'm Hugh, he returns.

That's a nice name, she says, and then feels embarrassed.

He thanks her, adding that she's a nice person, and you don't meet many nice people any more. She asks now what he does and he says that he trained as a painter but he mainly makes furniture. She says that her father used to make furniture, adding, embarrassed, that it was a kind of hobby and then suggests, feeling like a child pretending to have a grown-up conversation, that he could make the furniture for her café. He thinks this is a good idea, so they exchange contact details, with professional directness, and it starts to seem to Priss that she really might open a café, though it's not a thought she's voiced aloud before. When she looks up from her phone, Ben is standing beside them, stylish in his black linen jacket, looking at Hugh curiously. He smiles encouragingly at her, perhaps because she's blushing, and she wonders what she'd have to do to make him uncomfortably jealous.

Hugh explains to Ben that Priss has been telling him about her plan to open a café, and that he'd like to make the furniture for it. Ben looks at her, still smiling. Her café, he says, more as a statement than a question. And then he adds that he's bored, and asks if they can go. She's pleased to discover that she's been enjoying herself more than he has.

On the way out, they come to say goodbye to me, where I am standing talking to Vince and a couple of our younger editors. I'm glad that Vince has come — it shows solidarity with me, and with all we have stood for over the years, our commitment to spending money on talent, and avoiding the big auctions and showy names. He's pleased to see Priss. She's susceptible to older men, as I am, and she's not especially inclined to believe the allegations about him. Nonetheless, she's been avoiding him at the party, wanting to avoid awkwardness and also wanting to avoid having to ask herself if Vince really is someone whose strongest desire is to exert power by unbuttoning his flies and if this is therefore true on some level for all men. The thought of this repels her, negating the feeling of desire she has been locating in herself recently, which is fuelled by the knowledge of being found beautiful. You're so beautiful, she sometimes imagines Ben saying to her over and over again as he moves in and out of her. Talking to Vince, she feels that he is courteously admiring after all, but she worries that his respectful attentiveness has nothing to do with his lust, which he keeps hidden in a more secretive and threatening place. She wonders if this could be true for Hugh too, or for Ben. She's no longer sure what she invites when she wills men to look at her; she may be wrong about what the dance of eyes is saying. She's frightened of being left alone with her girlishness while everyone else gets on with a more violent, grown-up life she can have no part in.

Priss and Ben walk hand in hand along the dark street towards the Tube. They swing their arms and it feels like they are much younger. A childless couple in their twenties. The air is cold but she likes being under-dressed in it, enjoying the feeling of her body exposed to the night as the wind fills the space between her dress and her coat. She wonders who will mention the café first. They talk about Kirsty, about how she can follow up her early success and whether the excitement surrounding this second book is going to throw her off course. They talk about Vince, who's been a mentor to Ben as he has to so many of the younger men in publishing.

I think it's a good idea, he says, eventually. The café.

She turns to him, excited, and says that she just said it, to make conversation, and then knew it was what she wanted to do. It won't be useful for the world but nothing she could do would be, so she might as well do this, and it might make her happy. They are both surprised to hear her claiming happiness grandly as her right. He says that she could use the money from her grandfather. And it's true, there's

£30,000 sitting in a bank account. I don't know how much any of it costs, she says. Renting somewhere. Hiring staff. He says that she will find out. This is Ben at his best: able to make swift decisions and make others feel part of them.

Meanwhile, back inside the party, I have moved away from Vince, leaving him to talk to Susanne, and I am still circulating. I have watched Priss and Hugh meeting, have watched Ben watching them, bringing her to see me, escorting her off the premises. It's a habit I can't quite give up, watching Ben, however intense it becomes with Tom. And after all, Tom isn't here, and I am on public display, which always makes me feel lonely as well as happy to be showing off. So I would like to feel that Ben is thinking about me throughout the party, but I know that he's doing this less than usual because he's also wondering about Priss and Hugh.

Encountering Ben at parties these days, it's often as though I'm encountering Priss's Ben, and meeting someone I haven't slept with. There – I've said it now.

The party is almost over so Kirsty is wondering where to go next, and asking me if I'll come along. I have the excuse of the babysitter. I direct her to the nearest all right pub and walk part of the way with them. I feel proud of her and enjoy the restless energy of her friends. It reminds me of us at university. I think back to Priss on her bicycle. And as I enter the Tube I picture Priss emerging at Highbury and Islington, leaning sleepily into Ben, luxuriant in the knowledge of the awaiting bed, imagining their skin touching, at once comforting and shocking.

The interview with the nanny. We've all done this, with different degrees of entitlement and anxiety, interviewing the people to whom we are going to entrust our children.

I've always opted for the nursery. If I wanted a nanny to look after my child, I'd marry the nanny, Chris once said, in one of those memorable statements that misrepresent him, because he was stuck playing out an increasingly extreme version of the role he'd taken on within the marriage. So I didn't go down that route. Also there was a kind of safety in the nursery: in knowing that I'd know where Cleo was at any moment. But Priss has opted for a nanny. The word nanny has connotations as powerful as mother does, conjuring either a Mary Poppins or a sadist. For Priss, they're familiar figures from her childhood. Most of her friends in Derbyshire had live-in nannies, though few of their mothers worked: young, capable women who were seconded from the local villages and have since been pensioned back into them, relinquishing their freedom so that richer women could retain theirs. Priss's mother didn't want one. This wasn't the world she'd grown up in and she wanted to look after her daughters herself.

The nanny is going to look after Robert and Lena three days a week, so that Priss can begin work on making her café happen. There's only one candidate at the moment, an Italian woman in her late twenties. So this woman is sitting across from her on the sofa and Priss searches for openings within the conversation, as though pushing balls aside in the soft play centre, looking for the ground beneath. Priss announces that she's going to make tea, though the nanny has already said that she doesn't want any.

She's relieved to be alone in the kitchen. She cleaned it this morning, because tonight Hugh is coming for dinner, and she looks around now at the dark grey cupboards and counters, seeing a room in which she'll stand alone with Hugh. She remembers the first time she had a friend from school to play at home: the thrill of being alone together in the sitting room, and of lifting up her skirt to reveal her knickers and finding that she could be the leader, because the other girl immediately did the same.

Priss and Hugh have known each other for a month now, but this is the first time they will meet alone in a domestic setting. Although she suggested it casually, it's starting to feel less casual. It might be as clear to Hugh as it is to her that she wouldn't have proposed it if Ben wasn't away, and he may not guess that this is because of Ben's low boredom threshold. Ben seems pleased that she should have male friends, but doesn't want to be bothered with entertaining them himself. This won't be evident to Hugh, and she won't be able to enlighten him. These thoughts generate an erotic undercurrent which exacerbates her guilt at having a nanny in the house.

It's a bit of a mess, she says, that phrase we all say with the same unapologetic shrug, going back into the sitting room, gesturing towards the toys.

I'm used to it, the nanny says, but I'll be able to help you keep it in order.

Is this what Priss wants from her? Order? And then Priss herself will have more room in which to create disorder: to go out into the world and make choices large enough to be the wrong ones.

The bell rings and then Priss's mother unlocks the door herself. The children run in followed by Lulu, her mother's dog, yapping and jumping up at Priss and the nanny, who retreats from the little grey terrier. Priss pulls her back by her collar, disapproving of the nanny for being less confident than her children are around dogs. She walks back to the door with her mother, whispering that she doesn't know what to ask. Her mother says that she just needs to watch the nanny with the children and check that she's going to be kind. Priss's mother is encouraging her to start the café. She regrets not having a career herself, which perhaps she might have done if she hadn't married so rich a man or if her husband hadn't died in Priss's adolescence. Priss is grateful for her support but sometimes feels that, in her encouragement, her mother is saying that yes, she too is disappointed that she supported her during her admittedly almost free university education only to watch her squander herself on motherhood.

She observes the nanny with the children, thinking that this will soon be a familiar scene. She will come home from the café and look on as another woman plays with her children, wondering if it's appropriate to join in or take over. Both the children seem to know that good behaviour is required and she feels sad, as she has done since Lena was a baby, when she sees her trying to please, because some naturalness is lost. Robert gets out colouring pens and hands some to his sister. It's as though they are giving her permission to leave them, urging her out into the world of work like everyone else.

When the nanny leaves, Priss concentrates on playing with her children, determined to make up for the harm she is about to inflict on them with the nanny. But while she follows Robert's instructions, making Lego people talk to each other, she is waiting for the moment when she will turn their lights off and go downstairs, with half an hour to herself before Hugh arrives. The feeling of looking forward but also dreading has taken on its own momentum, and it's a different Hugh that she's anticipating seeing from the one she sees on their weekly lunches accompanied by Lena: more flirtatious, more urgent.

She resists sitting with Robert as he goes to sleep but he asks her to stand in the corridor for a few minutes and she gazes at herself in the mirror there, her skin gently tanned around the green eyes, her shoulders delicate against the dusky pink dress that she changed into while they put their pyjamas on. Next to the mirror there are family photographs, and she is there in riding gear with her sister. She hardly ever visited London at that age and she would have hated it if she had. It's odd to think that she's produced such urban children – frightened of horses, bored by fields. There's a kind of menace shrouding the photographs as she looks at them. That pink-cheeked girl, so at ease with her horse and her garden, doesn't know that she will lose the world she takes for granted, not so much because of their father's death, but because one day she will cease to feel that she's at the centre of her own life. She remembers that her sister rang earlier and that she should call back to check she's all right.

It's twenty past seven by the time she can escape from the corridor. She puts make-up on carefully, enjoying the speed with which life can be enhanced by the reflective sheen of creams and powder on eyes and cheeks. In retrospect, this moment of putting away the creams and turning from the mirror often feels the most promising point of the whole evening. It's certainly the time that the make-up has its highest impact, but tonight there's a slight relief in knowing that as the minutes pass she'll return to her everyday, homelier self. Then she goes downstairs, turns on the heat under the cassoulet and opens the bottle of wine that she's taken from Ben's supplies.

A text message appears from Ben. It disturbs her, making her feel that he's timed it for Hugh's appearance. 'Everyone here sends love. Miss children and you. Big hug to all xxx'. There's a silliness in these messages that husbands and wives now send each other. Once, she and Ben wrote to each other in careful paragraphs when he was away. We were the first email generation: it felt remarkable to us, to be able to send letters instantly across the ether. But now we all send these phrases, in which our phones predict most of the words. 'Nanny came,' she writes now, 'seems good. Children sleepy and cosy. Hugh about to come round. Miss you too xxx'. The reply is swift. 'Oh that's good – have a good evening xxx'. If he feels jealous of her he keeps it to himself, but his emotional privacy has never bothered her. She wants to feel loved – to be shown and told it – more than she wants deep knowledge of another person. This seems to be among the many things that have drawn her and Ben to each other: their desire to keep their inner lives private from each other and themselves.

The bell rings. He's always punctual, but this time he's ten minutes late. They kiss on both cheeks and she whirls around, girlish in her stockinged feet, while he remains in his shoes.

A glass of wine? she asks.

Yes, I brought some. You look nice.

She blushes, more out of awkwardness now than erotic tension. She feels frightened that his hopes for the night might really be as high as she's feared they are, and that she doesn't know how to diffuse them.

She explains that she was interviewing the nanny and had to look professional, though her pink dress is hardly the attire of a career woman and he might guess that she's changed.

How was it? he asks.

How was it? she echoes. Oh. I don't know, Hugh. Shall we sit on the sofa?

They go through to the sitting room, where he's never been. He touches the tweed curtains, which are flecked in the same dusky pink as her dress, and says that he likes them. It's a professional appraisal. She says that her mother made them and he examines the stitching, saying that they're well made. Priss realises that she likes them too, though she's never thought hard about it; she let her mother make those decisions. She suspects, though he's never said it, that Ben doesn't like them. This isn't his taste, though he's never really had a chance to find out what his domestic taste would be. She wonders if he minds this, or if he's happy, as she usually assumes he is, concentrating on work and leaving the domestic realm to her.

They sit on the sofa together and it's a relief to find that, talking about the nanny, she feels as natural with Hugh as she usually does. With Hugh it's easier to say things that she's ashamed of than it is with Ben.

After a few minutes they go back into the kitchen and he busies himself with helping, so that soon it's him stirring the food and laying the table and she is sitting looking into the glass of wine that she twirls in her hands. They are talking about their families, which turn out to be similar: well-off, contented marriages producing contented children, though in her case the contentment ended when her father died. It's odd they haven't had this conversation before, but also not odd, because their previous conversations have been practical, or sarcastic, with Hugh joking about her place in literary society. Now they are relaxing into the knowledge that they have a whole evening in which they aren't going to be interrupted by her children or his working day, so they go back, slowly, to the start of things, wandering comfortably, as though at the beginning of the kind of long walk they might have taken together in different circumstances, through the countryside of their childhoods, on a spring day like this has been.

Looking at Hugh across the table as he sits down, she thinks that it's reasonable of him to expect her to be attracted to him. He's an attractive man – his chest, like Ben's, is a chest you would like to lean against. She wonders what it would feel like to put her hand in his hair, and decides that this is hair, skin, a body that she would feel comfortable touching, that she can imagine lying naked next to in bed. She knows, as she allows that image to rest in her mind, that he's had these thoughts too. She's entering scenes that have already been given a kind of life over the month since they met. She knows that it's embarrassingly unusual to fantasise about men as rarely as she does and she's pleased to find herself doing it now. It doesn't add any awkwardness to the conversation, more a sense of conspiratorial closeness, because they both know that there's another incarnation of them, naked upstairs in bed as they talk.

They sit on the sofa with their ice cream. She draws up her legs and points her feet in under the cushions, noticing how much easier this posture is than the one she sat in with the nanny earlier. He takes off his shoes and draws his knees into his chest. She feels sleepy now, and wants to ask if she can lean against him, wondering if she would be answerable to anyone – to herself, to Hugh, to Ben? – in this transgression. As though he knows this, he puts his hand on her shoulder.

Come closer Priss, he says, come over here. Gratefully,

she twists round and turns her back to him. There's a sense of release, like when you put Lena in her bed when she's tired and she immediately smiles, clutching her elephant and her sheep to her face. He puts his hands in her hair and she feels her whole body prickling in response. He crunches her shoulders, hard in his hands.

You're stiff, he says. She's been conscious of his hands since she first saw him in his workshop, stroking the wood that he is using for her tables.

It would have been so simple, she thinks afterwards, in bed, to lean round and kiss him. There would have been no hesitancy on his part, their mouths would have known exactly what to do. They would have shut their eyes, while their tongues gently explored each other's lips and then, drawing back, they would have opened them, green gazing at brown, and smiled. He would have had more to say on the subject of her beauty and she would have been less embarrassed, more receptive to compliments than she was earlier. She wouldn't have taken him upstairs to the marital bedroom in which she has these thoughts, but she might have taken him to the spare room. There they might have stood, smiling seriously as they undressed each other. It could all have been accomplished so easily, and with grace.

So why don't they? Why does she, as gently as she can, not wanting to be abrupt or to suggest that she's uncomfortable with what has occurred, disengage herself, stand up, ask him if he would like coffee, walk back to the kitchen and break the silence between them with the noise of the coffee machine?

The decision is made without much thought and she doesn't regret it. But when he's left, when she's put on her white nightie and got into that expensively upholstered bed, when she's lived her way back through the evening as it occurred and as it could have occurred, when she's got up in search of a glass of water and returned to bed, she is filled with longing for her husband.

Stella

May

I suppose I should have mentioned the affair with Ben earlier. And I suppose – why don't I feel this more strongly? – that I shouldn't have had an affair in the first place with the husband of an old friend.

The whole thing began with us telling each other that it wasn't going to happen. Four years into the friendship, we suddenly became curious about each other, discovering how much there was to say and how much we wanted to say it, and how urgent it had become for both of us to expose to someone the private self that we kept hidden from our spouses. I felt like the only way to survive the sexual tension was to acknowledge that it was there, but to insist that we were grown up enough to resist its lure – we just wanted to make friends, we knew what we were doing. Of course, though, that meant that we felt freer than we had before, and so, writing to each other about work matters during a week when he was away at a literary festival in Sydney, we created together a fictional version of the affair that we'd have been having if I'd been there with him. It became, for those days, more real than our actual lives, the sex more erotic than most actual sex.

When we met again, for lunch in Regent's Park, we sat side by side eating our sandwiches, rationing eye contact because everything that our written alter egos had experienced together was there in every glance, and then he took my hand, or I took his, and it felt as though we really had performed all the acts we had written into being. And when we kissed under a tree in the drizzle – just once we said, to see what it was like – there was a sense of homecoming as well as exploration. So we gave ourselves three months. I was trying to get pregnant at the time with Chris; my real life was with him and Ben's with Priss. But we needed to work our way through this, we felt that we had to allow it to ourselves to stop it haunting us and making it impossible to concentrate on our marriages.

We really did believe it would end that autumn. And then, a year later when I had Cleo, we believed it would end definitively. But it went on – can I admit this? – for seven years. There's a narrative in which it was usually off rather than on, in which we were both absorbed in our marriages, in which I fell in love with several other men, and in which the resurgences of open desire, shocking each time in its completeness and force, were simply lapses into a past way of being. But there's another narrative in which this was itself a marriage, because we had both mentally evacuated ourselves from our spouses in those early months. As I entered my thirties and he entered his forties, we recreated each other, though with a lot of guilt on his side and fear of abandonment on mine. Who we are now – who I am now, with Tom – is unthinkable without those years of discovery, of honest mutual introspection, with Ben.

Where was Chris in all this? I kept trying to return to

him. There were periods of several months at a time when I managed to do so. He got the job he still has at the Science Museum and I became more interested in his work, and admired his energy and silliness with Cleo. She took her first steps with him, they had more jokes together than she had with me, though this sometimes made me competitive. I remember when I first started tickling her toes, and she called for me to do it again, I hid it from him, not wanting him to do it better than me and dislodge my bond with her. I enjoyed taking her to watch him play tennis and cricket on Saturdays, though, using her as an excuse to avoid talking to the other wives. We were both proud of him, and I felt waves of relieved desire, watching him leap forwards across the tennis court ahead of the ball, in better shape than the other men his age.

Look at Daddy, I'd shout, pleased to be able to say it. Daddy, the father of my child, a man who had been a kind of father to me when we met, giving me confidence as I emerged into adult life. Our love – and there was once so much of it – began as the kind of safe resting place that I still hope we can provide for our daughters. And even then, at those tennis matches, I continued to feel that he grounded me. He gave me the feeling that the disasters of the world were survivable, which I hadn't been given by my parents. But by that point neither Chris nor I was really curious about each other, or vulnerable to each other, or able to love the other person in a way that made room for their faults. Sometimes I felt that all the time he was waiting for me to do something wrong, to reverse the car into a bin or wash up badly, because there was a kind of masochistic pleasure for him in observing the carelessness of the woman he'd mistakenly married. And I was cruel too – dismissive of his friends (those teas after cricket where they'd tell me their uncomplicated political or cultural views), sometimes rude to them when I felt they didn't correspond to my image of the kinds of friends he ought to have.

As for Ben and Priss, I think theirs is a stronger marriage than mine was, though I've never really been able to understand it. Ben finds her a restful presence for all the reasons I found her restful when we lived together, I suppose. He admires her physically – her grace and stylishness – and he desires her all the more because she's seemed for long stretches of time to prefer a life without sex. He's glad to be protected from introspection, to get on with life without facing his fragility as he did all the time with me. If I was more disposed towards guilt, I might feel it about her, but I never have done. By the time that I became close to Ben, my friendship with her had already thinned, and we weren't confiding in each other any more. I'd withdrawn from her partly because I feared her plasticity: too often her clothes or her opinions reminded me of mine, though they seemed more striking on her. Also what I was taking from her in Ben felt like a side of him that she didn't want. If anything I felt like he was a better husband to her because I was there as well.

We haven't had sex for a year now. The last time was when I was just pregnant with Maggie. It was valedictory, I think, for both of us, after a party for a book prize. It was a hot May night and we felt claustrophobic in the squashed room. We escaped for a drink on our own and for the first time in almost a year it felt like it was possible to kiss, perhaps because my life was so much in flux. We kissed walking along the river, away from the party. He suggested a hotel but I'd promised myself never again to go to a hotel without spending the night, so we walked up to my office and lay down under my desk for the first time in years, lit by the torches on our phones, the manuscripts of many of the people we'd just seen at the party piled up around us, half read.

For me, it felt better that way, precluding nakedness, because I knew that nakedness might be too much. You couldn't give yourself fully to someone without the belief that you'd do it again, and having had that kind of absolute, surrendering sex with him, it felt depressing to do the same things with less feeling. But that way, clothed except for my tights and bra, I felt like it could be a different thing, though no less loving. I felt that for both of us the lack of beauty in the situation made it more beautiful. The hand on a cock through trousers, the mouth on a nipple – these weren't just mechanical.

The last time we'd had sex before that, the previous October at the same book-fair hotel we went to for years, I'd felt distanced from it. I had to be, because I was shutting off from the pain of disappointment; I knew that the life I'd imagined for us together was still lurking somewhere in my mind and I had to prevent it coming into consciousness again. Now I could be freer because I'd given up on the possibility of joy with him. There was love, still, but without joy. I was half conscious that joy could emerge once more from that love, if we allowed ourselves some form of future, but I felt strong enough to shut that out.

Thinking about Ben has made me realise that at the moment, I do not think very often about sex. This makes it easier, I suppose, to empathise with Priss. Sex matters. But the yearning with Tom – we have both said this – is for bodily closeness; the sex, and there is quite a lot of it, emerges from that.

When I first started having sex with Ben, I wanted more sex with Chris as well, and flirted with all the men I met at parties. Part of what was happening – I've seen this in all my friends, in different ways, though only recently in Priss – was that I was moving into a new phase of sexuality, as a woman in my thirties, and felt a new consciousness of the power of my body. Giving birth to Cleo added to this. I'd seen what my body was capable of and I felt somehow younger than I'd done before because I was at the beginning of this new phase of adulthood – a mother, a commissioning editor – and there was a sense of life opening outwards in its possibilities again, as it had at twenty-one. I fantasised about sex with most of the men I met. When they were married and when they told me, as they so often did, that their wives had lost interest in sex, I felt superior. I fell for their stories, pitying the men, looking down on the women, in a way that now makes me feel ashamed but which felt inevitable at the time. I couldn't imagine not needing sex to connect me to the world and thought that these women must be prepared to be less connected than I was.

But now with Tom, the better the sex becomes, the less interested I am in other men. I worry a little about my new monogamousness. I worry that I have misled Tom because at first we believed that we could be free spirited together. I assumed when I started going to see Moser that I'd be attracted to him, sexually, but part of what I like now about being on the couch is his disembodiment. I fantasise sometimes about living in his area – the clean, blossom-filled streets, the shop where I could hire different animal-shaped cake moulds each weekend – but I have little interest in him as a man with a body. I sometimes wonder about reflecting on this with him, but then don't.

And my male friends have started to seem less embodied as well.

I think this change has been to do with Maggie, as well as to do with Tom. I can't remember being able to look at anything for as long as I could look at her in the early weeks, when she used to lie next to me in bed, curled in the shape she'd acquired in my womb, smiling to herself as she fell asleep. Those moments were more intense than they were with Cleo because it was just the two of us this time, alone in the still, dim light of my room. It's a form of looking that's more like touching, because what I'm looking at isn't mainly the surface, the skin, eyes, mouth that other people might see. I go deeper into the softness, nestling inside her, losing myself in her compact little body as I might lose myself in the body of a lover during sex.

What's been odd is finding that these moments, when nothing else matters, are so readily available. Each evening, I know that I will feel this when I go into her bedroom and pick her up to do her ten o'clock feed. The surprisingly strong, feral smell of her little head, the feeling of a whole, squidgy body enclosed in my arms, the pride I take in her breathing and sucking, in knowing that I am keeping her alive. The physical attachment that I've felt to men, to two or three men, at odd moments – to the hollow beneath Chris's chest muscles, the top of Ben's head, and now to the top of Tom's shoulders when he leans forwards towards me – is recognisably similar to the attachment I feel all the time to Maggie's little body. And as in the case of the head, or shoulders, it's not a visual pleasure, it's a pleasure in the physical object, the small limbs reaching up inside my arms.

I've always dismissed women like Priss who seek more fulfilment in their children than their husbands. I've seen in the past few months that I'm wrong to do this because the point is that they've fallen in love. I've experienced love of this intensity only a few times in my life. It seems likely that many women haven't ever experienced it with a man. And yet it seems to be there easily with a baby; to be there in almost any moment you spend with them and to require so little input from them. Of course this makes all other feelings irrelevant.

Looking back, there's a sense of tediousness that overcomes me when I think about times when I've been obsessed by sex. I can understand how my older female friends seem so content to leave sex behind. Susanne, in her seventies, says that it just doesn't matter any more. My author Gemma, in her fifties, says that she is now beyond gender and expects the new challenges life offers to be spiritual. Yet both Susanne and Gemma are so sexual, not just in manner but in essence. So it can't be that they've moved beyond the erotic, more that they've found a new place for it in their lives, a place where they no longer need to feel the easy desire for your body you feel when young. Or perhaps they just don't want to talk about it any more.

In bed last night in my flat, both tired, Tom was cross with me because I'd been unsympathetic when his son rang earlier in the evening to tell him that he's stopped going to lectures because he thinks the other students are staring at him. Tom said that I expect him and Andreas to behave as I would in the same situations, and that I make no allowances in this for who they are. I felt miserable, lying there next to him but missing him because I missed the companionship we usually have. I tried to initiate sex and he tried to reject me as kindly as he could, which I'm grateful for now but at the time found infuriating, especially because he had an erection. He said it would be wrong to have sex across the gulf between us. I said that it would enable us to return to each other more easily, and that he must half know that, because he was aroused. He said that arousal is different from desire, that rape victims are often aroused but it doesn't mean that they want to have sex, and that my views on sex are wilfully uncomplicated.

I asked what he meant, while wondering if it would be easy to go and masturbate in the bathroom before continuing the conversation, because I was worried about making things worse by being so irritably frustrated. He said, lying back and talking to the ceiling, quickly, that I'm too dismissive of the allegations against Vince. That just because some women have wanted to sleep with him doesn't mean he wouldn't have forced himself on others. That sex, and what we want from it, and what it means for us, changes all the time, and so there may have been moments when Vince was using sex to feel empowered. We have to believe that there was something wrong about the encounter with Naomi Ayre, even if it's possible that she misremembered some of the detail.

I said, pressing my breasts against him in the hope of making his arousal as uncomfortable as mine was, that I just couldn't believe that any men get their penises out in public. Then I remembered a party at Mark's house a couple of weeks ago, where Mark's bright eighteen-year-old niece said that boys at her school regularly undid their trousers in taxis with them. Kay and I were fascinated, asking her one question after another about it, wondering if it was meant to be alluring or threatening. The girl found it hard to answer us. She was bemused by our surprise, and she found it hard to distinguish between the two options, giving the impression that it was just something you put up with. At her age I'd have found it horrific. I'd hardly confronted any naked penises by then. I said this to Tom and said I still couldn't believe any adult men did this, men who could have sex when they wanted to with consenting women.

Tom said, pulling away in bed more decisively and rolling on to his side, that the good thing about now is that no one can remain uncomplicated in their view of sex and that he finds it astonishing that I have managed to.

He went to sleep quickly and I moved around in bed, wanting him to wake up again, convinced that I'd only be able to fall asleep in his arms. The whole scene, more than any we've had before, reminded me of scenes I used to have with Chris, which depressed me. I hated the feeling that the version of me in Tom's mind was a less kind and sensitive person than the version of me in my mind, perhaps because I generally don't find it that troubling when people think I'm less kind than I am, but I therefore rely all the more on him to see the goodness beneath the briskness. And it was terrifying realising how lost I feel when I don't feel loved by him, because I saw how lonely I'd feel if we split up. I was still sure that if I could just persuade him to have sex, I'd know, the second he was inside me, that I was loved. I didn't ask myself how he'd feel, it was easiest to assume that he'd feel the same way I did. I am like all the men, I suppose, who tell themselves that the women feel as they do. Like Vince.

This morning I felt tentatively closer to him again, though we were carefully respectful in only touching through clothes and I think it might be a few days before I have the courage to initiate sex. There's a kind of tired greyness in feeling undesired, which makes me worry that male desire still matters to me too much, despite my protests last week, and that Tom may be right that I forgive men a lot because of that. I know about sexual violence, though I've never experienced it. I hear about it from Polly, in her work as a gynaecologist. But that doesn't seem to change my attitude to the men I know. Anyway, Polly is as susceptible as I am to pushy older men: she's having an affair with Sam, a consultant at work almost twenty-five years older than her. We're attracted to power, I suppose. Both of us would rather be spontaneously kissed than asked politely for our consent. Tom would say that's fine, but that I should know that power is dangerous and always open to abuse. But I'm not sure now that the conversation with Tom taught me anything except how humiliating and time-wasting I find sexual rejection. It still makes me cry, remembering lying there in bed next to him, feeling as though I had to restrain my hands from their impulse to touch.

Polly

May

Polly has just turned forty-one; she's a year older than us because she had a gap year before university, working. Her need to earn money then matters, because she used to insist on her lack of privilege. She became involved in the student union within weeks of arriving, determined to speak on behalf of the entire working class. She was proud that her father worked in a cheese factory in Somerset and that they drank tea with their evening meal, as she told us often, sometimes still drinking tea while she ate in James Street when she was tired or anxious and wanted to be reminded of home.

I suppose her decision to study medicine was a result of class. If she'd been less sure that her degree had to be practical, she might have studied English or music — those were the things she was most passionate about. It's useful now that she studied something that pays well, because since her father hurt his back five years ago she's contributed to her parents' rent, giving the money surreptitiously to her mother. This isn't the first time she has looked after her parents. She has done so in one way or another since her brother Ted died of spinal cancer when Polly was eleven and he was sixteen.

I think we got to know her because she sang in a choir with Kay, though I might have known her already because she was at my college. Kay admired her most, anyway, perhaps because she herself often fantasised about studying medicine. She likes the exactness of science and is interested in the peculiarities of the human body. She talks far more to Polly about her work as a gynaecologist than I do.

So Polly, now – Miss Polly Davis, as she is once more known – is a consultant at St Thomas's Hospital, just south of the river. She's young and attractive enough – athletic looking, with cropped auburn hair – that, since she became Miss, she's lost the respect of some of the patients she encounters, who assume that she's a nurse. But this evening, for the second night in a row, she's not at work. She finished at five o'clock and went to the gym for a cycle and shower. The day still flashes before her in a succession of images as it settles in her mind, large legs, slim legs, brown legs, pink legs, with all their lumps and blemishes, spread open in front of her, raised in stirrups. It's turned out, she says, to be true, what men claim, that no two vaginas are the same. And now she's sitting at the opera, wearing a black cotton shift dress that she'd forgotten, till she went through her wardrobe yesterday evening. And she's too caught up with thoughts of her patients and too conscious of Sam's body next to hers to give herself fully to the music, though it's one of her favourites and she'd usually have found in this, more than in almost anything else, an escape.

She's happy to know that they have so many hours ahead. Three hours here, dinner afterwards, and then bed at her flat. She doesn't know what lies he has told to gain this time with her, or how anxious he is that they might be seen by friends or colleagues who could make a chance comment to his wife. (Though she's starting to realise, and she finds this even more depressing than she finds the lies, that he doesn't go to great lengths to hide any of it because it's accepted that consultants in their sixties have mistresses as well as wives. It's another prize for having put in the long hours, working their way up in the profession, another aspect of her adult life that would mystify her parents, who she still takes pleasure in making proud.)

What would she like for her birthday? he asked, two weeks ago, and she replied that she'd like this, the opera and a whole night together, so he went off and arranged it. Her birthday treat. Now that it's happening, she's enjoying it, but is too self-conscious about her enjoyment for it to feel natural. He doesn't usually like opera, so she's wondering what he's making of it. She chose this one because it has psychological depth, but she's coming to realise that the plot is pretty silly. She's wondering, too, if there's a reason why, after half an hour in the dark together, he hasn't yet taken her hand, and if it would therefore be unwelcome if she should take his. Realising that it's this, most of all, that's stopping her from concentrating, she reaches her hand on to his lap. He takes it, squeezes it, and repositions their entwined hands upon her knee, where he strokes her leg through the flesh-coloured tights that she will reveal, on getting home, to be stockings. She looks straight ahead, able at last to give herself to the music.

She cries at the end. She always does. Old love, renounced for young love, with Strauss making all he can of the pathos – there's no restraint here. She wonders, as the three sing their extraordinary trio, if Sam is finding this painful, if he's seeing himself as the Marschallin, and realising that he must eventually relinquish Polly to a younger, more appropriate man, so that she can have the life that she deserves. But when it finishes, and she turns to him with her cheeks wet, he's charmed by her response, but does not seem to have been particularly moved himself. It's not clear that he's been following it. She's disappointed, and then feels embarrassed that it should matter to her so much, when she's had all these years to acclimatise to relationships, that the enjoyment should be shared.

She feels more easily connected to him again at dinner. They eat steak and talk about their weeks at work. Polly has always been hesitant to have relationships with colleagues, but she finds that she likes being able to talk about the thing — work — that occupies most of her time without having to turn it into an anecdote, or explain the technicalities. This time she knows that it will be more painful for him to talk about his week than usual.

So tell me about what happened, she says.

It was terrible, he says, and she is touched as she often is by his willingness to talk about emotional experience. We'd just given her a C-section, it went well, she had the baby in her arms, then suddenly she couldn't breathe, she had a cardiac arrest. She was brain dead and after twenty-four hours the ventilator was turned off. There's going to be a full enquiry of course.

It sounds like there was nothing you could do, Polly says, hating the platitude. She takes his hand across the table, looking at him as he looks down, suddenly confident that she is strong enough to help him.

I keep asking myself if we were right to give her a C-section, he says. She was two weeks late, and her first pregnancy ended with an emergency C-section. She didn't want to be induced, he's a big baby, it seemed like the right thing to do.

It was the right thing to do, Polly says.

Yes. But we both know that it might not have happened if we'd done it differently. It was so awful, Polly, when we turned the machine off yesterday. Her husband was there holding the baby, her mother was outside with their two-year-old. It still affects me so much.

Polly puts both her hands on his cheeks, as though warming him. As always, she likes the contrast between her pale skin and his dark skin. Her hands are no more white than his cheeks are black, she thinks, examining them; it would be more accurate to say orangey-pink and dark brown. She reaches her right hand back to stroke the softer skin on his neck. She wishes they could go home straight away and get into bed.

Let's have another bottle of wine, he says, summoning the waiter.

She's only had a glass and a half and she knows that he knows that she minds that he's drinking too much. She can tell that he's decided not to drink this evening, just as she's decided not to mind. But two bottles between them is his idea of not drinking too much, and minding but not saying anything is her version of not minding. It doesn't matter, she tells herself, he isn't her husband, it doesn't matter if he's slowly killing himself. But she minds the lack of focus that drink brings. She admires his mind – its combination of swift processing and careful thought. When he drinks he stops noticing things, thinks less quickly, is less observant of her. She's charmed nonetheless, as they abandon the conversation about the dead mother, when he proposes a toast to her on turning forty-one, and tells her why he envies her being in her forties, why she is more attractive at forty-one than she has ever been, why he is grateful, and moved, to be sitting here, sharing her prime with her. She thinks that he's better company than any of the other men she knows, than any of the men she's gone out with, and gives herself to this knowledge.

Arriving in her flat, a one-bedroom conversion upstairs in a Victorian terraced house in Camberwell, she takes his coat and hangs it on the hooks that keep falling off her wall and then, allowing her to navigate them safely beyond the coats, he presses her against the wall and kisses her. She has liked this about him from the start. The straightforwardness of his maleness. He doesn't expect, as some other men have done, that the desire should be reciprocal. He wants her body as an aesthetic object, he doesn't expect her to want his, and though she does, it's not the most crucial part of either of their pleasure. They go straight into the bedroom, where she removes her bedspread and cushions as she knew she would when she laid them out early that morning. With her white sheets and cream quilt, she asks herself sometimes if she's turning into a spinster. (At what age is spinsterdom foisted on us? It's unclear.) It isn't a flat that she can imagine a man imagining his way into. But it feels wrong to change it on behalf of this or of some other potential, more abstract lover, because she knows that the basis of what happiness she has now comes from self-sufficiency and that she'd be lost if she were to see a gap in her life where a man should be.

They lie down on top of the white duvet on the bed made for her twenty years ago by her father, who's a year younger than Sam. He caresses the outline of her body deftly and they're both pleased with the proportions of her shoulders, breasts and hips, which she thinks of now bent over the bike at the gym earlier, soaked in sweat that she quite enjoyed thinking was mixing with the sweat of the bike's previous riders. The sex is faster than usual because it's later and they are drunker – she as well as him – than they are during their hours here between shifts in the morning or afternoon. Clothes are pulled off quickly, hands gripped hard into flesh from the start.

He praises, as he always does, her wetness, and she wonders as she always does about the wife he's comparing her to. He rolls her over, stroking her shoulders, down to her waist. He comes quickly but she likes it, aroused by the feeling of him surrendering to her, liking those seconds when he's helpless, lost to himself, enclosing her body heavily. And then, with the mutual proficiency that characterises their lovemaking, she comes quickly too, first with his mouth and then again with his hand. They lie, faces close together, looking at each other.

I love you, she risks, and it's the second time she's said it, not knowing whether he will say it back.

I love you, Polly, he says, comfortably. She has forgotten that there is no emotional anxiety in this for him. He's done it before, will do it again. He believes it's a civilised way to live. So he can offer her love, but she knows that if called to define this love, he would describe something less all-engulfing than it is for her. She would like to talk more often about their feelings, but the language to do so doesn't come naturally to her.

As they lie in her bath, her foot caressing his thigh, she asks him what he told his wife he was doing tonight. It's foolish to ask a question she doesn't want to know the answer to, but she's not concentrating as she asks it because she's thinking of them as two anaesthetised patients in a white operating theatre, their languor the result of medical proficiency rather than sexual exhaustion.

A seminar in Birmingham, he says, with no suggestion that he minds telling her this, adding that it's the kind of place he wouldn't need to say much about afterwards.

Do you mind lying? Do you feel guilty? she asks.

I mind a bit but not enough not to do it, and I don't feel guilty, he says. I couldn't feel guilty about something that feels as right as being here with you.

I think most of the men I'm friends with would feel guilty, Polly says.

That's because they're younger. Your generation feels less entitled to pleasure than mine does. You're more moralistic. It's our fault, for fucking you up.

And now you're fucking me, she says.

Yes, but I don't think I'm fucking you up. I care about you more than you realise. And right now I think you want to turn around and lie against my chest and kiss me.

Sleepily, she does as bid. Once she can feel his chest against her cheek, her hair dampening in the bath water, once she leans up to kiss him and feels their mouths, still warm and moist, losing the separateness of conversation, she feels contented again. She strokes his chest hair. Here, in the warm water, lying against this solid body, is, after all, where she most wants to be.

They kiss again in bed and she's surprised to feel him hardening against her leg. She reaches down to touch his erection. This, she realises, is what she likes most about sex and why their affair, conducted now in brief weekly afternoons, is so unsatisfactory. The best sex isn't the sex that assuages urgent desire. It's the sex that follows, when ordinary arousal is gone, and when a new form of desire comes in its place, less bodily and more mental, creating a state in which the orgasms, though harder to achieve, remake you.

He pulls her on to his chest. She presses her breasts against him as she pulls him inside her. It is possible that they won't move much, that this might be just a quiet embrace, preceding sleep. But as he guides her gently up and down, clasping her buttocks with an expertise that he manages to make feel natural, all the divisions between body and mind disappear and she is lost to the sensation, deep inside her, of enjoyable tension. She isn't thinking about what will happen, so it's neither expected nor unexpected when she finds herself floating into the release of the spasms that eluded her when he was inside her earlier.

She shouldn't look at the clock, but she sees it as she turns off the light. It's 2.30 a.m. They have to wake at seven and then she'll be on call, with only short breaks, for forty-eight hours. They couldn't have known, when they chose the day, that she'd be given this shift, and she's been careful not to let thinking about the need for sleep intrude on the evening. She needs to sleep quickly now, but the wave of lethargy that was brought on by the orgasm is passing, and her thoughts are speeding up. When will they next meet? And when will they have a whole night together again? He shakes gently as he falls asleep and then begins snoring. She wishes that she had a spare bedroom, where she could go and read herself to sleep, but then regrets the thought, because on the days and nights when he leaves her on her own she always longs so much that he could stay, and now he's here, sleeping, beside her. She shifts in his arms and turns her back to him, trying to concentrate on enjoying the feeling of being enclosed by his body. But he's been half awoken by her movement so he moves too, turning his back to her until the only point of contact is in their spines, gently sloping towards each other and then away. As she falls asleep her thoughts turn disconnectedly to the women she has seen that day, many of them lying now beside men, as she is, many perhaps with unhappily racing minds.

It's Saturday afternoon. Polly and I are having tea, in a café in Kensal Rise – she's come all the way north to see me and we are childishly pleased with ourselves because we are sitting on the café sofa, though it's contrary to want our experience in cafés to be as close as possible to the experience we'd be having in the homes we have left behind. I'm pleased with the sofa because I have Maggie today, but not Cleo, and am enjoying the chance to spend much of the day holding her, which is rare now that I'm back at work. It's because of this, but also because I don't assume that childless women want contact with children, that I don't suggest Polly should take her until I get up to go to the loo. And then I see the eagerness in her eyes. When I come back, Polly is holding Maggie closely, though when she sees me she moves her mouth from her head. I offer to take her back and Polly says that she likes holding her, she likes babies.

How does she smell to you? I ask.

Good, she says. I was wondering just now if she smelt of you, if it means that I like your smell, if I like her smell. But I think she just smells of babies.

I never know if people want to hold her, I say, because I don't like babies other than my own, or didn't between Cleo and Maggie, though perhaps I will now.

I like all of them, she says, with their wondering eyes and their excitement.

We look together at Maggie for a few seconds.

Chris must miss her, Polly says, wanting to give me a chance to talk about Chris if I want to. Polly and I aren't close enough these days for it to feel easy to know how or where to begin to catch up on the more intimate details of our lives, though we both want to do it.

He must do, I say, but he never lets on that he does, because in the dynamics of our separation it's a punishment for me that I'm in charge of her all the time. When actually, now, except when there are things I really need to do, I wouldn't want to let her go.

Do you miss Chris?

No, I say, I think it's been several years since I loved him in the way that makes you miss someone, though I did miss him in our early years, as much as I've missed anyone.

Did you mind not loving him? she asks. She finds it awkward, talking like this, using the word love, but she has decided to overcome her awkwardness. We are both single women, now, and there's something to be gained in turning this into a proper friendship again.

It didn't feel like love was what he wanted from me, I say, and anyway I loved someone else for quite a long time, but he was married.

I offer her this because Ben feels safely in the past, because of Maggie and because of Tom. I haven't yet told Polly properly about Tom, partly out of guilt at finding someone so well suited to me this quickly, when she has been single for years. It's difficult, feeling such solidarity with my female friends, wanting to celebrate our independence together, but knowing that we all long to fall in love, albeit with a lover who can celebrate our independence at the same time as letting us sink into grateful, lethargic dependence.

I've been thinking that I should talk about Sam more, Polly says, with all of you, that I need to, because it's my experience as well as his.

She asks if I'm still seeing my married man and I shut the conversation down with a no. She wonders if this is because it's a man she knows. But she thinks that it can't be, because we don't have mutual acquaintances, except for college friends. I'm bothered by my own abruptness, so I open the conversation up again, saying that it was too much, for both of us, and that he wasn't going to leave so we had to stop. I ask if Sam will leave, and if she wants him to.

He's sixty-four, she says, her voice suddenly small, as though unsupported by her body. I don't think he will. He's had a lot of affairs before. He's very in control of his feelings. It would be crazy of me to want him to – I don't want to marry a man of sixty. But of course I do, in a way.

That's the problem with affairs, I say. After the initial excitement, like any relationship, they need to grow, but they have no room to grow, unless you can imagine, even in fantasy, that you might end up living together. With mine, we didn't do that, mainly because he didn't want to feel like he was leading me on. And so it had to end. Affairs need to remain an open question.

Does that mean that leaving a marriage is like leaving an answer? Polly asks, twisting her hair on to her finger near her right ear, but as she says it she's wondering if friendships need to grow too and if ours still has room to do so. Sam doesn't want to lead me on either, she says, though he said once that I'd be a nice woman to be married to. I don't think he thinks about this much. His life is ordered. The wife, the lover. At least he doesn't use the word mistress to me, though I guess he may use it with other men.

It's time for Maggie's milk, which I have in a bottle in my handbag. Polly cradles her and feeds her, enjoying the way that she relaxes completely into the delight of sucking, and for a few seconds I wish that I could be holding her instead. I ask if Sam feels guilty and Polly says that he doesn't. I say that mine did all the time. Sometimes he said he didn't, but then it would come out in other ways – moments when he had to deny me, or us. So he'd tell me how happy he was in family life.

Polly says that Sam says this is a generational thing, that his generation doesn't feel guilty. I say that this might be true, but I never felt guilty either. I just felt exhausted. By the scale of it. By the way that the pleasure so quickly turns into need and then it's not pleasurable, like drinking when you're addicted, it's just a relief, and so it leaves you more needy than you were when you started.

Polly thinks about it. She thinks that this is the point they're getting to now. After they meet, she feels depleted. She dreads getting into bed the next day because she knows that she'll still be able to feel the imprint of his body against hers, to smell him in her sheets. She feels sick, telling me this, and wondering if she should end it. Partly because of the coffee she's just been drinking, there's an unhealthy lightness in her head and stomach. Then she looks down at Maggie, who's drowsy, now, in her arms, lingering over the final drops of milk, and she feels a wave of longing that's more intense than anything she ever feels for a man.

I think I'm feeling broody, she says, stroking Maggie's hair.

If you want a child, that would be a reason to end it, I say.

It's not his fault, she says. He spends his whole day delivering babies but he doesn't know that I want them. I present myself as an independent woman, so maybe he thinks I want different things from women like his wife.

I know, I say, my eyes glistening, not so much from sadness as from the intensity of feeling that's behind what I'm saying. They all do, I go on. They think because you haven't managed to find ordinary happiness you don't want it. They think you're the strong one and that the weak women are the ones they need to protect.

So Sam is protecting his wife and not me? Polly asks. Is she weaker than me?

I don't know. Is he? Is she?

I suppose so – she's depressed. Polly minds the feeling that he is becoming generic. He does love me, though, I think.

Maggie has finished her milk and I take her back to burp her, smelling Polly's perfume on her as she leans into my chest, bouncing slightly as she's learnt to do on the Jumperoo at nursery. I ask Polly if the Me Too conversations have made her think differently about older men. I wonder as I ask it if it's a judgemental question and if she's heard about Vince. I explain that it's been on my mind, with the older men I'm close to. She says that Sam's worked his way through his junior colleagues, but they're colleagues nonetheless, not students. Then, after I've left the kind of pause that Moser would leave, she says that it's still an issue. That he treats it as a perk of the job. But she thinks that he'd say that they're equal, and it's a perk for her as well.

We look at each other for a few seconds. She rolls her eyes and then, simultaneously, we laugh.

She's standing looking out over the empty hospital playground with the opening of Fauré's requiem playing in her head. The playground is unusually well landscaped, funded by a bequest, and she often watches children playing in it noisily or listlessly, finding the exuberance painful because she knows that at least some of them will soon be going to die. It's a relief that there's no one there now, as she waits for Susanne, her last patient of the day, singing along with the Fauré, which she performed in a concert on Saturday. She likes being a soprano: there's a peculiar power in producing the highest note in the swell of sound, a sense that it's her role to declaim these unearthly truths. *Ad te omnis caro veniet*, she sings now. To you all flesh will come.

Polly usually worries about examining friends, and we've all been friends with Susanne since university, when we knew her as our friend Mark's mother. They're the kind of mother and son who have shared lives and friends into adulthood, so she has taken us all on, rather like Vince, who is himself a friend of Susanne's and may even once have published her. Now Susanne's been told that she needs a hysterectomy and wants to discuss it, so Polly has managed to get her added to her list.

When Susanne arrives she seems so confident about Polly's professionalism that Polly has confidence in it as well. She examines her, fighting an unexpected urge to laugh as she produces the condom and puts it on the probe, careful not to hurt her as she manoeuvres it inside. She gives a running commentary on what she can see and Susanne looks obediently at the grainy pictures on the screen. Then Polly leaves her to get dressed and she is seated at her computer again when she says that yes, it's a prolapse, and she does think that a hysterectomy would be the best way forward.

It's all right, Susanne says. I've got enough use out of it, two children, a lot of bleeding, I don't have any need for it now.

They smile at each other, relieved to be able still to rely on humour.

I think I'll be able to perform the operation myself, Polly says, if you'd like me to. How are you otherwise? How's Mark?

We both have books being published, Susanne says, which is fun. I enjoy picking up his children once a week. The joy of being a grandmother makes it all right to lose your womb. How are you?

I haven't made much use of mine, Polly says, my womb.

The smile feels more forced now, for both of them.

Do, Susanne says, do have children. When you get to my age it's the most important thing you've done.

Polly looks surprised and Susanne immediately assures her that there are many other ways to find fulfilment, what does she know? she only took two weeks' maternity leave, she had an au pair. And then she rushes off, telling her to come to tea soon, and Polly goes upstairs and, when there's no reply, opens the door to Sam's office. He's texted to suggest she should come at five, after her shift.

It's a familiar scene: the door left unlocked for her and then the neat shelves of equipment and books, the photograph of his children, two grown-up men she's never met, pictured here as shyly smiling boys with skin a few shades of brown lighter than Sam's. The photo is the only sign of his so-called personal life, a term Polly resents because she feels he is personal in his life with her. She sits down, thinking that she's hungry and going through the contents of her fridge in her mind, wondering if the courgette, carrot and sweet potato will be enough for her dinner. She wants to eat, but most of all she wants to see Sam and she wants to go to sleep. They are related desires, for peace. Before Susanne, she saw a woman with eight children, whose husband had given her a disease. She would like to think that her work here makes her a feminist, but often it makes her dislike the women, seeing them as weak willed, and it's easy to become dismissive of the sexual act itself, even of childbirth, with its repetitive corrosion that leaves you prolapsed at seventy. There's a tawdriness in all of it – in the uses these women make of their vaginas.

Sam comes in. She forgets, when they haven't seen each other for a week, how much pleasure there is in his smile, and how much joy in being the cause of it.

Come here, he says, and she stands up and leans into him.

He locks the door. There used to be an embarrassment in his doing this, but now it's just part of their routine. He pulls three chairs next to each other against the wall, so they can lean into each other as though lying on a sofa. They kiss. And she knows that she must have the conversation she has half planned to have, because even now, when she's so relieved to be relaxing in his arms, something important has gone.

What's wrong? he asks when she draws back.

I don't know if this is the right thing for me any more, she says, accepting the cliché.

She's grateful that his face seems to express a kind of calm sadness, rather than surprise.

What have you been thinking? he asks.

I don't always feel like there's enough here, for me, she says. It makes me wonder if you love me.

Perhaps you're wondering if you love me, he says calmly. We have no way of knowing if we mean the same thing by love, he says in the same equitable tone. Maybe the main question is what we have to offer each other. We're friends, close friends, and that's a big thing. We're passionate. Our bodies know what to do together. It's a rare combination.

95

Polly is silent. She knows that what he's saying is true. She appreciates that, unlike many of the men she has known, he's unwavering in offering what he offers. So all she can say is that she doesn't think it's working him being married and her being on her own. She gets lonely.

He says that he understands and he doesn't want to be selfish. Again, there's that sick feeling that she had when she first thought about losing him. She pushes herself on to say that she thinks she'd like to have children. He's silent. It's the question he's never asked, the topic she's never had the courage to mention, suddenly brought with surprising ease to rest between them.

I didn't realise, he says. I'm sorry. He encloses her small pale hands in his large dark ones and she wishes she could fit her whole body inside his. She's touched by his willing-ness, which is only partly characteristic, to see himself as at fault.

Would you miss me? she asks. If this stopped.

Of course I would, he says quickly, squeezing her hands. I miss you now, more than you probably know. There are days when I look around for you, wondering why you're not with me.

She wants to ask him why, then, he doesn't think of leaving his wife for her. But she reminds herself that she isn't always sure that she wants him to. It's possible that she only wants him to want to. She's becoming less confident that she knows what she thinks or feels, or rather that there's any kind of underlying reality to her thoughts or feelings.

He asks her what she's thinking and she says that she's wondering who he'll move on to next, though she hadn't planned to say it, and then wonders if it's too cruel. He looks hurt and she wants to look after him, but she's also curious about what he'll say. She watches his hands, which are clenched now, with his right thumb rubbing rhythmically against his index finger, as it often does when he's tense.

We both know that I have a track record, he says.

It's a perk of the job? she asks.

I think it would be like this in any job where it's so intense, he says. Where people care this much about what they do and work such long hours doing it.

Polly wonders if she should concentrate more on their equal need and right to sex. Why is she assuming that it's him doing the seducing, just because he's older. She wants so much to stop thinking. To suggest that he should just come back to her flat and go to bed for the last time.

I could do with a drink? she says.

Helena

May

Helena is thirty-nine, with brown eyes and blonde-brown hair. Like Priss, she is proud of her perfect posture, and I often envy the sense of deliberation that she exudes in the way she carries herself, which also makes you feel that her clothes have been carefully chosen and that she looks exactly as she intended to look, even when she's wearing the dark-grey tracksuit she often puts on at weekends, even when her waist thickens, as it sometimes does. She's a school friend of mine, as I've said, from my private girls' school in north London, a school for the rich but not the super-rich (I, one of Thatcher's luckier children, had an assisted place, and was always conscious therefore of how much wealthier my friends' families were than mine). This was a school where cleverness and achievement mattered above all else, but this was manifested less by a drive towards high grades than by a kind of frenzied celebration of ambition. We assumed that we'd go to the top universities and then excel in whatever unusual and creative career we decided on. We were a generation who didn't use the word 'feminist' growing up, but there were generations of feminists who made possible the belief that we adopted so effortlessly, though perhaps harmfully, that we should stride forwards towards the glory that was ours by right.

It worked for me. It did for Helena too. An excellent history degree, followed by an apparently effortlessly successful career as a documentary presenter. She was well connected, of course. Vince, as I've said, is her uncle, and was instrumental in arranging her first meeting at Channel 4. She made a success of it and she is the most famous of us now, a credit to the school.

We're both, in our different ways, ambivalent about the launch pad that propelled us skywards, both worried that there were sides of us that were ignored, leaving us unprepared to confront the failures that awaited us. The failure to get married in her case, to stay married in mine, and to have children when we wanted them. I'm at least half relieved that my children will have less expensive educations than I did – I'm not sure how well all our striving has served us, in the end.

Helena and I weren't particularly close at school but we were united in our European parents and our ambivalent Jewishness, though her family was grander than mine was. We became closer at university because our other school friends were absent and because the particularity of that schooling meant we had more in common than we did with most of those around us.

I was intrigued that she was bisexual, perhaps mainly because I was attracted to Kay who was determinedly straight, perhaps also because there was an element of desire in my admiration of Helena's centredness in her own body. At a party in our first year, I drunkenly kissed Helena's boyfriend, roused to attraction by my anger at how complacently rude he was being. Afterwards, she walked me back to college, worried that I might be too drunk to find my own way. I spent the journey berating her unapologetically for his boorishness and then, when she dropped me back at my room, kissed her. She was remarkably good humoured about the whole episode, but I don't think either of us considered kissing again. In James Street, our friendship settled into something more straightforwardly supportive. We talked about our sex lives, both appreciating the other's insight, but didn't initiate joint excursions very often unless they involved the others as well. Then, while I was married, I avoided her. I was convinced that she and Chris were attracted to each other and that they'd have been a better couple than he and I were. Helena would have been ready, years before me, to have all the babies he wanted, would have joined in with his sporting life, and wouldn't have wanted to work at weekends. I minded their chemistry and I minded the perfection of Helena's posture, until one day I stopped minding it and started wondering instead how we could return to being closer friends.

I haven't worked out why this is less appealing for her than for me, but it's clear that I've missed the moment for intimacy, and I usually assume that her distance now has something to do with the coldness of my intellect. She and Priss are still best friends (Helena was bridesmaid at her wedding and is godmother to Lena), which sometimes perplexes me, because Helena and I ostensibly have more in common. But Helena, who's gained more from meditation than anyone else I know, admires the ability Priss has to live in the moment. They go to yoga classes together in the evenings, they hum and breathe together. And I suppose loyalty counts a lot for both of them, more than it does for me, and they have a sustained, twenty-year friendship, where Helena and I have had something more erratic.

Helena's version of single life is more elegant than Polly's. She has a bigger flat, in a grand Victorian building in Stoke Newington with high ceilings and large windows. Each of its objects is carefully chosen, expressing an aesthetic of good, minimalist taste. But her flat, with all its beauty, feels less contentedly the flat of a single woman than Polly's more rackety one, perhaps because I know this to be the case, or perhaps because that kind of perfection seems to call out to be shared or at least admired. She moved into it specifically because it seemed like a good place to have a baby alone, and so, like the marital home we sold just before Maggie was born, it's been a space marked by the presence of a palpably absent child.

This is a question on her mind, today, as she sits at the hairdresser watching long sections of hair – blonde or brown depending on the light you see it in – falling to the floor. She knows that Veronique thinks that this butchery is a terrible idea. She knows that she's only just been able to stop herself from saying this, remembering that she's not the artist in hair she once dreamed of being, and that she has to take instructions from her customers.

Helena confronts herself in the mirror. She hasn't had hair this short for twenty years. It's grown gradually, without definite intention, so to cut it now is to assert a kind of control. In doing so, she has exposed herself to the world. Not just her neck but her nose and cheek bones seem more vulnerably stark, forced to speak for themselves, which they succeed in eloquently. Sitting there, upright in posture and features, the grains unsheathed on a stalk of wheat, she has reached the point where she's ready to face life in its most brutal radiance.

She asks Veronique what she thinks. She says that it's striking, and asks her what she wants from this new cut. Part of the point was to effect change, decisively. Helena looks into the remains of her green tea, observing the swirls of hair that have made it into her cup. She thinks that she wants a life where she's no longer waiting for the fairy tale she's always expected to live. She's assumed for years that she just has to be patient and soon a man or a woman will appear in her life and ask her to have babies with them. Now someone has appeared, but not in the way she expected, and she wants to be ready to say yes.

She and Aaron have been friends for a year, since they worked together on a documentary. They'd talked about wanting to have children, she'd talked about thinking about having a baby on her own. Then last week he said it. You'd be a great mother, he said, sitting on the bench in Regent's Park during her lunchbreak, eating the quinoa salad that he'd brought for them, in two Tupperware containers. And it was the first time anyone had said it to her and meant it, meant that he wanted her to be the mother of his children. She was surprised because the family he comes from – that large African family whose pictures fill his flat – is so different from hers. This makes it more flattering that he's chosen her. The haircut is a response to that. She is going to choose for herself. She hasn't told her producers that she's doing it, though she begins shooting the next series in two weeks.

She tells Veronique that she'd like a new phase in her life. She would like to be more herself. Veronique asks what she will do once she's more herself and she says that she might have a baby with a friend, a cinematographer. He's gay, she says. I'm sometimes gay. We can be parents together.

You'll be a wonderful mother, Veronique says. It is the phrase given to Helena by the world now it is readying her for motherhood.

Afterwards, going out into the street, she enjoys the feeling of the breeze on her neck. She feels streamlined. She has an image of herself cycling from James Street to the history faculty with hair this short and looks back on that younger self tenderly, glad to have protected her with hair in the years that followed. She goes into the Pret on the corner to have a coffee and no one recognises her. She feels like seeing someone, so she texts Priss, who replies inviting her over, and then walks into Bond Street tube, enjoying urban life today more than she usually does, her feet clacking in her new wedge-heeled sandals.

Priss is generously excited about the new hair, as she is about everything in Helena's life. It really doesn't seem to occur to her to resent Helena's success. She leads Helena into the kitchen, where Lena is sitting in her high chair in a fairy costume, eating her lunch.

Helena asks her if she's a fairy, thinking that she's generally better than this at talking to her goddaughter. There are a few more bites of pasta, eaten neatly, and then Priss takes Lena, easily compliant, upstairs for her nap. She comes back down and starts making lunch for herself and Helena, blending soup inside a pan. Helena apologises for adding to the domestic tasks but then thinks that they aren't experienced as extra burdens here, they're the essential components of a life. It's because Priss is better dressed than most stay-at-home mothers that she forgets this. She wonders what it would be like not always to feel that there's something else you ought to be doing, in a different sphere.

How are you? Priss asks, looking at her carefully. They haven't seen each other since Helena called, excited and frightened, to tell Priss about Aaron's suggestion.

I'm well. I think I really want to do this, to have a baby. It meant so much that he asked, that he was the one to suggest it first. He just suddenly said it: You'd be a great mother.

Helena didn't expect the tears that sit, unshed, in her eyes and is relieved that she's decided to come here if she's going to be in this mood. Priss hugs her and she finds herself sobbing, shaking as she does so, on her friend's shoulder. She explains that it's because no one has said it before that she's crying.

They should have done, Priss says, with unexpected fierceness, and they talk about how it would work.

I'm sad that I won't have the kind of family I grew up in, Helena says, like you have here.

Priss puts the pan of soup on the table and sits down.

Helena, do remember that it's not as perfect as it looks from the outside, she says. Any more than your life is as perfect as it looks to the people who watch you on TV and think you have everything, because you're telling us about Renaissance paintings, or Norman churches. You know that. You know that I've called you sometimes in tears on the days when I've looked at that clock and thought about changing the time, to make the hours go quicker until Ben comes home from work, and then he can't, as things have come up and he needs to stay late, and I wonder if he'd rather be there than here, and wonder what's happened to our marriage, that it's become all about me at home with the clock and him in the world, and talking about the children when we're here together. You won't have that.

They are both looking at the Victorian clock with its long hands marking out half past one. It's an object impossible to conceive of in Helena's flat but it seems possible that she'd have objects like this if she'd committed to family life. Like many of the things in Priss's house, it's a gift from her dead father's parents, who have shed possessions as they've aged. Helena isn't sure what honest response she can make.

He loves you, she says, he loves the children very much. He's proud of the family.

Priss laughs. I know! she says. It's ok. It's all changing now, with my café. We've leased the building!

Helena feels terrible that she's forgotten to ask about it. They talk about the café as Priss ladles out the soup and they both start eating. It's spicier than Helena expected, which adds to her sense of feeling newly lithe and awake.

You're a warrior, Aaron says, standing behind her at the kitchen sink, and he puts his hands on Helena's shoulders while she fills the jug with water, telling him how hard she has been working writing her next script. She likes him touching her. Now that there's so much at stake between them, the atmosphere feels curiously charged, as though they're lovers, waiting to see who might break the invisible barrier and lean in for a kiss.

Sitting on her sofa, she says that she's been thinking a lot about them having a child together. In fact she has thought about little else, in the two weeks since he said it. Now she feels as though they are a couple in a TV drama, as though it's not really her saying these things.

I have too, he says, all the time.

I was worried you might have changed your mind, she says.

I'm not going to change my mind, he says. I'm really not going to change my mind. If we go through with this, I'll be there all the way. I'm ready for parenthood. I want a little boy or girl to call me Daddy. I'm going nowhere.

She smiles, embarrassed by the phrasing but all the more pleased because of that.

I guess there's a lot to talk about, she says, about how it will work.

You're tense, he says, let me give you a massage.

She's rarely tense but it's true that she is now. He sits her down below the sofa and she makes noises expressive of pleasurable pain as he kneads her elegant shoulders and they talk about their days: the project he's been filming for a friend, the script she's been writing. She mentions, glad to have something to confide in him, that she kissed someone at a barbecue on Saturday, a younger woman called Clare.

I hadn't done that for years, she says, just kiss someone like that, the night I meet them. But we were flirting, all evening, you know what it's like, when you're having conversations with other people but you're still looking out for her. I was wondering if I had the courage to ask for her number, and then we were standing looking at the trains at the bottom of the garden and she asked, politely, if she could kiss me. And I said yes.

They do that, Aaron says, the young. They ask like that. I like it, on the whole.

Well they can't all do that, but she did. And then at the end of the party she said that she really liked me and took my number. So we've been texting. It's been so long, I don't want to get my hopes up, but it's nice.

She's craning round now, and it's starting to feel silly, being on the floor between his knees, so she wriggles free and thanks him.

Any time you want, he says. You're going to have a relaxed pregnancy.

Shall we talk about whether we really can make this work? she asks, and then, when he doesn't reply: Would you rather not discuss it?

If we were a straight couple, he says, we wouldn't talk now about who's going to look after the children on Mondays or Tuesdays, who's going to change what percentage of nappies. We'd just fuck. So I think we should do the same without the fucking.

I suppose so, she says. Maybe you could just tell me what a week, or a month, would look like for you, with a three-year-old child. I'm curious, about how you imagine her, how you imagine our life.

The need to plan. Helena has it less than some of us do but it's still there, the panic that sets in when you can't imagine the future. Is this a skill taught to high-achieving girls that we can never lose? Fifty years ago, we'd have been planning the menu for the week. Now we plan our careers and our domestic lives with the same sense that the future is achievable, and manageable. It's to his credit that Aaron respects her enough to take the question seriously.

I guess we'd split the week between us, he says, we'd both take the child with us to work.

Well there'd be nursery, during the week, Helena says.

Ok so there'd be nursery, that's easier. And in the summer I'd take her back with me to Zimbabwe.

Helena feels queasy, wondering why this hasn't occurred to her before.

How long would you want to take her for? she asks.

I don't know, maybe a month.

I couldn't not see my three-year-old child for a month. You must see that!

Maybe not, he says, but I always go back for a month, and otherwise I'd go back for a month on my own and then I wouldn't see my child either.

Maybe I could bring her halfway through, Helena suggests.

Yeah, maybe that would work, he says.

They are both bemused to be having so marital an argument about the movements of a non-existent child. Helena tells herself not to say too much. When she's imagined having a child with a real father, instead of a sperm donor, she's assumed that almost everything about it will be better for the child and for her. But now she sees that she hasn't allowed for the difficulty. Is she right, to think that the child will miss her the most? Aaron's body suddenly seems distant and opaque under the long-sleeved khaki T-shirt, the beige trousers which fit in well with her walls. She thinks how strange it is to be planning to conceive a child with someone whose body remains so unknown.

There's a lot to think about, she says, knowing that if she can name these fears to him they'll become more manageable, but knowing that it could make him less trusting. I guess I haven't thought enough about you wanting to do things with our child that would have nothing to do with me.

You just want a Sunday dad, maybe, he says.

His face has closed a little. She realises that she can't expect the same kind of communication she'd be having if this was a man she was having sex with. There isn't the same possibility of easing tension through touch, though the massage still hovers as a kind of encouraging presence between them. She tries to be as honest and precise as she can, because it's the only way that she knows to get through difficulties. She says that perhaps on some level she does want a Sunday dad, but on another one she definitely doesn't. She wants him to be involved. She wants him to be a different kind of parent from her. She just needs to get used to it, to his being a real person.

I sure am real, he says.

His transatlantic accent makes him seem young to her, though he's actually five years older than she is. It's also because he lives a studenty life, renting a room in a shared and very messy flat, where she now pictures her daughter staying overnight. She dislikes the prim quality she's starting to feel with him, and wonders if this is a feeling he will always bring out. She'll be the sensible parent, he'll be the one offering freedom and treats. She starts to feel the giddiness of loss and knows that it's because she's starting to doubt everything.

She says that he might be right that they shouldn't talk about it too much. He says that he's never thought this was a decision people should put as much thought into as we do here. His parents didn't plan to have children. They just appeared, one after another.

They look in her fridge for what to cook. She's a good cook, but she's keen to abdicate responsibility, to give him the feeling that he isn't being controlled by her. She has three eggs in the door of her fridge bought from the farmers' market, each a different shade of blueish pink, unusually elegant eggs, like everything else she owns. He suggests that they should make pancakes, and she agrees to this eagerly, convinced that it's exactly the right decision. They are just a little too insistently childlike, mixing the ingredients, tossing the pancakes. They both in their different ways know that they're making space for the scenes where they will do this again more naturally because they'll be accompanied by the child she's already imagining as a daughter.

They talk over dinner about their families. She's never asked him about his parents and his many siblings, or told him about her parents, both successful, both working in what she dislikes calling the arts. He says that she's his only friend who's so English, so part of the establishment here. She says that her mother isn't really English, she's Lithuanian, but she knows what he means. As always, she tries to downplay her privilege, laughing away her parents' success. But then he says that it will be good for their child to have all these contacts and she's pleased that there's something definite that she can bring to this, making it feel less likely that he will change his mind. The setting now feels oddly formal, the festive pancakes reduced to dinner on their plates.

She stands on her doorstep, waving him away. The evening has been disappointingly chilly and grey for May, but the sky is turning blue now as it darkens, and she finds the front gardens reassuring in their ordinary familiarity. The bins lined up outside each house ready for collection in the morning seem to offer a glimpse of functional communality which she reinforces by wheeling out the next-door bins on her neighbours' behalf.

She forces herself to consider the possibility that he isn't the person she should be doing this with. She'd rather not have to go to Zimbabwe with a baby, she'd rather not let someone else take her child across the world. When he first suggested having children together, she thought that their approaches to life were encouragingly similar. She can see now that their small differences will be distorted and enlarged. But then she thinks that this is true in any relationship and she wouldn't be thinking about it if she'd just fallen in love. Aaron is preferable to both the men she's fallen in love with in the past, as a choice to procreate with.

These thoughts have started to feel like they're clogging up her mind, and she pushes them away to concentrate on the main feeling, the heavy grey mass of disappointed grief that's squatting inside her because it has started to seem possible that the child she has spent the past fortnight learning to imagine into being might not be allowed to exist. The grief, once she confronts it, is so overwhelming that she sees that there is no decision to be made. As in a sexual relationship, she's too far gone to do more than simply let this play out. She breathes slowly in and out at the back of her throat, listening for her feelings. And as she breathes out she is expelling the grief, making room for the pale brown baby she's been living with for the past two weeks to come and take its place.

Aaron is in Helena's bathroom masturbating. It's only been five days since he was last here, but she starts filming tomorrow and she's ovulating now so why not? they both said on the phone this morning, why not try before they have time to change their minds?

She wants to put some music on, but isn't sure what would be appropriate. It's unusual, though not wholly unpleasantly so, to go so swiftly from friends to something curiously like lovers. He hugged her very deeply when he arrived and it occurred to her to suggest that they should have sex. Surely it would be no harder for him to emit sperm in bed with a woman than standing in her small, rather clinical bathroom. She wonders if he is fantasising about someone in particular, or if he's watching porn on his phone.

She chooses Handel. It seems unlikely to be taken as conveying an implicit message, even if Aaron were the kind of person who thought about implications, which he's not. Helena can't become someone who doesn't think about them, but she wishes to empty her mind. She lies on her bed and begins to meditate, imagining her womb readying itself for this potential child. She feels more sure than she will admit that this will be the time that will work.

She's only half present by the time that he comes in with the syringe, the sperm caught in it like a condom. We have all thrown so many sperm into so many bins over the years and now we harvest them carefully.

Shall I wait for you, or do you want me to go? he asks.

Go, she says, and I'll try to sleep.

He comes over and kisses her on the forehead, as though she is the child they're in the midst of conceiving. She has a momentary pang that this is not a man she's in love with, that she'll never have a chance to try procreative sex. But then he leaves and she props up her buttocks on pillows and inserts the syringe. She visualises the sperm making their way up into her womb. She visualises herself swimming as well, down a kind of river corridor of the kind she's been imagining inside her. And she visualises the baby, lying next to her in her cot, falling asleep on her breast in the bed, kicking her legs up and down when she wraps her up in the towel after her bath.

When the doorbell rings she's asleep, and she wakes up disorientated. With the long hours of daylight at the moment, it's hard to tell what time it is, but after a few seconds she realises that it's only five o'clock and Clare has arrived. They hug in the hallway; she isn't ready yet to kiss her again. She wants to brush her teeth after the sleep and she needs time to acclimatise to Clare because during the two weeks since the barbecue the person conjured by their messages has become further and further removed from the smiling figure facing her now. They go through to the kitchen and she puts the kettle on, to avoid the awkwardness of not yet knowing how to touch.

Clare's eyes are bluer than Helena remembered, her skin fresher. Her spiky blonde hair matches Helena's own. It was partly Clare's youth that attracted Helena in the first place, but now she wonders if the ten years between them are too much, if Clare is going to be able to handle the reality of Helena's attempts to get pregnant, if there is any point continuing if it's not going to last. With a man, she'd be able to contemplate the possibility of casual sex, but with a woman she can only imagine sexless friendship or love.

Clare asks how it's gone. They have been close enough, by text, for Helena to tell her what was happening before she arrived.

Fine, I think, she says. He did his thing, I put it inside me, he left, I fell asleep. So who knows what's going on now. The sperm are still swimming, I guess.

I've never had sperm inside me, Clare says.

Really?

I've had sex with men, but they've always used a condom or come somewhere else on me. So I don't know what it feels like.

Helena thinks back to the feeling of men ejaculating inside her. It hasn't happened for four years now and she hasn't had sex with anyone for two years. It's peculiar to think about this, as it doesn't feel like an accurate description of herself.

I used to like it, Helena says, the sudden wetness inside.

Maybe you're not really a lesbian then.

I'm not a lesbian, Helena says. I'm not straight either, I'm just glad that you're here.

You just fancy the particular person, Clare says sarcastically.

I fancy you, Helena says.

She puts her arms on Clare's shoulders and kisses her. They are the same height and their mouths are soft against each other. She leant over to reassure Clare, demonstrating that she's enough of a lesbian that she hasn't brought her here under false pretences. But once she has started kissing her, she finds that it's true, that she does want to kiss her, and touch her hair, and when she lets out a spontaneous moan as Clare runs her hands, hard, along her back, she wants to assure her that she doesn't usually make noises like this, without meaning to.

They could abandon the tea and go straight to bed, but they don't. Helena drains the tea bags carefully and puts them in the food bin and they carry their mugs through to the sofa where they set them down on the table and turn to each other again.

Helena says again, putting her hands on Clare's shoulders, that she's glad that she's here.

I'm glad that I'm here, Clare echoes. I want to be careful with you, though, to leave the sperm in place. Is it all right if I take your trousers off?

Clare lies Helena on the sofa and carefully removes her grey trousers, folding them up. It's the second time Helena has been treated as a child today. Clare runs her hands along her shaven legs. Helena says that skin is amazing, skin touching skin, both of them feeling through it and inside it.

They are kissing again and Clare's hand brushes lightly against Helena's knickers. Helena finds that she's much more aroused than she'd expected, and wants Clare to touch her there again. More purposeful now, she stands up and leads Clare to the bedroom. Standing next to the bed, she pulls Clare's top and trousers off, leaving her standing in her underwear. She's surprised by the strength of her urge to take ownership of this unknown body, to fast forward to the point where it will feel known and familiar. Her fingers are tense with force as she presses her way down Clare's back and along her arms. It feels as though this flesh, with its mixture of skin, bones and muscle, is both more and less than Helena is expecting: too slight in its fleshiness to satisfy the feelings it has provoked, while also so exquisite that the feelings continue to intensify and leave her wanting to be able to do more than simply touch it. Clare is plucking at the buttons on Helena's shirt and she helps her undo them and pull it off so that they mirror each other in their underwear, Clare's black and Helena's white, and then she lays Clare on the bed and leans down to press her teeth flat against the fabric of her knickers.

She is so aroused now that it's almost painful, a piercing sensation, but the way to assuage it seems not to be touched herself but to go deeper into the body of this woman. She undoes Clare's bra and takes almost her whole breast into her mouth, biting around the edges. She removes her knickers and presses her longer body against Clare's shorter one, her dark pubic hair covering Clare's smooth, shaven flesh. Clare is panting and lets out a cry and Helena thinks that perhaps she could make her come with these movements of her own groin. She wants both to hasten and to delay the moment of Clare's orgasm, not wanting to lose the sensation of this woman being in her power. She makes her way down Clare's body and grips hard against her legs with her arms as she uses her hands and tongue to open her outwards.

It takes longer than she anticipated. She worries that she

is doing it wrong. Just as the tension is rising it seems to deflate. She wonders about pausing and asking for instructions, she wonders if Clare is someone who doesn't expect to come. But then, unexpectedly, Clare begins to shake. Helena hears her cry as a surrender and seizes her whole body as her prize, enclosing it with hers. Lying like that, it takes a few seconds for her eyes to readjust to see this as the bed where a few hours earlier she lay meditating, this as the woman who an hour ago she was kissing tentatively, her body still unknown.

They lie facing each other. Helena tells Clare that she is beautiful. She has never been able to say anything like that as honestly to a man. She has a sense, unfamiliar but also familiar, of the world opening up, or of a world coming into view that she hadn't known was there, which they will explore together. Clare says that she isn't used to feeling happy because she doesn't do happiness like other people do, like Helena does.

But you're happy now? Helena asks.

Clare doesn't answer.

Helena asks if Clare will still come here and do this if she does have a baby. They look at each other, with a kind of mutually acknowledged foreboding present alongside their smiles. It's too big a question, asked too soon.

I don't know, Clare says. Not definitely not, and I do like babies, but I don't know.

Helena accepts the carefulness. She lies back again and shuts her eyes. The vision of herself in bed with a baby earlier has now expanded to include Clare and there's a luxurious restfulness in it, three bodies side by side.

★

She places the stick, horizontal, on the bathroom shelf. She tells herself to ignore the flashing egg timer and leave the room. She plays the first page of a Bach fugue on the piano, concentrating on breathing in time to the music. She thinks about the tasks she needs to do this afternoon and how different they will feel if she's pregnant. It's peculiar that these seconds, this minute, arbitrarily chosen in her day, is the minute when she might go from being just one person in a body to being two.

When she goes back into the bathroom, she's aware most of all of how cold the floor is on her bare feet. She breathes deeply, banishing the nervous nausea as she looks at the stick.

Pregnant.

That word that has carried so much fear, desire, pain and pleasure over the years for all of us. She has been right, then, to think that it's now that her life is going to start going according to plan.

Clare's phone answers with an anonymous message. She texts 'I've got news. Call me' and then calls Aaron. He's excited, asking what colour hair their child will have, will it be blond? She considers explaining to him that blond hair is a recessive gene. But she mainly wants to ask him not to jump forward. She isn't ready to think about the fully grown baby yet. She needs to adjust to this change in her body.

He suggests meeting straight away to buy something for the baby. She says that she has to work but could meet tomorrow. They make a plan and then he says that he'll call his parents. She panics, and reminds him that they shouldn't tell people till the twelve-week scan. But we know it's going to work, don't we? he says. She likes his confidence now and wonders if she should try to share his certainty. She says that he can tell his parents but should warn them not to tell anyone else. He reminds her that they're in Zimbabwe, so it doesn't matter who they tell, it won't be anyone she knows. It's true. She wishes she could feel less agitated. She wants to speak to Clare.

When she hangs up she finds a message. 'Can't talk. Tell me?' She takes a photograph of the stick and sends it with a message saying 'I'd love to see you. Can I come round today?' She doesn't need to work, she just doesn't feel ready yet to celebrate with Aaron. She plays more Bach, waiting for Clare's response as she waited for that word on the stick that would change everything. Her phone beeps. 'Congratulations. I'm really glad for you. Sorry – dealing with brother's crisis. Tomorrow? No champagne I guess?' It's disappointing and the starkness of Clare's text message style makes it worse. This has happened enough times now that Helena has to accept that it's a pattern, and that Clare seems to need time to prepare to see her. 'Can we speak, then?' she texts back. There's another minute's silence. 'I'm sorry. Difficult day. I don't want to be disappointing if we speak.'

Helena hates the feeling of losing control of the state of her own mind, on this day that should be all about the news of motherhood and not about Clare. The light shifts and half of her sitting room is lit by sunlight from the garden. She decides to go for a walk along the canal to her parents' house. She's remembering now why she was apprehensive about starting a new relationship at the point that she met Clare. She doesn't want her whole pregnancy to become shadowed by the fluctuations of a love affair. She has the rest of her life to fall in love.

Her parents are in the garden and her uncle Vince is with them. The flowers are blooming around the terrace – big blue bushes of ceanothus that are almost unnaturally bright. Helena remembers that she wants to get a cutting for her garden, though she can't recreate this sense of profusion on her smaller terrace. There's no sign of Vince's wife, which makes Helena think that he's come to ask their advice about the allegations. Her mother produces lunch and Helena thinks that it's the same kind of salad that she'd have made, served with the same implements. It's a thought that makes her want to cry, because she realises that one of the things she wants from this baby is to extend the string that connects her to her parents, continuing it beyond herself so that eventually she'll be sure it will never run out.

I've got something to tell you, she says. Her parents know what it is before she says it but Vince has no idea.

You've met someone? he says. You're making a new series?

Well, actually, both of those are true too, but Mum and Dad know about those. The big news is that I'm pregnant.

She stands up to hug her mother. There's a lot of banging into the metal garden chairs as they manoeuvre around the table amid the pots. Her mother asks when she found out.

This morning! the older woman echoes. And you're celebrating with us! We should have champagne.

Her father, who has been silent, goes inside to get some, pleased to have a task with which to show his appreciation. She sits, enjoying the feeling of her head and neck exposed in the sun, explaining the situation to Vince, who asks to see a picture of Aaron, and she finds one on her phone.

You'll have a beautiful child, he says.

We shouldn't really be telling anyone yet, she says. But I want to be happy now, and not in three months time.

They smile at each other, a smile that acknowledges the years of struggle that had to happen before she could be happy. She wonders how Vince really is, and whether he's able to concentrate on anything other than his splintering reputation. It's hard now, at some point every time she sees him, not to imagine him undoing his trousers, with a kind of sullen, vacant look on his face. Though she thinks of him as a kind man, his resting expression is a discontented one. Age has accentuated the downturn of his mouth. So she can imagine that there could come a threatening moment when he looked at you with cold sexuality devoid of affection. But his smile, which she's known for so many years, which once greeted her across the playground when he used to collect her from school, is always so warm that she never dwells on the more difficult image for long.

Her father comes back and pours the champagne she can't drink and they toast the pregnancy.

To the tiny embryo, Vince says. We're all cheering it on.

They all repeat it solemnly, to the tiny embryo, and she is grateful that this has felt so straightforward with the three aging figures who are looking at her now with anxious kindness. She says that she'll need a lot of help if it all goes well, but she's ready to do it. They dish up the salad and then Helena asks Vince how he is.

I was just telling the others before you came, I'm all right. I won't keep my job. But this might be the moment to go. It's not just the sexual world that's overtaken me. It's publishing as well. My future isn't digital, any more than my future is in asking women to sign a consent form before I take them to bed.

Helena and her mother exchange a brief, exasperated look, by way of acknowledging that they are committed to the issue of consent, even if they're not insisting on it now. Helena is irritated by how relaxed he seems, his legs splayed, his bare forearms upturned to the sun. It's possible that he's taking this too well.

Noi fummo i Gattopardi, she says, in her perfect Italian accent, and there are two decades of Italian holidays conjured up for all of them. They watched *The Leopard* screened on to the side of their villa three times over the years.

It's true, he says. And then in English, with an Italian accent, he completes the quote. We were the leopards, the lions; those who take our place will be the jackals, the hyenas. And the whole lot of us, leopards, jackals and sheep, we'll all go on thinking ourselves the salt of the earth.

The comparison, Helena thinks, is appropriately awkward. Does he mind being aligned with a character who has regular sex with a prostitute, who desires his nephew's fiancée? She imagines trying to explain all this to Clare, if she could get beyond the pretentiousness of the Italian-villa holidays. And she feels that it can't quite fit into their conversational world, and that it will be even harder to explain it to the child now developing in her womb.

It's Midsummer's day, but it's pouring with rain. It is wonderfully typical of Priss to have Midsummer's day as a birthday. At university, term was always just finishing then; in our year in James Street, we stayed on an extra few days to celebrate her turning twenty, entering a new decade together as we are now about to do again. But for Helena, there is little to celebrate now, and yesterday Priss wondered about cancelling the whole lunch party on her friend's behalf. Nonetheless, we are arriving and Helena sees me carrying Maggie to the front door of Priss's house, huddled in the rain, as she parks and waits for us to go in. I see her waiting, and accept this. She doesn't yet want to confront my baby.

For my part I'm sad because she doesn't wish to be close enough that I can support her in this, though I have sat in her kitchen bleeding away the remains of a baby myself. I didn't even know that she was pregnant, and it was Priss who she called in tears when she started to bleed yesterday and went to the hospital, Priss she asked to tell everyone what had happened, finding that she wanted the rest of us to know about the miscarriage even though she didn't want us to know about the pregnancy. It's interesting that she doesn't feel any envy of Priss in her easy fertility.

Standing talking to Priss in the hallway I listen for Helena walking up the path and pressing the bell. I hang back as Priss answers it and Helena comes in, wearing only black. Unusually, she's wearing a necklace, a thick band of silver given prominence by her low-cut top.

Helena, I'm so sorry, Priss says, hugging her.

It's my turn next.

I'm sorry, I say, but now you know you can do it, you'll get pregnant again soon.

Helena wants to interject that it's this particular baby that's been lost, but she knows that she can't say it without crying. We all walk into the kitchen, where Ben, Polly and Kay are sitting with a couple of Priss's local friends who we don't know.

Helena accepts Ben's offer of a gin and tonic, needing to claim the advantages of not being pregnant. Her stomach starts cramping and she has a sudden memory of Clare's hand touching her stomach yesterday evening when she came round, understanding that what she needed was to treat this absence as a physical pain. She wishes that she could be with Clare now, and hates not being able to count on Clare to be thinking about her. It's hard to know when Clare will not be too absorbed in her own unhappiness to remember her, and so every absence from Clare feels like a kind of death, because she can't rely on the mental connection between them. She wonders how long she should give herself before checking her phone.

Alisa, Kay's baby, has woken up and we place her on the floor with Maggie to see if they interact. Robert and Lena are playing outside in the garden. Helena sits on the floor with us and Kay passes her Alisa, wordlessly. She strokes the bare feet, the toes so remarkable in their details, wondering if she's right in thinking that she knows what it would feel like to have grown this body herself. She's pleased to find that it's possible to hold the baby without anguish.

She's lovely, she says.

Kay says, wonderingly, that she will probably never be this lovely again. I observe to Kay that we've turned out to be the kind of people who prefer babies to children, wondering if it's insensitive to express even such low-level maternal ambivalence in front of Helena. But Kay doesn't respond, she is closed in her own world. She looks thinner than usual, too thin to be the mother of Alisa with her chubby arms.

As the conversation continues, Helena glances over at Polly, who's talking to one of Priss's neighbours, who is still clutching the six-pack of beer he arrived with but hasn't got round to drinking, while his wife helps Priss with the food. Helena wonders if Polly is finding the inevitable talk about children boring.

How is it going for Vince at work? she asks me. How are you finding being back?

It's ok, I say. I'm glad to be back, but I feel a kind of anguish every day when I collect Maggie at nursery. And with Vince, it's complicated, but he seems all right, and if he leaves they'll make it as dignified as possible.

I saw him a few weeks ago, Helena says. He seems to accept it all. It sounds like Esther is genuinely standing by him.

Do you think the marriage has worked for Esther as well? I ask, because this has been on my mind, though I am self-conscious now, asking it in front of Priss and Ben and I avoid catching Ben's eye.

Yes just about, Helena says. My parents do, anyway. They really admire them for risking an open marriage for all these years. And I've always felt like he respects Esther, when they're out together. Like he's not eyeing up younger women, or he is, but he manages to make it more courteous than lecherous, and so somehow that's ok for Esther.

What happens if he leaves? Kay asks me, suddenly fully present. Will you get his job? Do you want it?

I wish that the alternative to her distractedness wasn't this inquisitive directness. Helena wants to change the subject again. Alisa starts to cry in Helena's arms and she hands her back and goes into the small loo under the stairs, taking her handbag so she can check her phone. She sees Clare's name on the screen and feels her chest tense with happiness. I love you, she mouths, spontaneously, as she opens it up, though she wouldn't risk saying it to Clare.

'I hope you're ok and there aren't too many pregnant women,' the message says. 'Come round after?' It's startling, how much effect these everyday words can have. 'Yes. Three o'clock?' she writes, knowing that leaving early will discon-cert Priss, but telling herself that it's her right to do this today.

She can feel already the relief of lying, clothed, on Clare's bed, their bodies squashed into each other, as the rain falls outside, and for the first time it seems possible that this is something she can rely on. When she pulls down her knickers, she finds that her sanitary towel is soaked with bright red blood of a kind that makes her worry she is haemorrhaging. She wonders if she should show it to Polly but instead she wraps it up and puts it in the bin, half-relishing her own disgust at her bloody hands because it feels better to confront the blood in all its lumpy horror in here than to maintain a fake equanimity in the kitchen while the process of destruction continues unseen.

When she goes back in, lunch is served, and she helps herself to a plate of the effortfully made salads that we rely on to proclaim our capacity to be both lavish and righteous. She sits next to Priss, because she's the only one of their friends she can trust not to examine her too closely, and they talk about Priss's plans for the café. It's half past two by the time the plates are cleared and Helena announces that she needs to leave.

Then she's driving towards Homerton, light-headed at the unreality of this day when the most important thing is that she's bleeding. She parks the car in another Victorian street, the front gardens here smaller than the ones in Alwyne Villas with their jubilant roses, and when Clare answers the door she wants to cry. She sees her hip bone exposed between her jeans and T-shirt and touches the pale skin wonderingly. It seems so peculiar to need someone so much, and for it to happen to be this woman, this particular, imperfect body, that somehow has such depths promised within the flesh, rather than any of the other, equally attractive and intelligent women she's spent the day with. Clare takes off her jacket and puts it on the coat stand, where it overlaps with her and her flatmates' coats. She says that the other two are out. Helena feels more comfortably that Clare's flat is their shared space than she has before.

Can we go to bed? she asks and Clare nods and takes her hand.

Helena likes the emptiness of Clare's bedroom today. There's a straightforwardness in Clare's distrust of unnecessary objects that Helena has come to admire. Clare draws back the duvet and they get under it clothed. The rain is falling loudly, as Helena imagined that it would, and Helena's tears are running down Clare's cheeks. Clare doesn't ask why Helena is crying but Helena wants to explain.

I'm happy, she says. I'm crying because I'm happy to be here. It's because I've been so sad that I'm so happy now, but I'm not crying because I'm sad. I'm crying because I need you and that feels ok.

Clare says that she likes her needing her, and there's clearly a cost to her in saying it. Their toes touch. Clare wraps her legs around Helena's. This is weightlessness, her body lost in another body, unsure where it ends and the other begins. It feels familiar, yet she cannot remember experiencing it before. The tears come faster now and she sobs silently against Clare's chest.

Stella

July

Last night I had the four of them round. I had a sudden urge for us to be a group again, without our children or their husbands, to see who we can still be for each other. I thought we'd cook, following the recipes together, like we used to do in our twenties, when Priss and Helena shared a flat. It was a silly thought, I suppose, to go back to a time when we were still playing at homemaking, given that we now all find domestic life tedious. And of course I was partly doing it out of curiosity as well — wanting to observe them. I wonder if they picked up on that.

Helena came first, punctual and neat-looking in beige high-waisted trousers, with a bottle of English organic white wine. Cleo called from upstairs for Helena to come and say goodnight, and I liked hearing them talking seriously about Cleo's teddies. When Helena came down I asked how she was but she changed the subject. It was only once Priss arrived, wearing a dark blue dress that almost matched mine, as her clothes so often do, and Priss and Helena were busy working their way through the recipe for buttermilk aubergine together, that Helena began to talk more, perhaps relaxed by the activity or perhaps better able to speak to

Priss than me. I busied myself with sorting out the kitchen.

I was relieved when Kay and Polly arrived – they'd walked from the station together and their faces were glowing in the evening sunlight when I opened the door. Kay sat down at the kitchen table – she said she was too tired to cook – and I felt embarrassed that I'd thought collective cooking was a good idea. I wondered if the others were humouring me by doing it, pitying me because I live alone and Tom doesn't like that side of domesticity. Polly chopped the onions to make the rice, rolling up her sleeves first in a way that made me think of her in scrubs. I opened the window as high as it would go and started to make a cake, scrubbing the oranges, thinking that I could have paid for a babysitter instead of spending £120 on ingredients I probably wouldn't finish, and we could be at Priss or Kay's house, drinking rosé in their gardens, instead of being trapped inside my tiny kitchen chopping things.

Polly asked about my day. I said that I'd had lunch with Vince, and I'd asked him about Sam, who Polly had discovered plays football with Vince – there are a group of men in their sixties who meet at weekends to play. Vince had talked about Sam enthusiastically, said that outsiders have to stick together: the black consultant, the Jewish editor. I'd wondered how they still manage to think of themselves as outsiders.

Kay said, talking unusually loudly, looking into her wine, that she finds their entitlement repellent, their sense of their prerogative to have affairs, to grope whichever women they please. She said she found it strange that Polly enjoyed having sex with a man so much older than her, and that I don't disapprove more of Vince.

I looked at Polly, whose eyes were red and watery from

chopping the onions. I offered to take over from her, glad of the distraction. I was trying to remember if I found Kay as tiresome as this at university. I've always described her as bracing, but I remember looking forward to seeing her more than I do now. I felt like I needed to say something, so I said that I could see that we only know one side of Vince and it's possible that he's turned on by exhibiting his own power. I said that if he really took his penis out, of course I disapprove of him, but I continue to find it hard to believe. And he is still Helena's uncle, whatever he's done.

Helena said, removing the seeds of a pomegranate with impressive neatness, that it doesn't matter whether he actually exposed his dick. He did something to this woman that made her uncomfortable.

Yes, Kay said. Why wouldn't we believe that? Why would she lie?

I wondered why Helena had hardened towards Vince and why I'd become his spokeswoman. I said that Naomi Ayre might be hurt by him in some way, professionally as an author. Or they might have had an affair that he ended. There are lots of reasons why she might want to lie, to punish him, lots of stories it's possible to imagine.

Kay stood up just as I started to sit down and we almost banged into each other, closer than felt comfortable. I noticed that there was a small patch of broken capillaries under her eye, a red bruise, and I wondered if it was the kind of thing that healed or if it was a permanent mark of age. She ran herself a glass of water, waiting for the tap to cool, and I had an image of her doing that in our James Street kitchen and of the lightness with which she moved then, the greater levity in her smiles. I felt suddenly very angry with Harald.

Polly started frying the onions and I found the homely

smell reassuring. It was a reminder that we'd all be friends at the end of the night, whatever any of us said about Vince. Polly asked, addressing me, how much we accept that it's a generational thing. That the behaviour of these men was more normal for that generation than for the younger one that's calling them out on it.

Pulling their trousers down? Priss asked, laughing rather overexcitedly, as she often laughs about bodily foibles. How could that be normal for any grown-up man? It's the kind of thing children do. Robert's in that phase now.

Having affairs, Polly said steadily, clenching both fists. Including with people they're working with. Like Sam. However hurt I've been by him, he has his own moral codes and he's living by them. He's honest about what he has to offer, he's loyal. He believes in sexual connection as a good in itself, which he's honouring. It's just that his moral standards are different from ours. Like Vince's are.

I said that I think we do have to accept that. And that I don't know how ashamed I should be that in some ways I like that world, that we're not allowed to live in any more, where it was socially acceptable, in some circles, to have affairs. Before people started regularly using the phrase 'cheating on'. Which I hate and which I tell my authors not to use.

I was cross partly because I felt ganged up on. Kay and Priss seemed so similar suddenly. I think they've become more alike in the last decade with their big houses, their two sensibly spaced-apart children, their lack of a work life they can believe in. In my mind they are still completely distinct from each other, because Kay is defined by brilliance, however perversely wasted, and because Priss seems so much more at home in her big house and the life it signifies. Even when they are both disapproving of sex, I see them as different, because Priss's views of sex seem to stem from virginal ignorance and Kay's from a kind of all-seeing weariness, as though she's lived many lives already. But I suppose other people don't see these distinctions, and maybe they don't see it themselves; maybe I project it all on to them because I need to feel that Kay is more similar to me than she is to Priss.

The aubergine was ready. Priss took it out of the oven and made it look exactly as it looked in the recipe picture and we sat down to eat, Kay and I squashed together at one side of my table. It was delicious, and I felt briefly vindicated, because this was better food than we'd be eating in a restaurant. None of us really has the time these days to cook for ourselves so it felt like something I'd offered them by demanding their participation.

I thought we'd change the subject but Priss asked Polly if she ever feels guilty about Sam's wife. I felt Priss looking at me and I worried suddenly that she does know about me and Ben and felt my stomach tightening with the fear that perhaps there are in fact things we could say that would end these friendships.

I don't feel guilty, Polly said. He's had affairs for years, his wife has chosen to stay with him, she's chosen their comfortable life, their large house and their dinner parties. I'm not taking that away from her. She may even have affairs herself. Why not? Why do people still get so hung up on monogamy? On families? Hardly any of the women I see at the hospital are in families of the kind we still force on ourselves. Sometimes, walking down the street, I picture one woman after another, still cooking similar meals in similar pans at six o'clock for their children, washing up and cooking again for their husbands after the children go to bed. Why is that something we need to defend on behalf of other people?

We all looked down at our plates. At the half-eaten meal we had cooked together, no longer so pretty, a mess of cut-up, mushy food. I said that I've liked having Maggie outside the structure of the family unit, but that I have to admit to myself there are times when I wish Tom lived with us all the time and that I'm happiest now when I'm with him and my children together. I said that lots of people, even open-minded people, have found the way we've done it very odd. Chris found it hard because it made him an absent father at the beginning – maybe Helena will find that too with Aaron. And older friends find it strange – Vince and Susanne.

I told them about the day that the blastocyst that became Maggie was implanted, when I went round to Susanne's house afterwards to rest. Susanne said that if it worked she thought Chris would want to get back together. I said that the way we were doing it didn't feel second best to me, and I thought we'd be better parents together when we'd stopped feeling disappointed in each other as husband and wife. It seemed too much to expect of ourselves, to be good parents and good lovers with the same person. She said that she was too old to understand. Her generation of feminists still wanted men and women to create children out of love, even if the marriages didn't last very long. She still thought that couples should stay together for the sake of the children, but our generation had separated our sexual and reproductive lives.

That's right, Polly said. The connection between sex and reproduction is arbitrary now.

I know, I said. But I still like it when men who are in love with me want to impregnate me. Sometimes I mind not sensing this desire in Tom, though I wouldn't want to have another child.

I feel like this is something we need to resist, Polly said, pushing her plate out of the way with unnecessary force, a large dent appearing above her nose as she frowned. The desire to be impregnated. The desire to be part of a family. The desire to be monogamous. They're dangerous desires. Especially in a world we can't count on – in a planet we've already almost destroyed.

Kay asked Priss, abruptly, if she would ever have an affair. Priss didn't seem offended by it, if anything she was flattered. I think she was enjoying the new bond she felt with Kay. She ran her hand through her hair with a kind of self-conscious languor, like someone being interviewed on television.

Sometimes I think Ben would like me to, she said. But I don't. More because of the children than because of principles – I wouldn't want anything to change for them. Also sometimes I just feel touched out by the children. As though more touch is the last thing I need.

Helena said that she doesn't think secret affairs are the answer to the conventionality Polly was complaining about. That she'd be prepared to have an open relationship. I said that Tom and I have talked about it. But right now I only want to have sex with him and it seems perverse to have sex with someone else on principle, although it may be that this is the only moment, when you're confident of each other's desire, that it's possible to do so without hurting each other.

Maggie started crying in her room next to the kitchen so I went in to settle her and then we went through to the sitting room, where I sat on the window seat with Helena, slightly cut off from the others. The talk was about children, and I felt depressed that we're coming to a point where we live partly through them, so I started reminiscing about university. I asked if they think we are still recognisably the same people, and they all said that we are, which surprised me, because when I think of myself then it's often in the third person, as though I can't identify fully with my younger self. When I walk past our old lecture halls or college buildings, it sometimes feels like I'm walking in the footsteps of someone else I know well, but like our bodies don't quite align.

Helena said that I've changed less than anyone else she knows, and that this used to make her angry with Chris, because he claimed that I'd become more independent over the years but actually it was all there when I met him. He was the one who changed, becoming a version of my mother, making me feel trapped by rules and disapproval.

I said that I can see their early selves in all of them, but when I picture them in their twenties they have the potential to develop into lots of alternative people who they haven't become. Kay said that she was glad that we don't have to do it all again, the becoming, and Priss said that she wished we could go back there just for a month and be nineteen again.

The good thing then was that even when things were horrible we expected everything to change, Helena said. But things were often pretty bad.

Do you remember the first party we had, I said, where there were people having sex in every bedroom.

I didn't even know the people I found in mine, Kay said.

And the time when Helena set fire to the kitchen, I said.

And the time that Polly hit Kay, Priss said, laughing.

We were silent, all I think embarrassed. The stillness in the room revealed how much motion there'd been in it before. I turned to look at Polly, where she sat next to Priss on the sofa. Her fists were clenched again. I was remembering – I suppose we all were – that scene. We'd all cooked a meal, perhaps that's what had brought it to mind for Priss. We were arguing about sex and Polly suddenly slapped Kay, quite hard, on the cheek with her palm. I can't remember what Kay had said to provoke her, but I remember us all continuing to eat afterwards, pretending to return to normality. Polly chewed away slowly and when she went upstairs, I remember Kay touching her cheek, stroking it questioningly, checking it was still there. For weeks afterwards we all tried to look after Polly, assuming that there was something wrong and that she ought, by the standards of the group, to tell us. We talked about it too much behind her back, we were so self-important and gossipy then. But eventually we forgot about it and I hadn't heard anyone mention it since.

I'm sorry, Polly said, smiling awkwardly at Kay. I was thinking, when you were talking before, that I didn't enjoy it there as much as the rest of you. I felt out of place, I felt like you all knew that your lives would be fine, and I couldn't count on anything.

I've always wondered why you did it, Kay said. Were you unhappy about something?

I've never told anyone, Polly said. Not even my sister. I've assumed it's something I won't tell people.

You don't have to now Polly, Priss said, quickly.

I have too many secrets, Polly said. It doesn't even matter now. An average hour in my life at work is more shocking than my whole life then. But that morning, I'd had an abortion.

We were all silent. No one except Priss was close enough to touch her, and Priss didn't. I was trying to remember whether Polly had a boyfriend at the time.

It was a man at home, she said. A friend of my dad's — they worked together. He wasn't that old. In his thirties. But he was married, and it wasn't serious. I didn't want to tell him, I didn't want to tell my parents, I thought they'd lose respect for both of us. So I couldn't tell my sister, and that meant that I couldn't tell any of you. Also it wasn't the worst thing that had happened to me. That was my brother dying. At the time, I didn't think of the abortion as a death. But, you know, recently I have. The baby would now be almost twenty. I don't mean to think like this, though. If I thought of dead foetuses as dead children, rather than just as messy clumps of cells, my life at work would be unbearable. You know that. You've lost babies as well now.

I looked around as we all tried to process it quickly enough to say something helpful. I can't remember the last time we were collectively so shocked. Kay asked if Polly could remember what she'd said, that made her so angry, but Polly didn't answer. Helena came across from the window seat and sat on the middle of the sofa, next to Polly, and hugged her.

It's fine that you didn't tell us, she said. But I'm glad that you've told us now. And I'm sure that you'll be pregnant again, and this time it will be right for the child to live.

Then Polly turned to Kay and said that although she didn't remember what she'd said, she did remember the feeling she'd had about her then, it was a feeling she had about all of us, that we took our luck for granted. Our right to be at university, spending our days reading books or acting in plays. Sometimes she hated us for it, and whatever Kay had said, it made her feel that she was incapable of understanding Polly's life, in which she was suffering under a burden she hadn't chosen.

Do you still think that about us now? I asked, recognising

the truth in what she was saying. She said that she trusted us more now to understand experience beyond our own. But she still thought sometimes that we complained too much.

Middle-class problems, Helena said.

But those are the problems we have, I said. And the answer can't be not to care about them. I said that sometimes, when Cleo is unhappy, I dismiss it, thinking that she's so lucky that nothing we do to her can be objectively bad, so we shouldn't worry about how she's taken the divorce. Sometimes, when I'm unhappy in my life, I tell myself that I'm being ungrateful and should just get on with it. But by that reckoning, Chris and I wouldn't have split up, and I think we did the right thing. These are the lives and the responsibilities we have.

I've had an idea Polly, Priss said, turning inwards so they could talk more easily across Helena. I suggested it to Ben after my birthday lunch, when I saw you all with children, and Helena trying to get pregnant with Aaron, and Polly on her own. You might think it's crazy.

We obediently urged her to say it.

Ben's such a good father, Priss said. And we've had enough children. Helena's having a child with Aaron.

So? Helena asked, smiling at her encouragingly.

I think Polly should have a child with Ben.

I looked at Priss, who appeared rather majestic in the excitement and certainty of her plan. And I looked at Polly, who was staring at Priss, and then suddenly her face crumpled and she laughed, crying as she always does when she laughs spontaneously like that, squeezing Helena's arm as though to share the gleeful awkwardness of it all.

Oh Priss, that's very kind, but, I don't think so. It might all be a bit too embarrassing for us, Ben ejaculating in my bathroom.

You could have sex, Helena said, laughing as well. We've agreed that we're not conventional!

Yes why not? Polly said. I'm having an affair with one married man, why not have sex with one of my best friend's husbands, while I'm at it?

I wanted urgently to leave the room. I felt almost certain that Priss was playing with me, that she knew everything, and was using this to show that she's more morally complicated than I've guessed. I was avoiding looking at her, and I was avoiding looking at Helena, wondering if she was also thinking about the time when I suggested to her that she should have a child with Chris, thinking that she must have told Priss about it, that it must have been this that gave Priss the idea. It was before we did IVF to have Maggie and I thought that it might save our marriage if he stopped blaming me for his lack of fecundity. We could all go on holiday together, I told Helena enthusiastically, the baby could be a sibling for Cleo. She said that if I wanted to go on holiday together we could do that, I didn't need my husband to impregnate her first. It was odd that neither of us was mentioning this now, that it had become unspeakable, like the fact that one of us had in fact already had sex with one of our best friend's husbands. I stood up, about to make up an excuse to go back to the kitchen, and then I remembered my cake, so I rushed down the corridor to the kitchen and found that it was burnt.

Oh fuck, I shouted (I only swear when I make stupid mistakes). Helena came through to help me scrape the top off, which took a while, and we brought it back into the sitting room to eat it. I felt so frustrated with myself, for doing this badly, my task for the evening. Polly put her arm round my shoulder in a way that I wish I could do as naturally with women as she and Helena can. And then we hugged and I cried. She said it was all right, I am doing a great job, I have a life that works.

I cry so much at the moment, I said, wiping my eyes with my hand, suddenly self-conscious because Priss was looking at me intently, as though I was a painting in a gallery she wished to imprint on her mind, and the suspicion returned that she knows everything about me and Ben.

Helena said that it's one of the things that surprises her most, about being at the end of her thirties, how much she cries. While she was briefly pregnant the sadness must have been hormonal, but most of the time it feels real. Like there's a lot to cry about, more than there used to be. Kay said that she's cried more since starting psychoanalysis, and I said that I have too, and that part of what psychoanalysis has shown me is how much effort I used to put into feeling that my life was ok and telling myself I was happy every day.

And then it was eleven o'clock. And none of us was free. We all needed to be in bed, and found it hard to imagine that once we could talk on for hours without thinking about whether we'd be tired the next day. Polly asked if we really slept much better then, or if it's something we imagine, looking back. Then in bed, thinking of them making their separate journeys across London, I wondered if we all have secrets from each other as big as Polly's abortion or my affair with Ben, and how I hadn't suspected at the time that something of that kind was wrong. I wondered what I'm doing, inviting Priss round and cooking with her like that, what claim I allow her over me if I think of her again as a close friend. I wondered whether she meant it, offering Ben to Polly, whether she'd have really gone through with it.

Recently I've started to see the affair with Ben as self-indulgent, because I find it harder now to think my way into the head of someone for whom sex is a good in itself. Also I think the idea that it was all about self-exploration was partly a lie, and actually I was looking for love, like everyone else, wherever I could find it. But it's impossible to be loyal retrospectively. I can't reverse without banging into things. Even if Priss might already know, it will change too much for it to be in the open. And it will create more drama than it needs to. Ben and I are so much less connected than we used to be, we only really meet through work now, or through Priss. We just have to keep acting as though the secret can remain a secret, hoping that it won't be found out.

I can still feel my way into the embrace with Polly at the end – the sense of being completely present to each other. I felt a kind of solidarity with those women last night that felt more important than any of our relationships with men. This is a new thing, as we approach forty. In our twenties, it was the men we followed with our eyes at parties, summoning them away from other women. Now I often most want to sit quietly in a corner and talk slowly and companionably to a female friend. It's not just companionable, though. Last night, it wasn't only Priss who looked at me in that intent, inquisitive way – almost with desire. Our own lives make more sense when we compare them to each other's.

Kay

July

Seb is shouting. Harald is shouting. Kay is silent: a spectral figure in her own home, because she has lost her voice. This is something that happens to Kay more often than it happens to other people and that she dreads. She fears not so much the loss of control as the loss of self. She fears that, voiceless, she will disappear. The fear is sustained from adolescence, when she lost her voice more often, tending to ignore the warning signs and to shout and smoke through the early hoarseness.

But in fact, when it happens, it usually proves restful. At university, she used to retreat from the world for days at a time into a nun-like sequestration. I remember having lunch alongside her in the James Street kitchen, feeling that she was oblivious to who else was coming in and out of the room, that anything I said or did would have less impact on her than usual. She can't retreat like that now but there's still a peacefulness, however noisy the house becomes, in knowing that she won't respond. Even when Seb comes and shouts close to her face as he is now, she's distant from him, able to forget that she's his mother.

The last conversation she had before losing her voice

was with Helena. She came round, yesterday evening, in Harald's absence. She was worried that Kay seemed unhappy at the dinner at my flat, and that we might collectively have failed to notice the extent of this because we were distracted by Polly's revelation. Kay was pleased to see her, as she's always pleased to see all of us, more than I'd expect given that none of us live up to her high standards of useful and intelligent action. I suppose she forgives us more easily than she forgives herself for failing those standards. They sat on the grass in the garden, their bare feet reminding Kay of her children, whose buckets had been flung out of the sandpit on to the lawn, and of that first summer when we all became friends. Helena asked, with visible concern, about Harald, outraged by his affairs, wondering what it would take to make him assume greater responsibility for the life he has chosen to live with Kay. They talked, Kay grateful for the sympathy but clear that she has no hope of Harald changing. And then she asked about Helena's life and suggested, as she once suggested to me, that the decision to have a baby on her own was a mistake.

She warned Helena that she didn't have enough income to be a single mother; she'd be unable to afford a full-time nanny and so would be left alone and breastfeeding and exhausted. She'd lose the best aspects of her life, the ability to go out when she likes, to make the programmes she wants to make. The relationship with Clare couldn't survive motherhood; if she cares about Clare then shouldn't she prioritise that and wait to have a baby together? Helena felt claustrophobic beneath the neatly accounted calculations. She felt that there could be no space amid Kay's elegantly arrayed pot plants and expensive garden furniture for her longing and grief. She wanted to say that love cannot be accounted, that there was a baby growing in her womb only a few weeks ago and that now she feels its absence as a kind of ache, all the time.

Kay knew all this. She's able to deduce what people might be feeling in moments like that, it's just that those feelings become less important to her than the urge to tell the truth and to correct the misapprehensions of others. The truth, as they sat there, had a kind of objective quality that it lost once Helena went home and Kay felt repentant for imposing her views on her when she could see in retrospect that all Helena wanted was sympathy. She went to sleep after Helena left, and lost her voice by the time she awoke, so there's been no chance to use new conversations to paper over the uglier debris of the evening. And she has spent enough time with Moser recently to know today that it was her own lost freedom she was describing and that she has to confront the regrets she has about choosing to conceive her children.

This is the worst day ever, Seb shouts at her now, his body clenched with rage. At least this sort of tirade suggests connection, assuming that his experience of the day matters to her.

He is angry because she told him, in a whisper a few minutes ago, that he needs to have a bath before dinner. He'd rather have dinner and then a bath, but Harald is making dinner and it's not yet ready, and she's determined to have him in bed by seven o'clock, counting down the minutes until she's left in peace. The bath is already run. It's cooling as he heats into rage. She regrets doing this and not just allowing him to miss a bath. But she knows that at some point within the next fifteen minutes it will be her who carries him, shouting, to the bathroom and forcibly removes his clothes.

Next door, Alisa has woken up, perhaps disturbed by Seb's cries, though in her waking she doesn't register distress. Alisa stops burbling when she comes in and raises her arms, expectantly. Kay picks her up, smelling the residue of contented sleep, grateful for this interaction where no words are required. She sits the baby down on her bed and kisses her with her fluffy penguin. Alisa laughs delightedly. Kay lies down on the bed and places the baby next to her, stroking her little chubby arms and thighs and smelling her familiar smell. She thinks that soon Alisa will start talking and then arguing and she will probably lose the only experience of unconditional love she has ever had. She wonders why we place so much value on words, on the endless movement of mouths into patterns of meaning that come in the way of intimacy.

Seb has gone down to Harald and there seems to be peace downstairs. This probably means that Harald has said Seb doesn't have to have his bath. Harald rarely shows enough solidarity to go along with her instructions, and today he's discounting everything she says because he's convinced that if she wanted to she could do more than whisper. The five minutes she lies next to Alisa are the most pleasurable five minutes she has had all day. She registers this as she monitors time passing, aware that the silence won't last for long. It's interrupted by Harald and Seb coming upstairs together, Seb running ahead.

Mummy, Mummy, he shouts, unable to accept that she won't reply till he's in her presence. He is angry again by the time that he comes into the room. Why didn't you answer? Daddy says I don't have to have a bath till after dinner. He says I can have one with him after that.

Harald comes in. There are too many of them, now, in Alisa's small bedroom. Kay feels too low on the bed, and stands up. She looks at her husband, with questioning, hostile eyes.

That's all right Kay, isn't it? He's not tired, we'll have a Sunday bath, to spend time together before we get caught in the week.

It's already run, she whispers.

What? Can you talk properly, please?

She tries and it comes out as a dry croak, which makes her think of a skeleton trying to raise its arm. Harald is dismissive, announcing that they will warm it up, or run another one. It's only water after all. Seb repeats it: It's only water, Mummy. Her whole body is clenched in frustration and when she closes her eyes to avoid looking at them, she fleetingly sees herself smashing her fist first against her husband's head and then against her son's.

The man and the boy leave the room together, running down the stairs, playing a tickling version of catch as they go. Kay lies back down beside Alisa but the baby has woken up fully now and is crawling down the bed, needing space. She takes her up to their bedroom, not wanting to go downstairs. There she sits on the carpeted floor in the bay window while her daughter crawls around the floor. She thinks about masturbating, to rid herself of the tension that's accrued in her body, but she would rather wait till the children are asleep and she can go to bed alone.

Ana is here. After departing for another fortnight, offended, once again, by the mess, she has returned, unannounced, on a Sunday evening, and she now turns on the hoover in the hallway, forming a kind of soothing counterpoint to Kay's silence. It's as though Kay's speaking through the hoover, as though she has emptied herself out and remade herself with only this one function, expressing herself with this constant neutral purr.

Kay shuts the bedroom door and puts jazz piano played by Keith Jarrett on the speaker. Although Harald has put speakers in every room, Kay usually opts for silence given the choice, but now she hopes to use the piano playing to give herself a voice. She likes this particular piece because it's repetitive and rhythmical and she enjoys the feeling that she doesn't know where it's going. She has fifteen minutes to listen to it before she needs to take Alisa down to feed her.

She can barely remember a time before each task, whether enjoyable or not, was allocated a fifteen-minute or half-hour interval. This for her, for many of us, has been one of the great losses entailed by procreation, the loss of unscripted hours. Somehow the men manage to avoid it. Harald going out to his writing room, Chris going to the Science Museum, have their working days as normal, then return and let events take their course. Yet Kay, who was never someone to clock watch, who wrote her university essays during open-ended night shifts at the library, has become someone who can only listen to music for fifteen minutes because after that her daughter will get too hungry to eat well, which could lead to her being too tired to sleep.

Then the door opens and Harald comes in, bare-chested, as he often is at home in summer. He offers to take Alisa down and feed her. Kay is surprised that he's remembered this, and, without her communicating assent or dissent, he takes the baby from her and shuts the door behind him. She lies down and pulls the bedspread up over her, although it's hot, luxuriating in its heaviness. She imagines what it would be like to lie here knowing that she's not going to be disturbed, complacent in the certainty that darkness will fall and lift again without the light bringing clamouring demands, without any requirement to leave her bed.

Stella

July

It's the kind of hot Sunday evening that makes me wish I was free and could wander through London, enjoying the crowds of underdressed people on the river. But I'm at home and I have spent the weekend wondering if I'm in the wrong life. Yesterday Cleo refused to go to her swimming lesson, and I had to drag her forcibly down the road. Maggie refused to eat and I spent hours mashing up one form of food after another, trying to persuade her to take it only for her to spit it in my face, crying or smiling. I eventually got them to Queen's Park, getting Cleo to leave the house by bribing her with the promise of ice cream, but the ice cream melted in her hands and she threw it on the grass in disgust. She started shouting, demanding that I should buy her another one, screaming that I didn't love her, making Maggie cry and causing people around us to stare. Throughout I continued to smile, rather manically, at passers-by, trying to convince them that this was a version of normal family life.

All through this I felt as though there was something both unbearably enviable and irresponsible about Tom's life. With Andreas in Germany, he lives as though he's childless and has managed to avoid the things that trap the rest of us – an office job, a mortgage – working as he pleases on the poetry magazine he edits and the poems and essays he writes. There's no obvious reason why he shouldn't live as he does. He doesn't ask for very much from the world, refusing luxury. But I envy him, and I envy Polly her freedom too, waking up on her days off with no one to think about but herself. I have to keep reminding myself that my life is no less irresponsible than anyone else's. It's not like I'm doing any good for others with my job or my children. They're things that I've chosen selfishly because I thought they'd make me happy, because I was caught in the ascent to grown-upness and was enjoying it.

It got better last night because Kay and my author Gemma came round and I asked them about whether they often think they're in the wrong life. Kay said that everyone constantly feels the way I do. She said that she often thinks it's a terrible mistake having children: you bring people into the world who you might turn out not to like, and they're there forever. She was exaggerating flippantly but there was also a sense of defiance and pride about it. Gemma said that motherhood, especially single motherhood, is an epic endeavour and I should learn to enjoy its terribleness. I thought about this while combing out the nits from Cleo's head this evening, and pressing out their lives in the sink. We'd agreed that she wouldn't shout at me, because I was doing this for her benefit, but of course she did, because she's a seven-year-old girl whose mother was hurting her. This is an epic endeavour, I told myself, as I combed my own hair afterwards, unsure if I had nits or not.

Gemma also said, in relation to Cleo and her constant complaints about everything I ask her to do, that she came to understand how her children felt when she won a big French literary prize and found that her schedule was now managed by her publicist. Deposited in the lobby of a French hotel, told that she had seven minutes to go up to her room before her next interview, she said that she went upstairs and had a sudden urge to throw the television out of the window like rock stars do. She understood why her children had such messy rooms. It's their only available form of protest.

When she said that, I did start sympathising more with Cleo. I realised that I find it hard to see her as a full person with a separate consciousness of her own. The otherness of our children is even harder to see clearly than the otherness of our friends, because we take their familiarity for granted. When they're Maggie's age, there's so little separating them from us, their little bodies are still ours to wash and clothe. Part of what makes moments like the one with the ice cream so hard with Cleo at the moment is that she finds our separateness difficult too, disliking the contrast with the charming baby beside her. She's torn between longing to sink back into babyhood and feeling ready to move into the next stage of herself, without quite knowing how to do it. Afterwards, she pretended that she couldn't walk, she could only crawl, and then when she pretended to take a few faltering steps she asked me to speak to her in the voice I use with Maggie when she does something well. It was heartbreaking, and it made me want to enclose her body within mine again, simplifying love.

Moser says that I should allow myself the unlived life. It's too late, as Kay says, to think of being in any life except our own. But I can fantasise about the life in which Tom and I are both free, and live near each other, and float in and out of each other's days, alternating intense bursts of creativity with intense bursts of sexual togetherness, still left with hours of extra time free for walking and reading and thinking. Fantasise about it, mourn it, get on with the life I've chosen for myself, see that Tom's life is less easy and more responsible than it looks on days like yesterday. But there are times when this is beyond me, when I feel a panicky drive to abandon him and my children and my job, and then wonder what I'd be left with, just me, endlessly writing away, alone.

It's Friday now, and reading my thoughts from Sunday makes me realise how quickly my feelings about motherhood oscillate. Today I encouraged Amy, my former assistant who's finally been made an editor, to have a baby, paid £104 for an all-day babysitter in addition to the £68 I was already paying the nursery in order to keep Maggie home because of her minor cold, and read in the news about the baby her age kept in a cage in America, who may never be reunited with his soon-to-be-deported mother. I feel guilty about Maggie's cold, which has gone on for two weeks and which Tom said yesterday is a sign that she is insufficiently relaxed in her life at present, shuttling between me and Chris and the nursery and babysitters. But I feel guilty also for being this attentive and extravagant in response to so middle-class a problem and doing nothing to help the babies suffering elsewhere.

I rushed home in the afternoon to be with Maggie while the babysitter collected Cleo. Kay came over, free from lessons because of exams, and we talked about the children in cages. We agreed that it's irresponsible to care so much, just because these are the children that social media has fed us right now. There have been children in cages elsewhere for years. She has been listening obsessively to the appalling footage of them screaming and has been scrolling through the Twitter feeds of the angry American women. She doesn't cry, she said, just sits there feeling furious with the people who have made these decisions, unable to do anything about it or to get on with doing the laundry or marking. After she left, I listened to the footage too. I did cry, a lot, and it made me realise how much I hate leaving Maggie at the moment, which may explain my rather arbitrary decisions today. I wish I hadn't needed to go back to work after five months: it was too early. Secretly, I agree with my mother and Priss, who both think it was cruel.

Is it because of the cages or do the cages affect me more because of Maggie? Surely there should be a kind of absolute quality to my feelings about keeping children in cages, which shouldn't be affected by my feelings about my own children. But the cries of those children don't really sound very different from Maggie's cries when she's left downstairs for too long in her pushchair – babies don't keep much distress in reserve – so one child's cry is going to remind you of another's, whatever the disparity in circumstances. And it's so hard to have logical moral views when it comes to anything to do with children. Everything is heightened and seen through your own experiences, whether you have children or not. I can't watch films any more in which children suffer without wanting to run home from the cinema and check on Cleo and Maggie. And now I can't separate hysterical terror at the fragility of my own two from compassion for the plight of the children in America. I describe myself as someone who never feels guilt, dismissing it as a wasteful emotion, but there's clearly so much guilt in my feelings about my own children, which feeds into my guilt about the children in cages. If I really wanted to help vulnerable children I'd go to help the refugees in Calais, or I'd lobby for the rights of asylum seekers here.

Kay seemed colder, less centred in herself, as though she's living at the edge of her life. She kept standing up and pacing, as if sitting down made her feel caged herself, and as if constantly on the verge of quitting the scene completely. Harald is away at a literary festival. She is finding that the arguments with Seb bring out a monstrosity in her that she loathes.

Polly

July

Dave is ordering food on his phone. He thinks it's quaint that she's asked for Chinese food. Apparently no one these days eats Chinese. Now that she's had her say on that, he doesn't ask for particular requests, going by ratings instead. They are having the most popular dishes from the most popular restaurant they've been offered. She looks at him. He is a man almost her age. His dark skin glistens. He has muscles of a kind she hasn't encountered in her bed before. But he's overweight and heavy featured and she's less attracted to him than she was to Sam, though if she told Dave this he would find it hard to believe and would see it as a sign of her fetishistic taste for older men rather than his own lack of bodily charm.

Dave is the first man that Polly has slept with since Sam. When she selected him from the grinning faces lined up on her computer, she told herself that choosing another black man had nothing to do with Sam and that this was better than going out of her way to choose someone different. Given that she has swiped Dave into her life, it's not surprising that he selects food by swiping away on screen. He's perplexed by her lack of internet life. He's even had to teach her to use WhatsApp. You're better sexually than you are textually, he said earlier this evening, which made her cross because she thinks, justifiably, that she's a good writer. Apparently he's been telling his friends that she's disappointingly unsexy when encountered by text message. And he doesn't know if she's laughing at his jokes. She needs to start using 'lol'.

Yet this isn't the whole story because they've just emerged from a very happy two hours in bed. She is astonished by his stamina. She had forgotten what sex is like with men who can keep pumping away at her for hours, even after they have come. She was so surprised by this that she had to ask to check that he'd come, the first time. She's had several orgasms as well and she didn't even mind when they broke her bed and Dave had to use her Ikea toolbox to put it back together, while disparaging both the tools and the bed itself, which Polly didn't say that her father had made. She tells herself that she's happy and relaxed and about to eat Chinese food with her lover. He wants babies, she knows this from his advert. He's well off, he has a job in media he describes as creative, though she doesn't really understand what he does or why the world needs it. They could have a future together, if she just learns to laugh demonstratively at the puns that he emits into the white boxes on her phone even more frequently than he emits sperm into her vagina. She has never been so close to the life that she wants.

They open the expensive white wine he's brought with him and sip it as they watch their food journeying towards them on his phone. He drinks less than Sam, which makes life easier, but she knew that about him from the internet as well. They talk about their parents. It's been a feature of her life since university that she is unable to be as dismissive of her parents as her complacently middle-class friends have been. She's shocked now when Dave criticises his father, perhaps especially because he's black and must, she assumes, have worked as hard for Dave's privileges as her own father did for hers. Dave is saying that his father has never found anything to make him happy, and therefore tries to stop everyone around him from enjoying themselves, issuing too many rules in his home and even expecting his children to obey them outside it. Polly asks if it comes naturally to him to be this disloyal. She is finding that an advantage of being with Dave is that nothing feels unsayable.

You don't get irony, do you Polly? Dave asks, and she says that it just sounds like cynicism to her. He says that everyone is cynical now, and she says that he can afford cynicism but she can't. She has to see forty patients a day. A lot of them are women in serious pain, inflicted on them by men. When it comes to the people who try hard to do the best they can, like her father, the men who aren't inflicting pain, she doesn't want to be cynical about them, even if they're gauche and silly and troubled in their own ways.

I know, he says, kissing her briefly on the lips. That's why I like you. You're not like the other women I know. You still care about stuff.

The food arrives. It's true that it's better than the food she'd suggested she might cook, which he rejected. She's never eaten Chinese food in this flat and it feels enjoyably novel rolling the duck in the little pancakes on her kitchen table, licking the plum sauce off her fingers, and she likes the thought that this whole experience, from the food they're eating to the sperm that's now leaking out into her knickers, has been summoned from a screen. It brings a liberating feeling that it could disappear as easily as it's appeared.

Afterwards, she suggests a bath, but he says that it's too

hot for one. This is the right decision, because they've already showered, because it is indeed too hot, and most of all because it's right that they shouldn't do the same things she did with Sam, who feels already like a ghost within their evening. They haven't talked about whether Dave will stay the night, and she's hoping that he won't want to. If he does, she fears that the moment of lying down to sleep will be the moment she most feels the absence of Sam.

There's the question of what they should do before bed. She's tired of talking, but doesn't think they've seen enough of each other to suggest watching TV. She's pleased when he proposes it though. There's a new series they both want to try, so they watch the first episode, competing to have more complicated theories about who might turn out to be the killer. Usually she likes watching things in silence. Eventually, after a few more dates, she'll have to tell him to be quiet. But now it's helpful, in the absence of shared experience, to have the images on the screen as a proxy life to make their way through together.

It's eleven o'clock when it finishes. Dave asks if he should stay the night. Polly says yes, because she doesn't know how to say no, and because she likes the thought of the warmth of his body against hers on waking. They have sex again. It's more direct and faster than it was earlier, he comes and she doesn't, and he assumes that this is enough for both of them, which it is. She wonders if he'd assume this with the younger women he's used to. At first, with Polly, he expected to come everywhere but in her vagina: on her legs, stomach and ideally face. Now he's used to having sex with a woman of his own age he's remembered the old-fashioned pleasure of exploding inside her, but it's brought the old-fashioned pleasure of complacency. He's stopped wanting to lick her

157

and this makes her miss Sam. She hopes that he won't fall asleep immediately but he does, lying on his back, and she lies next to him for half an hour before she decides to get out the sofa bed in the sitting room. She's working tomorrow, not early, but for long enough that she can't face doing it sleep-deprived.

This is the first time she's slept on the sofa bed. She finds her sitting room unfamiliar, with the evening's wine glasses still visible in outline on the table, and it takes a while before she can retreat inwards towards sleep. She thinks about motherhood. She feels sure now, lying a room away from his sleeping body, still able to hear his irregular breathing through the wall, that she will not fall in love with Dave. There's something he lacks, some suppleness of thought and feeling, that means she won't be able to feel her way inside him. She could see him a couple more times to make sure, end it, and order a new man from the internet. This is probably what she'll do. But now that Sam is no longer there, stopping her, as she believed, from having children, she's not sure she wants them. Also, telling us about the abortion has made her realise how much it had been in her mind. She'd been haunted by it superstitiously, as an act of destruction she needed to propitiate with an act of creation. But she can see beyond this now: she can see that it's all right to end up childless, even if she's been pregnant once, and that a live child would have nothing to do with the child she didn't give a chance to live.

If there's anything that impassions her, lying there with the street lamps visible through the curtains, it's the thought that she could stop seeing the next five years as a process of diminishment, in which her eggs lose their potency, as she's warned so many of her patients they will. She admires Helena in her frantic efforts to have children, and she can see the happiness procreation has brought to her friends. But talking to Dave, seeing how little he seems to care about his work, how little he worries about what he has to offer to the world in general, has made her see how much she still has to contribute as a doctor.

She is sore, now, from all the sex this evening, and she thinks that perhaps Dave should have checked that she wanted it to carry on as long as it did. She thinks that she wouldn't choose to spend time with a woman she liked as little as she likes Dave. This is a sign that she doesn't like being single: she's lowered her standards. But it's also because there's an element of attraction for her in hostility. The side of her that dislikes Dave can't be separated from the side of her that wants to sleep with him. He may be right not to check that she's happy and comfortable during sex. It may add to the erotic charge that they aren't interested in each other's feelings in bed. When he wants her to come it's because he finds it satisfying, both as a moment of climax and as a moment when her body and mind succumb entirely to a sensation created in her by him. It's not because he has a stake in her pleasure and happiness. This may mean that they are simply using each other for sex or it may mean that a relationship could develop where they care more about each other but where the impersonal feeling of hostility remains, and this is still alluring. This thought makes her miss Sam less. But she needs to stop thinking about men and go to sleep.

Stella

July

Today, during the train journey home from Tom's, I read a novel that has been submitted to me about a nanny. Halfway through it turns out that her own children, who we've seen as teenagers, are only fantasies. The real children died in a car crash five years ago, out for a day with their divorced father. At the point when the twist was revealed, Chris was driving Cleo and Maggie home from the seaside in what used to be our car. It was disturbing, all my anxieties about motorway driving suddenly given objective form. I stopped reading, and wrote emails instead, eating a KitKat and trying to enjoy the time away from the world before domestic life resumed, but then when I got home I turned back to the book, wanting at least to make use of the time while I waited and thinking that I probably wanted to publish it. They were an hour late and Chris didn't reply to my messages. I started to feel sick so I busied myself with domestic tasks, sorting out their laundry. In part of my mind I wondered if it would prove unnecessary for their socks to be in neat pairs, if they were killed, while also telling myself that if they were dead, the time wasted on sorting their clothes would be the last of my problems. Time, indeed, would become the thing I was never lacking again.

Among the scenarios I imagined was one where the children were killed but Chris survived. Part of what upset me was thinking that Chris would grieve for Maggie less than I would and less than he would grieve for Cleo. Maggie has not become the centre of his life as she has mine, though she will in time. Thinking this, I felt a loneliness on her behalf and on mine. But now that Maggie has been safely restored to me and I can hear her sleeping snuffily in her room as I type, I can see that there's also a pleasure in knowing that I love her more than anyone else does. And I know that there will be a loss for me and perhaps for her when she forms more relationships, coming to love Chris as much as she loves me, loving her grandparents, becoming a person in their minds as she is in mine.

The delight I felt in the children's little bodies when they did eventually come home brought a certainty that I am in the right life, that this is the only life I can be in, and that this is true for all my friends with children, however much we push against it. I picked Cleo up, finding it odd to feel her in my arms again, realising that the weight of her body is no longer familiar to me. I was relieved that there was equal fear and equal joy in my responses to the two children. It turns out that I don't love Maggie more as Cleo fears I do, it's just that there is no ambivalence in my love yet.

Meanwhile I continue to feel guilty about immigrant children, everywhere, and my failure to do anything about them. Tom and I argued about this yesterday, lying on the grass in the woods near his house. It was such a pleasure to be away from London and responsibility, to be out of the sun, to be somewhere beautiful with him. He was happy because he'd just sent an issue of the magazine to the printers, and their circulation is up. I was stroking his stomach under his blue T-shirt, plucking out hairs from his chest proprietorially, feeling so grateful to have found him, to have this unexpected layer of kindness and understanding in my life, to feel our bodies tessellating easily.

And then I wasted it, telling him about the disjunction in my Twitter feed between the literary news I keep track of for work and the news about the desperate children. He said that this was what was insidious about Twitter, and that the people sharing information about immigrant children are playing into their opponents' hands, behaving in exactly the way that liberals are meant to behave. I asked what the alternative was. He said it was to find new ways to share information, and new ways to resist, at the community level. The danger with social media and with liberal outrage is that it alienates the people on the ground in Texas or Calais, who have their own reasons to behave kindly to refugees, but now have no chance to find this desire within themselves, because they are caught between the noise of two groups.

I cried. In many ways I agreed with him. It's part of why I've put more effort into seeing my university friends recently, the feeling that we need to hold on to the real forms of community, rather than relying on the false satisfactions of the virtual ones. But I felt like there was no room for my confusion in his certainty, and felt as though I had to store my ball of messy thoughts up secretly to untangle later. He hugged me, but I could feel the beginning of distance in his touch, and I turned away from him, partly wanting him to draw me back towards him, which he didn't. We sat up. I said that I needed him to present his opinions as opinions rather than as truths that leave no room for other views. He said, his voice drained of character, that this is him – this is how his opinions are expressed and he wouldn't be himself if he wasn't like this – and I can respond by saying what I think. The problem is that I don't know what I think, and feel smothered by the apparent rightness of what he thinks.

There is a loneliness in all this that reminds me of being married. I often feel at the moment that all women are oppressed by all men. We hate them for their facility at forming all-engulfing world views and they hate us for feeling threatened by this. And women and men feel as though we're fighting for freedom and sanity against each other. This isn't how I experience men most of the time. But because there are moments when loving entails hating, because those are moments when the strangeness of the opposite sex comes into focus, it's so easy to be pushed into a state of mind where we hate all men, unable to gain enough distance on what is involved in hating the particular men we love.

We talked our way back to conversational ease but we didn't have the feeling of mutual relaxedness and good will that we usually have there and I didn't know where to find it. Part of the problem was that I was so hot, and so exhausted by these weeks of heat and the sticky stillness of the nights, that I felt detached from my own mind. It was only once we'd had sex later that evening that I felt easily connected to him again and could stop noticing the sharpness of our outlines, separating us from each other. This made me worry about what would have happened if I'd pushed him away too far to want sex.

He felt that the argument about arguing had been unproductive, but I think I am always going to have these moments of coming up against the unfamiliarity of another person's mind and finding this frightening rather than just mysterious.

It might be helpful if I didn't experience it so strongly as the woman in me confronting the man in him, but I bear the scars of a long marriage and I'm surrounded by women living under comparable burdens.

Lunch with Kay, who came into work. She wanted to tell me that she knows about me and Ben. Why now? And how long has she known?

We were sitting perched high on the stools in the window at Gail's, talking about our summer plans. She was wearing a high-necked black silk blouse, which made her face look very pale and which felt like it had been chosen in defiance of the weather and the hedonism of other Londoners. She was nervous and her hand, held in the air, was shaking slightly as she talked, perhaps because she was planning to ask me about Ben, though it may have had nothing to do with that, she may just have been hungry and caffeinated. She said that she's dreading the Italian holiday that she's diligently organised for the family and that she's been thinking about me asking her if she ever wished she was in another life. It made me regret asking it. I still cling to the idea that rational, unsentimental analysis is conducive to happiness.

I don't see how anyone can be fulfilled without children, she said, finding yourself doing the same things, year after year, as though you were still in your twenties. But they're going to make your life worse – how could they not? – and it's questionable whether it's even your life any more.

She spoke quickly, looking down, as though she had a duty to say it but wanted to get it done as hastily as possible. I admired her for her honesty, all the more so because it was clearly costing her something. But I blew out platitudes like the bubbles that Cleo has taken to following me around the house with, letting them rest briefly in the air between us before they dissolved. I said that there were moments when it was more fun to have children than not have them, going to the park on a Sunday afternoon, opening Christmas presents. I said that they go through so many phases, that some will be more pleasurable than others. I knew as I said it that I was betraying her. She was asking for shared courage in admitting the unsayable, rather than an assurance that her life was actually fine. It sounded like I was suggesting that, unlike her, I was a good enough mother to enjoy motherhood, that it just required a cheerful attitude. She looked at me as though from very far away. I didn't know how to shift back to a more collaborative mood and we were both silent long enough for it to be noticeable. Then she asked about Tom.

There are two, opposing versions of Tom that I present to my friends, both of them accurate. In one I have found the physical, emotional and intellectual compatibility that I've found with so few men. There is almost nothing that I can't say to him and feel will be understood. In another our lives are incompatible in their different levels of crowdedness, and he can't stride into our relationship with the certainty I want because he's too depressed about Andreas's depression, which he may be using as a way of displacing his own. Recently I've become tired of giving the negative account, because it leaves out the joyfulness of being together, so I give the positive one, and then people become envious, as I think Kay did, because I was describing a kind of quiet togetherness that she doesn't have with Harald. She started asking questions that chipped away at my image of him: what does he do all day apart from editing the magazine? how often is he in touch with Andreas? do I think it's irresponsible of him not to have found a way to live closer to his son? And then it was time to go and as we stood up I talked about going round for lunch at Priss and Ben's on Saturday, asking if she'd seen them recently. She asked if I found it awkward.

Awkward? Why? I asked, frightened that I knew what she meant. They are very particular moments, those moments when you determinedly will the old reality where the secret remains a secret to continue, while you can see the new reality looming into view. We looked at each other briefly and I found her inexpressive. Brown eyes are harder to read than blue eyes.

Because of you and Ben, she said, as she bent to gather her bags. And I didn't want either to deny it or to allow a conversation about it to begin, so I just said, Oh, not really, it's so long in the past – though she may know that it's not that long, even if it feels a long time now to me. I moved towards the counter to pay and she followed. I wanted some physical method of expressing my discomfort. I thought of the way that Priss hums, perhaps unconsciously, under her breath, when things are awkward, and wondered if I could perform a version of that. We both tried to pay, handing over our cards, and she managed, which I resented, though it's the end of the month and I was glad to save the money, which she won't notice spending. And so the encounter came to an end.

I have been wondering since then if she said it to test me or to clear the air, because she'd found the secret contaminating. In the first scenario she'd be uncertain in her knowledge and in the second certain. If she's certain, then how did she know? Either way, I wonder if she planned the conversation or if it was more random, provoked by me making myself sound like too devoted a mother or contented a girlfriend. She was reminding me, accurately, that my narratives about myself proliferate and contradict the narratives that they displace. Where does it leave us now? I think it will shift the dynamics in the group, turning Kay and me into more of a pair within it, locked into intimacy by our shared secret. I don't think she'll tell anyone else, she'd have nothing to gain from doing so. But I feel uneasy. It makes me long for James Street again, for the time when I had no secrets from them.

Priss

August

It is midnight and they are scrubbing together, Priss and Hugh. In ordinary life they don't scrub. She outsources it to a cleaner, he makes his peace with grime. But this is work, or what's going to count as work for her, a café that she can't expect to make the kind of money that a mother who really needed to work would need to make. She's called it Lulu's, after her mother's dog. It's opening tomorrow and she can no longer remember why she's doing all this and is becoming increasingly embarrassed that she is. Why this café, rather than another one? Why any café? What made her think that this is what her life should be about? How do we know what our lives are meant to be about?

She has been crouching but she has no energy left even for that so she sits on the floor, scrubbing slowly, repelled now by the smell of the cleaning products and rubber gloves. He's finished doing the furniture so he comes to help her.

Priss, this is the last part we're going to do, he says. And then I'll open the champagne.

She's grateful, thinking how unlike Ben he is to bring champagne, but also unlike Hugh. He puts the bottle in the freezer and carries on, getting out the paint stains she was failing to remove from the floor. He lifts her hands on to her lap, peels off the pink gloves and scrubs around her.

Then he's standing with two glasses, looking at her. She feels unusually available to him, sitting at the round wooden table made by him with her head propped up by her right hand, because she's no longer concerned about what she looks like. They clink glasses and congratulate each other. He asks her how it feels, and she says that it does feel like a thing she has done, making this place. She may not be adding much to the world at large but she is adding to hers. And to mine, he says, holding her gaze when she looks down, but they both know that his role here is finished and this is partly why she's so tired, she has moved into a life that will no longer have the enlivening energy of his presence.

When they leave, the night is warmer than they'd realised, and they agree, talking more loudly and energetically now, that they're not ready to go home. She thinks of warm nights like this in the Peak District, and wishes she could be there now with Hugh, lying on the cooling rock after swimming in the river. The image of the water and stone makes the café they've just left feel flimsy and temporary and she tells Hugh about this thought, confident that he'll understand. They wander around Newington Green where there are still clusters of people, younger than they are, at the end of picnics, with half-drunk bottles of beer and wine spilling on to the grass. She thinks how strange it is that the physical sensation of her bare shoulders warmed by the still night air is exactly the same as it was when she was the age of the women reclining on the ground.

It's not that late, really, she says as they sit down on a bench.

They are colluding, so that they will have more time

together, so that they will have the moment that will clarify who they are for each other. It's been years since either of them has had one of these moments and they both feel that it's owed to them by a world in which they have paid their dues and not asked much in return. Priss calculates the duty to pleasure ratio in the lives of her friends and husband and decides that she needs a boost of pleasure to balance the books. Hugh puts his arm around her shoulders and she leans into him. It feels straightforward. He tells her that she's very beautiful and that sometimes he has found this embarrassing, and that he's grateful when he can focus on a task, like scrubbing the floor, so he can stop looking at her. She thanks him, regally. She does not think that compliments need to be returned, like tennis balls.

He kisses her. It's fifteen years since she kissed a man for the first time. It feels more unfamiliar than she expected. His tongue in her mouth feels too much, too soon in the relationship and too soon in the encounter. With Ben the kisses start with lips, and tongues are introduced only as they're moving towards sex. She leans back, withdrawing the interior of her mouth, offering her lips. He understands. The kisses become more delicate, and she feels the beginning of arousal. This is the start of learning to read each other's bodies. It's a process that could go on for years if they wanted it to, and she feels wearied by the prospect, knowing that she doesn't want to confront his naked body, to see the penis that she can feel pressed up against her as he leans back and pulls her on to him, smelling so much more of himself than she expected.

When they release each other they talk, too soon, about what it means. He tells her that he loves her. She doesn't know how she'd find out if she loved him. She knows that she loves Ben and her children and her mother and sister. It feels both too easy and too difficult to identify this particular mixture of desire and need as love. He asks about her marriage and she realises that he has imagined a life with her. This makes her feel that he can't know her as well as she thought he did, can't know what the whole messy enterprise of family life means for her. She tries to explain this and he assures her that he understands it already.

A young couple walks past them, coming closer to their bench than is necessary, laughing loudly at something they're looking at on the woman's phone. Priss wonders if they've been laughing at them as well, if people are looking at them, thinking that they're too old to kiss so seriously on a bench, guessing that it's an affair.

I know that you won't leave Ben, he says. I just wonder who I am for you.

You're a conspirator, she says. Since I've known you, I've felt like a real person in the world, because there's an adult I respect who respects me. I think Ben respects me now as well.

I don't want to feel that you're using me to improve your marriage, he says.

I don't think I am, Hugh. I'm here because I care about you. It's a kind of side effect that the marriage feels better too.

He asks her if she feels sad when they're apart and she admits that she doesn't. She gains happiness from knowing that he's alive elsewhere, thinking about her. But it's two o'clock, they are almost the last people here now, and she wants to go to bed. She doesn't like the way that the magic is dissipating and it's turning into an account of their responsibilities to each other. She returns to his chest, enjoying the feeling of her nose against the buttons of his shirt, wondering if she can feel the texture of his chest hair below her face.

We should go, she says.

He hugs her again. They stroke each other's backs. She says, panicking, that she'd miss him if she didn't have him in her life. They kiss, and it's more arousing, because the possibility of loss always brings for her a need that can become physical. This time she's the one to introduce her tongue into his mouth, and she feels her body clench, alongside his. But she stands up and shakes off the confusion of the night. And then he walks her home in silence and they part with a whispered goodbye.

The next day, we all arrive at once. Priss's mother counts thirty-one adults and nineteen children. There are too many people for a space of this size and we spill out on to the pavement, eating homemade doughnuts in a range of colours. Priss and Ben stand at the centre of the café, ruling their new territory. Ben seems at home here, more than I'd expected and more than Priss expected. He pours champagne for people as they arrive and explains the flavours of doughnuts. Hugh sits on one of his chairs, on his own at a table which has filled with children. He sees Priss asking Helena if she'd mind going over to talk to him. He's not very friendly to Helena as a result, but she stays, asking questions warmly, and he succumbs. He is easily flattered by the attention of women and Helena's interest is genuine, because there is no one else she would rather be talking to. She has no agendas, in these situations, and is here to support her best friend.

Priss looks around, pleased that we're all here, but frustrated that this space, which she's thought about so carefully, is too full. She is ready for Monday, when she'll leave the house at eight o'clock and come to work, and people will arrive and use the tables as they're meant to be used. It feels wrong that she's serving tea for free to her friends yet again when this is meant to be her employment, not an extension of their home. She smiles at Hugh, shrugging her shoulders by way of expressing this, but he's talking to Helena now and doesn't see her. Helena is stroking the wood on her chair, asking him about how he made it.

The kiss feels as though it's secretly present, like a soft stone she's carrying in her pocket where she can put her hand in to touch it when no one is looking. Robert and Lena come to ask her for another doughnut, and she says no, aware that they will become more difficult to please now, and directs them to the corner where she's left paper and crayons. They moan, as predicted; Robert is already saying that he's bored. But she's able to keep them at a distance because of the kiss in her pocket, which she now feels starting to press against her, like Hugh's erection.

Ben taps his glass and proposes a toast to Priss and her café. It's easy to forget, watching his awkwardness as he loiters, how confident he is when he's given centre stage. He doesn't get enough opportunity to show off as an agent and he enjoys making this speech now, letting it last longer than it needs to. Priss thanks him and the waitresses, thanks Lulu for giving her the name and then thanks Hugh. Their eyes meet for the first time in a while but he looks away, resisting her.

As soon as she can, Priss joins him at the table. Helena talks appreciatively about the café, and Priss and Hugh are united now in gratitude to Helena for affirming so determinedly that this is worthwhile. Then Helena gets up, ready to mingle, and they're left on their own.

Thanks for the thanks, he says, but he sounds more gloomy than grateful.

She puts her hand on his shoulder and says, as quietly as she can without whispering, that last night mattered to her.

Ben's good at speaking, he says. He's a good husband for you.

Thank you, she says.

He is taking it in, the reality of her marriage. She pours them both a glass of warm champagne and they clink them, acknowledging the continuity with last night. Ben comes over and sits down, asking if they're enjoying themselves, as though he is now the sole host. He takes her hand and she wonders if he'd mind if she gave her other hand to Hugh.

None of them proffers a topic of conversation so they look around. Priss can no longer remember who all these people are. She has barely had a chance to speak to her mother, who she sees is playing with Priss's children, making the dog do high fives. She waves at her mother, and at me, where I'm talking to Polly, taking refuge in the childless as I don't have mine with me. Kay is outside with hers, helping Seb to lock and unlock the clasp on the high chair that Priss has taken out for Alisa. Priss thinks of all the parents who will placate their bored children in that high chair over the months that follow and feels exhausted. But she should be looking after her friends so she gets up and leaves her husband and her lover to talk.

Stella

August

I found out about the kiss from Kay. Priss told her about it on Wednesday, the day after she confessed it to Ben. They'd been to the cinema and afterwards, drinking a bottle of rosé under all the hanging greenery in the pub garden, both pleased to have escaped their children for an evening, not thinking, as I would have to, about how much each extra half hour was costing with the babysitter, Priss said to Kay, I kissed Hugh on Friday night, the night before the café opening. And Kay being Kay immediately asked her everything about it. She passed the details on to me at lunch on Monday, eating Pret salads on a bench in Bloomsbury Square, whole sprouts of broccoli sticking out of our mouths awkwardly because they're too difficult to chop inside the box. I didn't want her to ask how I felt or to point out Ben's hypocrisy in minding, so I changed the subject too quickly for it not to feel abrupt, planning to think about it properly afterwards.

I found it very odd not to have heard it directly from Ben because it felt so much part of our story. When we were together, he was always half hoping and half fearing that Priss would liberate us by having an affair herself. I wanted to find out how he'd taken it now it had almost happened, though I distrusted my curiosity and my urge to direct events as they played out, editing their lives. I texted him to suggest a drink and he kept changing the time, making our window smaller and smaller until it was almost invisible, so I was irritable by the time that we met, and then became much grumpier when I discovered that he'd brought Priss's mother's dog with him. We'd met on Piccadilly and we sat outside a pub for a bit with Lulu yapping and then gave up and walked down to St James's Park, banging into people along the way. As we walked, I interrogated him rather coldly about Priss and he answered abruptly but then stopped and accused me of talking about her dismissively. He was right, but the feeling of being judged by him hurt more than I allowed him to know.

Once we were in the park, we both relaxed. He apologised for bringing Lulu – they're looking after her all week and today he'd offered to take her into work. It seemed absurd to me, when they're rich enough to afford a dog walker, when Priss could more easily have her at the café she's named after her. But I suppose I resented it because it reminded me how committed he is to family life and how determinedly helpful he is to Priss's family (he'd spent the weekend building her sister's bookshelves). This makes me suspect that he was never as serious about me, or about the prospect of an actual relationship with me, as I was about him.

This is also why he minds about Hugh more than I'd expected him to. He thinks that Hugh has callously jeopardised a happy family. (Did Ben not do the same with mine?) The minding seems to have been good for Ben and Priss as a couple. She has discovered that she's able to suspend her longing for Hugh, or so Ben believes. He has discovered that there's more to her than he'd allowed in recent years and that he's still capable of jealousy. They are having more sex, though I didn't want to know about this. And so Hugh is becoming a bit player in their marriage, as happens so easily. One of the worst things about marriage is the way that it allows couples to devour other people. I can see this in me and Tom already, the way that we have allowed our friends to provide entertainment for us, summoning them and sending them away again without giving them the chance to disturb the fundamental mood of the evening, which is ours. It's why Polly was right to leave Sam, even if the new men she's meeting are proving less satisfying than he was.

Lulu slowed down and the three of us ambled together – it felt like a caricature of a couple walking their dog. As we walked, Ben and I brushed against each other, just enough to show that it wasn't accidental. A cyclist went by and he held me back, which was a shock – the feeling of his hand, hard against my collar bone. We sat on a bench and he took my hand briefly. I wondered if he wanted to get even with Priss: to avoid the humiliation of one-sided infidelity. I reminded myself that I wasn't attracted to him when we first met – I don't generally fancy blond men. He stroked my fingers and I realised that I missed the way that in affairs the touch of finger on finger can carry the full intensity of bodies meeting. Tom and I rarely linger on those early moments of touch now.

What about you? I asked, as Lulu leapt up on the bench with us and Ben tried to still her in his arms like a baby. Have you been fantasising about other women?

Yes, all the time, he said, and it was the first time he'd acknowledged thinking about anyone other than me. But I don't want to do anything about it, he added, at this phase in my life.

When we walked to the Tube, I felt much calmer than I had an hour earlier. The wistfulness I still felt in him was a relief and I could relinquish him back to his marriage without worrying, as he must with me, about being directly replaced. I was careful to resist drawing him back in, knowing that there's nothing to be gained for either of us from allowing the erotic charge to flare again, and that I have nothing to offer, and much to lose, if I allow myself to become regretful about the ways Tom doesn't yearn for my body as much as Ben did. And so he has gone back to his life, and it seems that I'll hear from Kay about what goes on in it, because she seems to feel more loyal to me than she does to Priss.

When I got home, Maggie was in bed and Cleo was sitting on the sofa in her pyjamas, waiting for me to put her to bed and tell her nightmares to go away. As she sat on my lap, clinging to me while I said goodbye to Rosa, the babysitter, I found that I felt more connected to Rosa than I did to Ben. I'd been worrying about whether she disapproved of me, going out two evenings in a row, or was irritated that I'd asked her to stay late without much warning. But then I realised that she knows that I never want to leave the children, that she doesn't judge me as a mother any more than she judges herself for leaving her own teenage daughter in order to look after mine. I worry so much about what the babysitters think about me, flusteredly paying them more than I need to sometimes, because my life is so precariously dependent on them. So it brought a rush of relief to feel that we were a kind of couple as we considered remedies for Maggie's cough and Cleo's nightmares, realising that she is as invested in their recovery as I am. Would I feel more rivalrous with her if I were still married to Chris and he were having some of these conversations with her? We are so conditioned by the structure of the couple, so much better in twos than threes.

This morning, in bed here in my flat, enjoying the way divorce has restored the weekend lie-ins that I thought were gone for decades, I started stroking Tom's thighs, less because I was aroused than because I thought I quite easily could be and it seemed a shame to have a whole childless night on our own without sex. Tom asked, suddenly, what I meant by telling a whole table of people at the pub last night that I'd lost interest in men. Had I thought about how it reflected on him?

I was surprised. I think of him as being so much inside my head that I expect him to read my mind, and know what I mean when I say things. And I think of him as being too self-confident sexually to be affected by something like that. What I'd said, at the pub celebrating his friend Christina's birthday, was that it's a relief to discover, at thirty-nine, that I'm not going to mind becoming less desirable as much as I feared I would. I was probably showing off to the younger women there (Christina had just turned thirty) when I said that I am frequently bored when I read manuscripts where young women write about desire. I'm bored by their pleasure in their own bodies, especially when they don't know how self-satisfied they are.

I apologised to Tom. I was rather touched by his wounded pride. I told him that I still find my own body pleasurable enough, in bed with him, or on show to the perhaps two other new men a year I find attractive. I'm still interested in sex – I like writing about it. But most of the men at parties bore me. I thought he might enjoy my flaunting that. And

I think that they don't realise the price they are paying, the young women, in responding to any man who happens to desire them by turning their petals outwards, pleasingly.

Tom said, rolling on to his back and picking rather unappealingly at a broken fingernail, that if we don't find new ways to reanimate desire we will abandon the field to incels, puritans and *Love Island*. He's right, I suppose, once again, and now I think that it's because of my sustained confidence in the erotic to remain at the heart of everything that I can renounce it so casually. It's almost as if my faith in the erotic is so strong that the actual men I know feel inadequate to even associate with it. That's why I dismiss the young women: because I feel they are missing the point. And I trust Tom to know that I'm not talking about him, because I'm talking about a world of surfaces, which is different from our private world of bodies.

I felt protective of him, as we stopped talking, and he allowed himself to become aroused. I felt the vulnerability in his excitement, I could feel the need for me that made every touch of my hips or buttocks arouse him more. I liked the fact that he likes different bits of me – my bottom, the skin at the top of my thighs – from the bits I like myself. Sex makes room for that separateness so much more easily than conversation does. I brought him inside me, more quickly than I usually would. I wanted to hold him there, tightly, and pressed my back hard against his chest, so that it felt like he was moving within my body, rather than moving in and out of it.

He had to go straight afterwards. He needed to drive back and wanted to get there before Carla called. She calls him every day at the moment because Andreas has dropped out of university and she seems to depend on berating Tom, blaming him for Andreas's lack of confidence and telling him to do something about it. Tom finds that the language she uses closes down the possibility of discussion, but Andreas doesn't want to talk himself so this is Tom's only way of keeping in touch until he goes there next week. After he left I felt bad, thinking that I need to be a consoling presence, ushering him towards life, but that instead I say these things about sex that he finds put a wall between us, making him trust less in the reality of our bodies together.

When did I become so disillusioned with the men I know? Which men? Vince? Yes, I suppose I'm coming to think that he might well have exposed his penis and that even if he didn't do it on this particular occasion, he's been doing things like this for years, relying on women finding it gratifying enough to be looked at that they will forgive moments of passing aggression. My friends' husbands? Yes, I feel contempt for Harald and his affairs now, although I don't really believe in monogamy. Even Ben and our affair seems foolish because I can't recapture the seriousness with which we imbued every sexual act during those long nights at the book fair and in the emails we wrote about them afterwards: we cared so much about what our bodies looked like together. Tom? Yes insofar as I find it silly that he's attracted to so many women, and worry that I'll lose respect for him on those grounds. But also no, because he's had enough sex that I trust him not to take desire itself too seriously, and to see that what we have is different because it's primarily about bodies merging. I want to be looked at by him too and sometimes mind that I don't think he looks at me enough. That's why I liked feeling him become aroused when he touched me this morning — because touching felt like a form of looking. Perhaps not as much has changed as I think it has.

He said a few days ago that he doesn't like the way I bond with my women friends by collectively disliking men. It's true that we do it. There must be a way to enjoy the new closeness I feel with women without feeling that we are fighting for a world populated only by us. There's a sense in so many of our conversations of men as expendable when they're not there and disappointing or even dangerous when they are. But this is false because at the same time we devote so much of our energy to loving, forgiving and looking after the individual men we are making our lives with. This is the case even for Helena now, with Aaron, and it's more straight-forwardly true for me with Tom, so perhaps he's right that there's an element of betrayal involved in every generic conversation I have about men. Yet now I feel I'm betraying my women friends, because we do also mean what we say. And there have been times for me, for all of us, I think, when it's being able to say these things that enables us to keep going.

Helena

August

Helena and Clare are on Helena's grey sofa, eating strawberries out of a bamboo punnet that Helena bought from
the farmer's market, more successful than the rest of us at
avoiding plastic. Helena is seven weeks pregnant again,
and is tentatively happy, but she's wondering if it's a bad
sign that she and Clare haven't yet kissed today. Is it because
Clare has a cold or has their desire become less urgent?
She's too tired to think hard about it. She doesn't know
if Clare understands how tiring the first months of pregnancy can be. She's worried that her new exhaustion is
drawing attention to their age gap but it turns out that
Clare is tired too, or at least that's what she said when she
announced they had to go, halfway through the lunch
with Helena's parents they've just come home from. It's
the second time this has happened at a social occasion, so
she can't let it go without discussing it, though she doesn't
want to spoil this moment with the strawberries, which
feels more intimate than anything else today. The sun is
beaming through the patio doors on to their bare knees
and Helena has the comforting feeling that they are two
school friends released from lessons on a summer's

afternoon in the stripy summer pinafores she and I used to wear.

How are you feeling? Clare asks.

Pregnant, Helena says.

Is that good or bad?

Bad, Helena says. But if the scan with Polly goes well next week I'll start to believe in it more and enjoy it.

Oh, Clare says, I wanted to say, I don't think I'll be able to make it.

Helena holds Clare's eyes for a second and then looks away, irritated by how many times a day it's possible for someone to inflict these wounds.

Why? she asks.

Clare explains that the producers of the documentary about rape that she might direct have emailed asking her to come in for a meeting and she has said yes. Helena wonders why Clare didn't try to move the meeting. Did she resist announcing that she had a girlfriend or that she had a pregnant girlfriend? She wonders about suggesting that they ask Polly to change the time, but she doesn't want to because Polly is doing it as a favour, before her shift starts. Anyway, perhaps it doesn't matter to Clare to be there. She shuts her eyes, not wanting to look at Clare while crying.

I'm sorry, Clare says again. I'll be there afterwards.

Why did you want to leave lunch? Helena asks.

I was tired, I couldn't do it any more, being a girlfriend on show to parents, she says. And then in a softer voice: Look at me.

Helena turns her head back to Clare and opens her eyes. Clare rubs away the tears with her fingers.

I hate being someone who cries this easily, Helena says.

Do you think it's my fault?

Yes! Helena replies – it's the only logical answer.

They look at each other, wondering if they can survive this conversation.

I'm not used to being in relationships, Clare says. I need more time before I can think for both of us and be part of a couple. This isn't my baby, it's a baby you're choosing to have that could take you away from me. I don't want children. Most of the time I think it's irresponsible to have children – I can't stop thinking about all the factors involved in these decisions, the planet's resources being used up. All I know about the future is that I want to make films, and that the money I saved is about to run out, so soon I won't be able to pay the rent. I have to make decisions around work, because there's nothing else I can allow to matter. I can't make films without other people's support, and I hate this, because I hate having to rely on other people and on being sociable. So now that someone I like has finally appeared, wanting to make films with me, it feels like it could really happen. And I have to be clear, in each small decision I make, that I'm opening myself to that.

It's a long speech for Clare to make and she seems tired by it. She looks away and starts pushing down her cuticles with her thumb, which makes Helena want to intervene to shield the nails from harm. Helena takes Clare's right hand and squeezes it, relieved to feel the desire to look after Clare reawakened. It's easier now that it's explicit. Helena agrees, in principle, that it's irresponsible to have children, but has long ago accepted the messiness of her own thinking. She finds it harder to sympathise about work. She tries to think back to the beginning of her career, when she cared about work like this, but she never believed in the creative act of making documentaries in the way that Clare does. And success came so easily that she didn't have time to learn how ambitious she was. She doesn't think there's ever been a moment when she would have prioritised her work over a lover, but she never had to worry about earning enough money to survive. And she sees, or is trying to see, that she can't only believe that Clare cares about her if she shows this in exactly the way that Helena would.

She wonders how much Clare's rent is and why she's never asked her this. We are all squeamish about money, our group; our year of house-sharing taught us how to split costs without embarrassment, but it didn't teach us to reveal our incomings or outgoings, and we don't tend to know much about each other's finances now. We all spend hours thinking about how we're going to pay our rent or mortgages and how much will be left once we've paid them. Helena is saving now so she can pay her mortgage while she's on maternity leave; I worry about how I'd pay mine if I lost my job or if the death of book publishing comes even sooner than we expect it to. But we don't talk about it as much as we should do, and it's both surprising and unsurprising that it's taken Helena and Clare this long to mention it.

Helena wants to say that Clare doesn't need to worry about money because she could come and live with her, or Helena could lend her some. She can't quite say this, though, because at a point when Clare is loosening the bond between them it seems inappropriate to suggest a solution that involves tightening it. Instead she says that if Clare's money is running out, perhaps she should get a part-time job, and that Helena could see if there's anything going at Channel 4.

If I work it will take up all my energy, Clare says. You don't see how much effort I put into just going out and meeting people. Having to go to work would make me feel worse and then I wouldn't be the enthusiastic and creative person I need to be if I'm going to convince people to let me make films. You don't see how close I am to giving up, all the time.

She is talking now in a voice that Helena hasn't heard before: panicky, cold. It feels as though Helena has become an enemy, pushing her towards a crisis. Helena pulls back quickly, fearing that she could do serious damage to Clare and that this could become a conversation in which they split up. She puts her hand on her stomach, as though to reassure the baby that she hopes is growing there.

I'm sorry Clare, Helena says. I do want to help you and not make it worse. I can see that you can't come to the scan but it will be hard on my own.

I know, Clare says, but I'll be there with you, in my own way.

Which is not being there.

Yes, Clare says.

They laugh, uncertainly, trying out a version of themselves that's less strained. Clare pulls Helena towards her. They kiss for a while and then Clare suggests sitting in the garden. Helena wonders why she doesn't want to go to bed now, and whether it's because she's waiting for Helena to initiate it. She fills a jug of water, appreciating the elegance of the jug and of her sink, thinking that her flat and its objects are things she can rely on.

They sit at the table outside, and Helena minds feeling boxed in by yet another set of chairs and tables in a day that should feel more expansive. She starts deadheading the dahlias within reach of her chair, wondering if Clare will mind her doing this as they talk. Clare says that she found it hard talking about Vince at Helena's parents' house. Helena thinks back to the conversation. She asked her parents how he was, if there was news; they said that it looked like he'd leave his job by Christmas, but the woman wasn't going to go to the police. She asks what Clare found hard and she says that it's the way they all accept he's in the right. That he's entitled to his well-pensioned retirement, and a lot of sympathy from all of them, while the woman is left feeling like she's spoken out and it's had no effect.

I agree that we need to take her seriously, Helena says, but it's had some effect and we'll never know if he did it.

What do you think? Clare asks.

I think he probably didn't do it, but I'm open to the possibility that he did, and definitely that he made the woman uncomfortable.

And yet you still see him? Clare asks.

What else can I do?

Listen to women.

Helena smiles, involuntarily, and then regrets it, seeing the effect on Clare, who starts to shout.

Do you know how many women are raped without the men being punished?

But he didn't rape anyone, she reminds Clare, as gently as she can. No one is saying that he did.

But if they were, Clare says, then you'd all still think he probably didn't do it. Not Vince. Not Helena's favourite uncle who got her job for her. It's other people who rape.

What do you want me to do? Helena asks, genuinely perplexed, wishing they were still on the sofa so they could touch easily.

Have you tried asking him if he did it? Clare asks.

Helena laughs, thinking that it's so obvious a solution, but none of them thinks of doing it. She doesn't know if this is because they don't expect to get an honest answer, or if it's because they're somehow too English to ask such a direct question, even though her mother and Vince are in many ways so un-English – more contrary, more direct. She can see that her laughter is irritating Clare.

I could do, she says. I could ask, but if he says he didn't do it, and I don't know whether to believe him, then what can I do?

Face it, Clare says, that you may have to sacrifice something to be a moral person.

Helena is confused. She doesn't know how this conversation happened, or where Clare's antagonism came from. This time three days ago, they drove off in Helena's car and spent a whole evening in a field in Essex, lying with long shadows on soft, wild grass, threading daisy flowers on to a stalk, moving fluidly between conversations and orgasms. For the first time in years, she allowed herself to think that she might be capable of getting life right. So she became complacent enough to expect today to be a continuation of that, but they are doing this instead.

Clare abruptly stands up and goes inside, the back of her bra and the bird tattooed between her shoulders visible in outline through the thin white top that billows over her shorts. She comes back immediately, holding her sunglasses, and stands leaning against the patio doors. Looking at her, Helena is struck again by the arbitrariness of this choice. Why has she put all her hope and determination into this one particular woman? It has turned out that this is a woman with stubborn views, unable to make room for the complex feelings that make Helena hope that in this instance a man is telling the truth and a woman is lying. It occurs to her that she could just give up on Clare. She could tell her that it's over between them and that she wants her to leave her flat. She'd be left with her baby and her friends. She could wander back to her parents' house and apologise for their abrupt departure. Clare's volatility, Clare's depression, Clare's lack of money, Clare's slow-starting career – none of these would then be her problem. She finds it hard to tell if this would be a lonelier life or not.

Helena stands up too, with no definite intention, and Clare comes towards her and puts her hands on her shoulders, without speaking. She brings her face close to Helena's and they both draw in their breath, smelling each other. There is such need in this, it feels like a chemical addiction, the need for this mixture of perfume and salty sweat and the skin that has come to feel so familiar over the past months that it's an extension of Helena's own skin. Helena puts down the jug and places her hands on Clare's head, kneading her head through the short hair. She realises how tense she must have been, for this to provide such release. And now her hands are on Clare's back, running up and down it with increasing speed and force, and their mouths are locked, hard but without much movement of lips. She takes Clare's hand and they go back inside, into the bedroom.

Clare comes quickly and Helena feels proud of her lover's orgasm. Afterwards, they lie together, entwined, and enough time passes that they realise they must have slept. Now when Helena looks at Clare, she is fully familiar again. Each knobble and crevice of her body feels loved and known, yet seen as though for the first time, with the kind of clear-eyed vision that results from disappearing into a place beyond selfhood where there is only sensation. They shower together, and go back to the kitchen, and Helena suggests making dinner, but

Clare has to go, because she's meeting her mother, who she has not yet suggested should be introduced to Helena.

After Clare goes, Helena checks her email, where she finds a series of work messages, which include a brisk note from a French producer, cancelling a programme she was due to make for him. Helena cries, more at the curtness of tone than at the news itself, which she doesn't particularly mind, and then she sits at the kitchen table, wondering if she can allow herself to be this tearful.

The relief of seeing Clare as a stranger earlier, she now realises, was a relief at feeling that it would be possible to give up on her own neediness. She's exhausted by herself as a wanting person. She would like to be someone who wants less from others, but she feels like this can only happen if she gives up on wanting altogether.

She wonders what would have happened if they hadn't had sex. Afterwards, they agreed that it was all they'd needed, and that they should have done it much earlier. But there's a danger, she thinks now, in using sex as a kind of drug, to occlude their separateness. It stops them having to see each other's more awkwardly shaped edges, where they can't fit together.

She imagines texting Clare to tell her that it's over, and wonders how she'd respond. It feels like a reckless temptation, like longing to throw yourself off the cliff that's frightening you. There'd be so much gained by it: the time saved, as well as the thicker skin she could develop. But her life would thin as her skin thickened. She sees how much she's been changed by the gradual process of allowing herself to love. She can't remember what it was like to have day-to-day experiences that she wouldn't later describe to the person who cares about her more than other people care. She has grown used to her body's expectation of loving touch. So perhaps she needs to accept the relationship as a given, like her parents do. Or perhaps to see Clare as only one element in her life; as someone who is here but might not be here forever, unlike the baby, who she's becoming more hopeful is here to stay. She thinks of Aaron, with a warm sense of his presence. She can see him standing next to her in his small neat leather shoes.

Polly

September

It's the end of her shift again. She returns from the window, where she's been watching a four- or five-year-old boy going up and down on a slide that's slightly too small for him, and she opens the folder in front of her. It's a six-year-old Gambian girl who's been referred urgently. She sends the nurse to summon her, resisting her own dread. The girl comes in, holding the hand of her mother, both looking down.

Fatoumatta, Polly reads from the folder. Did I pronounce that right?

The mother nods, looking at her now, and smiles. Fatou, she says.

Fatou continues to look down and Polly asks her mother how she can help.

You need to look at her, the woman says, and looks down again.

Polly asks the girl to remove her knickers and helps her on to the bed. The girl looks uncomfortable, with her head raised awkwardly, but she is trying to be good here. She looks rapidly at her mother, seeking reassurance or approval, but her mother is avoiding eye contact. Polly clenches her hands, feeling frightened about what she is going to find.

She lifts up the brightly patterned skirt, slowly. This is one of the most extreme cases she has seen. The girl has been sewn shut and has become infected. There's pus coming out of the swollen skin. She should have come days or even weeks ago. Polly pushes the skin back as gently as she can with the forceps. She knows how painful this is but, though Fatou flinches, she doesn't cry out. They will need to operate. She would like to do full reconstructive surgery but their budgets are too limited; she will only be able to open it up and heal the infection.

When was this done? she asks the mother. Was it done in this country?

There's anger in her voice that she regrets when she sees the tears falling on Fatou's cheeks. There's no point being angry at the mother. She can't believe that this woman would have freely chosen this for her daughter. But she is angry because, in this room where they are all safe, the mother doesn't express anger herself, doesn't name this as a barbarity and beg her to reverse it if she can.

You too? Polly asks. Do you have this as well?

The mother nods, still looking down. Polly dries Fatou's face carefully with a tissue. There are tears in her own eyes which she doesn't attempt to conceal when the girl finally looks up at her. She has large brown eyes. Polly has rarely felt this much tenderness towards a patient and is disturbed by how much she enjoys the experience of herself softening. She can feel what it would be like to fold this body into her arms, how it would crumple in towards her, how they would sob together.

She tells them that she will need to operate. It's an emergency and if there's space she would like to do it this week. Mother and daughter look at each other, frightened, and

Polly feels that she loses something as their bond reasserts itself. She is not sure how much English Fatou understands but she seems to take in all the details of the operation as she explains them. She asks if it hurts to pee and the girl nods. She promises that soon it will stop hurting, that she's going to do her best.

Polly is not able fully to concentrate with the patients that follow. She is waiting to cry, but doesn't want to do so with the nurse present. Afterwards, she goes upstairs to Sam's office, longing to sink into him as she has imagined Fatou sinking in towards her. He is there but there's a male colleague with him, an American consultant called Richard who she knows a little. Sam looks surprised to see her, not displeased, but stiffly formal. Richard looks at her with open amusement and then leaves. She realises that she'd have never been this reckless in arriving without warning when they were sleeping together.

I'm sorry, she says, I wasn't thinking.

But Sam assures her she did the right thing and asks her what's happened. She explains. She leans against him and cries. He holds her close, burrowed into his chest so that she can't breathe. It's exactly what she imagined him doing and she finds it a little disturbing that Sam remains the person with whom fantasies are most easily fulfilled. She reminds herself that this is not Fatou being comforted, that nothing has changed for the girl.

Sam tells her that there's nothing she can do. She must just do the best she can with the patients who come to her. Their lives before and after they arrive in the hospital are not her responsibility. They wait for his familiar beige kettle to boil – an ugly cast-off from the marital home – and talk about the last few months. He laughs, bright eyed and admiring, at her anecdotes about Dave and she wonders if she's making a mistake in allowing her love life to sound so unsatisfactory. Eventually she asks him if he's sleeping with anyone else and is surprised that he is, though if asked, she'd have said that she'd expect him to be. She knows that if she suggested going to bed together, he'd be delighted. They'd go back to her flat, perhaps immediately, and he'd be as much hers as he ever was. She looks at his hands, which are clasped together on his lap, and thinks that she'd like them to touch her instead. But she knows as well that this wouldn't be enough for her, because he could belong to any number of other women this way too. She sees herself suddenly as an enticing jar of liquorice allsorts in one of the sweetshops that were a feature of both of their childhoods: special and tempting but easy to close up again because there are sherbet lemons in the next jar.

He senses that she's troubled by his answer and returns the conversation to her work. His careful kindness makes her feel half grateful and half resentful. He asks when she will operate on the girl, checks his own timetable and suggests that she come to see him afterwards. She says that she will, knowing that she will need it, though she would like to resist this need. And then she goes downstairs to collect her things.

On the way down she finds Richard. She suspects he's been lurking outside Sam's office, waiting to see how long she'll spend there. It's foolish to think that people don't know about the affair. He walks with her to the locker room, though this isn't his department, and waits as she collects her things. She is conscious of his bodily presence, the thin sheen of stubble that she would not like to kiss, the wavy blond hair just slightly longer than you'd expect. His face seems altogether too large, even though each feature is regular within it. They stand there, with her shoes and coat in her hands and then she changes her shoes and he catches her when she loses her balance, standing on one leg. There's an exchange of anecdotes about their days in which he's just witty enough to raise it above the banal, making her think that he must have an effective doctorly manner. She can imagine feeling relaxed if she was giving birth under his watch; he'd turn it into an amusing escapade, promising that she'd be back to normality soon.

Where are you going now Polly? he asks. I've finished too, maybe you'd like a drink?

She considers saying yes but there's something about his tone, the assumption that she'll agree to it, that makes her say no.

Oh, he says, putting an arm against the wall behind her and leaning in so their faces are almost touching. You don't want me. What don't I have that he does, I wonder.

He is smiling, keeping the tone jokey enough that she can't call him out on it. Polly tries to keep her anger under control and to seem less disturbed than she is. She slides away from him and he doesn't resist, standing back to let her go, laughing as she trips over the coat that she's carrying. He seems to think that he can allude to the affair with Sam as though it's common knowledge. She hates the implication that she's had sex with one senior consultant so is easy prey for any others who ask. What bothers her most is the suspicion that he might be right. In different circumstances, with just a little more finesse on his part, she could have been attracted to him. As with Dave, the way that she dislikes him may be more compatible with the erotic than some forms of liking are. Even the scene in the locker room has a harshness in its outlines that energises her, however enraged she remains.

Out in the street she calms down. She's free, he can't threaten her, she is not one of the vulnerable girls who she sees in her consulting room. But the excitement of the encounter, its horrible erotic charge, has awoken adrenalin in her that makes the thought of going to bed early less alluring than it was half an hour earlier. She decides to walk fast along the river first, to exhaust herself.

Walking as the final film of pink fades from the water and the sky, surrounded by people charging towards their evenings in packs or couples, she thinks about her body and how little it has been put through despite the abortion, and despite these occasional moments of pressure: less than almost all of her friends', so much less than her dead brother's, or all of her patients'. She is thinking – and it's a thought that seems to result from the encounter with Fatou though she doesn't quite know why – how much she needs her body to remain unchanged now, which means avoiding even apparently natural changes, like pregnancy and birth.

On Tuesday, she gave Helena her early scan, hugging her when they heard the heart beat and saw the tiny sac on the screen. After Helena had allowed herself to feel relieved, she was solicitous of Polly, aware that she'd once got to almost this point herself, and aware that she'd now be the last in our group to have children, and could end up as the only one without them. Without this being spoken, Polly found it hard to reassure Helena that she wasn't envious. She couldn't say that although she was pleased for Helena, she couldn't bear the thought of those changes set in unstoppable motion once again inside her own body. She'd loathed her fortnight of being pregnant at university – loathed the nausea, the feeling that her breasts were changing against her will – it felt like an alien was crouching, waiting to take over her body from within. Now she hates the prospect of her stomach swelling with the expectation of her vagina being wrenched open. As she swerves out of the way of a man walking towards her, looking at his phone, she unwillingly imagines the tearing flesh and the emergence of another human body into the world, a new creature to expose to pain.

She thinks of Sam, telling her she can do no more than she does already. It isn't true. They can all do more, though they find different ways of coming to terms with the little they do. She has never talked to Sam about what it was like to watch her brother dying, though she once mentioned that it had happened. He didn't ask more, which she took for a lack of curiosity but has come to see as respect for her privacy. She has now slipped back into the old habit of talking to Sam in her mind and she is telling him about her mother's grief. Her mother knows the worst that can happen and now she, like Fatou's mother, has to endure the knowledge of her two daughters in the world, exposed to its brutality. It strikes Polly now that it's not because Fatou's mother is not angry that she doesn't allow herself to be outraged on her daughter's behalf, but because she is gathering her strength to protect Fatou from further assault.

Polly tells the imaginary Sam that she doesn't want to live with those fears. She hates the thought of the inevitable selfishness of parenthood, which makes the single life of your own child matter more to you than hundreds of other children, so that you put more effort into placating whims than alleviating suffering. Right now, she owes more to the Fatous of the world than to any imaginary creature she might conceive.

Stella

September

I have been at home all day with a fever, crying much of the time. I cried in the car this morning on the way to Moser because I felt so full of pity for myself and because being hot and shivery made me want to explode. Then at lunchtime Tom called to talk me through how to medicate the evening enough to get through bedtime with the children and I cried out of gratitude, because he was being nice to me, and I don't seem to expect that. I'm still on Day Nurse and Migraleve now, lying on the sofa with my laptop and a cup of half-drunk peppermint tea that I'll probably leave unfinished because I like to save a little of things, because this allows me to believe they will never run out. Lying here, I've been enjoying the clarity that comes when a fever goes down, and I've been thinking about how much we all cry at the moment.

These tears: mine, Helena's, Polly's. I wouldn't have expected it as a child, that we should continue to cry so much this far into adulthood, but it seems to be related to our age, to being on the cusp of middle age: those stalks of wheat, shivering in the wind that I pictured the day I banged my head against the car. I was right then to see us awakening collectively into these as the only lives we will have, and seeing ourselves with unusual clarity as real people in a real world, and finding that hard to bear. I feel at the moment – I think we all feel – so exposed, in a way I didn't expect to feel at this point in my life.

Real people, the real world. We wouldn't have been allowed to use the word 'real' as undergraduates; we had to remember that reality was a construct. But I use it at work, urging my authors to make their scenes more real. And it's the right word, I think, for the feeling of these middle years being the years in which we imprint ourselves on to the world we've found ourselves in, and of the traces we leave on other people having a kind of physical actuality. Love itself feels so close to pain at the moment, whether it's love for my children or for Tom or for friends: the men with whom the love is a marker of the unlived life we might have had together; the women whose feelings overlap so closely with mine that our separateness is a source of pain. So the tears are both because we see how glittering with possibility life has become and cry in wonder, and because we feel ourselves getting it so wrong, day by day.

I can understand why, seeing this, Polly would decide not to have children. If you do have children, they become the main answer to the question of how you imprint yourself on the world that is now revealing itself to be real. If you haven't had children by the point that you see this question opening up before you, then there's a kind of responsibility to find other answers.

Today I had lunch with Vince and Cliff Carson, our CEO. We went to the Japanese noodle place by Holborn station: it was Cliff's choice – he's trying to avoid stuffy (by which he means expensive) lunches but is never prepared just to eat a sandwich in the square. I forget what a gossip Cliff is. As we sat slurping our soup, packed tightly against other lunchers on uncomfortable benches, he asked us rather excitedly what we thought of the editor of the American literary magazine who's under fire for commissioning a piece about being a victim of Me Too from a talk-show host who had lost his job after being accused of assaulting women.

Vince looked to me to say something and I wondered whether Cliff was genuinely oblivious to how awkward this conversation was going to be, or if he just enjoys controversy, like the American editor himself, who claimed in an interview yesterday that journalism at its best should make room for unpopular opinions and that it's really not his concern whether the talk-show host actually has bitten, choked and punched women, as twenty have accused him of doing, adding that he certainly wouldn't have commissioned the piece if he'd been accused of rape. His interest, he said, was in the question of what happens to men who are innocent in the eyes of the law but guilty in the eyes of the world.

I said to Cliff, keen to make my position on these matters clear, that I'd found the article unpleasant but the interview much more so. I hated the editor's complacency. He didn't seem to care. I hated the suggestion that we're not serious minded if we can't stick to the abstract questions, without getting sidetracked by whether the man really did punch women in the head.

How do you know whether he cares, Stella? Cliff said, picking his bowl up to drink from the side. Privately, he cares a lot, I'm sure. But professionally, he doesn't think it's his business to care. He's interested in freedom of speech. He wants every voice to be heard.

We've never heard every voice, Vince said. It was a fallacy. So there's going to be a period when we prioritise the voices we haven't been hearing from, which means those particular voices, the voices of abusive white men, can't be heard.

I was grateful to him for saying it. I realised that I'd been wondering, since reading the American interview, if Vince has similar standards. Rape – too shocking to contemplate; biting and choking – well, why make a fuss about it? Also I've realised recently that I no longer think all opinions are equally valid, as I did when I was young, and as the American editor seems to think. And I've started to think that those phrases that we use so glibly – 'innocent until proven guilty' – are phrases generated by a judicial system that is itself patriarchal. I hadn't planned to mention any of this to Vince, the whole thing had been starting to make me feel too queasy to think about, but it was a relief to hear him saying something similar, saying that he knew his voice had had its day.

Walking back to the office, I thought that whatever I believe about the facts of these cases, and we have no way of knowing whether the talk-show host bit and choked these women or whether Vince inappropriately exposed his naked flesh, I do now believe that neither Vince nor the American magazine editor are the people to lead literary culture further into the new century. I admire them both, I'd rather work for them than for many women of similar status, I believe that they see the best in the women they respect and avoid obvious sexism in the workplace. Publishing is hardly an industry where women have been silenced, and they've both employed their share of women. But women, collectively, are too bruised and too angry about our bruises to be led by men stuck so bewilderedly in the old world.

As we went into the editorial meeting, I found that I was

struggling to keep down my rage with Cliff. I felt most angry with him for the coldness of his judgement. He'll probably sack Vince. He cares too much about public opinion not to. But it won't be an emotional decision. He won't feel for the women Vince may or may not have assaulted and he won't even feel for Vince. Then, once we were sitting down, I had a message from Chris complaining that my trip to a literary festival on Sunday morning would interrupt one of his two weekend lie-ins. I looked around the room and found that I hated the men present, Cliff and Vince in their tailored suits and the two younger men in self-satisfied patterned shirts. I hated the way that they expect women to look after their children and to fit around their plans, hated their certainty that theirs is the worthily objective point of view and that the women who find this upsetting are being partial and illogical. And I hated their sense that anything short of rape might count as tolerable erotic play, and hated the knowledge that in some moods I agree with this – certainly I can see that hatred is a part of love.

I had an image of the paper plane that Cleo and I made at the weekend, decorated with the lightning that she feels invading her body when she's angry. We made it so we could send it away, banishing the anger. But I started wondering then if I'm right to encourage her quietly to expel her anger. Perhaps I should be urging her to amass it instead like the pocket money she has recently begun to save, powering her with the momentum she'll need to explode out on to the world, clearer eyed than I am.

Then there was a lot of fuss because my former assistant Amy spilt a cup of tea on the antique table. Cliff summoned the receptionist to clear it up but Vince started old-mannishly trying to join in with his handkerchief. Amy was self-conscious and I saw her looking at me and realised that I am expected to give some kind of signal to the younger women on how we should treat him. So I went and assisted too, by way of showing that he's not yet a pariah, raising the number of unnecessary helpers yet further. And then we all sat down again, and Vince and Cliff together, charming, complimentary, apologetic, proceeded to reject the proposal I'd worked up with a young author wanting to write about female adolescence. No one defended it except Amy. Leilah, the poetry editor, said apologetically that she thought it was formally reactionary. I was required to remain bland and cheerful, unfazed by rejection, sympathetic to Cliff's concerns about the marketplace.

We need to back horses that will definitely win now, he said.

And through all this I missed Tom, who has gone to Germany, with an aching physical need and at one point I even fantasised about resting my head against Vince's comforting looking russet-coloured jumper. I felt that I was disintegrating and that I could only be held in place by a man.

Kay

September

Kay wakes up feeling sick and vomits just before she's due to leave the house. It reminds her of being pregnant and how much she hated that daily occurrence of the contents of her body brought out into the world. Afterwards, she feels fine, relieved to have had her period recently enough that she doesn't have to worry about failed contraception. She assumes that it's something she's eaten but still feels entitled to call in sick to work, glad to miss lessons that increasingly feel like an internal struggle to avoid shouting at the students, covering them in the bile she has just flushed away, blaming them in their lazy complacency for stamping on the corpse of literature. It seems strange now to think that when she first started to teach, she believed that she was changing people's lives by introducing them to books she loved.

She decides to go to bed for the day and then to walk to her session with Moser. At half past two she will drink a glass of vodka, by way of marking the A level class that she hates most, toasting the absent girls, with their absent stares, their certainty that this is boring but it doesn't matter, because the interesting part of life is still ahead of them. That's one of the things that most enrages her. Sometimes she'd like to show them a film of their lives at forty, to demonstrate how much less interesting it is than their lives now, and that a time will come when they can't be complacent in the present. There's a violence in the thought, a desire to slice into their tight skin, or to stretch it apart and leave it wrinkled. It's like the feeling that makes her grip her son's arm too hard when he's complaining, reminding him of her greater physical power.

Just after she's got into bed, she hears footsteps downstairs and the noise of the cleaning cupboard being emptied. It's not Ana's usual day, but there are no usual days any more. If they were different sorts of people, they would mind the lack of privacy enough to sack her, not knowing when they'll have a stranger among them, not knowing when she'll decide to stay late into the night. But Kay doesn't usually mind Ana moving around the house in the evening, a ghostly addition to their family. Even when Harald's there, Ana doesn't interrupt intimacy; if anything she makes the lack of intimacy less noticeable. Kay does, however, mind her being there now.

She puts her trousers back on and follows the noise of the hoover into the sitting room. Ana must have noticed that the door wasn't double locked, but she doesn't seem to have looked around for the house's inhabitants and she doesn't register any sense of Kay's presence so Kay switches the hoover off at the wall. Ana turns round and Kay finds herself repulsed by her greasy hair and face, wondering why she doesn't bestow the kind of care on herself that she determinedly gives their house. The two women face each other, unsmiling.

You didn't tell me you were coming today, Kay says.

Ana says nothing in response.

I'm ill, Kay says, I'm afraid you need to go home, I need the house to myself.

Ana says something in Bulgarian. There's a challenge in it, but it's a conspiratorial one, an acknowledgement of their texts. Kay has never spoken Bulgarian out loud before, but she tries it.

Съжалявам. I am sorry.

Ana stares at her and then turns dismissively and throws the hoover on to the floor.

I leave, she says.

Kay says it now in English. I am sorry. And then she shouts. The thing is that I am here too. My life may look easy but it's not. I don't know how many more of these days I can endure.

Ana leaves the room, and Kay hears her walking downstairs, and then slamming the front door. The thought that she might not come back provokes no feeling in her. She leaves the hoover where it is and goes back upstairs and gets into bed. She is composing sentences in Bulgarian in her head. Не знам как го правят другите хора. I do not know how other people do it. Всеки ден. Every day.

She sleeps throughout the morning and gets up at lunchtime, hungry enough to eat some of the tomato soup she made for the children. She takes it outside where the sun is directly overhead, dividing the garden sharply between light and shade. She can't remember what she does when she has free time. She has no wish to read, to cook, to watch TV; she would quite like to exercise but doesn't yet want to leave the house. She goes from room to room tidying the toys away, removing traces of her children as Ana hoovers away their fallen hairs and flakes of skin, and then she puts together a new chair that has been sitting flat-packed against the wall in her study, waiting for Harald to do it. She finds that there's an enjoyment in following the instructions, correctly. She becomes absorbed enough to ignore time passing and it's three o'clock when she drinks her vodka. With each sip she imagines a girl in the class she's missing. She pictures herself standing before them, laughing coldly. Then she imagines throwing the liquid in the glass at one and then the glass itself at another. The cracked glass grazes the girl's face, producing the look of shock that she has never managed to bring on in class. Then there is blood and the girls start screaming while Kay calmly leaves the room.

The walk to Moser takes an hour, mainly along the river. She isn't looking forward to seeing him but it doesn't occur to her not to go. It's an excuse not to be there when Harald brings the children home. For once it will be her rushing in just as it's time to leave the house, saying goodnight to the children and then leaving them to the babysitter because tonight is Mark's birthday party at his mother Susanne's house. She enjoys the walk, in graceful afternoon sunlight, enough to have another period of forgetfulness, able to accept for a while that this is her life, walking across Hammersmith Bridge on a Tuesday evening, gleefully pleased each time she overtakes another pedestrian, though she doesn't know what she's proving.

She describes her day to Moser when she arrives, examining his ceiling and then letting her eyes rest as usual on his bookcase, wondering if she would like the European poets she has heard of but not read, thinking that he is perhaps one of the few remaining people she would like to talk about books with. She describes her argument with Ana, the chair, the vodka, the fantasy about the girls. He is silent and she keeps talking, wondering how long he will leave her to speak.

Well, what do you think? she says eventually.

He says that she is not very good at dwelling in silence with him, this is something they should both notice.

She says that she's paying over a pound a minute for this, and has set aside time for it. How would he know what it's like to have no time to yourself, ever, when he's in his consulting room from eight in the morning till seven at night, leaving all the childcare to his wife? Then she says that she longs for silence all the time but that doesn't mean she wants to be silent here. Or perhaps she wants it too much, and fears that if she has it she'll never speak again. Sometimes she thinks that the first sip of a strong drink has the pleasure of silence. Like diving deep into a swimming pool.

Blocking out all the noise? he asks.

Yes, she says, and stopping everything going on above the surface mattering as well. And then if you drink enough, you can't hear your thoughts either.

She says that the most disturbing noise at home at the moment is the noise that Seb makes at Alisa. He claims he's doing it to make her happy, and it's true that she smiles at it. But it's a terrible screech – it sounds like a howl of pain or a battle cry. It makes her want to shout at him to stop. But she holds back, telling herself that she needs to give him the autonomy to make the noises he wants to make, especially as it does actually succeed in making Alisa laugh. She thinks that maybe she hates that noise so much because it reminds her how much she hates the sound of her own thoughts, and it makes her scared that Seb hates his as much as she hates hers.

He is silent. This time she doesn't urge him into speech. She lets her mind wander. She talks more about the chair she put together earlier, wondering why she decided to do it. She talks about Ana, wondering if she'll come back or not. She notices that she doesn't have a clear image of Ana in her mind when she mentions her.

I've been thinking about desire, she says. I've started to think that all my friends desire more easily than I do. If I do desire anything, it's to overcome desire altogether. I don't see much use any more in my body, my silly legs lying here in the jeans I chose to put on today for no obvious reason. Stella's probably told you that she thinks I'm prurient, pushing her to talk about the affair with Ben. But I think in fact it's envy. I want to hear her talking about desiring someone else's husband because I can't imagine what it would be like to be the kind of woman who desires other husbands. Even Priss has turned out to feel more desire than I do, kissing Hugh. Helena desires to have children in a way I've never done. I find it hard to judge Harald as harshly as everyone else does because I'm starting to think I envy him his affairs, more than I disapprove. He finds it so easy to desire all those women, and to be so active about it. None of them seem worth it to me, but then nothing seems worth it to me. That was the gratification of making the chair earlier. For two hours it felt necessary to put screws into wood in the correct order. I think the relief of drinking isn't really the feeling of getting drunk, it's more about noticing a desire in myself for drink. Perhaps I'll let myself become an alcoholic just out of the desire to desire.

You want to tell me about the urge to drink, Moser says. You've mentioned it a few times. You want to know that I'm hearing it.

Kay says that she disapproves of alcoholics because of the loss of control. But maybe it's possible to be a clean, neat alcoholic, without the squalor.

Do you want to become an alcoholic? he asks.

She opens her eyes and doesn't know where to rest her gaze. She says that she imagines her life as an alcoholic and it looks emptier and less responsible. Maybe there are other ways to escape her life that she's not thinking of. There's the fantasy where she moves in with Ana, who she sent away today. Is it possible that her life could be more empty but also more desiring?

It could be, he says, but they have come to an end.

At home, the children are fed and Kay remains distant enough from the scene not to insist on a bath. She goes up to change, inspired by the flatness of her stomach after a day without food to put on a black dress, which Harald, coming up to change once the babysitter arrives, smooths down with approval that feels more professional than lustful. Nonetheless, when he grips her inner thigh in the taxi there is wanting in it.

We are all there when they arrive. Weeknight parties these days begin punctually. Because we have all been to so many parties in that house, it feels more like Susanne's party than Mark's, and their friends have merged over the years in a way that my parents envy, minding the way I keep them apart from my friends and my publishing life. It's Susanne, as always, who has baked, and there's a birthday cake so we all sing happy birthday and then cluster around Mark, who seems happy in the slipstream of his wife Thea's excitable, nervous brilliance. She makes speeches, about her friends, about books and films, about her own drunkenness, and there is a sense that this is all for his benefit, because it's his party and they are, at least as far as it's possible to know, that rare thing, a happy couple.

As it gets going, the party starts to feel different, and Kay is excited by this. There's a collective pleasure in being out without our children. The younger generation – classed here as anyone under fifty – starts drifting into the front sitting room where there is coke being passed around, brought by an artist friend of Mark's we don't know. Kay and Harald both take some. Kay realises, as it takes effect, that alcohol is the wrong drug for her, she likes this clarity better, this energetic geniality with the world. Harald, high, is worse than he is usually, more aggressively confident, less aware of others. But what Kay usually dislikes in him becomes attractive to her again when she's in this mood and she's reminded that there were reasons she chose to be with this man even if there are choices they have made – the children now almost forgotten in the peculiar intensity of the party – that negate these. Harald takes another line but she remembers that she'd like to sleep tonight and comes into the back room, where I still lurk, avoiding the drugs.

We confront each other, in our mirroring black dresses, from our very different evenings. The talk here is of book prizes and publications as we sip our wine. I look with frightened envy on Kay and the altered strangeness she has brought into the room. She gets from seeing me a wearying reminder that this is her real life, old friends with their talk of books. And then Susanne comes over to us and says that she's tired of standing, asking us to sit on the sofa with her and tell her the gossip. Kay would rather not sit down, she's reluctant to lose the fragile energy of the last hour, but she does so anyway. Susanne's black cat appears through the cat flap and comes to sit next to us, immediately purring and licking us as we stroke her white chest, soliciting more affection. Susanne asks us what's been going on.

I say that the talk is all of the various editors under fire but regret saying this because the magazine editor, who's now been sacked, is a close friend of Susanne's and I worry that Kay might not know this, or might not handle it carefully in her current mood.

It's so sad, Susanne says. I don't know what to think. He made a mistake, but surely it didn't need to lead to this.

He didn't let the women editors at the magazine read the piece, Kay says, making me wonder why she knows so much about it. He wasn't curious about the experience of others. Biting and choking. It didn't matter to him.

I'm so old, Susanne says, leaning over to stroke the cat, who is now wriggling on her back, clutching Kay's hand with her paws in a way that makes Kay worry she'll draw blood. I'm probably wrong about everything, but I don't think it should have happened like this, I don't think you should have to lose your job for one mistake because a group of people don't like a piece you've commissioned or how you've talked about it. I'm old enough to remember a time when we thought freedom of speech was more important than that. Who will be next?

I say, drunk enough to be indiscreet, that it will probably be Vince. I've heard that there will soon be more complaints about him. Susanne shakes her head worriedly and says that we don't want a world run only by women, that isn't the answer either, but she probably shouldn't be saying this. People are leaving and Susanne gets up to say goodbye, followed by the cat, who has abruptly lost interest in us. Kay says to me, leaning in and talking seriously, as though she's telling me something I urgently need to know, that Harald has heard that Susanne once had an affair with Vince. I say that it's just as likely to be true or untrue but why would it matter, they are friends now, they are old, and he won't have a job for much longer. Kay says that it means she might know more than we do about him, because she's seen what he's like in bed.

All this matters right now for Kay primarily because she's curious about Susanne, about whether Susanne has moved beyond her femaleness in old age, as she can feel herself beginning to do. Susanne flirts, it's her way of existing as a social being, but she says openly that sex is over for her now. Kay thinks that it might be only people for whom sex is over who can understand these questions and who can forgive men their maleness as she is unable to forgive her husband.

Kay goes back into the front room and finds that they are dancing and have overtaken her, they're drunker and higher than she is and she wants to go home. It could be hours before Harald wants to so she's grateful for the deadline of the babysitter. She goes upstairs to the loo and finds Priss, who's there without Ben, looking at the paintings on the staircase, early works by famous painters who are friends of Susanne's.

It must be wonderful to live alongside these, Priss says, and Kay wonders what it would take to make herself believe that it was wonderful to live alongside anything.

She asks about the café and they talk about their children. Kay warms up, more than she expected to, finding that she is more curious about the sleeping patterns of Robert and Lena than she is about the machinations of the literary world. They have this in common, their distance from the shared world of their husbands. She suggests that they should meet for a drink soon, and Priss says that yes, Ben is encouraging her to go out more.

I bet he is, Kay says, not sure what she means by it or what tone she has said it in, but with the image of me in my black dress still flickering in her mind. And then she orders an Uber and goes to find Harald in the crowd and says that she's going and he can come along later if he wants.

I'm exhausted, he says, leading her outside. But you look great tonight, Kay, what a great evening.

Stella

September

Is it your madness, or hers? Moser asked this morning. I'd been describing a dream about Kay at a kind of water party, isolated at the end of a narrow stream of water, her long dark hair falling witch-like over her face, breaking down. She was screaming, loudly, in a way that made me see that there was madness in her as an immanent possibility all the time. I went over to her, away from the party, which Harald seemed to be wilfully hosting regardless of her state, and asked if I could help, feeling awkward in my sanity, and she stopped and looked at me and reached out a hand to touch my face and said, You're so pretty, how are you so pretty? But you're pretty, I said, bemused that she didn't know this. And then she turned away, violently, and resumed her wailing, taunting me with it, so that now it felt that I was in the presence of hostility as well as craziness.

Come over here, Harald said, so I went over, and attempted to join in the festivities at this so-called party, as I put it to Moser. And I felt disloyal to myself as well as Kay, ignoring the presence of madness.

So whose madness is it? Is it mine? Moser, if anyone,

would be able to tell me which of the two of us is more mad. But we are all mad, I suppose. Those of our age and class who have set ourselves up, societally, to be the sane ones, the builders of nations, the employers of others.

On the way back I went to a yoga class, where I spent the first half hour distractedly looking forward to doing balancing poses and then finally, standing on one leg, my body horizontal suspended between ground and ceiling, I felt almost as peaceful as I was instructed to feel. I have been balancing a lot recently, without knowing why I like it so much. There's a side of me that enjoys liking the things that everyone around me likes, which must be why I've started looking online at jumpsuits. I don't expect to be particularly good at balancing because it's Helena's thing, as writing is meant to be Kay's, baking Priss's and singing Polly's, but in the evenings I look forward to standing on one leg after putting the children to bed, and I think of all the other women across the suburbs doing the same. It's possible that it makes me saner than going to Moser does.

So many of my friends stubbornly persist in believing in the talking cure. We hope to talk our way into a relaxed relationship with our own madness, greeting the unconscious on friendly terms. But I've started to worry that all the talking to Moser just makes me rely all the more on logical thought to solve my problems, trapping me in my insistent and illusory rational world. It's another version of the matching Tupperware containers of children's food I stack up in my new freezer, asserting control over the unknown. I need – we all need – to stop feeling that we can bring our lives into being at a conscious level. I think now that this was what Susanne was objecting to when she thought it was odd that I was choosing to have a baby in such peculiar circumstances. She finds it strange how I make these decisions with such faith in the primacy of the conscious mind. Psychoanalysis hasn't worked yet in stopping me from doing this. It may be saner because more easily, pleasurably insane to stand on one leg or to read my horoscope as my younger colleagues seem to be doing. At least the words we use in yoga – Virabhadrasana, Pranayama – are open in their magical thinking.

And then I came home to read manuscripts and spent the whole day on the sofa addictively watching the Kavanaugh proceedings, which I want to call a trial, though it isn't. Judge Kavanaugh, nominated for the US Supreme Court, challenged for assaulting in adolescence a woman who is now a professor of psychology, Christine Blasey Ford. Today she took the witness stand before the world, telling us that she's a hundred per cent sure that her attacker was the man standing before her while he railed against her, shouting and crying, blaming a political conspiracy.

I find it impossible to feel any nuance, watching it. I feel furious with men who try to discuss it as a many-sided political event. She is obviously telling the truth, I said repeatedly at work yesterday, otherwise why would she seek this kind of destructive attention, this kind of pain. She went forward before he was nominated, she was doing her civic duty. But it was so long ago, said Martin, a younger man who usually prides himself on how right on he is and who last week I overheard observing ruefully that Vince will probably have to leave. Why not come forward earlier?

For me the ultimate proof is that she had two front doors built on her house in case of attack. How much more proof do you need that someone is frightened? And now I hear Moser's voice, asking me who is frightened, and Tom, who reminded me gently on the phone from Germany that yes we know that she's frightened, we know that she believes she was assaulted by this man, but there's such a thing as delusion, so it doesn't mean she really was.

Nonetheless this man, this repellent man, shouting at her for ruining his career, open in his assumption that anything you do in adolescent drunkenness can be excused, is likely to be on the Supreme Court. And the President of America tweets his outrage at Christine Blasey Ford for taking Kavanaugh on, assuming that she's making it up. And at ten to six when I rushed back out into the September evening sun to collect Maggie from nursery, I felt I was swimming through the water towards Kay, wondering how anyone can expect us to remain sane.

Andreas is in hospital after falling off a roof. He was sitting on it last night, drinking, with a friend, and then fell and broke his arm. The friend called Carla who summoned an ambulance and then called Tom, who reached the hospital at the same time as the ambulance and saw Andreas, semi-conscious, as he was rushed to have his stomach pumped. Tom and Carla stood in silence in the waiting room, blaming each other and themselves for his self-destructiveness, though according to Andreas they should be blaming the world at large. The apocalypse is already happening, he told them when he came round, which is the kind of thing that Tom might say.

I woke up to a message telling me about it and I've been on the edge of tears all day when not actually crying, distraught by the pain of this boy I have never met but who might in other circumstances have been my son. When I spoke to Tom on my way to work, shouting over the noise on the tube platform, I told him that he's not responsible and he snapped back that of course he is, what kind of father would he be if he didn't feel responsible? It's true, this is how high the stakes are for all of us when we sculpt our lives into shapes that include the creation of new people.

I have a picture on my phone of Andreas not much older than Cleo that Tom sent me a few days ago, when Carla and Andreas wanted to go through old photos. Andreas isn't smiling in the photo, and I can see more of Tom in him than I've seen in photographs of him as an adult. Now I have to picture that delicate, drinkable skin bloody after his fall. I find myself having endless imaginary conversations with him, though I have no way of knowing what he sounds like. And I feel for Carla more than I ever have before. I'm more aware of our shared vulnerability as mothers, and I've been imagining her blaming herself for wanting a life away from Tom. Perhaps we should remain in families who can care for one another after all. Do we risk our children's lives when we search for new structures of support and fail to find them? Should I feel guilt towards my daughters for seeking my own happiness and then making myself more vulnerable with Tom? But Andreas survived. And he's been repentant today. He's promised not to drink like that again.

It was a great relief getting home from work to my daughters and gathering them in my arms, promising myself that I'll do all I can to protect them. I thought of Tom and Carla gathering Andreas to them when he was a small child, offering him the same promises. I find it unbearable not being able to see and touch Tom. I can't comfort Andreas: it's not my role. But I know that I have it in me to comfort Tom, to hold him fiercely to me. The things we say on the phone – all the analysis of the past and the future, my attempts at advice, coming out tinnily through the WhatsApp call – feel wrong, and make me worry I am making things worse. For once I distrust thought and words. The best moment of the phonecall was when we both sobbed, without speaking.

Kay

October

Kay and Priss are waiting for me, at a tapas restaurant on Wardour Street. They've met for dinner and I'm joining them for a drink but have texted to say that I'm held up at work. They're on their second round, Priss drinking wine while Kay drinks something called a Bubblebath cocktail, and have ordered some calamari. Everything is wrong with the restaurant that you'd expect in Soho on a weeknight, the service slow, the tables too close together, the suited men at the next table shouting their news. But Priss's skin glistens under the low lighting in the expensive make-up that has proffered the new radiance it promised, and Kay likes the way her pink cocktail glows on the gold table. Kay has rushed there from the children's bedtime and is pleased that she's starting to feel drunk, getting a floating feeling in her limbs. Priss has been swimming first, making the most of her new life as a woman entitled to ask for things for herself. They are talking about their children's ailments.

I arrive, wearing a blue dress bought in yesterday's lunch hour from a shop I usually think of as too young for me. Kay notices it, thinking that the sleeves are too baggy for my shoulders and that I look too determinedly fashionable.

She thinks that it would look better on Priss. I sit down, but am still distracted by the long phone conversation I just got drawn into at work, which I tell them was about Vince. A young editor from one of the big conglomerates telephoned, ostensibly about an author we have stolen from him, but actually because he wants to work with me if I take over Vince's job. I tell them about him, outraged by his assumption that I have so little loyalty to the man who has not yet left the building, and about how he then went on to hint at worse accusations which are soon to come out.

I say that I'm more confused about Vince because I'm so angry about Kavanaugh. I hate the thought that Kavanaugh has been given a seat on the Supreme Court but I don't know if it's right that the literary world should take the hit. The New York editor, Vince – they're hardly Kavanaughs.

Kay swirls her drink in her hands and says, talking quickly into it, that she doesn't see why we're all so convinced about Kavanaugh's guilt. Just because Christine Blasey Ford is so calm and ordinary doesn't mean that he is a monster, despite his anger and entitlement.

She's got nothing to gain and everything to lose, Priss and I say in slightly different formulations at the same time: why would she do this if it's not true?

She believes that it's true, Kay says. But women over the centuries have had rape fantasies about men in power. Anyway, even if it's true, it's no worse than a million other cases like this so why do we all fixate on this one. We're not even Americans. We don't know the names of anyone else on the Supreme Court. It's because he's the rapist and she's the victim that suit our collective unconscious. The most repellent form of masculinity, the most self-apologetic and innocent yet psychologically knowing form of femininity. I think I hate her as much as you all hate him.

She turns to look at us now she's finished her speech. Priss is very upset, I'm less disturbed, partly because I've heard similar arguments from other people and partly because I've hardened myself recently to Kay's provocations, but my instinct all through this has been the same as Priss's so I argue alongside her. We say that if he behaved like that in what was effectively a job interview, lying about everything from drinking ages to his adolescent schedules, how can we trust him in a position of power? We say that he doesn't need to be on the Supreme Court, it's not like we're suggesting he should be put in prison, we're just suggesting that there might be a better candidate. We say that part of what's so upsetting is the rhetoric around it. There's Trump publicly proclaiming Kavanaugh's innocence, assuming that there's no point listening to the accusations of women.

But why would you expect anything else? Kay says, finishing her drink swiftly.

She's bemused by our ability to be continually surprised by the awfulness of awful people and she despises us, suddenly, for siding with the supposedly innocent. She pulls back her hair in a tight ponytail and orders another cocktail. Priss holds up her hand as Kay orders, signalling that she's had enough.

I have to go. I've said I'll pop into the end of a book launch, though after that phone conversation I'd rather not see Vince, whose author's launch it is. They wish me luck and I leave, banging into one of the suited men at the next table as I do so and leaving the restaurant alongside him. I wonder as we compete for a taxi if anyone still finds these London evenings energising.

Kay was warm as she said goodbye to me, hugging me with unplanned vigour, but after I've gone she feels irritable again. She is the one, out of all of us, who's put up with the worst sides of masculinity for years, in Harald, so she feels that we've come late to this. What gives us the right to expect the world to be a morally sanitary place? She is angry with me for my ease in rushing into the restaurant and rushing off to my party, enjoying my job, enjoying my evening. It is clear that I find life more liveable than she does, and this seems unfair, given that I have lived at the expense of others. She finds Priss irritating too, for standing up for the victims of predatory men without realising that she is a victim as well.

She wonders if she should go home after this drink, she doesn't feel like she has much ordinary conversation to offer and they've just turned the music up in the bar. But home is no more tempting than being out is; she can't face Harald, she can't face the inevitable night wakings from Seb, she can't face feeling locked inside her own mind. The word 'home' itself feels wildly inaccurate as a description of that house in which she almost never feels sheltered or relaxed.

Priss asks her about work and she remembers that she's curious about how Priss is finding running the café, and starts asking her questions. How much money are they making? how much does Priss see of the children? do they mind her going out? is Ben still taking some mornings off to be with them?

Priss answers, pleased that her life has now become a subject to be discussed, and then Kay asks how much she sees of Hugh.

He comes to the café, Priss says. A couple of times a week, when he knows I'll be there. We chat, he reads.

Have you kissed him again? The question is abrupt and Priss laughs, embarrassed, but finds that she wants to talk about it, her moment of complicated conquest, and that Kay makes this easier with her directness.

No, she says. No, I think it was a one-off.

Because you don't want to? Kay asks.

Reddening, Priss says that she does want to, in a way, of course. But she likes the memory of it, as an experience in itself, before things get complicated. And she wants him to be free to meet someone else, and she doesn't want to hurt Ben.

Don't you think it serves them right, these men, if we have affairs too? Kay says. Otherwise we're stuck in the 1950s, living the lives they con us into.

Priss looks at her, surprised. This is not what Kay usually says. She agrees that perhaps it would be acceptable for Kay, because of Harald, but she thinks that Ben is different.

What about Ben and Stella? Kay asks, her voice quiet and neutral.

Priss tries not to show how shocked she is, but her eyes widen involuntarily as she looks away and then back at Kay. She feels it churning through her, like a noxious liquid that Kay has poured into her mouth or eyes from her pink glass.

Ben and Stella? she asks, reddening.

Together they look at the seat that I have vacated and at my empty glass. Kay nods quickly and looks down. Priss wants to pretend that it's not a surprise but she doesn't sustain this.

Are you sure? she asks.

Yes, Kay says, Stella's admitted it to me. You really didn't know?

Kay rouses herself out of the haze of drink into a state

of urgency. She knows that what she's done is serious and doesn't want to make it more miserable for Priss, and she knows that she owes me loyalty as well. But she's finding it hard to concentrate, suddenly conscious most of all of how much she hates the atmosphere of the tapas bar, with its fake nods to the Mediterranean, its off-the-peg classiness, the gold wallpaper and lights that next year will be ripped out to be replaced with interchangeable alternatives. She would like to tear it all out now and start again with something more truthful. But Priss is asking her if it's still going on so she has to talk to her, and she decides to be as accurate as she can.

Kay says that it's been over for a couple of years and asks if she'd rather not have known.

Maybe, Priss says, thinking back to the conversation she had with Ben about kissing Hugh, wondering if he tried to tell her then that he'd lapsed as well.

Priss feels empty now, as though her stomach is hollowing out as her life does, but there's also the excitement of recognition because she's allowing herself to know this thing that she already knew in some part of her mind. And there's a kind of charge running through her body that she knows will lead her, tonight, to Hugh. She can picture him opening the door of his flat, can picture herself crossing the threshold as though in a film, unsmiling, removing her coat and standing still while she waits with pleasurable anticipation for his response.

Kay doesn't want to go home but she sees that the evening is over for them. She tells Priss that if she wants to go and talk to Ben then it's fine to leave her here. Priss tries to pay. She transferred money from the restaurant to her account on the way here with which to do so, proud to be earning

228

a salary finally. But Kay doesn't let her, insisting that she should leave immediately. Left on her own, Kay texts me a short factual message. 'I just told Priss about you and Ben. Sorry. I thought she probably knew already.' She orders one more drink, which she makes herself sip slowly, reading the news on her phone without taking much of it in. Then she starts to feel too energetic to sit still so she goes outside, planning to walk around.

She walks down Shaftesbury Avenue towards Piccadilly Circus, not sure where she's heading. The important thing is to keep moving, so she doesn't run blindly around the maze of moral implications. She is drunk enough to suspend her knowledge that actions have consequences. She could walk now into the street and would not be responsible for what happens next, for the tooting and braking that would ensue.

There are too many people here so she walks in the direction of the river and then east, keeping close to the water when she can, wondering what it would feel like to touch it — cold enough perhaps to numb feeling altogether. She remembers the year, just after we finished university, when we all used to go for evening river walks together in the docklands, with water bottles filled with gin and tonic in a rucksack, wanting to get to know London's edges. She turns inland, abruptly, and walks through the City, with its banks and churches: two worlds that mean nothing to her and that therefore come as a relief in their inscrutable grandeur. Everything is large enough here that it is easy to feel she doesn't matter at all.

Suddenly — without enough warning — she is in Shoreditch and the streets are filled with people again; she resents them for pushing her up against the recognition that she is a person too. There is a crowd about her age going into a club, so she follows, though she hasn't been to a club for years. When she sees the queue to deposit bags she almost turns round again, but she waits in line, goes straight to the bar to order a double vodka, and then launches herself on to the dance floor, feeling as though she is diving into a swimming pool, using her arms to push aside the bodies resisting her path. The lights are a low combination of red and grey. The music is loud and regular, with no discernible words, and brings a feeling of release; it feels like she's going inside her own body, as though she is her daughter, back in her own noisy womb. Now that she's in the middle of the floor, she stops moving her arms, and stays almost still, surrendering to the physical pain of the assault on her ears. She'd forgotten what it felt like, losing sensation in her body because there is noise pumping through it, making her vibrate, but it turns out to be exactly what she has been seeking over the past months, when she longs to inhabit a world without claims. There are no claims on her now, no sense of past or future. She shuts her eyes, wondering if she could stay like this forever, wondering what would happen if she failed to emerge out of this comforting cave.

Stella

October

I didn't get Kay's text until a couple of hours later, with Tom. He'd joined me at the pub after the book launch, and we were on the bus home. I felt sick, but I also couldn't believe that it was real. At first I was smiling, grinning even, as I sometimes do when I hear bad news and haven't properly taken it in. Once I did understand, my first instinct was to text Ben, to decide our story together, managing the situation. Tom said that I should leave it, that if they're to repair their marriage they need to learn to rely on each other and that Ben needs to stop feeling that I understand him better than Priss does and give her the chance to understand him. He was right. There's a selfishness in my wanting still to have the kind of understanding with Ben that he doesn't have with anyone else, and it stops me committing fully to my friendships with the group. Tom has his own reasons for wanting the friendship with Ben to lapse, though; I think he's more jealous of Ben than he allows himself to know.

Tom put me to bed, carefully, and sat up reading in the sitting room. He only got back from Germany on Sunday and I am anxious that it's too soon for my emotional crisis to dominate our relationship when he is still so nervous about Andreas. Lying in bed, I worried that we would split up, that we're too preoccupied with our own frequent crises to be there for each other. I felt better once he came to bed, and I lay turned towards him with my head under his armpit, squeezing his leg, hard, with my hand, intermittently squeezing it even more tightly because I wanted more of him than I could access by touching.

I was awake for a few more hours, imagining conversations between Ben and Priss, me and Ben, me and Priss, recriminatory conversations with Kay, self-justifying conversations with Helena, who will probably dislike me now, and with Polly, who will look back on our conversation about affairs and find me dishonest. I wonder if other people spend as much of their lives having imaginary conversations as I do. Last night I was trapped in them. I tried listening to podcasts on my headphones, but I was deafened by the inner voices that are all a version of my voice because I seem unable to grant people otherness inside my head. At one point I wondered about waking Tom up to talk to me, which made me remember a phase with Chris I'd forgotten, when he used to talk to me for hours in the night during my weeks of insomnia, telling tenderly inconsequential stories about his day and listing the seven dwarves and the seven wonders of the world. He took on my sleeplessness as his responsibility, as he took on my parents, my safety and, for a few years, my happiness. I felt a wave of remorse for my own ingratitude, in needing what I found in Ben more. And I felt sad, because Chris and I are no longer able to honour the grace of a marriage that we allowed to become ugly, and because Tom and I are now too old and encumbered to take responsibility for each other with that careless ease.

Then this morning, Ben emailed me, a short factual email

of the kind Tom might have advised, saying that Priss has found out, that she's angry but they're talking it through.

I read it just before I arrived at Moser's. During my session, I was furious with Kay, who I still haven't replied to, and was asking myself where it leaves me with Tom. Despite my night-time regrets, I realised how glad I was to be no longer in a position where I'd have to explain it all to Chris. It made me grateful to be in a relationship without secrets – though perhaps I'm naive to think that's possible. But I could still feel the loss of a kind of safety net with Ben, as though I was left risking everything on one person. Now that Tom is back from Germany we are very close and very careful with each other, but can we be everything for one another, as Priss and Ben will have to be? I feel ready to try it, and yet I can't say *our* sofa, as Tom does, about the sofa I think of as his. *Our* bed, he says when I am there, but I often end up sleeping in the spare room, claiming my bed, a bed he has never slept in. My boyfriend; our bed; will I be able to say those again?

Lying on the couch, feeling my throat become tight with the effort of producing all those words with so little sleep, I asked myself why Kay exposed me, half wanting my explanations on her behalf to pre-empt whatever she'll tell Moser on Monday. There's her commitment to truth. She'd have disliked the thought that Priss was living in ignorance about her own life. It's a side of Kay that hasn't been affected by psychoanalysis and the realisation it brings that we are all living in ignorance about our lives. But even if she wanted to increase the truth-telling in the world, her decision to speak last night feels unplanned and volatile.

It seems ridiculous now that we're both seeing you, I said.

Are you angry with me for taking you both on? he asked.

233

It was odd having so direct a conversation without looking at each other and I wondered about turning towards him, but felt too rule-bound to do so. I said it seems unprofessional, but I guess that he must regret it, and maybe it's not his fault. None of us was to realise that her life and mine would become so entwined. He asked if I was wondering if we'd become so entwined because we're both seeing him and I said that it seemed a self-important thought. But then what am I paying him for, if I don't believe he's capable of being a central figure in my psychic life?

I was silent for a while. He observed last week that I use my sessions to talk a lot, and it made me picture the room with an imaginary other woman on the couch, using her time for unconscious reverie, instead of wasting his time with well-constructed stories about her days. It was good to be quiet for a while today. Eventually I said that I felt deluded, thinking that I could have the affair with Ben without it affecting the group. It's meant that I haven't been honest with any of them, for years, and there's a kind of relief now in thinking that I might be able to talk truthfully to them eventually, if they still want to be friends at all. Then I felt depressed, because most of them will probably dislike me, and confused, because I disliked myself too, and felt suddenly curiously united with Chris in doing so. Yet I used to be sure that I didn't subscribe to a value system that made it immoral to have affairs.

Used to be sure? he asked. Have you changed your mind?

I believe in kindness, I said. I think I have been unkind.

Polly

October

Polly arrives at Priss's café a few minutes late because she's been on the phone to Tomas, the carpenter, who's building her a new wardrobe and has found that it's more complicated than he'd expected. He's now going to bring all his tools to her flat to reshape the wood that he'd pre-cut. She trusts him to do all this, though he's temperamental and last time he came he shouted at her neighbours when they tried to deliver a parcel. If anything, his volatility makes his generosity to her feel more genuine, though she'd rather she didn't have to spend her time second-guessing the moods of strangers. She wishes she wasn't still so dependent on men to do the jobs her father once did for her.

Lulu's doesn't open till noon on Sundays, so they will be on their own. Kay has called Polly, telling her about the affair and its revelation and asking her to look after Priss. Polly is the only one who's not busy with procreation or children, so she is apparently the one who has time to care, before she goes on to have lunch with Helena. Also Kay wants everyone in the group to be involved, needing the groupiness of the group to assert itself because she's worried that she might have completed the destruction that I began with the affair.

Polly has followed Kay's instructions, but she finds that in fact it's hard to care, though a few months ago, if she'd been told about it, she'd have been astonished by the affair and angry with me. At the moment she feels increasingly sure that if you choose to embark on a sexual relationship, you open yourself to the pain that ensues. She knew what she was getting into with Sam. She never felt guilty because his wife knew what she was getting into as well. Sexual relationships happen, it seems to her, of their own accord. Life is a kind of *Love Island*. Throw people together and see what kind of mess they can make of each other's lives. Now she believes that Priss, me, Ben, Kay, anyone else who has a view on it, is mistaken for expecting these relationships to be anything less than complicated, random and fraught. Yet she is the one deployed to console Priss, who has finally discovered this.

She dislikes the café when she arrives, with its cake stands and smugly mismatched crockery. She realises that since it opened, she has come to view it as a symbol of futile effort. Priss greets her at the door and offers her a choice of tables, playing at being a working person in a way that still feels unconvincing to both of them. Polly examines Priss clinically, noting that her eyes are slightly redder than usual and that she bites the inside of her cheek as though it's a necessary action she's been interrupted in. She wonders if this is a sign of suffering, and if it matters if it is; certainly this isn't suffering as she sees it on the operating table.

Sitting down, Priss thanks her for coming. You must have a lot of other things to fit into your weekends, she says. Polly nods but then says, by way of keeping her own ego in check, that she would probably just be on another internet date. Priss asks how this is going and Polly shrugs to indicate helplessness in the face of the inadequacies of the dating marketplace.

I've thought about that, Priss says, over the past week. I've thought that I'm lucky to have found someone, that this may be enough, without him needing to be perfect.

Polly is enraged by the platitudes. She wants to tell Priss that she doesn't think she's lucky, she doesn't wish she had Ben in her bed as well. That's not the take-home lesson from this, that Ben is a covetable prize.

Priss goes behind the counter to make coffee, doing that thing she does of humming tunelessly under her breath. She tells Polly, apparently talking at random, though also responding accurately to her thoughts, that there are moments when she finds the good taste here excruciating. She's one woman with good taste catering for others, while they all hide the more troubling details of their lives.

Polly warms up. You can't do anything more than that, she says, as Sam said to her again after she operated on Fatou, during that week when everything suddenly changed, though she doesn't want to tell Priss about James yet.

Priss puts the coffees on the table and sits down, neatly. Her skull is always visible beneath her skin, with its high forehead and angular cheekbones, but this is more pronounced because she's lost weight. She's wearing a black polo-neck jumper and trousers, which makes her look rather impressively austere. Looking at her friend, Polly is struck by the oddness that each female body, whose almost identical interiors she knows so well, should have its own arbitrary coating of skin and then clothes, and that we should assign so much importance to the differences between our coatings when we are all, as someone says every day on the Brexit phone-ins she listens to in the mornings, united by our shared humanity. She wants to tell Priss that none of this matters, none of the ways that we insistently differentiate ourselves from each other with our particular appetites or skills. We are just breathing, bleeding creatures. And thinking this, she feels more warmth towards her, because it doesn't really matter whether she likes or doesn't like this woman who she labels as her friend, they are two random, clothed bodies coinciding, and they might as well do what they can to make this process less absurd.

But how are you? Polly asks, and Priss, sensing that this is finally an expression of genuine concern, tells her that she is finding it difficult, discovering that there were months of her life, important ones, perhaps years, that she was experiencing falsely. She may have been happy, but it wasn't a real happiness, because the man with whom she was happy was thinking all the time about someone else, and was probably wondering about leaving her. She's always feared, she says, that she can't be enough for someone. She lets the thought trail off and says that what's worse is discovering that Ben can't be enough for her either. Shyly excited, she tells Polly that she went to have sex with Hugh, the night that Kay told her, and has done it again twice since. She thinks she needs to carry on.

Polly, who doesn't think of herself as shockable any more, is shocked. She wonders why she's here, if Priss is in fact fully able to look after herself. Polly thinks of Priss as being unusually prepared to let life be what it happens to be, but it turns out that in fact Priss is shaping her life actively, even rather frantically, with the café and now with this love affair.

Does Ben know? Polly asks.

Yes, Priss says. He finds it hurtful, but I'm hurt by him. What's clear is that I need to do all I can to live my own life.

They regard each other across the table. Priss ties her hair back with what Polly remembers from childhood as a scrunchie, which she takes from her wrist, and then unties it again. Polly examines her and decides that she stands by her original diagnosis: she does look more fragile than usual. She says that she would like a jam tart after all, so one is produced from a cake stand, the jam a fluorescent orange and in the shape of a heart. Priss says that she made the pastry with Lena yesterday afternoon and Polly thinks that this may matter after all, Priss rolling pastry with her children. She thinks that she would like to sew Priss and Ben together, like broken flesh, with thick, surgical thread.

Afterwards, Polly realises that she didn't tell Priss she was going to Helena's house next. She seems to need secrets today, protecting her from being a bit player in her friends' dramas. She listens to Amy Winehouse on her headphones as she walks to Helena's, singing along, enjoying the anonymity of being this far away from the hospital. There's a pleasantly touristy feeling to loitering in an unfamiliar part of London, walking slowly past the people squashed up together at the bus stop with their shopping and phones, all waiting to be bussed further east. Looking at their hair, their clothes, their postures, she half scorns and half admires them for these frantic efforts at individuation, defying the sameness of the bodies whose cells are dying in billions by the second.

Helena is waiting for her with lunch laid out on beautiful pale grey crockery. Polly cannot remember the last time she cooked a celeriac; she is not sure she ever has done. She examines Helena's bump and tells her that it's a perfect sort of bump for sixteen weeks, though this isn't something she really knows about. Certainly, it seems a precise flattened sphere, as sure of its own right to protrude into the world as it's neat in tucking itself away. Helena asks if she'll scan herself if she gets pregnant and Polly says that she doesn't think she will get pregnant. Helena, anxious about the unequal distribution of babies, says she'd recommend doing it on her own.

It's not because of the lack of men, Polly says, beginning to eat the celeriac which tastes much stronger and more recognisable than she'd expected. I've actually met someone. I wanted to tell you. He's called James. Not the kind of man I usually go for. Public schoolboy. Entrepreneur. It's quite serious, I think, which is surprising, but it doesn't make me want to have his babies.

Helena smiles, suddenly relaxed, which makes Polly realise she wasn't relaxed before.

Does he want children? she asks.

He has a son already, Polly says. And an ex-wife. It's the first time I've talked about all this so early with a boyfriend but he says he'd have them if I wanted to, but he'd rather I didn't want to. It's interesting, because with Sam it felt like his not wanting my babies meant he didn't love me enough, but with James it feels more that it's because he loves me that I'm enough for him. He doesn't need babies as well.

They're silent as Helena takes this in and then says that this may be how Clare feels. Polly notices that Helena's back is rounded in her chair, her shoulders more slumped than she has ever seen them. She asks if Clare's said this and Helena says that at the moment they don't talk about the pregnancy. She told Clare when the twelve-week scan was and waited to see if she'd say that she wanted to come, but she didn't so Aaron came instead. Sometimes she thinks Clare will leave her when the child is born and is just waiting it out in the meantime.

If that was really true she'd leave you now, wouldn't she? She wouldn't bother to wait it out.

I don't know, Helena says, wiping away a tear elegantly with the back of her hand.

She mutters something apologetic about hormones and Polly says that it's all right, she's used to hormonal women, she sees them all day. This may be part of why she doesn't want to do it herself; sometimes it feels like she's had twelve babies already and she looks down in the shower expecting her womb to fall out of her vagina.

Is mine going to do that? Helena asks.

Probably not, Polly says.

How did you meet James?

Oh – it's a funny story, Polly says, wishing she'd brought some wine. At Sam's party. He and his wife had a party, and he invited me, as a colleague, because he thought I needed cheering up, I think. It was odd seeing his house. It all felt more ordinary than I'd imagined. Lots of things that I wouldn't have chosen – a poky kitchen, an ugly poodle – which was a relief in a way. And I needed to talk to people, so I talked to the men my age, and there was James, a neighbour of Sam's, who didn't know many people. I'd just ended it with Dave, and decided to stop internet dating, and that I wasn't going to have children, and that I didn't need a serious relationship in my forties. James asked for my number. I didn't really think about him afterwards, but it's turned out that it's surprisingly relaxing, having someone being kind to you whenever you need it, not fearing that he might be about to disappear or wishing he would.

Yes, Helena says, getting up to clear the dishes. Maybe a serious relationship isn't what I need either.

I'm sorry Helena, Polly says. It doesn't mean that Clare doesn't love you, just because she disappears like that.

It must be a relief finally to have decided not to have children, Helena says.

It's a relief to get beyond thinking they're mine to want. It seems absurd to me that we can decide to create another life.

There's no other way for anyone to be born, Helena says, washing up the saucepans by filling the washing-up bowl with warm water in a way that Polly finds unhygienic, though it's how her mother does it. My child will have a better life than the majority of children in the world, so I think it's all right to create this life, even if the circumstances wouldn't be generally perceived to be ideal.

Polly says, needing to say this but not wanting to criticise Helena, that she wouldn't feel consoled by this. It's because her child would have such an easy life, compared to her patients, that she thinks she should be improving the lives of other children, rather than bringing another middle-class child into the world. Helena asks if she's going to do anything to try to make a difference to those children, and Polly, sensing that this isn't asked mockingly, says that James has worked in Gambia, where some of her mutilated patients come from, and that she might volunteer there. She says that sometimes we have to do things that are clichéd, if we feel strongly enough, because often they're good things.

Helena turns back from the sink, surprised that this should be a concern.

Of course it's worth doing, she says. It's so much better to act than to complain on social media like everyone else does.

Polly thinks that Helena doesn't seem cut off from other

people in her pregnancy in the way that the rest of us have been in ours. She tells Helena that she hasn't told any of our group about her plan because she's worried that we'll think she's just a 41-year-old whose fertility is running out, seeking distraction.

Helena wants to go to the park. Once they start walking they stop talking about themselves, relieved no longer to be looking at each other. Polly lets her arms wave as she walks and she thinks that Helena is like Priss in always seeming in control of her limbs, while she's not quite sure where hers should be placed. They talk about their absent friends. Helena asks Polly how Priss was this morning, which makes Polly feel silly for not mentioning to Priss earlier that she was seeing Helena. She wonders if she kept it a secret because there's a side of her that resists group life and even friendship, however much she yearns for it and minds the ways that her friends have retreated into their families. Talking about Priss, she finds that she now feels more loyalty to me than to her. Sensing this, Helena holds back, and some of the closeness of the afternoon is lost. Together, they move towards criticising Ben and find that this brings the possibility of renewed unity, though it's not clear why he should be any more culpable here than I am.

Kay

November

Kay sits on the blue sofa, looking out at the sea, wondering when exactly she decided to leave. For the last few days, she's been separated from the world by a layer of gauze of the kind that she put on Seb's knee when he fell over, voluntarily it appeared to her, on the way home from nursery on Friday evening. She had done everything right, getting there early, bringing him a snack and a drink, but it made no difference because he was in a bad mood, goading her to behave badly by refusing his snack and scraping back his feet along the pavement. She dragged him along, just a little but enough to be uncomfortable, holding his hand with one hand and the pushchair with the other, until he fell. At home there was the stinging ointment and then the gauze and as she put it on, with Alisa sitting on her lap unusually quietly, leaning her head against her chest, Kay thought that this was the gauze that had enveloped her, pressed smoothly around her body and face, draining colour and feeling from the world so that now it was tempting to stand up, allowing Alisa to drop to the floor, and to shut the door abruptly and go downstairs and make herself a gin and tonic, unable to hear their cries.

This, she said calmly to Moser yesterday morning, is depression, this inability to feel. If she told Harald she was depressed, he'd nag her about getting medication, but to medicate would be to assume that there's a happiness that's hers by right, or at least that she wants to see the world in full colour. In fact there's been a relief in the gauze and the feeling it brings that no mistake she could make would matter because neither she nor the people who populate her world are real. If there's been any pleasure over the past week then it's a pleasure in the lightness that comes from feeling she can say whatever comes into her mind because nothing she says or does can affect anything.

It sounds as though you are in pain, Moser said, and she said that she is angry with her husband and friends for thinking that their trivial lives and careers matter, with her children for their ceaseless needs, and that yes there is a pain in this, and a rage with herself for having made choices where she is responsible for the lives of others. Moser was careful with her, he didn't push her, it was the first time that she had felt looked after by him. It was a relief, but it didn't give her the urge to look after other people in turn. She just wanted to go to sleep.

She has a school friend with a cottage in Cornwall. She texted her when she woke up this morning, asking if it was empty, got back a message saying that it's free all winter if they want it, just let them know the dates, replied saying how about today and packed her bag and took a train. She enjoyed the journey, rocked gently for five hours, able to calibrate her bodily needs for lunch, coffee, cake without responding to anyone else's demands. And now she's alone in a house as the sky darkens over the sea outside. It's a rough, deep-blue sea, far below her, on the other side of the cliff that's red with autumnal gorse. If she leans her head out of the window she can see the coves, where the small triangles of white sand seem insignificant compared to the large black boulders surrounding them.

She texts Harald. 'Gone away for a few days. Hope you three are all right.' She doesn't list them by name because her calm in this empty room could be disrupted if she even writes the name Alisa. She needs to keep the image of her daughter out of the room's weightless emptiness. And then she turns off her phone and goes up to the second floor where she gets into the big bed with the thick duvet that crunches as she shapes it around her body, half compliant. This is how to make life bearable, she thinks, to focus only on sensation from moment to moment. As she falls asleep, she listens to her breath passing lightly in and out.

She wakes up in a world without responsibility but then realises that it's only a room. She's frightened, thinking how unreal the world would become if she could discard responsibilities forever. She goes outside with a torch, wanting to get close enough to the sea to feel its spray. She walks along the cliff, adjusting to the feeling of the cold wind on her face and to the texture of the stony ground, until she finds a path down. She's only wearing trainers and it's steep and rough but she risks the descent, using one hand to hold the torch and the other to lever herself down more gently. She's slipping and balancing, slipping again and balancing again, unsure if she's walking or swimming, thinking how absurd it is ever to think you're doing more than slipping, slipping and just about holding your balance before you slip again.

She shines the torch down towards the sea. She's still only a third of the way down. She wonders about abandoning the descent and climbing up again but she's committed now to the attempt, which feels no more arbitrary, no less rational than anything else she's attempted in her life. Slipping again, rebalancing and looking down, she finds that she's less frightened than she is curious about what falling might feel like. At home last night she tried to cut the skin of her wrist with a knife, wanting to draw a gentle stream of blood, and found that it was more difficult to do than you'd think, given how many people cut themselves in this way. This has left her wanting to break through her invincibility, willing blood to appear.

She rests for a minute, crouching on the path, grateful for the noise of the waves, which has supplied the unexpected answer to her need for silence by making thinking impossible. It's less a lapping than a constant roar that seems to come closer and then recede, comforting in its imperviousness. She feels it pummelling her, caressing her. She sets off faster and when she trips, she makes the mistake of holding on to the torch. She finds herself on her front, scrabbling with both hands to get a grip on the gorse, which she does, but there's not enough to hold on to and she slips down further. She can only slow the fall with her hands, pressing on to the raspy strands of gorse, at once bristling and tenuous. Then there's a rock pressing into her face, gashing it, and her whole body feels bruised, and then the incline finally levels and she lies face down on a slope and when she turns round she can see the sea just below her, lit by the half moon. She lies there for longer than she should, thinking that it's surprising that it should turn out to be so easy to go to a place where you could die without anyone knowing about it. All that's required is a train journey to a friend's second home, and an everyday adventure that becomes potentially fatal only because it's taken alone.

She clambers down and tries to walk, not sure if she'll be able to do it. She's aching but she doesn't seem to have damaged any limbs. What hurts is her face and when she touches it her fingers are covered in blood. She is very cold and she knows that she has to get back up to find help but first she sits on the ground and looks out at the dark and roaring sea, distinguishing its outline from her stretch of sand. She's tempted to lie next to the water and wait for the waves to pull her out. She slumps down, wondering what the waves are saying, fitting phrases to them that eventually become the repeated words Go away, Go away.

She has lost track of time, but it's probably half an hour before she gets up. She's stiff and numb from sitting on the ground in the cold and she struggles to identify her limbs and organise them into motion. Then, using the light on her phone as a dim torch, she manages to locate the path that she was thrown off and scrambles up carefully, finding this easier than the descent. The gorse when she touches it feels less hostile, less peculiar, but this doesn't make it less sinister, because she knows that it has death hidden within it. She'd rather not see anyone now but she walks dutifully inland to the pub, the Tinner's Arms. Entering it, surprised by the ordinary warmth of fire and wood and conversation, she stands awkwardly in the doorway for a few seconds, not sure how bad she looks.

People gaze at her in their clustered groups, alerted by each other's stares, a few lone drinkers ignore her, and then a woman rushes forward, warm but efficient.

You're hurt, she says, and takes her back behind the bar into a room where there is a brown bird in a shoebox with a bandage round its body and a small hot water bottle beside it. She sees Kay looking at it and says that it's a turnstone that she found earlier, with a broken wing. Fred, her boyfriend, who's the landlord, thinks it's too much, her desire to look after everything, but what can you do when confronted by pain. She's Scottish. Kay wonders how she's ended up here. Her face is stinging so much that it's hard to think about anything but she surprises herself by being curious about this woman.

I'm Sheila, the woman says, unwrapping gauze from a well-organised first-aid box. Kay introduces herself, and then Sheila touches her cheek and Kay yelps in pain.

It's a deep cut Kay, she says. You could go to hospital or I could wash it here. I know what to do but it will hurt.

When Kay tested the knife on her wrist, she was seeking physical pain that could bring clarity to her mental state. It's here now and she must face it. She tries to experience the next twenty minutes as a kind of duel, in which she and the pain are gripping each other in an angry embrace, both needing the other to respond with full force to prevent themselves from toppling. When she has finished, Sheila stands back and asks if she wants to look in the mirror. She helps her up and Kay sees the scratches and the gauze across her cheek.

You'll have a scab on your face, Sheila says, and then you'll probably have a scar.

Kay touches the gauze gently. Even if she goes back to her life, which she now realises she has been expecting to, she'll be required to keep explaining her scar by describing the day she took a train to Cornwall and hurled herself towards the sea. It's not only this that upsets her, it's more straightforward vanity as well. She is surprised to care so much, when she knows that she thinks about how she looks less than her friends do. Sheila touches her shoulder. It feels natural for her to touch any part of her now.

You are beautiful, she says, you will still be beautiful.

She takes Kay back out to the bar and sits her at a table. A few people smile at her and then look away, comfortably enough that they don't seem to be avoiding her. A man comes over from behind the bar, attractive, with an accent that surprises Kay by being so like her own.

You must have had a bad fall, he says. What can we get you, a glass of wine, some food?

She looks at a menu and asks for sausages, surprised to find that she's so hungry. When she sips the red wine she realises how cold she is and starts to shiver. Sheila comes and sits at the table next to her, saying that she's ordered food as well but they don't need to talk, she'll just be there if she wants to. There is an ease of companionship here that Kay rarely expects. This certainly wasn't what she came to Cornwall in search of. She finds that she wants to talk, and she smiles at Sheila, with the smile that she has at these moments when she wishes to please, which is more diffident, more youthful than you'd expect it to be. She asks if Sheila has been wondering what she was doing, clambering down to the sea in the dark.

I'd just arrived, she explains. I wanted to get closer to it.

From London? Sheila asks, and nods, as though it has all made sense.

Sheila tells Kay that she lives up the coast in St Ives, the seaside town where Kay's train arrived that morning, a place Kay remembers from her childhood as jolly and sandy, another world from these bleak cliffs. Sheila says that she's here because of Fred, the man who took Kay's order, describing him again as her boyfriend, apparently unfazed by claiming him as hers or by using the word boy to describe a man in his fifties. Kay is briefly envious of Sheila's life here with him, the life she has in a pub at the edge of the world, protecting birds and women from pain. Sheila tells Kay that they have both been in Cornwall for twenty years and together for five. He has children he rarely sees in London, she has none. They make their money from the pub and from giving guided walks in the summer. They live separately and between them they have two dogs, who she summons now from behind the bar, black labradors that settle at Sheila's feet. Their food arrives just as Sheila starts asking about Kay.

She has no children either, Kay says, looking down at her wedding ring as she cuts her first bite of sausage, but she's married, to a businessman – it's a word from our childhoods – who's away travelling, so she borrowed a friend's cottage and travelled down here. She's a writer, a novelist, but they won't have heard of her. She's unknown. Sheila nods, saying that they have a lot of writers here, because of D. H. Lawrence. He lived here, a few houses away from Kay's. Kay is irritated. She doesn't like D. H. Lawrence and she is tired in general of male novelists.

Her face still stings but the exigencies of the evening have resulted in a feeling of peculiar peace which she's in danger of losing, with this talk of novels, so she sips her second glass of wine more rapidly. And then the music starts. Kay didn't see them setting up, on the other side of the room, but here they are, two violinists, playing reels. Sometimes, Sheila says, she sings alongside them. She taps her feet, excited, and then gets up to welcome them, abandoning her half-eaten risotto. Kay looks around. It seems that everyone knows each other, that they are here to encounter the music together, enclosed by the dark evening, committed to the idea of the companionship of the local pub. The few who don't join in, men drinking at the bar alone, turn inwards. A couple of people smile at her as she catches their eye, but she doesn't know if she wants to be welcomed into this. She orders a third glass of wine, deciding that it will be her last.

Stella

November

She's gone. When she talked about wanting to escape her life it seemed like a fantasy. I didn't think she'd actually do it.

I came back from an afternoon meeting, out with a potential new author and her agent, and found messages from Harald. He'd got the 'gone away for a few days' text, rushed to collect the children from nursery, and then left messages for Kay and all her friends. He has no shame about being abandoned by his wife, or about outing her as crazy. Eventually, just before I spoke to him, he'd found the friend who'd lent her the cottage and was apparently – I had to hold the phone away from my ear because he was shouting – very distressed. She'd thought she was lending it for a family holiday, and it turned out it was for an act of abandonment. Harald wanted me to look after the children so he could go straight there and get her back. I persuaded him not to and said that he needed to prove that he could manage with the children on his own.

After I spoke to Harald, I went out for a drink with Vince and told him what had happened. I hadn't realised how much he knows about Kay and Harald, but he's known Kay, I suppose, since he visited us in James Street, cooking us all those dinners. It turns out that he took her seriously as a potential writer then and even read some of her student work, because he said that she'd write again after this, claiming that it will unlock her, that now she'll stop caring so much what she thinks of herself and just do it. She'll be able to see herself as separate from Harald so it won't be a choice between his writing and hers. He said that I should take time off and go and see her. I felt he was saying this as Helena's uncle, that I'm still for him the 21-year-old whose foremost duty is to that particular group of friends. He didn't know how horribly complicated a prospect it is for me to see Kay, because he doesn't know about what she said to Priss. Though he always turns out to know more than I think he does, so perhaps he knows everything.

It made me realise that, in all my ambivalence about Vince over the last couple of months, I've forgotten how insightful he is. I felt loyal to him again. I even wondered if I loved him. As we left the bar I realised that I'd forgotten to ask about him, or hadn't wanted to. So I asked how he was and he said that Cliff has asked him to leave at Christmas. A delegation of prominent poets have written to Leilah and Cliff, threatening to speak out and to go elsewhere.

What would we be without the poetry list? Vince said, adding that he cares too much to wrench us down. As an independent we rely on good will, and he doesn't want to divide us or to make Cliff defend him or force him out.

There wasn't time to say much. We hugged and I smelt his familiar after-shave, thinking that we've known each other for so long that he has the familiarity of a former lover to me. I was agitated on the way home, watching the minutes go by on my phone and wondering if Maggie would still be awake. I was missing her with a kind of frantic fear, terrified that I might not see her again. It was as though it was me who'd abandoned my children, as though Maggie was waiting apprehensively, unsure of whether I'd be coming home. After Rosa the babysitter left I went into her room and leant over her cot and smelt her and cried.

On Saturday, Tom and I went to stay in a cottage in Suffolk for two nights. Maggie vomited just before I left but I thought it was just because she'd coughed and brought up her milk. Then, as we arrived, Chris texted to say that she had vomited again so I spent a lot of the time that we were away feeling as though I was in two places at once and not knowing if I should go home to look after her. Tom and I told each other that it was good for their relationship that Chris was looking after her when she was weak. But I worried that she didn't know where I'd gone or if I was coming back and that it was a mistake to stay away simply because I don't like changing plans.

It was odd being by the sea knowing that Kay was by the sea somewhere else. I spent a lot of time imagining her days and wondering if she finds the sea comforting like I do, or more blank and threatening, like Tom finds it. She's been a background presence in my mind most of the time since she left, and the questions I ask her in our imaginary conversations became more urgent with Maggie ill.

I've been realising yet again that I don't make allowances in my thinking for how different people are from me. Because I wouldn't leave, it didn't occur to me that she would. It matters to me on principle not to judge women for leaving their children because I felt so misrepresented when Chris felt that I was abandoning Cleo every time I went away on work trips. And yet I do judge Kay, because the way she's done it seems intended to signify abandonment to herself and everyone around her. This has worked, as far as Harald's concerned, so I worry about Alisa in particular, and how she's experiencing it. But by the same reasoning I could worry about how Cleo experienced my going away when she was that age, when Chris saw me as abandoning her. And now that Chris judges my absences less, because divorce makes the dividing lines between our parenting shifts clearer, I've taken on his old views myself, and so I felt guilty for my absence the whole time that I was away.

Because of this, I felt unmoored within my life, and experienced everything more confusedly. On Saturday afternoon, sitting in the café by the power station, looking out on to the darkening sea, I got an email from Kirsty Kennedy saying that her friends have been urging her to withdraw her next book from us and that she doesn't know what to do. It feels obvious that this is because the company hasn't been clear enough about Vince or made any statements, and I wondered if the only way to save it is to get rid of all of us and replace us with young women who speak the language of today. Perhaps Kirsty and her friends should take over. Tom said that this was a destructive fantasy but that I did have to make a statement to my authors and that I should call Kirsty and have an honest conversation with her on Monday. Loyalty to Vince is an indulgence now that he's agreed to go and I can't take refuge in ambivalence any longer, given my position. I became angry and told Tom that he'd never had a proper job and that it therefore wasn't fair for him to tell me that I do mine badly. He said that it was me who was fretting about doing it badly. I'm the one who covets prizes, he doesn't, and now I'm worried about losing a prizewinning, bestselling author.

I worried that all my authors would leave and that my career was over, which made me worry all the more that Maggie's illness was somehow caused by my going away. Instead of seeing her as ill with a vomiting bug that would pass, I found that her illness imbued her with a more abstract and agonising fragility. I woke Tom up with these thoughts on Sunday. I could hear the sea at the back of the house and it felt like it was a whirlpool of disintegration, waiting to claim me as it may be claiming Kay. Tom pulled me down, beneath the duvet, wanting to carry on sleeping together, as tired as I was by the noise of my thoughts. I tried to remind myself that this was hard for Tom to talk about reasonably, because Andreas is so much more definitely fragile than Maggie is, and because it may be partly my experience of Andreas's vulnerability that makes me so frightened about Maggie.

That afternoon, walking along the beach at Cove Hythe in the last of the light, the sea calm, the sand wide and flat, I talked about Polly not wanting to have a child, and how part of me finds this difficult to understand, given that she wanted to before. Tom said that he's always amazed by the ease with which people make that decision, to create life, and that he finds life almost unbearable even when it's bearable and that sometimes he regrets having forced another person into the world.

You wouldn't want Andreas not to exist, though, I said pedantically, and he said that if Andreas says he wants not to exist, wouldn't loving him involve not wanting him to either?

But if he died, you wouldn't want to be alive yourself, I said, turning to look at him as we walked across the sand. He shook his head.

We stopped and looked out at the water, leaning into each other. Feeling supported by his body, I wondered what it would be like to get back to London and not have him beside me. I felt vulnerable because I felt so protected by his presence and knew that I couldn't continue to feel like that. I reached under his coat to find his jumper and then pulled it up to put my hand on his skin, pinching him, finding it hard to live with my need. I saw, more fully than I have before, that Maggie and Cleo will always be fragile and that this will always be almost impossible to bear. Now when Maggie cries it's because she feels entitled to the well-fed, well-rested, well-loved norm of her days. Gradually she'll discover that those expectations are unreasonable, that you can't count on life being pleasant. And then she will become more vulnerable rather than less, she'll start having nightmares like Cleo does, and soon she'll be exposed to more danger and more pain. I felt as though I'd never be able to rest unthinkingly again because there are people alive whose deaths I would never recover from, whose bodily presence I rely on to feel at ease. I felt sorry for Tom, because he hadn't chosen to impregnate Carla, sorry for Chris, because he'd changed his mind about wanting to impregnate me, and yet they have all this fear of pain to endure. I couldn't think about it any more without screaming. I changed the subject and we went in search of fish and chips.

Then that night, as we were going to bed, there was a message from Chris saying that Maggie was worse again and that Cleo was now ill too, and I wondered what I was doing there, and thought about driving back to London straight away. I cried and Tom comforted me, his T-shirt wet with my tears. I couldn't bear it, I said, the sense of fragility, the sense that everyone around me is broken, that I have brought children into the world who are so intolerably delicate, that Kay who loves her children is too unstable to be with them, that Tom half wishes that neither he nor his son existed. We walk through the valley of the shadow of death, he said, but that's where the action is, that's where life matters, we comfort each other along the way.

It seemed so late in life for me to confront that as a possibility. I said that I still live as though goodness and effort are rewarded, even though the books I most admire tell us otherwise, tell us that collapse and failure and disintegration are waiting to engulf us. I said that there was a brief moment, when Maggie was implanted, when I was able to resign myself to chance, knowing that we have no control over our lives, but that I'd stopped living like that, I'd made decisions as though I did have control, and now it was clear that I didn't. Vince could turn out to be abusive, my career could implode, Andreas could be wilfully self-destructive, Maggie and Cleo could get ill, Kay could give up on everything. Tom said that sometimes effort is rewarded, that love begets more love, with my children and with him. I went to sleep feeling excruciatingly vulnerable, painfully conscious of my love for Tom and for my daughters, and thinking that the most honest way to live would be to remain on that precipice as Tom does and to find a way to make it liveable, but that I didn't think I had the courage to do it.

Priss

November

They take their glasses of champagne and sit opposite each other at one of the little tables. Priss wonders if it's a mistake to think that their marriage is going to be repaired at a small plastic table in a sweaty bar, facing each other without touching. The increased eye contact that's part of the allure of going out for a drink with your lover can feel more like surveillance than intimacy in the wrong circumstances. Now, looking determinedly into his eyes as they clink glasses, she feels that her husband is a stranger. She checks her watch, hoping that they can go outside soon and skate, but they have an hour in here first. This, indeed, is the point of the expedition. He thought they needed time to talk.

There have been moments over the past fortnight where she's felt that her mind is enmeshed in his in a way she's rarely experienced before. Arriving back on Wednesday night after being with Hugh, she felt Ben's pain clamouring for attention. At first she tried resisting his efforts to initiate sex but then she succumbed, thinking that perhaps he was right that she owed him this. It may have been the most intense sex they've ever had. She didn't think she had it in her, physically, to come again, after the hours with Hugh. But once Ben began touching her, she found that she was still receptive, as though a switch in her body had been turned on and Ben's touch could be a continuation of Hugh's. For the first time, she wanted her husband to be violent in his thrusts, wanting even to be hurt, and he may have sensed this, or may just have been too angry to care what she wanted, because he pushed inside her with an aggression he'd never used before. She cried as she came, shocked by the scale of her own pleasure and by the feeling of her body being turned inside out. And afterwards Ben cried too, and when he said that he didn't deserve what was happening to him she was far enough inside his mind to think that he might be right, though logically she still thought that this was precisely what he did deserve.

Either way, something has to shift. Hugh has started to say that he isn't always going to be there as a toy for her, so soon she'll have to choose between the two men. They all know that she's not going to leave Ben, however much she's forgotten about her children over the past few weeks. So she wants to tell Ben now that she'll give up Hugh, and that she'll try as hard as she can to forgive him. But she wasn't prepared to confront him as a stranger like this. She's used to the quiet closeness of their life at home. This has been supplanted by the peculiar intensity of the past fortnight, which has made him alternate between lover and stranger. She's always suspected that their marriage is less intimate than other marriages, but if this is what real intimacy feels like then it's agonising.

She leans over to straighten the collar of his shirt, which has been ruffled by his coat. She feels him enjoying the action, liking the sense that she is proprietorial when it comes to his collar. Two of the bar seats by the window become free and Priss suggests that they should move there to watch the skating. It's a relief to be able to look out on to the colder world they will soon enter. She feels as though she is outside in the cleaner air, looking in at them. And then Ben takes her hand and she finds that he settles into familiarity again, his blue eyes and delicate nose and mouth losing their strangeness as they come into focus. They point out the good skaters and Ben loyally assures her that none of them are as good as she is, though it's been almost a decade since they last skated together – they have never taken Robert.

They talk about the last time they were here, in the skating café at Somerset House, about to go on the ice, and agree that it must be exactly ten years ago. They reminisce about the flat they lived in then, in Islington, with the roof terrace where they used to drink hot chocolate on winter evenings like this one and to sleep outside in the summer. Priss thinks, hopefully, that perhaps this is all Ben wanted, to reminisce, that he might not want to have a conversation about their problems after all.

Then suddenly there are only fifteen minutes left and he is suggesting they should go outside. She thinks that she must say something, must say the thing she has come here to say.

I know that we can't carry on like this, she says hurriedly. I'll give up Hugh and I want you to promise not to do it again.

Not to have affairs? he asks.

But she doesn't mean that. However unacceptable she'd look now to her younger self, she's come to see that she can't expect a lifetime of fidelity. Her expectations need to be lower than they were, or higher.

You lied to me Ben, she says, as she's said every day for

three weeks. The words mean less and less the more she repeats them but now she sees herself stabbing him with them up and down his chest, wanting to find a way to hurt him with the pain he's inflicted.

I promise not to lie to you again, he says. But I want to know. Do you want me more than you want Hugh? Or is it only because of the children that you're not leaving me?

Of course I want you more, she says, surprised that he's asked.

She stands up and they walk outside. She puts her white Russian hat back on, straightening her back, enjoying feeling regal as they survey the ice they're about to enter. After the hairdryer-like heat of the bar she is glad to feel cold. As they walk around the edge of the rink, he asks her if anyone has heard from Kay. He says that he still doesn't understand it. If she needed time off, why didn't she just go away normally, why this disappearance, leaving everyone to pick up the pieces? He's heard that Harald is worried she's becoming an alcoholic.

Priss thinks that it's a reason not to be part of a group of friends, these overheard voices and our willingness to believe them.

You've never needed to run away, she says, walking more quickly in her impatience. You don't know what it's like, the endlessness of everyone depending on you to be responsible. Kay works hard, but she still does more than half the tasks at home. It's not just the time spent with children, it's the constant thinking about their needs before your own that gets exhausting, feeling that your mind is never at rest.

She almost cries as she says this, and she realises how much she's wanted to point this out, over the past six years, how much she has resented his mental life continuing as it was before, while there's been almost no room for her in her own mind.

She wants suddenly to go home and have sex and stop thinking. She does not like this feeling of disliking her husband. But they move towards the queue for skates and soon they are laboriously lacing up the heavy steel shoes and then lurching clumsily as they walk towards the rink. She leans into him, worried that if the skates feel this alien she will no longer be able to do it. But then they slide on to the ice and she is instantly exultant, delighted to rediscover the peculiar freedom that comes from being able to glide at will. At first, she and Ben skate slowly together, holding hands, but then, without warning, she lets go and glides off, powering herself fast across the middle of the rink, laughing as she performs a figure of eight. After so long away from the ice it's as though she's gaining this power for the first time, and she smiles as she circles a man her age carefully observing his own feet as he tries not to fall. This, more than her home, more than her café, is the territory she has been given to rule.

Eventually, she returns to the area where they came in, and finds Ben there, practising against the side.

I've forgotten how to do it, he says, his body tense with irritation, but they both know that he was never any better than this — it was just that in the old days she made sure to keep hold of his hand.

I love it, she says. I love being here. I can't believe we haven't come for so long.

Go, he says smiling. Go as fast as you want. I'll be waiting for you.

They skate slowly along together again, holding hands, and she's glad to have time with him without needing to talk. It was the right thing to do, coming here, though it felt dangerous to try to recapture their past. Their grey woolly coats are well paired, and she thinks that they must look like a distinguished grown-up couple to anyone watching. People wouldn't be able to guess that they are in such a peculiar phase of their marriage. Then she skates away, depositing him carefully at the side of the rink, promising to come back quickly.

What an odd skill to have, she thinks as she speeds off, one that she uses so rarely. She only went skating once at university, she and Ben have only been a handful of times. All those hours at the rink in Sheffield, watched over loyally by her mother, the silly outfits, the trophies. Skating and horse riding. She should have developed a talent that would be more conducive to success in adult life.

A little shy to be showing off, she tries out the beginning of one of her teenage routines, lifting a leg at a time in the air, finding it strange to be doing this in jeans. She is aware of admiring glances, and sees two men pausing to point at her. She looks round for Ben to see if he's watching but the ice has become more crowded near the entrance and she can't see him. As she skates over she sees a crowd gathered in a tight circle and some fluorescent-jacketed staff appearing. She joins the circle, thinking that she might be able to help. It's only once she's right up against the crowd that she sees who it is.

That's my husband, she calls, finding the word 'husband' surprising after her lone turn on the ice.

Priss, he says, holding up his hand, and she goes over to kneel beside him, more self-conscious now about her ease on skates, as though she's been caught showing off when she should have been focused on him.

He says that he can't move and that it's his back that hurts. The onsite medic appears from wherever he's been lurking, and instructs the staff to carry him off the ice. Priss follows slowly, awkward again in her skates, not wanting to risk hurrying. They lie Ben in a small room next to the shoe hire where he shouts in pain, insisting that he can't move. While they summon an ambulance, Priss collects their shoes, phoning her mother to ask her to take over from the babysitter as she does so. Almost immediately, they are settled in an ambulance, Priss self-conscious in her Russian hat with a large male shoe in each hand. She puts them down so they can hold hands and Ben's grip is stronger than she expects. She feels repentant now for not holding his hand all the time on the ice.

Ben is becoming calmer. He tells her that he was proud, watching her skate, and thought he was up to skating over to find her but someone banged into him along the way. He looks exhausted, his face grey and oddly featureless in the yellow light. Priss suddenly has a sense of them as old. It feels foolish to want to be admired or to worry too much about who has had sex with whom when soon this will be the reality of their lives, two frail bodies supporting each other as best they can. It's the first time she's been in a vehicle with the siren on and she thinks how much Robert would enjoy it. She tells herself that the worst that can have occurred is that he's broken something that will mend. She realises that she's spent the week since Kay left fearing that something terrible is going to happen and that there's a kind of relief in thinking that this may be it, and now they can set about recovering.

They're going to St Thomas's Hospital and Priss wonders about texting Polly but doesn't want to disturb her if she's at work. When they arrive at A & E, there's a group of about ten people, mainly women, heavily made up and dressed as though for a summer evening. They're talking loudly and everyone else in the room is watching them. It's unclear what they're all there for; perhaps they're waiting for someone. Priss watches Ben lying back, watching the women. She thinks about Hugh, and how when she's with him she knows that he doesn't take in the presence of any women except her, and she thinks it's odd that he doesn't know that she's here.

The nurse takes them to a cubicle for their assessment. Together they help Ben get into a gown to be examined, turning him around on his trolley. Priss finds it hard to subdue her movements so soon after the skating. She wonders if the nurse finds her too flushed or energetic or just too full of her own personhood in a place where you are meant to be as quietly selfless as possible.

Pushed and kneaded by the nurse, Ben admits that he might be able to move a bit. Priss suppresses irritation with him for wasting the hospital's time and making her so worried. The nurse pronounces him more likely to be bruised than broken and books him for an X-ray. They go back to the waiting room, where the dressed-up women are now gathered around a man who's just emerged, his face bloody and bandaged. Priss watches the women touching him, asking how he is, and imagines what it would be like if all of us were here, me and Kay and Helena and Polly, doing the same with Ben. She finds that she likes the thought and thinks that perhaps she wouldn't mind us all having sex with him as much as she's minded just me doing it, remembering suddenly that reckless offer she made to Polly, to have his babies. She turns, laughing, to tell him this thought, planning to ask if she should text Polly and tell her to come and find them after all. But he's fallen asleep with his mouth slightly open.

She shuts her eyes too, in the chair next to him, and when she opens them the room is almost empty and seems darker. She wonders if they've lowered the lights on their behalf. Ben's eyes are open and she leans down to kiss him on the mouth. He responds urgently, with his tongue.

I'm in so much pain Priss, he says, and they both laugh.

Maybe life can glisten like this even in ordinary marriage, maybe they don't need the excitement of the past weeks to make it do so. He holds her close, bent over him, and his pain seems to be a force flowing through both of them, warming their blood, making them glow.

Kay

November

Every morning after breakfast, Kay walks over the cliffs to St Ives. Today she has taken her usual walk across the fields, which lasts three hours. Occasionally, she goes for the five-hour walk along the coastal path. It's years since she's walked rapidly like this, her feet in a self-perpetuating rhythm that seems to have nothing to do with her mind, the mud oozing as she presses it down. She's bought hiking boots, which help with the sharp lurches, but there are moments on the rockier bits of the coastal path where she feels as though she's about to lose her balance again and dive into the sea that still seems to summon her down towards it, its roar a kind of siren song. If it was summer she might have swum, as a way of offering her body to the water while knowing that she can take it away again, enjoying the normality of an everyday holiday act. But there's no temptation to swim in this squally cold, so the contact with the water must remain a fantasy, more alluring by the day.

In St Ives each morning, she buys food for the rest of the day and brings it home on the bus. She then goes to bed again, until it's dark, partly because she finds the long evenings easier to dispose of than the days, though she doesn't go out at night either. She regrets arriving in the pub in the way she did that first night. She'd like to go back but feels that the people there would claim an intimacy with her that she wouldn't be able to bear, partly because she wants it so much. She imagines Sheila, lightly touching the scab that has now begun to form on her face, asking about her writing, and it frightens her. So she stays home, drinking the glass of whisky she's allocated to herself each evening as a kind of medicine.

She hasn't spoken to the children in the week she's been here, which feels like longer to her, so may do to them as well. There's a hole in her heart where her love for her children has been plucked out, ruthlessly, and put under the bed in one of the rooms she doesn't sleep in, for safekeeping. She hasn't spoken to anyone else either, just sending one text message each evening to Harald, telling him that she's fine and will come home soon. She scrolls through all the messages on her phone rapidly, not wanting to take them in. She knows that eventually she could be here long enough that everyone's lives will cover over, eliminating the gap she has left in them, like the wound on her face which will eventually leave only a faint scar.

She doesn't think about very much, it's easy not to. Sometimes, walking along the path or around the house, she thinks about Harald. This begins with bodily need, experienced on the skin. If she lies down and touches herself at these moments, anywhere on her body, she feels the rest of her body tensing in expectation, as though unable to believe that she's there alone and that there can be no element of surprise. If she makes herself come it happens quickly, and the brief fantasy at the moment of orgasm is of Harald, gripping her hard with a counterbalancing force, like the pain she confronted with Sheila. Sometimes she wonders if she should try fantasising about Fred in the pub instead. Her memories of their brief exchange are erotically charged, perhaps because of her wondering admiration of Sheila's physicality and the curiosity it brought. But this doesn't translate into arousal and so she's drawn back to images of the husband she has abandoned and who she assumes has long since stopped fantasising about her.

After one brief, jerky orgasm that seems to make no difference to her body's restlessness, she wonders if she made a mistake in marrying Harald, and tries to imagine the other kinds of men she could have been with instead. She surveys the carousel of husbands, settling on Chris and Ben. They have less appeal than Harald does: Ben is insufficiently masculine, Chris too normal in his sportiness, his practicality. The appeal of Harald remains his definiteness. By being so wholly himself he removes the need for her to have a visible personality and gives her the freedom to live privately the inner life that she then despises him for being unable to imagine. But these thoughts don't interrupt the peace for long. She can always look out to sea and empty her mind again. She is surprised now that she enjoyed going to see Moser, because all the noise of talking to him feels like it's part of what made her life in those months so hard to bear.

Just before she instructs herself to go to bed, during the hour after midnight when thoughts are most likely to start churning in her mind, she often relaxes by hoovering the house. She does it slowly, methodically, like mowing the lawn, tracing straight lines up and down the carpeted empty rooms. She envies Ana her job and her commitment to it now, with an envy that means she can no longer think of them as secret conspirators. She's ignored Ana's text messages, her angry questions about whether Kay is coming back, as well as everyone else's, though sometimes she hears them in her mind at night and replies to them mentally in Bulgarian.

Now she is in St Ives and she has almost finished shopping for the small selection of things she plans to eat today. The woman at the checkout recognises her and asks if she's on holiday.

Are you on your own? she asks next, looking at Kay's deluxe one-person cottage pie and single courgette.

She says it kindly – she is the right age to be Kay's mother – but it disturbs Kay to have to answer yes. She wants to say that there is a couple and a family she could be in if she wanted to, and that she has chosen this peculiar situation as she has chosen her uninspiring dinner. She avoids eye contact as she flashes her bank card at the machine and turns to leave. The bus back to Zennor comes swiftly and then, just as it's about to go, Sheila rushes on with her dogs, breathless from running, happy. She spots Kay and comes to sit across the aisle, the dogs wandering between them.

I almost missed it, she says, and Kay wishes that she had, but she's also pleased to see her. Sheila looks closely at her face, with professional interest, and says that it's healing well and the scar won't be too large. She talks about her car, which is being repaired, and Fred and the pub. There is live music again tonight. Kay had forgotten that it's Tuesday again and thinks briefly of the day she'd be having in London, at school and with Moser. Sheila asks if she'll come along and she says no, she has work to do.

On your novel?

Yes, she is working on a novel, she's in a crucial part of it now, she has to be alone with it. Sheila has picked up on her changed tone and she seems relieved that she can put it down to this.

I'm sorry, you were thinking, I interrupted you, that's like me, I talk too much, Fred says it too, you need to be alone with your thoughts.

Kay doesn't reply and they spend the rest of the journey in silence, but this is no longer the silence of oblivion, because Kay finds that the person in her who wishes to please has been reawakened and that this makes her dislike Sheila for disturbing her. At the same time, she admires her, responding again to the energy and physical ease, and she feels angry with Fred for telling Sheila that she talks too much, wanting to find a way to contradict him. She decides that she will say goodbye, as warmly as she can, at the end of the journey, in the hope that these thoughts won't continue too insistently once she's home. She practises it inside her head. Goodbye. Goodbye. Goodbye. She wonders if she can then have her glass of whisky when she gets back, instead of in the evening, or if today she can allow herself to have two.

It comes out naturally. Goodbye. She smiles, not the false smile she has prepared but the diffident smile from the previous meeting. Sheila seems reassured by it, and turns away easily towards her afternoon of talk and chores, urging her to come to the pub later. Kay goes back to her house feeling depleted by the encounter with her own warmth, reminding her that there's a life other than the one she's living now. Something needs to change in the rhythm of the day so she gets out the hoover and works her way across the sitting room, moving out towards the sea and then back again, wondering if the hoover would be strong enough to crash through the glass of the window, taking her outward, over the cliff. The sea itself needs cleaning in its grey dullness; it's peculiar that water can look so dirty. For once, she doesn't want to sleep, she remains too energised by speech and by her reawakened curiosity about Sheila, about what it feels like to be her and to proceed through the day with such energy and such certainty that her energy is required by the world.

When she arrives in the pub, not sure until she actually approaches the front door that she's definitely going there, the music has already started and there are more people than last week so all the tables are taken. She thinks about retreating but she's been spotted and two men make space for her at the bar, ushering her to a stool. She smiles at them and watches the music carefully, hoping to suggest that this is why she's here. Sheila is sitting by the violinists, stamping her feet in time to the music, her whole body alert to it as though she's conducting lightning, and she waves at Kay but doesn't come over to join her. Kay's had a whisky at home so she orders another one and then thinks that it's a mistake because she sips quickly when nervous so it's swiftly gone. She moves on to red wine, worrying that it will look like an odd combination of drinks. Fred arrives behind the bar from the back of the pub and says hello to her, more warmly than last time, wearing a soft black jumper that she would like to stroke.

How are you? he asks.

I'm well, she says. I've been walking every day to St Ives when I'm not writing. I love the coastal path.

He seems as surprised by her speech as she is and looks at her more intently as he agrees on the pleasantness of the coastline. She gives him a look of mock helplessness, as though to say that this is the best she can do at small talk and she should be rewarded for trying. He nods, as though in acknowledgement of this, and she wonders if they are flirting.

Sheila comes over during the musicians' break and kisses her on both cheeks, her lips on the scab a shock that makes her realise this is what it will feel like now, to be kissed. She says that she's pleased she's there and asks if she's enjoying it. All this announcing of mutual pleasure is becoming tiring. The men beside her at the bar know Sheila and she introduces them as Phil and Dan, both heavy grey men in their fifties. They ask Kay where she's from.

We're fed up with Londoners down here, Sheila says, but you don't count, you're a local now with us, so we won't give you any grief.

Kay thinks that she has enough grief of her own, though she doesn't know what she is grieving for. The men are farmers and she asks how the year has been.

We've had a bad harvest, Phil says. After the hot summer.

It must have been lovely here, though, in the sun, she says, and then she regrets saying something so frivolous, as both men shake their heads.

Not if you were working, Fred says from behind the bar, and she says of course not, finding it tiring to have to keep guessing the right thing to say and hoping that the music will start again soon. Sheila goes back to the musicians.

The only thing that Kay knows about the Cornish farmers is that they have voted, en masse, for Brexit, if the reports are to be believed. She is curious about how they feel about it now, and also feels an urge towards antagonism swelling within her, partly because she's tired of sustaining the friendliness tonight's encounters require.

What about Brexit? she asks. Are you worried about what will happen then?

Fred looks at her and rolls his eyes in disbelief at what she is getting herself into, and she regrets severing their connection. He goes back into the room behind the bar. It's Dan who takes her on now, who tells her they are not racist, they want foreign workers, but if she thinks they can't survive without handouts from the EU then she's wrong. She didn't mean that, she says, not sure what exactly she did mean. She asks for another glass of wine, wondering if three drinks will strike them as unwomanly.

It would be easy now, she knows how to do it, to say something silly and charming and to bring the conversation back into a safer realm. They'd talk about Cornwall, they'd talk about the music, and then retreat again into silence. But she is overcome with the need to convince them that hers is the only possible logical position.

Perhaps your farms can survive, she says. But can you? What will you do when the NHS collapses because there are no doctors? What will you do when you go to hospital and they don't have the drugs that you need?

There is no conviviality now between her and the men. She wishes that Sheila or Fred would return, she wishes that she was back in her cottage, facing the empty evening, and for the first time she wishes that she was back in London negotiating the small differences of her friends. Unexpectedly, Dan touches the right-hand side of her face where her scab is, his touch somewhere between aggression and care.

Who did this to you? he says. Did you go to hospital?

Phil says that Sheila helped her, he was here when it happened. Kay is surprised it looks like an injury given to her by someone else and pictures a rock hurled at her face, frightened now.

I fell over, she says, and he laughs, his hand still on her cheek. She wonders about removing it but she doesn't want to touch him. She avoids his eyes and looks across at Phil, who's looking down.

You want to watch yourself Kay, Dan says, pressing hard enough that it hurts. You don't want it to happen again. A woman on your own in that white cottage.

She looks from one to the other.

Don't worry, you're safe among people like us, Phil says, nodding at Dan.

He releases his hand and she wants to leave, but to walk straight out of the pub would be to show her fear and there's nowhere else that she can go. The music starts and she catches Sheila's eye as she leaps up in excitement and beckons to her to come over. Kay goes towards her, thinking that this will be a chance to say goodbye. The music is a fast reel now and Sheila is dancing a kind of jig, kicking her feet into the air. When Kay approaches she takes her hand and puts an arm round her waist and dances her in a circle. Kay is surprised by the sudden movement into joining in, but she breaks off as soon as she can and says in Sheila's ear that she's tired, she has to go.

Walking home she berates herself for thinking that it could be easy, that she could just have an enjoyable evening at the pub like anyone else. It would have been hard enough without her scab, but with it she's too much a target for curiosity, and too visibly susceptible to harm. When she gets in, she double locks the door, angry that she can't erase Dan's words or his tone from her mind. She goes to bed, thinking that she will stay there later than usual the next day, grateful that her head spins as she lies down.

Helena

November

When she wakes up, the rhythm of rushing feet from her dream feels present in her bedroom. She'd been running, with her mother and a boy she knew in the dream to be her brother, over a flat plain of hard mud scattered with patches of grass. They were running as fast as they could and she'd taken the boy's hand to drag him along with her.

Waking after a dream, there's often a feeling of sadness, because she misses the strange freedom of the inward wandering. Now she wills herself back into the world of the dream. She pictures her mother, running without seeing where she's going, and realises that this is not her mother's face but her grandmother's. The eyes are wider spaced, more obviously foreign, the hair wilder, the nose bonier. So the brother she acquired there might be Vince. It's the first time she's dreamt herself a sibling and she's moved by the certainty of kinship she felt with that boy – the knowledge that he was hers to protect.

Her mouth feels dry after the sleep and her eyes are still willing themselves shut. It's seven o'clock, but it feels much later in the evening. She didn't mean to have such a long nap and is tempted just to brush her teeth and get back into bed. She lies stroking her stomach, hoping for a kick. My daughter, she thinks, and then she says it aloud. My daughter.

She went to bed because she was lonely. She doesn't want to go out any more, when she doesn't have to; she's too exhausted, too clumsy in her heaviness, and at her happiest she no longer feels much need of the world. But she knows she should still push herself into socialising. Even now, if she stays at home, she'll be depressed by nine o'clock. Her flat, with its growing cache of baby paraphernalia, feels oddly impersonal at the moment despite the definiteness of her taste; she depends more than usual on other people to locate her. She runs through the people she could see in her mind. Clare is at home but working, she saw Aaron two days ago, her parents yesterday. She does not feel like seeing her work friends at this point in pregnancy when work has ceased to interest her, and the axis of adultery has made all members of the group except Polly unappealing. This is the least close she's felt to Priss in years, which makes her realise how sheltered she was by the knowledge that she had a best friend, even when they didn't see each other that often. Over the last few weeks, the sympathy for Priss that followed the revelation of Ben's affair has been replaced by what feels like physical disgust at Priss's affair with Hugh. It seems so determinedly self-destructive, so vain, all the more so because Helena can't at the moment imagine voluntarily undressing in front of anyone.

Last night, at three in the morning, Helena woke up to Clare pulling her grey nightie up and stroking her way up her thighs. When Helena transferred Clare's hand to her stomach, wanting it there on the bump instead, Clare moved away silently and turned her back, leaving Helena feeling horribly alone but still unable to contemplate sex, even if it had become the only way for their bodies to lose the estrangement she hated.

She looks at the yoga timetable on her phone, and finds an eight o'clock class that she thinks would be gentle enough for her to go to. She started doing yoga years ago, long before it became fashionable and all her friends started doing it too. This is the longest – two months – that she's ever not been. She hasn't minded feeling hunched, hasn't minded the sense that her body is becoming an incubator for her child, and that it's out of the question now for her to believe herself to be attractive during sex. But she has to find something to do in the evenings and that calm grey studio bedecked with indoor foliage is the only place she can think of going alone this evening.

The dream has made her miss her grandmother. She pictures herself in the double bed they used to share when she went to stay in her tiny flat in King's Cross, lying next to the older woman in one of the lace nighties she used to lend her. If her grandmother was alive now, Helena would summon her over and submit to the interfering bustle as the older woman reorganised the kitchen and the baby's room, accepting the wisdom of experience, of survival. She wonders what her grandmother would have made of Vince's situation and imagines the shrug with which she'd have dismissed both Vince and his accusers. She found the younger generations naive for expecting people to be better than they are.

For the ten years before her grandmother's death, it was only Helena who saw her regularly, Helena to whom she talked, in the final year, about the war. Neither Helena's mother nor Vince could cope any longer with the intrusive commentaries on their lives, and Vince was angry about childhood slights that Helena has never been particularly curious about. Helena knows that their childhood was harder than hers was, that her grandmother's standards were more arbitrary, more cruelly inflicted. But in that decade when she was the only point of contact between the generations she thought that they should take it less personally.

She wonders where they were, on that hard, dry mud. It feels like her grandmother's childhood that she was witnessing there, in Lithuania, rather than anything from her mother's childhood in London. She wonders about going to see her mother, so they can talk about her grandmother. There would be a pleasure in summoning the dead woman and the unborn baby as imagined presences in the room, celebrating the strength of the matriarchal line. But Helena and her mother have never found a way to reconcile their very different feelings about the dead woman, so they wouldn't be able to talk easily about her. Also she doesn't want to rely on her parents too much. She needs to form her own family now, not to allow her daughter to become an extra child in theirs, so it feels more sensible at this point to depend on her friends.

The minutes pass without a decision and she starts to feel that she is close to falling back asleep. Noticing this reawakens her, and she finds that she is crying, wishing that she could call Clare and suggest meeting, wishing that they lived with the assumption that any time they were both free would be spent together, while knowing that if she were Clare's age, and not pregnant, this is not how she would want to live.

Abruptly, she gets up and changes her clothes, apparently on her way to yoga. She puts on her new maternity coat, bought for her by Vince last week. A couple of days after their shopping trip, her mother told her that there had been two new allegations, claiming he was violent during sex, so

Helena no longer knows whether she's right to enjoy the soft grey wool with which he chose to clothe his niece and her unborn daughter. Helena's mother said last night that she's planning to have a talk with him, making it clear that they can't continue to sympathise with him unless he gives them some account of it. And if he doesn't? Will Helena ceremoniously return her coat?

He told her, when they met for their shopping trip, that Esther had been pregnant once, and that she had lost the baby and was told not to try to conceive again. That phrase, Helena thought when he said it, losing a baby, as though you might just have put it down somewhere and forgotten about it, as though there remains a chance you might find it again. Vince said that they didn't tell Helena's parents at the time because they didn't want them to feel sorry for them, or to have to hide their own happiness in procreation. Also, he said, Esther feared that there was an unwomanliness in being infertile. This news surprised Helena because she'd always assumed, as her parents had, that Vince and Esther chose not to have children. They were too committed to work, to each other, to leading an experimental modern life. It disappointed but also relieved her that they should have turned out to be like everyone else. But it's yet another secret revealed. She is fearful that there will be more and that she is becoming too tired and too stiffly inflexible to respond to them.

On the walk to the studio, she eats a packet of crisps, enjoying feeling awakened by the salty crunchiness as she breaks them up in her mouth. This is the first noise she has made for a while; it's louder than her trainers on the pavement. She stretches her arms back and rotates her neck forwards and backwards, preparing to stretch. There's a kind of brightness in the darkness, the stars visible in the clear sky.

When she arrives, she is shyly pleased by the fuss made of her by the yoga teacher and the women she recognises without knowing their names. They are glad that she's returned, that by her presence she is affirming that they're right to think these hours spent defying stiffness and gravity matter, because she still needs this even as she moves into a new life.

She lies on her side with her hand on her bump, thinking that for the first time today she feels she is in the right place, even though she's unsure that she'll be able to do more than listen to her breathing and roll her knees from side to side. As she rolls, she feels the baby kick, and she wonders if she's right to think that she will be less lonely when her daughter is born, and if it's naive to love an unborn creature this much. Other women talk about taking a long time to bond with their babies, but she feels she has bonded already. She has never felt that anything is so wholly hers. Though she wouldn't say it aloud, she believes that her daughter belongs to her already more than she can ever belong to Aaron, more than she and Clare can ever belong to each other, more than she feels that Lena and Robert belong right now to Priss, who Helena blames for gambling their future happiness so carelessly, even if the happiness of life in the nuclear family is something that Helena hopes her own daughter can live without.

She pulls her knees up, feeling her thighs squish against the bump, thinking about her grandmother's pregnancies in 1950s London, living alongside a husband who had little interest either in her or the unborn children, if the reports she gave Helena fifty years later are to be believed. Her grandmother was no less lonely than Helena is despite her more peopled household. Possibly she was more so, feeling the ambitious working life she'd imagined for herself in Lithuania slip away, delegating to her two children the burden of providing her with a place in the world, and then watching them do so with such aplomb that it took them away from her, leaving her lonely again.

They are rolling on to all fours now, and Helena likes the sense of the weight in her stomach pulling her down as she tries flexing the abdominal muscles she has not used for weeks. She arches her back in time with everyone else, enjoying the familiarity of an action that feels more right and less arbitrary than any of the actions she might perform during sex. She hopes that in a few months she'll give birth in this position and she pictures herself doing so now, breathing as deeply as she can to help her daughter fight her way into the world. This is all she can offer her, she thinks, a body rooted in the earth by its limbs, ready to fight alongside her.

Stella

November

I am shattered, having just got back from two days away, spent mainly on the train. Harald begged me to go. Helena didn't want to travel, Priss couldn't leave the café, Polly was busy at the hospital. He offered to have Maggie overnight, which was thoughtful enough to play a part in persuading me, though in fact Maggie stayed with Chris and he sent me proud messages while I was away, reporting on her progress with crawling. I think that he's happier than he was a few months ago, less shocked by the gulf between the life he's living and the life he set out to have. He's started looking me in the eye again when we meet.

It had been years since I took that train, close against the sea, and it brought more of a holiday feeling than I'd expected, edged with apprehensiveness because it's a part of the world I associate with marital holidays. While I was on the train, I edited half a dystopian novel, providing marginal comments on someone else's vision of apocalyptic doom, booked a room at the pub, and texted Kay to say that I was on my way and would be with her by five. It was strange to picture us having an evening on our own, away from all our children, by the sea. Anticipating it, I wasn't sure if I disliked her or not, or how we'd broach the question of her betrayal, or whether I'm right to be angry about it given that my betrayal of Priss was much greater. She didn't reply.

I took a taxi, enjoying the way the landscape became wilder and more remote as we approached Zennor and then the sea came into view, brilliant, rough indigo against the reddish purple and green of the gorse on the cliffs in the evening sunlight. I found that I recognised the pub and its garden from a day we'd spent there years ago, when Cleo was the age that Maggie is now. I left my bag in my room, pleased with the view of the cliffs. And then I walked to Kay's house, grateful for the torch which they'd given me at the pub, wondering what it would be like to be there alone for two weeks, as she's been now, thinking that it must feel like two months or two years.

When I got there I saw her in the sitting room upstairs, silhouetted against the window. I didn't know if she'd have got my message, but she wasn't surprised to see me. I was struck by her scab, which she told me about matter-of-factly on our way upstairs, and by her hair, which seemed greyer than usual, scraped back into a bun. I wondered what we'll look like in old age: will we all have buns by then, or cropped hair, will we still wear the same clothes, continuing with the taste we developed in youth rather than adapting to what old ladies are expected to wear? She opened the bottle of wine I'd brought, saying that we'd have a drink, and then go back to the pub for dinner. And we sat down on the pale-blue holiday-cottage sofa. She asked straight away if Harald had asked me to come. I said he had but I'd wanted to as well, I'd been worried about her and I liked Cornwall. A Cornish mini break? she asked caustically. But in a way it was.

I pulled my legs up and sat cross-legged, facing her across the sofa, which made us both more intimate and more adversarial. I looked beyond the bun and the scar now and saw that she looked well, her body springier than usual, her skin clear. She asked – concentrating in a way that made me feel these are not the thoughts that occupy her days and that she was reluctant to summon images of her London life – how Priss had been. I said that I hadn't seen her, we'd both been avoiding each other, but I'd heard from Polly that things had moved on and she and Hugh were now sleeping together. Kay hadn't known this, so there was the satisfaction of bringing interesting news. She raised her eyes in mockery of someone but I wasn't sure if it was me or her or Priss. We both agreed that we'd underestimated Priss; we hadn't thought she had it in her to have an affair herself. She asked how Ben's taking it and I said that I'd heard from Polly that he's humiliated by the public cuckolding and he's more angry than you might expect. We both laughed and then I started resenting her again, needing more of an acknowledgement of what she'd done. So I asked why she had told Priss about me.

You've never been reckless, she said, standing up and walking over to the window, as though in a scene in a play. You talk about being free but you've never known what it's like to walk right up to the kerb and want to stride out into the traffic. Or to lie with your head over the edge of a cliff, longing to fall. The kind of desperate boredom that brings the need to court disaster. You think that everyone is always emotionally lucid. We're not. I'm not. Priss isn't. She's known, anyway, in the same way we all have.

Do you think I'm a terrible friend? I asked, thinking that she was right, I criticise her for expecting other people to think as she does, but I do the same thing.

Not really, she said, sitting down again. She asked if I thought she was a terrible friend.

Yes, I said, but then I smiled and asked what she'd been doing there.

Hardly anything, she said. I walk, I shop, I eat. Mainly I sleep. The days feel the right length. Not too long. I can't imagine now how I used to do all the different things I did in a day.

I asked if she thought she'd be able to do them again and we had another version of the same conversation we always have, about whether we have chosen our lives. She said that she couldn't imagine that anyone, offered the choice, would choose her London life instead of her Cornish life. Why would anyone choose a life with too much in it instead of a life where we can do nothing? I repeated the words she'd once said to me, about how if you don't have children and nothing changes, you could end up feeling that you aren't really living. And then I asked if she missed Seb and Alisa.

Not really, she said again. Before when I've left Alisa, never for more than a night at a time, I've missed her horribly. Even Seb, I never stopped missing him, though he was getting bigger. But this time, it's like they don't exist. And if they do exist, they're in a busy world, their own world, which has nothing to do with me, busy with their routines, their connections. Alisa's about to stop being a baby. It might be better that she doesn't have me, holding her back in it because I'm worried that I'll stop loving her when she grows bigger. Do you miss yours?

I said that I don't miss Cleo any more, when she's away for a night, because I'm so used to her being with Chris. But I miss Maggie like a kind of missing limb, in a way I'd only ever felt with men before. I never sleep as well when she's not there.

I'm glad that you've finally allowed yourself to think of yourself as a good mother, she said. You know, you're kinder and more vulnerable than you think of yourself as being. That's rare.

It touched me, her saying that, partly because it's true of her as well but I was suddenly too shy to tell her that.

Then she asked if I'd missed Ben like I miss Maggie, and I said yes because I felt like this was the moment to say something honest about Ben. She asked if I'd felt guilty about Priss at the time and I said that I hadn't, perhaps because the point about the kind of desire you feel when you're falling in love is that it's so self-righteous, you think you're feeling more intensely than anyone else and therefore are subject to different laws.

I was looking at the dark window as I said it, the sea's invisibility made more peculiar by its noise, like a cat purring in the dark. I wondered how much calmer I'd be if I spent two weeks as close to the sea as she is, wondering if it's as crazy to attribute spiritual power to a large, energetic expanse of water as it is to read our fates in the stars, and wondering if I'll admit to anyone that I looked up my and Tom's astrological compatibility on a website and found that everything it said about us was true.

It's funny, she said. We're all friends, but it's funny how little we know each other.

I looked at her scab, thinking that it must feel rougher than it looks and that we'll still talk about her scar years later, remembering our evening by the sea.

I've been thinking that too, I said. We don't know each other, and we like each other less when we feel known ourselves. It's too exposing.

We've all turned out to be worse than the others thought we were, she said. Even Priss.

I know. What will we do next?

Have you ever stolen anything? she asked.

I said that I'd stolen things occasionally in supermarkets when I couldn't be bothered to queue and that I'd enjoyed experiencing myself as someone capable of breaking the law. She said that she used to quite often in her twenties, trying to work out if she had a moral system or not. This surprised me, because I think of her as being determinedly law-abiding.

I think about this kind of thing all the time, she said. In that darkness. It's made me think that the only way I can return to my life is if I accept that we're all terrible people most of the time. Cruel and selfish. All of us, our husbands, our children.

We both looked out to the indiscernible sea again. She poured us both a second glass of wine, which I didn't particularly want, and then took the bottle downstairs to the kitchen, rationing herself. When she came back, she asked, impulsively I think, if I'd missed her, and I found it endearing because it suggested she'd missed me. I said that I had missed talking to her, but I'd had lots of imaginary conversations with her in my mind. She said that she'd missed me since our rupture. She'd often thought that we should be closer friends than we are. That it was her who'd make a good close friend for me, now, from our group, more than Helena, though she knows I'd like it to be Helena, because I idealise her. I said that she was probably right but that I could see too much of my own coldness reflected in her. We both live too much in our minds and not enough in our bodies and I don't like the thought of us as two cold women, dissecting the people we know.

You assume that Priss doesn't think, and I don't feel, she said. We all think. We all feel.

I said that I'd felt closer to her since we both had our second babies.

But now I've left mine, she said.

I suddenly found the absence of our babies frightening. I was scared that we'd both get sucked into the darkness outside and never go back to them and I pined for home, picturing Maggie clutching her lion as she shook her head from side to side, going to sleep in her cot.

You'll go back to her, I said. It's good for Harald to have his turn. To really see what it's like, day after day, having to think of everything. I've found that side of it quite funny, watching his outrage. Like when Chris had Maggie for two nights in a row and told me it was exhausting, because you have to keep washing her bottles and clothes.

We laughed. As always, I found it depressing, the ease of bonding by laughing about the inadequacies of men, the ease with which we reach for a dismissive sneer. And since then I have found the thought of Alisa, waiting night after night for Kay to put her to bed, almost unbearable. Today I wondered about going round to do it myself, though I know I'd be no better for her than anyone else.

It was exciting entering the night air. I thought of Kay, climbing down on the first night, and felt tempted to try it out myself, wanting to compete with her or maybe just to be her. She told me about her conversation with Dan and Phil as we approached the pub, half regretting her suggestion we should go there. But there was no sign of them, and dinner was warm and jolly, with red meat and red wine. I couldn't really connect it to the pub I'd had lunch at with Chris and Cleo – this time it felt like somewhere to escape the sea rather than to be alongside it. She asked if I wanted to ask her when she was coming back and I said that of course I did. She said she'd come back when she'd been there a month, I could report that to Harald if I wanted to.

Are you planning to see Priss? she asked.

I don't know, I said. I'm not avoiding her any more. In some ways I want to get it done, our first meeting, and then we'll know if we're capable of becoming friends again. But no opportunities have come up and I don't want a one-on-one conversation, I don't want her to ask me questions about the affair.

I didn't ask if Kay wanted to meet again before I went home. It felt like enough. So this morning I went for a walk on my own, part of the same inland walk to St Ives she goes on every day, half familiar because we took Cleo along there in a sling. And then I turned back and came home. On the train I looked at photos from that Cornish holiday, finding that Cleo looked less like Maggie and more like herself now than I'd expected her to, and that the pictures of Chris carrying Cleo on his back made me envious of Kay, knowing that when she feels like it there's a marriage she can return to which would people these scenes, however exhausting we both find family holidays by the sea.

Looking at the pictures made me miss Chris smiling at me in the approachable, boyish way he smiled there. Even though I know that there was more resentment than affection by then, the photos were a reminder that there was affection, and that we were still open to enjoying each other's company in a way that feels impossible now. I felt sorry for him, because I can see again how much he had to offer a wife but that I was the wrong wife to choose, and neither of us could have known it at the time. I felt sorry for Cleo as well,

pictured grinning stickily in a high chair and waddling determinedly up and down on the beach, because she had no way
of knowing that she'd lose that contentment, that confidence
in herself as the only beloved child of two parents whose
almost constant presence she could take for granted. I was
struck again by how strange it is that she's become someone
who has private thoughts, and that I don't have access to her
in the way I did then and do now with Maggie. That's what
she minds when she worries that I love Maggie more, and
yet she insists, rightly, on her privacy.

I spent the final hour of the journey thinking about what
to do about Vince because Cliff had just emailed, saying that
he'd agreed with Helen, his absent partner, that we need to
make a statement and that it should be me who does it.

I tried to draft one but couldn't do it, and then the train
suddenly crowded with people getting on at Reading from
their separate journeys, ending the feeling of otherworldli-
ness that Cornwall had given me. I felt angry with Cliff, for
pushing the responsibility on to me, though I also know that
I'm the one who's chosen to stay and take Vince's job when
he leaves. I felt angry with Vince as well, for putting us in
this position in the first place with his uncontrollable appetites. On the Tube home I wondered what Kay would think,
wondering if she'd think it was inappropriate for me to be
the one to keep the company's name clean when my own
name is tarnished. And then I felt irritated with her for caring
about me and Ben so much. It happened, and now we are
different people from who we were then. The revelation
seems rather belated. What can it matter now, that we once
loved each other, that we once believed the world was turned
on its axis by the act of fucking? What's the point of judging
me now for who I was then? But that's precisely the argument

293

that lecherous men use, and I don't accept it there. I don't seem capable of understanding anything. There are moments when I envy Kay, looking out at the sea day after day, never dealing with insistently questioning children, never talking to Moser. I've understood why I like standing on one leg so much. You can't think about anything else while you're doing it.

Polly

November

Polly's sister has come to stay, wanting a week in London. They're sharing the double bed. Getting into it each night, Polly likes the smell of Ella's perfume on the neighbouring pillow, a familiar smell that's exotic in this setting. She feels embarrassed, discovering how easy it turns out to be to share a bed with her sister, when she seems incapable of sleeping next to a man. James said, when she mentioned it on the phone, that it was because she's never properly grown up, which feels unkind when she thinks about it now though it didn't at the time. Certainly Ella remains her closest friend, even now she's in her forties. It's because she was so close to Ella that she didn't look for a best friend at university, preferring to move more casually among our group, though this is occasionally a source of regret. Since the relationship with Sam ended she's wondered if that was what she was seeking in him: an unlikely best friend.

They're waiting for James at the Italian restaurant at the end of her road. It's empty, and Polly is conscious of the pink-and-white tablecloths, the black-and-white photographs of film stars on the walls, wondering what James will make of the place. He's coming to meet Ella, and Polly is excited about seeing him, though it will be odd, but perhaps interestingly so, not going to bed together at the end of the night. Helena will arrive in time for pudding. It feels suddenly like a lot of pressure, all these encounters that she's responsible for. But now James is here, leaning over to kiss Ella on the cheek and Polly on the mouth, ordering a bottle of wine from the menu that he's apparently already had a chance to study, talking to the waiters in exaggerated Italian. Ella is hungry, so Polly suggests they should order food straight away, and James asks for a steak, because he thinks it's silly to eat pasta in a restaurant. They sit back and take each other in and James says what an excellent place to come, what a great wine list.

Polly has a sense of their collective good health. Ella and James both have winter tans and she's proud to be able to present them to each other. James still seems, encountered like this, to be an unlikely piece of good fortune. It's appropriate that he should have ordered meat: there's something pleasantly meaty about his torso as he puts an arm around her now, she can imagine the flesh on the two sides of his chest as supple chunks of steak. His thick blue shirt brings the suggestion of James in a shop, comfortable choosing it, trying it on (a quick reckoning with blue eyes and curly blond hair in the mirror), saying that he'll take three of them, handing over the money without worry or regret. She admires qualities in him that she couldn't condone in herself: his worldliness, his confidence that he's fully himself, and therefore different from everyone else and that this brings its own privileges and rewards. He's an attractive grown-up man, affirmed by the world, who wants to make a large amount of space in his life for her. This may be the first time this has happened. Ella goes to the loo and he puts his arms around Polly to kiss her. I've missed you, he says, squeezing her tightly enough that it almost hurts, and she says it back, meaning it. She thinks of how many men she's said this to in her life, three even this year.

When their food comes, Ella asks James about his work in Gambia. Polly hadn't expected her to do this. Ella is suspicious, she realises, of someone who is rich but claims to be doing good work in poor countries. Polly usually shares this suspicion, but she accepts that this isn't how James became rich, that was the decade in the hedge fund, and now his projects – it's an educational IT project in Gambia – are not primarily about money.

Nonetheless Polly finds, as the two take their positions, that she is suspicious as well. She realises that she has never actually asked him the question, have you taken out more money than you put in? She asks it now, and he laughs. She asks why he's laughing, and he says it's because it's naive to think that any businessman – that is the word he uses – wouldn't do that. He couldn't afford to lose money. The point is that he's doing it responsibly, that he's taking aid money given to schools and delivering – that is the word he uses too – the things they most need to improve their educations.

I won't take out more money than I put in, when I go there, Polly says.

No, but it's a kind of holiday for you, Polly. You've made enough money, you don't need more, you don't have a family to support.

Polly and Ella look at each other, and she feels that their bodies are united in their tense slightness in contrast to his relaxed bulk. She knows that Ella now feels apologetic for bringing out a side of him that Polly may find difficult to reconcile herself to. Also Ella is rueful in her knowledge that in fact Polly does have a family to support: she has taken on the burden of supporting their parents alone because Ella makes barely enough to live on. And Polly feels embarrassed that Ella will realise that she hasn't felt able to tell James about her material circumstances, however close she hopes they are. She knows that Ella will know that this is partly because she's taken on her father's own shame about being supported by his daughter and partly also because Polly doesn't want James to ask why their father doesn't claim benefits, if he can't work because of his back. The truth is that she is shielding him from having to admit his own need, just as she's shielding him from her brother's death by providing the help that he would have accepted from a son but finds almost impossible to accept from a daughter, leaving her in the absurd position of giving the money secretly. This all feels too complicated to explain to James, who will offer advice that she does not feel ready to receive.

Now, all they can do is change the subject. But the new topics they try don't work, they move from one to the other, Polly still too wounded by his comments to relax and give the encounter the enthusiasm it needs. James asks Ella thoughtful questions about her work which she doesn't respond to at length. She's unable to give a positive account of her labour on a magazine that doesn't pay its staff and unwilling to talk instead about her fears that the magazine may fold or about the exhaustion that results from balancing this work alongside the things that she does for money. She seems unnaturally still in contrast to his suppleness. Polly is conscious of the way his whole face moves all the time, changing shape as he talks. She imagines herself reaching out a hand and deftly swivelling his mouth upside down.

While they wait for Helena, James announces that he's going to have a cigarette, though he hardly ever smokes, and has to buy a packet of cigarettes to do so. Polly asks Ella if she minds if she joins him, though she smokes even less often than James does. She takes one now, standing with him, because it gives her something to do and she wants to be near him and not talk, hoping that this will be a way to stop feeling so angry. They are both silent, and then he asks her if she's all right. No, she says, and it would be easy just to turn inwards to him, to let him comfort her for his own inadequacies. But she doesn't, she continues to stand upright and alone, while she explains how much she disliked the things he said about his work in Gambia, and about her being different from him.

You don't know how much money I need to earn, she says. You don't know anything about me.

I'm sorry Polly, he says, with an unconvincingly fervent look of regret. I didn't mean to patronise you.

But it's impossible for it to be unsaid, so anything he says now won't feel true, and she's aware of Ella waiting for them inside. She goes back in, and shrugs her shoulders at Ella, who apologises to her too, saying she didn't mean to show him up. James returns and they examine the dessert menu while they wait for Helena, who appears looking relaxed and pregnant in a beautiful soft grey coat, as though she hasn't just crossed London on a soggy evening. Polly is surprised by the force with which she feels Helena's special-ness, much more than when they last met. She's surrounded by visibly pregnant women at work, has witnessed it repeat-edly in her friends, but occasionally there are still these moments when she feels left behind in ordinariness by a woman who has been chosen by the gods to enter a magical realm. This feeling settles as they talk. Helena and Ella are pleased to see each other, and Ella becomes more talkative under her questioning. James asks Helena well-informed questions about the documentary-film world and seems genuine in his interest in her pregnancy, recalling details of his ex-wife's pregnancy, which Polly has never heard him talk about before.

Polly wonders what Helena makes of James. She seems to like him as she has, over the years, liked most of the men Polly has introduced her to. They talk easily and quickly to each other, and Helena seems to be able to tease James in a way that Ella isn't. Polly has wondered before whether being bisexual might mean that Helena has higher standards in men, because their maleness doesn't grant them exemption from her usual standards in the way that it does for Polly. But now she thinks that perhaps because Helena is less invested in loving men, she's less invested in hating them as well, and therefore finds them generally more tolerable than she does.

They are all examining Helena's bump now; Ella touches it so James does too. Then James gets up to pay the bill, waving aside suggestions from Helena and Ella that they should contribute, and Helena tells Polly that he's wonderful, with warmth that feels genuine enough for Polly to feel once again that he is. It occurs to her that all this might have nothing to do with sexuality, that Helena just doesn't share Polly's tendency to wonder whether she really likes the people she thinks she might like, and that this is a difference Polly has appreciated in James as well.

Outside, Helena looks more tired than she did in the restaurant and Polly wonders if she might be finding the pregnancy a strain after all. Polly encourages her to get a cab home, but Helena is saving money for the baby, which leaves Polly feeling bad for suggesting she should cross London at night. James offers to walk Helena to the station and then, just as Polly and Ella arrive home, there's a message from him, which Polly reads in the kitchen as she waits for the kettle to boil. He is saying that it was great to see her and how much he liked Ella and Helena. 'I wish we could have sex,' he says.

She knows that if it was him in the flat with her now, instead of Ella, the argument in the restaurant would produce a sexual charge. She could turn her rage and his callousness into bodily strangeness, which would then be dispelled by shared pleasure. How can we know if we're shirking the problem, when we overcome our fear of otherness through sex? She can't decide whether sex gives new, more generative forms to their differences or represses them. She looks out of the window at the night they've left behind, picturing James still walking around in it. There's an erotic intensity in her vision of his coat billowing behind him as he lunges forward, a man roaming the city who she could summon to bed if she wanted to.

I'm still angry, she says, sadly to Ella, going back into the sitting room with their cups of tea. I want to tell him exactly what he's done wrong, presenting him with a kind of check-list. But I don't want to lose him, and I can feel the life that we're going to lead together slipping away when I feel angry. I don't think I can find a man who doesn't make me angry. At least this one makes me happy as well.

Ella says that she has learnt in therapy to be less frightened by her own anger.

We couldn't be angry, she says, as children. When Ted was alive, we were too frightened of him to be angry. And then we worried that if we were angry we'd die, like he did, or we'd cause someone else to die. His tumour obviously had nothing to do with his anger, but I've realised that it felt to me like one minute he was shouting at us and hitting us and the next minute he was in horrible pain. And then when he was gone we had to be quiet and good, for Mum and Dad's sake. I've been thinking that when you didn't tell me about the abortion it was because you thought it was your fault, you didn't think of blaming Evan. But it was his fault, more than yours, Polly. And we have to feel angry, all women do. It's the only thing that keeps us going at work, carrying on commissioning articles despite all the abusive comments. It's not the same as hatred – it's more constructive. When I was talking to James about his work in Gambia, I didn't dislike him. Did you think I did?

Polly lies down on the sofa, putting her feet on Ella's lap. Ella squeezes and pummels them and Polly realises that she has felt all evening as though constantly ready for an emergency.

I don't know, Polly says, prepared to accept that Ella might be right. But I know what you mean about Ted. No one else in the house got angry and then the person who was angry was suddenly dead.

She is wondering what life would be like if she allowed herself to be as angry as she could be. She senses that there's more anger than she knows about, kindling inside her, and that James may be better able to cope with it than she fears. She imagines conversations at work, fuelled by anger, conversations where she challenges the cuts being made and looks higher up the chain for answers, or where she insists that it is in fact her duty to find out who is mutilating the girls who end up in her consulting room.

Ella is saying now that her therapist says that the strength of anger is that it presupposes the possibility of change. We wouldn't get angry if we didn't think it could have some effect on the situation we're angry about. Polly considers this and finds that she agrees. She wonders if it's therefore a hopeful sign that she's more angry with James than she ever was with Sam. Perhaps it's not that Sam didn't provoke her anger, it's that with James she can believe enough in their future for the anger to feel worth bothering with.

Stella

December

I've just come back from Kay's house. When I arrived she was decorating the expensively sumptuous Christmas tree, and it felt as though everything was back to normal. Ana was there, she had helped Kay position it and hoovered up the stray needles. I'd brought Maggie and she and Alisa sat on the rug next to the tree playing with decorations while Kay and I put baubles on the branches. Neither Chris nor I had been planning to buy trees this year but as I decorated Kay's tree I felt like it was unfair on Cleo: like we need to do what we can to make it a normal Christmas, however much we both dislike it. After all, the normal families – Kay and Harald in their clean and perfect house with their large and perfect Christmas tree – are just as abnormal as we are.

The decorations were brighter than I'd have expected. Deep red shiny baubles. I couldn't picture Kay buying them, which reminded me that I can't picture Kay buying anything for that house. It's as though everything has just appeared there, for her to live alongside. I asked if Harald had bought them but she said it was her, so I tried to imagine her choosing them in John Lewis.

Towards the end of it, I sat down cross-legged on the

floor in my woolly dress, and Maggie and Alisa both came over and crawled on to my lap. Kay sat down too and Alisa went over to her. She said that Alisa had become clingier since she came back, and that she was glad because she'd heard about other children who transferred all their affection to their fathers when their mothers went away. I said that something of this had happened to Cleo when I went away in her early years, and that it still feels sometimes that she is more Chris's child than she is mine. She cries when she misses him, and she doesn't cry when she misses me, though that might tell its own story, about being able to take me for granted. Kay said that for several days after she returned Alisa cried every time she came into the room and every time she left it. Her job is covered till Christmas so she's taken Alisa out of nursery because she feels that neither of them can stand the daily separation. Yet one reason for the absence was that the proportion of her days that she spent with her children was making her claustrophobic.

I said that perhaps it was family life that made her claustrophobic, rather than time with her children, and she said that it might be but there was no other way she could do it. She didn't think she was able to look after two children without help from another adult. And she worries that without Harald she'd become so brittle that she'd snap in half.

Maggie crawled over to the tree and started shaking the branches, making needles fall, which made me worry she'd get them in her eyes. I carried her over to where Alisa was playing with the toys and they started touching each other, somewhere between patting and hitting. We laughed at them and I realised that I finally feel confident that my friends have accepted Maggie's place in our shared world. I no longer feel so hurt by Kay telling me I shouldn't have her. Perhaps it's better that she did, and that she extracted the secret of the affair out of me, because it's tested us and it's turned out that we can forgive each other our knowledge of each other after all. However hard it is to be known, it is better than not being known.

I asked Kay how much she and Harald have talked about her time away. She said that even with Moser, she finds that there's almost nothing to say about it. She went away and then she came back. There is no meaning to it. I found it difficult to imagine what it might feel like, not to need to find meaning in my actions. I looked at the blank grey wall behind the tree, thinking that I share Kay's attraction to emptiness and that our efforts were making the room less beautiful.

As we put the final decorations on the tree, Ana came in to clean up the needles that had fallen, which made me wonder if she'd been waiting outside, listening to the conversation, though she doesn't strike me as curious in that way. Harald texted, saying he and Seb were on their way back, so I left because I didn't want to discuss my statement about Vince, which is now online. Also I didn't have the energy to confront their marriage, and to wonder if Kay is right to allow it to resume.

Her time away has shifted something for me – perhaps for all of us – making me see the craziness and the contingency of our lives. What would it be like to go away and not come back? How do people gather round in your absence and fill in the gaps you've left? Her return makes the fault-lines – the sense of struggle involved just in staying the course – so visible that even an ordinary day at her house is dangerous to witness. I need to amass my energy and concentrate on keeping going.

★

My car, for the past fortnight, has stubbornly resisted its destiny as a car with a single owner. First there was a puncture last weekend, just as I was about to drop the children at Chris's and set off to Tom's. I called Chris and he came round and put the spare tyre on, his mood fluctuating between grumpiness and gallantry because we remain unsure how to be together, and he is confused when divorce looks most like marriage. I agreed to replace three tyres when the man at the tyre shop suggested it, determined to be a dutiful car owner. But then this weekend it happened again, in the same wheel. I summoned the RAC, expecting to be admonished for calling them out unnecessarily, but it turned out that this was a normal request for them, we are no longer expected to change our tyres ourselves.

This time the garage – our usual garage where they still assume that I'm married – found that one of the valves was broken, so the tyres hadn't been punctured at all. It was a gentle deflation, not a rupture, Moser observed this morning.

And then yesterday I took the children to soft play, after school, in Swiss Cottage, celebrating the feeling of getting towards the end of term by taking the afternoon off work and spending an hour among coloured balls, with Maggie laughing excitedly as she watched Cleo sliding towards us. When we got back to the car, I couldn't find the key in my handbag. Knowing how pointless it was, I took them back to the café and then to the play area, Maggie wailing with tiredness now but Cleo more grown up than she had been all afternoon, shocked into responsibility by the feeling of emergency that had come upon us. We went from one cage to another, pushing the brightly coloured balls aside in search of the key we knew we wouldn't find. And then there was a text message exchange with an irate Chris, who eventually gave reluctant permission for us to go and let ourselves into his flat in search of the spare car key. 'I left you because you were always wanting independence,' he wrote, 'and this is the best you can make of it.'

When we got back to the car with the key, it turned out that it was already unlocked. What did I do with the key? Did I put it down somewhere while I was assembling the pushchair? Chris is right. Owning the car alone was my reluctant final gesture of independence and I seem unable to commit to it or to do it well. I still fear that the car and I might not be able to cope with each other on our own.

Sometimes I have fantasies of selling the car and buying another one, imagining a painless car-owning future akin to the painless versions of family life and sexual love that I like to project into the future as well. But I know that I can't afford to do it and also that there can be no more wilful acts of change for me. The car and I have to learn to survive alongside each other.

Kay

December

It's Saturday. Kay and Harald have agreed that on Saturdays she will have the day off to write. He's offered her his writing flat but the thought of it makes her feel queasy, not so much because of all the sex he must have had there as because of all the unnecessary words he has written at the desk. So she's come to school, though she hasn't been here since she went away and doesn't plan to come again on a weekday until she starts teaching again in January. She's avoiding the staffroom and has gone instead to the A level classroom where she's taught *Hamlet* year after year. She likes it, empty of girls and their gaudy bags, only her laptop on the triangular tables that she joins into a perfect square before she begins.

When she pictured herself here, she didn't know if she'd actually write. She thought it might be like her weeks in Cornwall, time to do nothing at all. But she opens her laptop and empties the screen except for a large white document. And she writes for three hours, sparse sentences narrated by a woman who is glacial, detached. It is not pleasurable, in itself, but she is not seeking pleasure. There is a definiteness in it that makes her more sure of existing than she is usually, even as she disappears behind the black lines and curves appearing on her screen. In the past, she's said that one reason she doesn't write is that she dislikes her voice – the white, middle-class voice our group shares. But she doesn't feel hindered by it now, the way she's writing feels more universal. This may yet turn out to be her vocation after all.

At one o'clock she stops, coveting the four hours that remain to her, wanting to find a way to use them as slowly as she can. She goes to the staffroom to deposit her computer, and finds that it's as sparse as the classroom, the mugs all cleared away into the cupboard, the rectangular grey sofas clear. She lies down on one, not intending to sleep, just to enjoy the feeling of being more at home in this room than she has ever been. But she shuts her eyes, thinking that this feels a little like being on Moser's couch, and she doesn't resist the drowsiness that starts patterning her thoughts into floating chunks of text, her brain still forming the words she has recently been writing.

Afterwards, she feels she has gone further into herself. There's a particular satisfaction in realising that she has not left behind her life in Cornwall, that it might be possible to sink into some partial version of it in this unlikely setting. As she leaves the school, she thinks that she wants her writing to be like the fields she walked through to St Ives: clean and impassive and sometimes shimmering but shadowed with a brutality that makes it real, because you could disappear into that landscape without anyone noticing. She thinks that it's those fields and cliffs that have finally taught her how to escape her spoken voice.

She goes out to the Caffè Nero near Hammersmith station and finds that she is sitting across from a woman with a tiny baby. It's the first baby this small she has seen close up since Alisa became too big to be called a baby, and it brings a moment of physical longing that surprises her, on this day that's all about escaping motherhood. She finds that she is staring at the baby surreptitiously, glancing repeatedly at the soft arms and legs, listening for the little noises of pleasure that it makes as it nestles into its mother. She did not have anything like this longing as Seb moved beyond babyhood, and she thinks that this must be what Harald feels when he longs for an attractive young woman. Now when she looks, she catches the mother's eye and they smile at each other. Her covetousness turns out to be acceptable.

How old? she asks, and is told two weeks. She reaches out, before she's had time to ask herself if it's an appropriate thing to do, and strokes the pale brown foot which pokes out from the Babygro.

Would you like to hold her? the woman asks, and Kay is surprised by the offer, which is not one she'd have thought of making.

Then she is holding the baby, and it feels unexpectedly right that she should have left her children at home to hold this baby, a tiny girl who smells of someone else's milk. She says that she has a 1½-year-old. They grow up too fast. She finds that it's all right to admit to being in a café on a Saturday without her children. They talk now about sleeping and feeding and crawling, the easy conversations that make possible a community of parents everywhere, however much we resist it. Then the woman leans over unexpectedly and touches the scar on her cheek. She asks how it happened and Kay says that she fell, adding that it was by the sea, as though this will make it more explicable. The woman nods and shows Kay a small scar on her own wrist. Then Kay returns the baby and walks towards the park. She is going to stretch out this final hour of light.

Stella

December

These changes. Yesterday I turned forty, last week Maggie turned one, together we are growing into ourselves. Few birthdays have felt so right to me. The relief of being through my thirties. Here I am, with greying hair, a wrinkling stomach, a back tooth missing, ready to embark on middle age, though glad to note, as I walked down the corridor to my office yesterday in a felt dress, that my legs were still better than most of the younger women's. Walking along, catching men's eyes, I realised that I am thinking about sex again. There's that curiosity: what do they see in me, what do I see in them?

We are very particular in our vanity, I think, we women of forty. I talked about this with the whole group, who came into town for a birthday lunch for me. It was Kay's idea – she'd planned to come for lunch, and she brought the others along as a surprise. She'd remembered, I suppose, that I wanted an opportunity to see Priss, who looked well, blazing with the physical self-confidence that comes from knowing that there's a luminous hologram of you installed in someone else's mind. (I miss that feeling, I suppose, though I distrust it. Does that mean I'll want it again?) Helena was much bigger than she was when I last saw her and seemed well, as straight-backed and centred in herself as she was before she was pregnant. She said that she'd been sleeping better. Polly was radiant. She has handed in her notice at the hospital and will leave in March.

Kay seemed awkward as she brought them into the café – we went to Bill's on Kingsway. I liked her embarrassment – it protected me from my own – and there was a kind of tacit apology in the whole gesture, an admission that I value these friends and that in telling Priss about the affair, Kay had acted as though I didn't. I tried not to think about Priss in her particularity and just to enjoy being a group again. We talked about how we feel about turning forty, now that Polly and I have done it and Kay and Helena are about to join us. Polly and I agreed that we've ceded the field to the younger women with more relief than sadness. There's to be no more experimentation with make-up or hair removal, though Polly revealed, with touching pride, that last week she got a small tattoo done on her shoulder, a silhouetted sparrow in flight. We all have our grey hairs and our scars, the one on Kay's face now a more natural part of her face, proof alongside the C-section of all she's undergone in the last decade. But there is a satisfaction in our distinctiveness, in legs, eyes, cheekbones, whatever it is that we happen to pride ourselves on. We know which features are here to stay, we know we can conduct the erotic through our bodies like lightning as we swim further out, conserving our breath because there is still a long way to go.

The food came – how many hundreds of meals have we eaten together over the last twenty years? – and I thought that it's impressive that we all eat properly, curries and fish rather than just salads. I couldn't remember when exactly that changed for Polly, who used to just pick at her food when we ate in public places. Helena had read my statement about Vince, she said that she admired it, and thought I'd done a good job making clear my commitment to the importance of female consent while also saying that the allegations remained unproven. Priss congratulated me on the news that I'll get his job. It was the first time she'd addressed me directly and I could sense everyone looking at us, wondering how we felt. I couldn't decide if she really seemed different from how she was before – she sounded so happy and energetic, but perhaps she always sounded that way.

I said, looking at her too intently because I wanted to make sure I was talking to her directly, that I feel too young to be a publishing director but that I still worry that I'm so old I'll become a source of embarrassment to my younger colleagues, schooled as I am in the old ways of thinking.

Helena said that sometimes she feels that way with Clare, but she thinks it's fine if we allow ourselves to learn from the young. Clare feels her anger with the offending men so passionately that it makes Helena more hopeful that there will be new possibilities for desire once the old world has been cleared away.

Polly said that she thinks the thing that Clare's generation does much better than us is to express anger. That girls of our generation learnt not to express it and maybe not to feel it, to see it as frightening.

I said that I thought she was right. As a child, I found my mother's repetitive haranguing and my father's sudden eruptions of anger almost unbearable. My love for Chris couldn't survive all his shouting, and I was terrified when he provoked anger in me. I didn't think I was managing to teach Cleo that anger was something we could both live with.

Who do you feel angry with? Kay asked me, with an

excitement in her tone that made me think she was suddenly enjoying the conversation.

I said, not expecting to have the answer so easily ready, that I'm angry with Chris, for making me feel for years like I was a bad mother, for making me feel ashamed of taking my work seriously. I'm angry with Harald, for not seeing that Kay has a right to go away when she needs to, even if the circumstances of this weren't ideal.

I've been angry with Harald, angry with my children, with my students, even sometimes with my cleaner, Kay said. Going away I stopped feeling angry, I felt numb instead. I don't know how to feel angry again yet. I don't know if I want to.

I'm angry with the men who've seen sex as their right, Priss said. And have made me feel frigid if I don't happen to want it.

It was an odd thing for her to say, just at the moment when she's outed herself as a sexual being. I wondered if she was angry with me for making her feel frigid, by desiring her husband more than she did. I felt suddenly that I wanted to say something about it, that I wanted to have the affair openly there between us, but it felt unlikely there would be a good chance to do so.

I'm angry with all the men I've dated who've made me feel that I have to suppress part of who I am to please them, Polly said. I'm angry with the man who got me pregnant and the men who didn't. And I'm angry with all the men who've hurt the women I see at work. Who've forced them to have sex, or too many babies, or have just gone straight out and mutilated them, or sent the women back to cut more girls when they refuse to do it.

We looked at each other, surprised by the clarity of our

speech-making. Our plates were all empty and Helena stacked them. Kay and Priss were both leaning their heads on their hands in a way that made them look younger than they are. I said that maybe this is the kind of conversation students now have in their kitchens. I can't remember what we talked about in ours, but it was more passive. Did one boy like us, or another? We had no agency, in those days, except around our work. We didn't even call ourselves feminists.

Polly said that she knew what I meant. And that she's been thinking that there's something so peculiar, almost non-existent about our generation, coming of age before the internet, before the millennials. We're old-fashioned in bed. Sex is still more about touching than looking for us because we didn't grow up accustomed to porn. She thinks this is part of the appeal of older men for her – they feel more contemporary than lots of the men our age.

It's true, Kay said, as the older man at the next table got up to leave, almost hitting her head with his rucksack. We still believed in literature. We became ourselves by being Jane Eyre or Isabel Archer. We thought that nothing was going to be as important as writing the novels that would shape the minds of our children. But books won't matter to them.

She sounded sad, as though she was mourning the loss of her own youth. I wanted to touch her, she was stiffly upright now and I wanted her to bend so I could cradle her in my arms. I wanted to say that I still believe in the books she'll write. But I knew that what she was saying was probably true.

The coffee came and it turned out that Priss had made me a small cake which the waitress brought out plates for. It was a shock, it felt invasive to me, though I didn't quite know what she was invading. I think that because it's the kind of thing a mother does for a child, it infantilised me, and took away my sense of agency. I thought of the hour in the café kitchen she'd spent making it that morning, wondering if it's possible to make a cake maliciously. I thanked her, effusively, and she laughed. Rather than hearing malevolence in her laughter, I tried to hear a kind of merry acceptance of the cruelty of a world where she ends up baking a cake for her husband's former lover.

Helena asked how we all feel, watching the news at the moment, do we feel angry? I said that I more often feel sad, and helpless. Like it's too much for me to bear. Priss said that sometimes she turns it off. She hates the undifferentiated onslaught of government resignations, coups in foreign countries, climate disasters. She finds it too alienating an experience being upset by footage of suffering children in earthquakes or wars and then being assailed by financial news and football scores that are somehow meant to form part of a connected world.

I said that I don't let myself turn it off, it feels like I'd be silencing people. But I don't do any good by keeping it on, I added, worrying I'd made myself sound too smug or that I was accusing her of silencing others. Polly said that she's found watching the news easier, since she allowed herself to feel angry. She sits there thinking of what can be done, rather than feeling helpless. I said that maybe that's a reason not to have children. You can cope enough with the footage, without breaking down, to think that you can do something.

There are plenty of mothers who can cope enough to act, Kay said, rightly, and I was relieved to hear her sounding briskly disapproving again – I've missed that since she went away. I agreed that even if it's being a mother that makes us feel more strongly about certain things than we did before, it doesn't invalidate the feelings. Part of the problem is that when you're a mother getting angry about the treatment of children, there's something embarrassing about the feelings, because they're so personal.

Embarrassment, Priss said, smiling the same merry smile. Perhaps that's the biggest problem of being middle class and white and English and a woman, finding it embarrassing to take ourselves seriously. I'd have done so much more with my life if I hadn't felt embarrassed.

Yes, Helena said, with both hands placed on her bump, regally. I've been thinking that too. We have so much power between us, if we can take ourselves seriously, with our grief and rage and love and desire.

And our laughter, Polly said, laughing. Don't forget that.

Maybe that's what we'll do in our forties, I said. Learn to use our power.

It felt — I hope for all of us — wonderfully like we were a group again, taking on the world collectively, more potent because we had confronted our capacity to cause pain. And then Polly had to rush off and I offered, spontaneously, to pay for everyone, though my December budget is absurdly tight. Priss said that it was their turn, I'd provided the food for our last gathering. And Kay said that Priss had made the cake, so she and Polly and Helena ended up splitting it, and I disliked the pettiness of the discussion, after our grand statements about our power.

Kay walked me to the office. She told me off, along the way, for banging into people on the pavement. It's always irritated her, as it irritated Chris, the way I find it hard to second-guess which direction the people around me are going to walk in. She asked how it had been to see Priss, and we agreed that it seemed too good to be true, her happy alertness, but that the affair with Hugh may turn out to be what she needed, however suspicious we both are these days of sex as a solution to life's emptiness.

Kay asked about Maggie's birthday, and I was touched that she remembered. I said that over the past few weeks she and Cleo have become equals, little people in my life and in Chris's. I say 'my children' easily now, instead of my baby and my daughter. Looking at Maggie, touching her, I don't feel the same in-love feeling. It's more of a social relationship, with a separate person in the world. Kay said that this had finally happened with Seb as well, and that it was important this should happen to me, so my relationship with Cleo can be less hollowed out. I agreed, and said that the most vital thing is that Maggie's bond with Chris is equal now to her bond with me. But that I mind the loss of that rare experience of single-minded love, now there are years of ambivalence and complication ahead.

And then I went back to work, where I spent the afternoon thinking about Priss. I texted her thanking her for the cake. 'It was my pleasure', she wrote back. Is that really her pleasure, I wondered, making a cake for her husband's lover when she could spend the hour doing her nails or reading or being kissed from head to toe by Hugh. I realised that I've despised Priss for her obliviousness, over the years, and now I despise her for pretending to continue with that obliviousness, even if it's exactly what I'm doing. It's impossible to imagine being open with her. I've started to see her as a version of Chris or my mother – someone I need to protect myself from being known by in order to have the space to be fully myself. Yet I want so much to be at ease within the group again and I can't see how that's possible without talking about it. Tom says that I place too much emphasis on talking things through, that there are other ways to be connected and to recover, that shared experience and kindness can do that work too. Perhaps this time I have to hope that he's right, and in the meantime I have to allow Priss to continue with her perverse pleasures. What will she think of to do for me next?

In the evening I celebrated with the children. Cleo had been shopping with Chris and had bought me a book about feminism, which I found a little barbed as an offering from him, but perhaps the younger women he's been dating have succeeded where I failed in alerting him to the existence of the patriarchy. Then Tom came to take me out for dinner, unexpectedly full of delight about my birthday and our lives. We held hands as we ordered, my second meal out in the day, and when the drinks came, we toasted my forties and the divorce, which came through last week, and which made me more sad than I'd expected. I said that it makes me feel frightened, to have lost the whole structure I'd built up to protect me from the world, and old, to have finished everything we connect with youth. Tom listened sympathetically, but I think he's more straightforwardly pleased about it. I am no longer owned by my husband so can be owned by him instead, should he wish to do so. For a spiky moment I thought that it was too easy for him to be pleased, given that he's not taking responsibility for me. If I lose my job, now, there's no one to help. I'm left with my children, my flat, my bank account, and my beleaguered car.

We joked about Brexit, which has limped along in parallel with my divorce. The parallels will stop now. Is it possible that Brexit won't go through? That this will turn out to be a comedy of remarriage of the kind that hasn't taken place in my life?

Lying in bed, I thought about lunch, and was pleased they'd all come. I thought that perhaps Priss and I will be able to talk properly once the affair with Hugh has finished, seasoned adulterers comparing our liaisons. I thought that the point may be, as Tom says about the leavers and remainers, that there's not really that much difference between us. We insist on our minor differences: I am the one who never finishes her tea, Polly finds it hard to choose which cake to have because she's tempted by all of them but tempted also to renounce cake altogether. We characterise ourselves, like characters in novels. But we'd look almost identical to most onlookers in our wealth, our privilege, our freedom of choice. And more importantly, these characteristics are so arbitrary: we could swap them between us at will. The real feelings – the love, desire, fear, anger, laughter – are the same, whoever experiences them. There's an ocean of experience and feeling which we just dip into. Yet we insist on each other's otherness, even as we fear it. Because our sameness disturbs us even more.

Kay

December

It's her last session before the Christmas break. It's getting dark outside but he hasn't turned the light on and she closes her eyes, thinking that she would like to fall asleep here, and that since she went away it has become more possible to fall asleep at odd times and places. She is telling Moser that she has missed Alisa over the past few days, when she sent her back to nursery so that she could write.

Every day when I see her again I feel as though she's changed, she says. It's like I'm meeting a stranger. I feel guilty because I'm leaving her.

He asks if she thinks Alisa misses her and she says that she might do, but it's probably not doing any harm.

That's the important thing, he says. He's not going to stop her beating herself up about it, if that's what she wants to do, but it's probably not doing any harm, or no more than the ordinary harm of being alive.

Last night I dreamt that I was in hospital, Kay says, and Alisa was in special care, as she was when she was born. I wake up in the night and realise that it's been days since I last saw her, and that they must be hiding her from me. So I go down, and look for her, and can't find her, and I know she's dead, and I don't know if it's my fault, for not going down to feed her, or if she died of her own accord, and therefore they didn't bother to tell me it was time to feed her, so that's why I haven't gone down. Then I wake up.

You wake up in the dream, or outside it? he asks.

Inside the dream, she says, I wake up, and go into her bedroom, and see that she's there, she's alive and I feel so much better, I feel ecstatic with relief. I see that I've been given a second chance to look after her and nothing could matter more than this. And then I woke up in real life, crying, and waited till morning, until it was time to see her.

He asks if she thinks she's been neglecting Alisa and she says that she hasn't since she went away. She wonders if she's the baby in the dream as well. Whatever happens, one of them is going to be neglected. He asks if she can bear that and she says that she thinks she can. Her voice seems to come from deep inside herself, rising with her breath. She wonders if she really is going to sleep, able to be silent with him at last.

Going outside, she's relieved by the shock of the cold and the metallic taste of the streets after rain. She looks at the wreaths on the doors, noting which are real and which fake, and peers in at people's Christmas trees, a whole wasted forest of them accumulating as she walks, wondering if insight is always on the side of loss and despair. She isn't sure whether her relief at no longer being in the room with Moser is a sign that it was a productive session. She thinks that psychoanalysis has turned out to be very different from what she thought she was doing in the spring. Today he was doing more of the interpretation for her than he usually does, perhaps because since her trip he feels more responsible for her, more aware that there could be tragic consequences for the people around her if she's in an unsettled state of mind. This makes her wonder if she now thinks of him as siding with her family against her, thinking that her children's needs matter more than hers do. But she knows that this isn't true. And she's stopped trying to understand what goes on in that room now.

She goes to pick up Alisa and finds that today she hasn't notably changed in the seven hours they've been apart. There's still something surprising every time, though, in her particular fleshiness, in the way that the two-dimensional image in her mind becomes so instantly and fully three-dimensional in the little person who runs towards her. She forgets now that she was ever unable to walk. Yesterday, on the Tube home from Moser, she found herself looking at early baby photographs, missing the creature sleeping on her breast, experiencing the loss as a form of death. She feels guilty that she never felt this with Seb.

Her mother brings Seb home. They have been Christmas shopping and are both exuberant about their finds. Seb wants to tell Kay what he has bought but his grandmother stops him and Kay wonders for whose benefit she's insisting on secrecy. She can't see it as a strength for children to learn to keep secrets.

And then Harald is there, and her mother immediately leaves, though she has complained in the past of feeling like a paid servant who's expected to go as soon as they're home. Kay can't remember what it's like not to feel like a servant – surely it would be better to feel like a paid one. But that's not quite true, now. She has her time off to write.

Harald lifts Seb up to face him and Kay wonders if they're aware of how absurdly similar they look. It never stops bemusing her, that her body should have served as the incubator for the cloning of her husband, doubling the number of small round brown eyes in the house, surveying her. Before he takes Seb off for his story, Harald asks her courteously about her writing and she realises that it's years since she has asked him about his. She looks up at him, wondering if he's making a point, but it seems that he's not, and she remembers that this is part of what attracts her to him, that what in some moods she sees as a lack of subtlety is also a generous straightforwardness. She asks, feeling oddly formal, about his writing and he says that he is rewriting. She realises that she can't remember and may never even have known what this novel is about. She isn't sure what her own novel is about either. It seems at the moment to have nothing to do with her, to appear word by word on the screen as though someone else is manoeuvring her fingers or is there in her place and she is somewhere quite different, back in Cornwall perhaps, which she sometimes feels she never left, still watching her feet endlessly treading the muddy coastal path.

He waits, as he has waited several times since her return, in their bedroom while Kay puts Alisa to bed. She goes in as she knows she is meant to, not asking herself whether this is something she wants to do. He has made them both gin and tonics and he hands her one without speaking. She looks at him, wondering if it would be possible to see him again as an attractive stranger, but wondering at the same time if marital seduction is always coercive. She tries out the thought that she has no alternative. That there is no moment, from entering the room, to accepting the gin and tonic, to lying down and eventually putting her hand on his crotch, that she has any choice over, though once it's set in motion, it's usually her who accelerates it rather than him.

This is something she can change, so she becomes passive.

She stops moving or touching and waits for him to touch her. He asks her if she wants him to carry on and she says yes. He removes her clothes, looking at her as he does so, and then removes his own. Her skin is cool, so he pulls the duvet from under her and wraps her up to her breasts, which poke out, the nipples still large from breastfeeding. It is difficult to conceive this body, with its stretch marks and scars, as an object of desire, but this is what they must learn to do again together, as she must learn to be aroused by his erection, which points out at her, as he comes round beside her and gets into bed.

It is peaceful, leaning against him, his hand in her hair, and she wonders if this is all he wants as well, if they will just go to sleep like this, and if that would still count as a sexual act. But letting go provokes desire and she leans into him and then shakes when he runs a finger across her hip bone and down her thigh. They kiss, and the pleasure now is in the wetness of tongues, reminding them of all that lies beneath the skin: nerves, blood, crevices. She would like him to lick her. She would like to take him in her mouth. She pushes his mouth down her body and relaxes into his skill. The desire now is absolute enough to be cold. It makes her more desiring that he has done this with so many other women, not because she is jealous but because it gives the act a neutrality that is itself arousing. She grips the bedstead as she gets closer to coming and it feels as though she is being pushed hard against it and then, as she comes, breaking through it, pushing through the wall behind. Her eyes are shut and when she opens them he is next to her. They kiss, and it is not love that she feels as she pushes her tongue further into his mouth, wanting more, but greed. She wants this to continue. She wants to do it all again.

Stella

December

I went to Cornwall, on my own, on Boxing Day. I was staying at Tom's, minding feeling landlocked, minding that I'd left my children behind only to find myself surrounded by Tom's extended family. So I got in my car at seven in the morning, before Tom was awake, not sure whether to go away for the night or just to drive for a couple of hours and come back. I found myself driving past junction after junction on the M5. It was surprisingly quiet and I went fast, much faster than I usually drive, pushing at ninety, feeling rather sorry for the car as the engine strained, but not sorry enough to slow down.

I followed the signs to St Ives almost without meaning to, and then took the turning to Zennor. This was my moment of escape, and the only way I could do it was to follow Kay, wanting to be somewhere I'd been with her but wanting most of all to inhabit the landscape that she still inhabits in part of her mind. It's rare to find yourself exactly where you want to be but I was sure I was in the right place, coming round the bend and seeing the sea. The sky was clearer and lighter than it had been in November, the gorse darker green, the sea darker blue. I hadn't booked anywhere to stay, but luckily the pub was open and had a room available. So there I was again, eating a sandwich in bed, tapping on my laptop, having the Boxing Day that I thought Kay would most like to have.

I got up to go for a walk. I'd never tried the path there that goes closest to the sea. They said at the pub that it was too late to make it to St Ives before dark, but I thought I'd just go for a short walk and turn back. I texted Tom, first ecstatically, with pictures of the sea he doesn't long for as Kay and I do, and then more beleagueredly, describing the unexpectedly soaking path. There was water gushing down the gaps between the stones and I had to cross a waterfall, drenching my walking boots. I made my way to the inland path, getting trapped in a lot of thigh-high gorse as I did so. And then I walked back in the rain, thinking of Kay and wondering what I was doing, appropriating Kay's adventure, wondering why I have become so addicted to being inside her head.

Back in my room I got into bed, unsure what to do for the rest of the afternoon, thinking about Boxing Days we had while I was still married, Cleo playing with her Christmas Playmobil sets as she would be right then in London without me. I pictured Priss and Ben driving back from an energising afternoon on Hampstead Heath with the children, him stroking her hand at the traffic lights under the soft rabbit-fur muff that I imagined him buying her for Christmas. I pictured Helena, lying on the sofa at her parents' house while her mother and Aaron tended to her needs for tea and massage, growing into their new family constellation. I pictured Kay, who I hoped by now would have told Harald that it was his turn to look after the children for a couple of hours and retreated to bed with her laptop, in turn imagining herself by the sea I'd just walked alongside. And I tried to picture Polly but realised that I didn't know what she was doing for Christmas – I wasn't sure if she was on call at the hospital or not.

The thought of Polly made me smile, realising how much I admire her at the moment, how of all the group it turns out to be Polly who is getting the most from adult life, confident that she has a role to play in the world. Spontaneously, I called her. She was in the middle of cooking dinner for her family in Somerset. Hearing the sound of everyone talking and laughing in the background made me miss the afternoon I could be having with Tom's family and worry that he might be missing me too, and that my absence might make Andreas's absence feel more painful.

Polly was delighted with the whole Cornish escapade, as I recounted it, but heard the loneliness in my voice, and heard my need of friendship, or perhaps she recognised her own.

Let's meet, she said generously, astonishingly. I'll leave them some casserole and bring some for us. Let's meet in Devon, tonight.

It turned out she was meeting James there the next day; they'd borrowed a house from a doctor friend of hers. So I left behind the sea I'd driven all those miles to reach and drove for another hour and a half to find a cottage at the end of a dark lane with the front door unlocked and Polly inside, a Christmas miracle, lighting the fire with her hair flaming red against it, so much herself, so living a body under her green jumper. She stood up and we hugged, both of us laughing and crying, and I found in my gratitude and exhaustion that I had nothing to say.